Dear Reader,

A novel virus, influenza A(H1N1)pdm09, aka swine flu, hit the United States and quickly spread across the States and the world when I was writing *Wolf Fever*—a warning of gloom and doom, harkening back to the deadly 1918 flu epidemic.

As I began writing this tenth-anniversary letter, an outbreak of a novel coronavirus, SARS-CoV-2, and the disease it causes, COVID-19, was in the news. And this epidemic soon turned into a pandemic, with most countries of the world trying to keep the coronavirus from spreading throughout their populations until a vaccine can be found. The death toll continued to escalate, and life as we know it has changed. Maybe forever. Pandemics will continue to be a topic of discussion, both in the real world and for fantasy and science-fiction writers who will take the epidemic/pandemic concept in all different directions.

As a writer, one of the most interesting ways of inventing a new story is to ask: What if? The swine virus immediately made me think of canines getting the flu—and yes, there is a canine-specific influenza. Kennel cough is a canine respiratory disease. Neither of these highly contagious canine-specific diseases can transfer to humans. The same goes for human influenza and colds. The viruses are species specific. That means if you're sick or you have a dog that is, you can still cuddle your fur baby until you feel better or they do.

But what if you're a wolf and human too?

You've probably seen stories about villains bioengineering viruses in an attempt to take over the world. I've seen tons of movies like that. So what if a sinister wolf pack used this strategy to take over Silver Town, a very profitable town run by wolves since its inception? And what if the wolves of Silver Town contracted the highly contagious virus? Normally, they heal twice as fast as humans, but since this is engineered differently, they can't get rid of it. But wolves can't have human viruses, so the best way to get rid of it is to shift. Right?

Simple solution, but a wolf designed the virus. He knows that.

So what if...

That's how I research and write my stories. Often something in the news will give me the idea, and I'm off and running with it. Consider these interesting tidbits:

Did you know that wolves each have a unique howl that they use to identify themselves to one another? Humans are only beginning to be able to understand this sound analysis. Did you know that alphas wake up the wolves in their pack to get them started on the day? Did you know that their voices can express emotions, just like humans'?

Social and family-oriented, wolves are like us in many ways. They deserve to raise their families, just as we do. And they actually help the ecosystem (unlike us, so often). They were hunted to near extinction, but gray-wolf populations began to recover after they were put on the endangered species list in 1978. The gray wolf was dropped from the endangered list in Idaho and Montana in 2011 and is again being hunted for trophies. And last year, the U.S. Fish and Wildlife Service proposed ending federal protection for the gray wolf throughout the lower forty-eight states.

What if they're hunted to extinction...for good this time?

Humans and loss of habitat threaten the survival of this noble canine. Fight for the wolves!

Terry Spear

WOLF FEVER

TERRY SPEAR

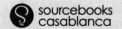
sourcebooks
casablanca

I dedicate Wolf Fever *to my manager, Sheila Slater, who is battling breast cancer like a real trouper and who sends me fun emails about wolves and wolflike characters while reading all my books on her reader! My thoughts and prayers go to all those who are fighting this insidious disease.*

Copyright © 2010, 2020 by Terry Spear
Wolf in Mind © 2020 by Terry Spear
Cover and internal design © 2020 by Sourcebooks
Cover art by Craig White/Lott Reps

Sourcebooks and the colophon are registered trademarks of Sourcebooks.

Published by Sourcebooks Casablanca, an imprint of Sourcebooks
P.O. Box 4410, Naperville, Illinois 60567-4410
(630) 961-3900
sourcebooks.com

Originally published as *Wolf Fever* in 2010 in the United States of America by Sourcebooks Casablanca, an imprint of Sourcebooks.

Printed and bound in the United States of America.
OPM 10 9 8 7 6 5 4 3 2 1

CHAPTER 1

THE WAXING MOON WAS CALLING TO HER. *AGAIN.* LYING on the soft mattress in Darien Silver's guest room early that spring evening, Carol Wood tried to sleep. But she felt the growing white sphere begging her to shed her human frailties and run with the magnificent grace of the wolf, strong and agile, with purpose in every stride in the crisp, cold Colorado night air.

She did *not* wish to be one of them—at least as far as being a part-time wolf—no matter how much several in the pack had encouraged her to embrace this new side of herself. The moon would soon be whole, but deep down, she rebelled against the wolf's curse. Because it *was* a curse to her, just the way her premonitions and psychic touch often were.

She'd grown up with her revved senses and had realized she couldn't do anything about that aspect of her life, once she'd learned it wasn't normal to have the abilities she did. But now to be—she squeezed her eyes tighter and rolled onto her back—a *wolf...* No matter how much she wished the truth could be changed, she knew she'd have to deal with it before long.

With all her heart, she prayed to keep her newly acquired bizarre condition—shifting—at bay. Her body tingled with heat and her mind with apprehension. Even in the darkness of her half-asleep mind, she fought the change, fought the feeling she was losing control of her physical form. Fresh tension made every nerve ending prickle while she clutched the comforter underneath her chin.

The heat, like the sun shining on a bright and warm Caribbean afternoon, invaded every pore, signaling the unwanted craving to shift. She moaned, tightening her hold on the comforter, her nails digging into the white eyelet. The moon was growing day by day, just like the damnable desire to shift. No, not desire. *Compulsion.*

Then, as if her psychic side finally gained some ground against the wolf, her second sight kicked in. The room and the need to shift dissolved into blackness, and the wolf in her vision appeared again like a lucid dream.

As big as it was, with massive shoulders, broad muzzle and forehead, and long legs, the wolf had to be a male, standing proud and tall, watching her from the edge of the spring-green forest. Cloaked in rich bluish-silver fur with a lighter mask and with his ears perked like an alpha male's would be, he panted until he caught her gaze. His amber eyes focused on hers: the wolf wanted her. Beckoned her to come to him. But not as a human.

As a wolf.

Even in her visions, the scene was one of cajoling, begging her to recognize her destiny, to give in to her wolf's half. At least that was the way she viewed him.

Carol refused the wolf's alluring gaze and the moon's sensuous serenade.

But the moon *commanded* her! Aroused her to do its bidding through its seductive pull, yanking her abruptly from the vision.

The heat invading her body intensified now, like a fever that couldn't be squelched. Never had the shift overtaken a vision in progress. The urge was growing. Yet she knew she still had some influence over the shift, like those born as *lupus garous* had an inborn ability to prevent humans from catching them during the conversion. Like them, if she wanted to change, the shift happened in a flash. And since she hadn't just automatically shifted, she must have some control.

Still, her muscles twitched with need as she shrugged off the comforter and blankets. She lay in her silky gown on the soft mattress in the pack leader's chilly guest room, ready to yank off her garment before the transformation took over in case she couldn't stop it. She envisioned the horrifying image of getting hung up in her gown as a wolf. Trapped, snarling, and growling, she'd try to free herself until she woke someone in the household. He or she would find her struggling in a cocoon of silk—furry legs kicking and sharp, wicked canines snapping.

She gritted her teeth and pressed the palms of her hands flat against the soft mattress, battling the moon's domination. She would not give up control and shift! Not when she couldn't rule her paranormal abilities. Not when she would now have to relinquish control over her physical form as well.

But more than that, she feared the shift would change her forever. *Forever!* Doomed to live life as a wolf with the conscience of a human. Even a single moment as a wolf could permanently seal her fate. At least that was what she thought a new vision was telling her, yet she couldn't know for certain. That was why fear consumed her to a greater degree every time the damnable shift threatened to overtake her.

Cursing her fate, she ground her teeth and clenched her

hands into fists, her fingernails biting into the palms of her hands, and attempted to think of anything that would halt the raging need to shift.

She visualized Lelandi, the pack leader's mate, throwing a first-ever All Girls' Night Extravaganza the previous week exclusively for women in the pack—complete with wolf-romance writer Julia Wildthorn's latest novel made into a feature film, *Wolfly Desires*, popcorn, margaritas, and lots of laughter. They were still finding popcorn underneath cushions and beneath the couch in little clusters. Carol smiled at the memory, hoping they could repeat an activity like that soon.

But then the heat rushed through her body again with a new wave of warning. Every muscle tightened, preparing for the fight. As if she'd called to the gods of psychic phenomena and they'd taken pity on her, her thoughts began to blur, and she knew her psychic sense was trying to take control again.

Holding her thoughts hostage, the dreamlike image showed an out-of-focus man, dressed in red and white stripes, who had knocked her down and was holding her there. Instantly, her blood cooled, the need to shift withdrawing. A scrap of relief trickled through her. She focused, trying to see the mental picture more clearly, attempting to determine who had tackled her and why. Annoyance was the driving feeling she experienced from the encounter. Not fear. Loss of control, maybe. But the strongest emotion was definitely annoyance.

The vision grew mistier, the man's shadowy face becoming hazier and the red and white stripes blurring into pink until they faded completely from her mind. She was in control again—of her thoughts and her physical form.

Taking a deep breath, she rubbed her arms, which were covered in chill bumps. Once more, she'd successfully stopped the change, and she felt some measure of triumph in overcoming the need to shift. She shivered. The compulsion grew stronger every month with each full moon. She could also shift anytime a crescent moon appeared— waxing or waning. Only the royal wolves, whose roots had not been diluted by strictly human genetics in their recent ancestry, could shift during the phase of the new moon.

She feared that one of these times, she wouldn't be able to conjure up a vision quickly enough or maybe not at all. The arrival of her visions was as unpredictable as the timing of the craving to shift. But what if she did manage a vision and the shift superseded it again? Worrying about that wouldn't change a thing.

She meant to dream up a fantasy world that would distract her so she could fall asleep again, because she desperately needed the sleep, but her thoughts drew back to the wolf in her vision earlier. He would come for her. Why? She didn't have a clue. But she knew she couldn't put off the inevitable.

Her ragged sleep interrupted, Carol stared at the white eyelet comforter, canopied bed, and antique dressers filling the guest bedroom at Darien Silver's home and making her feel like a fairy-tale princess. She snorted. Right, like Rapunzel locked away in the tower. Except that Carol had chin-length hair. She had no long, golden tresses to toss out the second-story window, allowing her princely rescuer to climb to her room and take her away from her imprisonment.

She touched the bed beside her where her tabby cat

would normally sleep. Poor old Puss. Stuck at the kennel until Carol learned to control this wolf-shifting business. But for now, her cat was happy, sprawled out on the receptionist's counter every afternoon greeting customers, even though Carol wanted him home with her. She suspected Darien didn't worry that her shifting into a wolf would frighten Puss to death as much as he really wasn't fond of cats.

She sighed. Darien wasn't just the owner of the silver mine and the leather-goods factory, nor was he just on the school board, the hospital board, and every other board in Silver Town. He ran the place...as a gray *lupus garou* pack leader, along with his triplet brothers, Jake and Tom.

Lelandi, the red wolf, was his mate. And Carol was now a red like her.

With her skin covered in a light sheen of perspiration, compliments of her continuing night terrors of being attacked and the shifting urge she continued to experience, she rose from the bed and walked toward the room's sole window. The filmy nightgown she wore caressed her skin with every step, her bare feet pressing silently against the springy golden carpet.

Not believing how upside down her world had become, she touched the place on her throat where five months ago, a feral red wolf had savagely ripped her open, turning her into one of their kind. No scar existed, not even a trace of one. She sighed deeply. She'd known for some time that a wolf would turn her. Damned psychic visions. But she hadn't seen how or when or what the ramifications would be. Nor had she realized that the change would force her to take a mate sooner rather than later.

Once she'd had the vision of what they truly were before she'd been turned, everyone had scrutinized her—Darien, Lelandi, his brothers. And the rest of the pack. They had watched her and made sure she didn't slip and spill the guarded secrets of the wolf kind once they realized she knew what they were because of her psychic visions. They had supervised her, barely ever allowing her out of their sight.

She was still a danger to them. An unknown quantity. A newly turned wolf who could fight the shift, which was an oddity in itself. But something more about her was off. She could see glimpses of the future. And sometimes she could touch an object and gather a psychic impression from it. This bothered them too. Even Lelandi, who had become like a sister to her, was troubled somewhat by Carol's paranormal abilities.

She sighed. She would never truly fit in, never belong. Yet for now, she was stuck under Darien's thumb, living with him, his mate, and his brothers until he could secure a mate for her. *Barbaric!* But it was the only way to ensure their safety and hers.

Not that she was going along with it.

She pulled aside the heavy, pale-blue velvet drapes and the matching silky sheers, her wolf senses allowing her night vision so that she didn't have to turn on the lamp. She peered into the forest and actually could see, as if the woods were merely cloaked in shadows. Chilling the air further on this cold night, a stiff breeze tugged the branches, making them dance to its tune.

Then she saw *him*, the wolf from her visions, stepping lightly out of the woods, watching her, and catching her eye. Her lips parted in surprise, and she took a shuddering breath. Who was he? She still didn't know all of Darien's people in their wolf forms. Someone who was guarding the house? Watching that she didn't leave in a crazy attempt to run away and start her life anew without Darien's intervention? That would be plain ludicrous. She could never manage on her own, nor did she want to live that way.

Because of the wolf's posture—his ears perked, his head lifting even higher—he had to be an alpha. It wasn't one of Darien's brothers. Someone from another pack then? Someone who wanted to fight Darien for leadership? He'd have to battle Darien's brothers also. Jake and Tom would never allow some outsider to take over the pack.

The lone wolf's gaze settled lower, studying the way she was dressed. Could he see well enough from that distance to note that her nipples had grown hard against the silky gown in the chilly air? Observing a wolf and realizing it was probably a wolf, who would have a man's desires even in wolf form, seemed surreal.

His gaze returned to hers.

Somehow, she was tied inexplicably to him, although the hazy visions weren't clear enough to tell her how. She didn't feel any apprehension, nor fear. He was safe, she thought.

Taking matters in hand, she would find out just who he was and, if she could, why he was here. She yanked the drapes closed, then with as much wolf care as she could manage, she slid a drawer open, hoping not to alert Lelandi, who was sleeping in the master bedroom down the hall.

Carol often got herself into trouble because of everyone's heightened sense of hearing. She kept thinking they could foresee things as she did. Not at all. They were just very good at eavesdropping to spy on what she was up to. Not in a mean way, of course. But to protect her and themselves.

Intending to find out who the stranger in the wolf coat was, she yanked out a sweater and a pair of jeans and began to dress. If she could get close enough, she would be able to smell and recognize him if she ran into him later in his human form.

She hated how everyone watched her every move. She felt as though she lived in a glass exam room where everything she did or said was monitored. But what was said behind closed doors rattled her even more. She was one of them, but *not*.

Yet—she tilted her chin up a hair as she left her room and then crept down the stairs with the utmost caution— she wasn't about to lose the person she had been before the change. She smiled as she got to the bottom of the stairs without signaling Lelandi that she was up after retiring to bed early and was planning an adventure she was certain none of them would approve. Now she only had to cross the living room to the back door and hopefully unlock, open, and close it without drawing attention.

The house was quiet, Lelandi also having retired unusually early to bed. Darien and his brothers were working late at the leather-goods factory as usual, so for once, Carol wasn't being monitored closely. Because she'd been so tired from her nursing shift and unable to sleep when she had the chance, no one expected her to leave her bedroom before daybreak.

Slowly, she twisted the handle on the door to the back patio. Without anyone's permission or supervision, she'd be free for a few precious minutes and prove she could manage her own life without disastrous consequences.

Disgruntled with himself for slinking through Darien's forest as a wolf so he could watch the house for any sign of Carol Wood, Chester Ryan McKinley hated his obsession. Even now when his PI practice had taken a back burner to his position as mayor and pack leader of Green Valley, he couldn't give up thinking about Carol, whom he'd met five months earlier while investigating a murder case involving Darien's pack. Ryan had found a lot of evidence against the murderer, but Carol's testimony had solicited the confession and the truth of the matter.

Long-legged and stacked, with hair the color of the golden sun and eyes as deep and mysterious as a shadowed blue lake, she had often worn a troubled expression during the investigation. Most likely due to the mess she'd gotten herself into as a human. The fact that she'd managed to get into such a predicament bothered him more than he liked to consider. As was his rescuing nature, he'd wanted to save her from her plight, ensure she didn't become one of his kind, and shield her from what they were.

But how could he have? She'd recognized his kind were *lupus garous* through strange visions, or so she had said. There had been no way to change events. During an ensuing fight between gray and red *lupus garou* packs, a red had bitten her and turned her. Ryan sure the hell wished *he'd* been protecting her.

Carol had been an innocent, unprepared for what would happen and unable to fight back. He imagined she'd never before witnessed wolf combat, which for a human had to have been extremely unnerving. Although every ounce of logic he possessed told him that people couldn't foresee the future, something about her—maybe her sincerity, the fear she'd exhibited, or the notion that she couldn't have learned all that she had through any other means—chiseled away at his wall of doubt.

Most of all, he admired her for her fortitude and dependability. She hadn't panicked or fought against her fate. Now he was sure Darien would be pushing for her to take a mate. For life…that was how they mated. That she would need one bothered him more than he liked to admit. Those who were born *lupus garous* could do with or without having a mate. Their choice. But a newly turned *lupus garou*? Allowing a new wolf too much freedom was too dangerous.

The drapes suddenly were thrust aside in the guest room Lelandi had once used. And there, standing in the window in a diaphanous gown of pale-blue silk, the blond pondered the woods. Almost as if she knew he was there watching for her. Which sent an unexpected surge of feral desire through his bloodstream. What was wrong with him that she had such an effect on him?

Her appearance in the gown at this early evening hour surprised him. Had she worked a long shift at the hospital?

The lovely rounded form of her breasts and nipples, peaked in anticipation of a lover's touch in the nearly see-through gown, became the focus of his attention. *Hell.* Not intending to enjoy the sight of her as a voyeur or to give in to his wolfish yearnings, he stepped forward so she could witness she was not alone. He meant to encourage her to close the drapes and return to bed, to warn her that the wolves in these woods were much more than just wolves. They were also men, like any of his kind, with earthly desires that needed to be sated.

Instead of closing the curtains, she challenged him with those eyes of hers. What had caught his attention about the woman, even during the investigation, were her classically attractive facial features—the high cheekbones and the perfect skin, framed by golden hair, and the large, striking blue eyes that could swallow a man whole. When she had spoken, full kissable lips had captured his attention more than once. She wasn't movie-star gorgeous, having instead the wholesome, girl-next-door look, but that appealed to him even more.

She frowned at him and then yanked the drapes closed. Good. She'd finally come to her senses.

He couldn't let go of the notion that the nurse thought she had the ability to make psychic predictions. It was the principle of the thing, he told himself. He intended to prove to himself, and to her, that she had come by her information about the murder through means other than some form of sixth sense. Either she had subconsciously learned the truth, or she had meddled in the investigation and was unwilling to tell about it.

Yet something deeper plagued him about the woman. Some elusive feeling that she could be in trouble. *She* could be trouble—that was more like it. Any newly turned wolf certainly could be that.

He tried to tell himself his being here wasn't about anything other than resolving the doubts that plagued him; although…something else bothered him, and he just couldn't put his finger on what.

Ears perked, he sat on his haunches, unable to take his gaze off her window and thinking of her returning to bed and then buried under her blankets. The unsolicited wish that he could be with her, snuggling and heating her up, flashed through his brain. Hell, he didn't need to be side-tracked any more than he already was.

Despite the case having been solved and his having no real reason to come back to Silver Town, Ryan was attending the spring festival the next morning to learn more about Darien's celebrations. Like he'd done before, Ryan would take the information back to his own people who wanted something of what Darien and his people had—a town run by the wolf kind.

But Darien had only *reluctantly* allowed Ryan to investigate as an outsider to discover the murderer in the pack. He was sure Darien wouldn't favor seeing him again under the circumstances, not when Ryan intended to question Carol further about her visions.

Darien sure wouldn't approve of Ryan lurking about his woodland estate early in the evening. Especially when Ryan didn't have one good reason for being near Darien's house like this, no matter how much he tried to convince himself he did.

A click on a back-door lock got Ryan's attention, and he quickly rose and backed into the woods to keep Darien or his people from seeing him. The door opened. Ryan's jaw dropped.

Little Miss Nightingale stepped out of the house onto the flagstone patio, peering in his direction. Not dressed warmly enough for the out-of-doors this evening, she wore a robin's-egg-blue tam that was perched on top of her head, a matching fluffy sweater that caressed her perky round breasts, pale-blue jeans that showcased her shapely legs, and a pair of fuzzy blue slippers that made her feet look twice their size.

He raised his brows. Hell. She had no business coming out into the night looking the way she did—soft and cuddly and vulnerable—with no way to defend herself in the event someone dangerous was lurking about. What had she intended to do? Search for him? Ask him his business?

At first, she stood stock-still, just staring into the woods. At the very place from which he watched her through a grove of Douglas firs. But he didn't think she could see him.

And then? She rubbed her hands together as if she were on a wolf-hunting mission and stalked toward the woods, headed straight for him! The notion that she'd hunt him down appealed on a strictly primal level. Her hell-bent determination wreaked havoc with his need to keep this on a purely professional basis. Willful was how he'd describe her actions. What if he'd been bad news?

But he wasn't, although right now, he had the strongest urge to circle around her through the woods and stalk her right back. A game between wolves. A competition. And more. Which made him wonder if she'd understand their wolf ways, not having grown up learning them. He also was curious just how far she'd go to discover who he was.

Instead of tracking her down, he moved deeper into the woods, as if luring her into his trap, and listened to her steady footsteps. They were more hurried now as she tried to reach the forest before he disappeared for good, he figured. Or maybe the fact that he wasn't in plain sight gave her more courage.

She stopped only a few feet away, the gray-green leaves of a Douglas fir brushing her arm, her eyes searching the dark woods as he watched her. His heart beat harder— the urge to hunt in his blood. Then she lifted her nose in a wolf's way, trying to catch his scent. Seeing her react the way his kind would—smelling for scents, tilting her head as she listened more carefully, attempting to track him down like a wolf on the hunt—he felt a new wave of respect for her wash over him. He hadn't seen this side of her before. It suited her.

Quickly, she turned her head, and when she saw him, her eyes widened. Luminescent. Huge. Bewitching.

Unable to help himself when he should have been annoyed with her impulsivity at leaving the house without protection, he gave her a slight smile. The woman would be his undoing.

What now? He wanted to force her to return to the house. On the other hand, he'd probably never get another chance to question her in private like this. He laughed at himself. Yeah, he'd shift, stand here naked in the cold as a human, and question her as if she were a suspect in one of his cases. He'd make such an impressive and frightening inquisitor that she'd quickly spill her story.

He took a deep breath and inhaled her feminine scent. Sweet like peaches and jasmine mingled together in a tantalizing combination, it triggered the lingering memory of when he'd managed to get close to her before. But not too close. Darien and his people had made sure of that. It was as if she were a fairy-tale princess in a gilded cage, and only those in Darien and Lelandi's close inner circle were allowed to draw near.

A feeling of satisfaction swept through him that he finally had a private audience, although it didn't do him much good while he was in his wolf form. He didn't smell any indication that she was fearful, which could have gotten her in trouble if she'd come out here without worrying about his intentions.

"Who are you?" she asked, her brow deeply furrowed as she wrapped her arms tightly around her waist, defensive but firm in her stance.

He had half a mind to shift. She'd asked a question she knew he couldn't answer any other way. What would she do then? Run screaming for the house to alert Darien and everyone inside? He'd shock the hell out of the woman, he was certain.

He swung his head toward the house in his wolf's way, ordering her to return.

Determination etched in her brow, she shook her head. "Shift. Tell me what you want."

Without his express permission, his jaw dropped again. He couldn't believe she'd order him about. Him, an alpha male and pack leader. She smiled a hint, her eyes narrowing. *Devious.* Appealing. She didn't think he'd shift?

She had asked for it. He stood taller, tail straight out, summoning the urge to change. Her brows lifted a little.

Heat poured through every blood vessel, spilling through every vein and artery. His muscles stretched, re-forming, and then in a flash, he was standing as a man before her. The cold breeze swept across his heated naked skin, and he expected Carol to vamoose or, at the very least, stare him in the eye to avoid looking at his nakedness.

A whisper of an intake of breath caught his attention, but she quickly recovered and took her fill of him, her gaze drifting all the way down to his bare feet, appraising him in an unhurried manner. He'd never had a woman peruse him in such an arousing way.

She snapped her gaze back to his face. "You look nice and healthy to me. I thought maybe you needed medical attention."

That was when it dawned on him. Miss Nightingale wouldn't be bothered by his nudity. She was used to seeing naked men. Why did that thought irk him? Maybe not so much that she had seen a lot of nude men, just like their wolf kind would when shifting, but that she didn't think *his* maleness was special in any way. Just...*healthy*. Yet he could have sworn she looked him over in much more than a clinical manner.

"Well?" she prompted.

"To the point, Ms. Wood—"

"Call me Carol. If you're going to talk to me in the dark forest without a stitch of clothes on, it seems silly to be so formal."

"I'm—"

"Chester McKinley. I didn't recognize your wolf form, but I remember you so gallantly wanting to help Lelandi find her sister's killer, no matter how much Darien disapproved."

The tone Carol used didn't sound as though she was impressed with Ryan's gallantry. In fact, she seemed downright irritated to see him. Despite her tone, he couldn't shake loose of the fascination she held for him.

"I go by Ryan."

She hesitated to speak and then asked, to the point, "So, *Ryan*? Why are you here? Does Darien know?"

"No. I wanted to speak to you about—"

Lights suddenly flooded the back porch, and Jake yelled, "Here! She's taken off into the woods this way!"

CHAPTER 2

"Oh, no. Go," Carol whispered to Ryan in the dark woods, at once sounding vulnerable and desperate. Darien and his brothers were sure to be on the warpath as they searched for her. "If Darien finds me with you and you're…" She motioned to his nudity, her gaze lingering lower. "There'll be hell to pay."

"He'll smell me anyway and see my wolf tracks." Ryan couldn't pinpoint why he delayed leaving. Maybe he was worried he might have gotten her into trouble because of their actions. Yet the inexplicable feeling kept gnawing at him that when he had wanted to question her during the investigation and after she'd been injured, Darien hadn't allowed it. Ryan didn't like to be thwarted in any fact-finding mission he set out to accomplish. And he wouldn't be this time either.

"Go," she pleaded.

"Tomorrow, I'll speak with you at the celebration."

"Darien won't allow it. You know he won't."

At that, Ryan felt a stab of guilt. The only reason he came here was to see Carol and prove she didn't have any special abilities. For an instant, he thought she sounded hopeful that he wanted to see her about some other matter, something more intimate. Which struck another chord deep inside.

He had to remind himself that his own wolf pack hadn't had a newly turned wolf in a couple of decades. So he wasn't

used to the notion that someone like Carol might have difficulty adjusting to pack life where a leader had to ensure
the newbie didn't stray far and cause colossal problems that
couldn't easily be resolved.

"Carol…"

She shook her head. "Go, now. I'll try to see you
tomorrow."

He ground his teeth and listened to the hurried footfalls
headed in their direction. Then he shifted and, at a wolf's
loping run, took off for the river to hide his tracks again.
Eventually, he'd return to the bed-and-breakfast and settle
in his room for the night. Although he might not be able to
keep the room if Darien learned about it.

Ryan had wanted to face Darien and his people and
explain why he had been there tonight, knowing they'd
question Carol mercilessly about what she had seen in the
woods. Although as a naked man, he'd have had no chance
to explain himself, especially when he couldn't come up
with a half-logical reason to explain it to himself.

"Carol!" Darien said, his tone sharp but worried.

A pack leader carried the burden of keeping all his
people safe, Ryan knew only too well. He headed toward
the river and thought he saw a flash of red fur. Coyote?
Another red wolf? He glanced back in the direction he had
come. Couldn't have been Carol, and he doubted it would
have been Lelandi.

Unless it was that sneaky cousin of Lelandi's, Ural. Or
some other member of her family. Why slip around in the
dark out here in the woods like he was doing? Ryan's spine
stiffened as he considered what might have happened to Carol
if she had encountered whoever this was alone in the dark.

He had never liked coincidences and rarely believed in them. His PI instincts pressed him to investigate the red in the event he could be trouble for Darien's people.

With a quick twist in the wolf's direction, Ryan dashed in hot pursuit after the red.

The image of Ryan in the nude was still foremost in Carol's thoughts as he raced off in his wolf form. Although his eyes, pools of darkened amber, were entrancing enough to nearly make her forget anything else. Dark coffee-colored hair curling around his ears had somewhat softened the hard, angular planes of his face, a shadowy stubble adding to the sexy ruggedness. She hadn't seen him in five months, but that amount of time didn't diminish the way she had remembered him—the way he had studied her months ago when she explained to Darien what she'd envisioned and helped him bring the murderer to justice.

Ryan had observed her the same way just now. He seemed to be intrigued with her. Most likely because he'd never met anyone quite like her. At least that was what she thought.

But then she was back to thinking about his naked body. Healthy. *Right.* Sleek, hard muscles toned to perfection, darkly pebbled nipples and an indented navel meant for licking, skin glistening, his sex stirring even as she had admired it, jutting out from a bush of dark-brown hair, muscular legs, and large feet, all *very* well proportioned, caught her imagination. She'd definitely not seen him in *that* way before.

She had believed that once she had turned into one of their kind, seeing a naked man built like Ryan wouldn't affect her. She guessed that was a naive thought. Especially when she had to take a look at his package—twice. Would it make any difference if she had been a *lupus garou* for eons and had seen others strip and shift whenever in a pack?

Maybe. Like living at a nudist colony and being used to seeing everyone nude all the time. No big deal. Even though the pack members didn't shift all the time. So they weren't often naked in front of other pack members. And they changed so fast that, to the naked eye, the shift was mostly a wondrous blurring of forms.

She had thought she wouldn't be affected, being a nurse and trying to look at him in a clinical way while maintaining an air of aloofness. *Right.* She hadn't succeeded. Now she couldn't shake loose the image of his powerful build, thinking how it would be with someone like him in the throes of passionate lovemaking. Her face flushed at the thought.

"Carol!" Darien snapped again. She recognized the fear in his expression, although he often schooled his face to hide such emotions.

He stalked toward her, dark hair, dark eyes, a warrior ready to do battle. His brothers flanked him, all eyes on her, tensions running high, their postures ready to pounce if she attempted to run. Where was she supposed to run to? She was clueless about so many aspects of being a *lupus garou*.

Lelandi had warned her how vulnerable she would be on her own as a newly turned *lupus garou*. But she didn't want to live alone either. Despite the pack's restrictions on her, she still loved the whole lot of them. She loved their

protectiveness, their caring, and the way they seemed clueless sometimes as to how to deal with her uniqueness.

Even so, she thanked God that she hadn't yet changed
into a wolf. But the urge to shift would make it impossible
for her to fight it forever. She had no plans to go anywhere.
This was home, such as it was, and at least she worked in the
hospital, now that she was one of them—*kind of*. Working
as a nurse had been the job she'd dreamed of since she was
a girl and had broken her leg. She wanted to help others in
need, just like the medical staff had helped her. So this was
it for her.

"I'm coming," she said in a grumpy way as Darien and
his brothers drew closer. She really wished they wouldn't
watch her so much. She was fine and didn't need them hovering over her like a bunch of old motherly hens. "I thought
the three of you were at work."

Jake and Tom looked her over as if to ensure she was
okay and then quickly searched the surrounding area, trying
to locate Ryan's tracks.

"Is that why you left the house? Because you thought I
wouldn't learn of it?" Darien took her arm and escorted her
back to the house. He turned to peer over his shoulder at his
brothers, took a sniff of the air, and grunted. Towering over
her, Darien gave her a hard look.

"What the hell were you doing out here alone with
McKinley? Just because my brothers and I weren't home
and Lelandi was sleeping, that doesn't mean it's safe for you
to be running around in the woods by yourself at night."
Then he considered her, his eyes narrowing. He shook his
head. "He'd better not want you for a mate."

Her lips parted in surprise. She should have known

Darien would recognize who Ryan was, but why would a gray pack leader be interested in a newly turned red wolf? Then again, why in the world would he want to see her so badly, potentially incurring Darien's wrath?

She sighed. Ryan was virile, rugged, and sexy with a body that wouldn't quit. Hell, he was a feast for impoverished eyes to be sure. She hoped she'd acted less like a schoolgirl who hadn't seen goods like that on a man in a long time and more like a nurse concerned with his medical needs. But more than his physical good looks, Ryan was protective and caring and dedicated. Was he really interested in getting to know her better?

She smiled, each step becoming springier as she headed for the house. She'd always had a thing for alpha males. Not that she had any intention of being bossed around, even if one had her best interests at heart. Her fascination with alphas was that they were a challenge. Betas didn't hold much of an appeal.

But then her step slowed. When he'd been here before, she had read in his posture and in his censure that he didn't believe in her psychic abilities. With that kind of attitude, he couldn't be interested in her.

She stiffened and cast a look over her shoulder in the direction he'd gone. So then what was he *really* doing here?

———

Later that night, after not locating the red wolf who had run off in the woods next to Darien's house and irritated beyond reason, Ryan came to the conclusion that the *lupus garou* was wearing some kind of hunter's scent concealer.

Otherwise, Ryan would have caught up to him at some point. Which meant the red was up to no good.

Sneaking through Darien's territory, the red had been careful not to mark the area, just as Ryan hadn't, although the instinct was hard to control as an alpha in wolf form. Ryan had smelled the scent markings made by Darien and other pack members when he had crossed the invisible boundary into Darien's territory earlier. The markings were a warning to other wolves and predators that the land was already occupied.

Ryan came across wolf tracks and red fur snagged on a pinyon pine branch, but the smell of the wolf's current location eluded him. When Ryan sniffed the fur left behind, there was no odor at all.

He traveled after the red wolf for a couple of miles, but the trail led to a river and stopped on the rocky bank. Even though the trespassing wolf was Darien's problem, not his own, a nagging thought continued to plague Ryan as he turned and headed through the forest to town. Why had the wolf been watching Darien's house?

His actions didn't make any sense, and Ryan couldn't help worrying about Lelandi and Carol, the only two red wolves in Darien's pack. Except for Lelandi's doctor from her former red pack, who was on loan to Darien's pack for the time being. But the doctor lived nearer town, not close to Darien's home. And he was a male. Which made Ryan believe that the red male lurker was interested in Carol or Lelandi. Or both.

Reluctantly, Ryan followed the tree line and finally reached the back side of the Hastings Bed and Breakfast, where his rented room looked out on the Douglas firs, perfect for privacy. He'd left the window open so he could easily let himself back in. When he jumped at the opening, though, he realized too late that someone had shut the damned thing.

His front paws hit the glass pane hard, and he grunted and jumped back. *Hell.* Swinging his head around, he saw Bertha Hastings, the owner of the establishment, peer out the kitchen window. For a while, she just watched him, not recognizing him. A lone wolf. Not of her pack. An outsider.

He sat and waited.

Bertha's round face lifted in a happy countenance with springy silver curls tracing her cheeks where they'd fallen loose from a bun and a dash of white powder on the tip of her pert nose. Did she finally recognize him? She hadn't been at the battle when the reds and grays fought. And he hadn't been in his wolf form at any other time when Bertha had been around.

She opened the window, lifted her chin, and breathed deeply. Then she smiled again, this time her eyes matching the cheerful greeting.

She knew it was him. He took a breath of relief as she disappeared from the window. Then the back door opened, and she motioned for him to hurry inside. He hesitated, concerned she might have some human guests about. More vigorously this time, she again waved for him to come in.

With a loping gait, he hurried into the kitchen. The scent of strawberries and whipped cream, sugar-powdered cakes, roasting duck, and spears of asparagus grilling in olive oil met with his approval. He took another whiff, which made her smile.

"Dinner will be served in a couple of minutes. What are

you *really* doing here, Ryan McKinley?" Bertha asked as she pulled a key off a rack and hurried down the hall, the key clinking on its chain.

He guessed, as many years as she must have lived, she didn't believe he was just attending the spring festival the next day as he'd said. He followed close behind her, wanting to slip into the room before a human guest saw him and went into hysterics.

Bertha unlocked his door and let him in. "I closed the window because heating this place is difficult enough. I didn't realize you'd taken a run on the wild side. I do have an electronic wolf door in the kitchen if you need to go out. No human guests are staying at the bed-and-breakfast right now, so feel free to come and go as you please in whichever form you prefer."

He'd seen the wolf door when he'd first checked in, but he hadn't wanted Bertha to know he was headed out, figuring she would have been curious about what he was up to. And he hadn't known if she had any human guests, although that could have changed if one had checked in while he was on his run.

She motioned to the bedroom with its floral prints in varying shades of green on white backgrounds, dark forest-green walls, white furniture, and a vase filled with fresh green-and-white carnations. The place made him feel as though he were staying in a room in the forest, minus bugs and weather problems.

"This is the room Lelandi used when she first arrived. She sure brought a hornet's nest of trouble with her, although in the end, it all turned out for the best," Bertha said and then raised a brow. She gave a resigned sigh.

"You aren't planning on stirring up the town also, are you? I should warn Darien you're here. But I doubt you're any real threat. I take it you're not here to see Lelandi this time." Then Bertha's brows both elevated as if she'd worked out the mystery on her own. "Oh, not Lelandi. Carol then?" Her lips curved up in a sly way.

He waited patiently for Bertha to leave, but she seemed preoccupied with sorting out why he was here and letting him know what conclusions she was drawing from the situation.

"Oh…now I see. I'll leave you to your business." She turned to go but stopped and said over her shoulder, "Darien's getting ready to encourage one of our pack members and Carol to mate. So if you're interested…" She sighed. "I shouldn't be saying so since you're not one of our pack, but I think you could handle her best of all since you're an alpha and patient to boot.

"She puts on airs that she's strong and doesn't need anyone to look after her while she's supposed to take care of everyone else. Don't believe it. Under that competent, no-nonsense, skilled nurse is a woman who needs someone for moral support from time to time. Jake would be a good candidate for her, but they quarrel a lot in a lighthearted way. And Tom, well, I'm not sure what he's thinking half the time. You might want to step in and make a bid for her. I can only say she'd be worth it."

She smiled broadly, then closed the door and left Ryan in peace.

He didn't like hearing that Jake was quarreling with Carol. After all she'd been through, she needed someone who was supportive and not confrontational. He shifted and threw on his clothes, thinking about what Bertha had said about him being patient. Yeah, he guessed he could be described in that way. Also methodical, dogged, and thorough.

But in the market for a mate? He shook his head. All he needed were answers.

His cell phone rang and he grabbed it. *Rosalind.* "Hello? What's wrong?"

"Did you see her?"

No matter how many times he told his sister this was strictly business, he couldn't convince her. "I plan to see her tomorrow." At least that *was* the plan.

CHAPTER 3

THE NEXT MORNING, APPREHENSIVE AS TO WHETHER Jake or Tom had caught up with Ryan last night, Carol hurried to dress in jeans, her favorite soft violet sweater that always made her feel ready for any adventure, and a pair of tennis shoes. If the brothers had had heated words with Ryan, no one had said a thing about it to her. Which made her worry more that they were hiding the truth from her.

Sneaking away to see Ryan privately was going to be a real challenge, *if* Darien and his brothers hadn't warned him off and Ryan still managed to slip into the festival. Not knowing what to expect at the spring affair, since only wolves were allowed and she hadn't been to one before, Carol had been excited to participate.

She had barely slept, wondering what Ryan had wanted of her and hoping he hadn't gotten into a lot of trouble with Darien and his brothers the previous night. Not to mention that twice more, the damned hot flashes had invaded her body, an annoying prelude to the shift. Thankfully, she'd been able to stop it both times with a recurring vision of the man in red and white stripes.

Festive pipe-and-whistle music could be heard playing in the meadow near the woods, and that lifted her spirits. Darien's pack gathered in the meadow for wolf-only functions due to its private location, and the music made it sound like a fairy troupe had descended on the area.

Downstairs, she smelled bacon frying. Had to be Jake. He was always up the earliest and loved to cook.

Then the aroma of rose and lilac wreaths pelted her senses—the fragrance of spring and summer. The roses and lilacs had arrived compliments of the local florist shop, while the rest of the flowers were grown in Lelandi's own garden. Everything from the staircase to the fireplace mantels was decorated in nature's finest: pine cones, feathers, crocuses, tulips in red, purple, and yellow, and a soft sprinkle of white lights—as if a floral garden had found a warm, cozy niche in a spacious wolves' den to escape the still-cool spring weather.

What really enlivened Carol's step was the notion that she would meet with Ryan again and learn why he wanted to see her. *Was* he interested in her? It wasn't that she didn't want a mate; she simply wanted some choice in the matter. So far, she hadn't been attracted to anyone in the pack except Darien's brothers, and they weren't showing any interest back. Maybe the reason she'd had the vision of Ryan was because he was the one meant to sweep her off her feet.

Or not. Her visions could be irritatingly deceptive, unenlightening, or just plain ominous.

When she entered the kitchen, Jake's back was facing her while he turned bacon in a cast-iron skillet. "Morning, Carol," he said without turning around.

She lifted her nose and took a whiff of him. He had a spicy scent, a fresh woods smell—as if he'd just been outside and brought in another load of firewood. Even though it had been five months since she was turned, she wasn't used to everyone using their sense of smell to know she was around. She kept thinking they had psychic abilities like she

did, although Lelandi assured her they didn't. Except for
Lelandi's strange ability to feel her brother Leidolf's strong
emotions.

Leidolf. He was now a red pack leader in Portland,
Oregon, and totally intriguing. He had been single and very
available but not interested in a newly turned red. Nope, he
was a royal. That meant his lineage could be traced close
to the first lupus garou, and very few humans had tainted
his family's line. Carol would have tainted it big time if he'd
ever thought of mating her. But only a couple of days ago,
Lelandi had sprung the news on them: it looked like her
brother had finally met his match.

Jake scooped some eggs onto a plate, rousing Carol from
her thoughts about Lelandi's brother. Jake was an interesting character. He was tough, hiding his emotions, and dark
and brooding like his older brother, Darien. But unlike
Darien, Jake wore a beard, and his eyes were nearly black.
Whenever he had the time, Jake headed into the wilderness,
not to hunt or fish or be a macho man but to take pictures of
wildflowers. And he played down the fact that he did.

"Eggs, bacon?" he asked.

No longer did she crave fruit for breakfast. Eggs and
bacon were much more her style now. She let out her breath
in a heavy sigh, hating all the changes she'd experienced.

Jake cast a small smile at her over his shoulder. "Don't
tell me you used to be a vegetarian and have been keeping it
secret from us these past few months."

"No." She didn't even bother to hide the annoyance in
her voice.

He chuckled. She'd heard him arguing with Darien, that
she needed a mate and in a hurry. But Jake wasn't offering

himself. And as sweet as their youngest brother, Tom, was, he didn't seem interested either.

So what did that leave her? A mess of males of various ages, all bachelors, who were dying to locate a female for a mate because females were so rare, or so she'd been told. Sam the bartender was a hunk, but Silva and he were a match, although they were still in the courtship phase of their relationship. *Lupus garous* did not have casual sex, so that meant the courtship would probably end soon, as hot and heavy as the petting was getting between them.

"It'll get better." His tone more serious, Jake set the plate piled with eggs and bacon in front of her. "You'll adjust."

"Right." She didn't believe she ever would.

"Darien says you're fighting the change. Five months." Jake's gaze pinned her with the accusation. "Can't put it off forever, and if you keep trying, it's bound to get you in trouble."

"I've heard the lecture before, Jake."

"Yeah, but you should heed the warning." He finished his coffee and went back for more. "If you don't change, you'll force Darien's hand to ban you from working at the hospital."

She stifled a gasp. Darien couldn't take that away from her. Could he?

Jake cast a sympathetic look at her. "You won't have any control over the change pretty soon. All of a sudden, you'll be ripping off your clothes and turning wolf anywhere at any time. Wouldn't bother the rest of us, but what would human patients think? We can't let them know what we are. And you're a big risk right now."

She couldn't allow the shift. She'd felt the urge growing

as the full moon approached, but from what Lelandi said, anytime the moon was out, even half-moon or crescent, *lupus garous* could change. And they had to at least once during the cycle. Lelandi didn't have to, being a royal. She could change anytime or not at all. Except for one time: when Lelandi had feared for her brother in his fight to the death with Larissa's murderer, she hadn't been able to shift back right away.

Carol thought that was part of the reason she herself feared if she shifted, she'd be a wolf forever. But the vision she'd had worried her even more. The red doctor from Lelandi's former pack, Dr. Weber, would shift and then be unable to shift back. At least she thought that was the case.

Certain Darien and the rest would all shake their heads at her in disbelief, she hadn't voiced her concern to anyone yet. But she had to. Lelandi was like a sister to her now, and if anyone would believe her, Lelandi would. Or at least Carol hoped she would.

Sitting across from Carol, Jake smiled. A gleam of mischievousness sparkled in his eyes as he paused, his fork carrying a scoop of eggs to his mouth. "Ready for your coming-out?"

She ignored him and poked at her eggs.

"Darien won't wait much longer. Not when ten of the men in our pack are insisting he make you available to court."

Her lips parted for a second, and she couldn't disguise her surprise quickly enough. Darien hadn't allowed the men to get close to her? To an extent, she was relieved to think the bachelors hadn't just been avoiding her because she was such an oddity. And that Darien was concerned enough about her well-being to wait until she was more ready for this.

But she was incensed that she would be treated like a heroine in some historical romance. *Available to court. Right.*

"Oh, come on, Jake. It sounds like medieval times instead of the twenty-first century!"

She wrinkled her nose in annoyance at the disagreeable thought. Even though she loved *reading* romances like that, she didn't want to be treated like one of those women. Although, in the fictional versions, they always *eventually* ended up living happily ever after.

"Hey, when a shortage of women existed in the Old West, women were prized. You should feel honored. Besides, we've told you we base a lot of what we do on age-old traditions. When a good thing works..." He shrugged.

"Honored? Ha! All a man wanted then was a woman to darn his socks, cook his meals, and warm his bed."

Jake smiled. "No need to darn socks or cook meals here. Warming beds"—he raised a brow, his smile still lingering—"that's another story."

She gave him an annoyed look. "I feel pushed into making a decision I don't want to even consider right now."

He shook his head, his tone an attempt to be reassuring. "You're not going to be made to do anything right away."

She didn't believe that for a minute. And "not right away" meant what? She had days? Weeks? A few months to make a decision? She understood their concern—that she had to be watched constantly, that a wrong move on her part could put them all in jeopardy, and that having a mate would help her adjust more easily to her new role. Still—

His chestnut hair lighter than Jake's and his eyes more

amber, Tom sauntered into the kitchen and cleared his throat. "Give it a rest, Jake."

Tom was always her knight when she needed one, but even he had kept his distance as far as any kind of emotional attachment since the Thanksgiving feast. She'd wondered if Jake and Tom had only stuck close to her then because Darien had told them to watch her, to keep the other males away from her until he said the timing was right.

She harrumphed under her breath, and Jake raised his brows. "Got something you want to share?"

She cast him an irritated look and chomped down on another piece of bacon.

"Mervin's *real* interested," Jake said.

She didn't care that Jake was teasing. She was tired of the conversation.

"Jake." Tom slanted him a warning look. Being the baby of the triplets, even only by five minutes, Tom couldn't help that the pecking order was well established. Jake wasn't about to listen to his younger brother.

"Get free haircuts if you mated with him," Jake persisted.

"He's the barber. He doesn't cut women's hair." Carol knew Jake's comment was intended to ridicule her for having a chin-length haircut and not growing it longer like other *lupus garou* women. *That* she wasn't going to change.

"A bunch of us are going for a romp through the woods late tonight," Tom said casually. "Did you want to go with us, Carol?"

"Thank you, Tom, I'd love to." *Not.* Poor Tom. His heart was in the right place; he kept trying to make her feel like one of the pack. But she couldn't shift. Not willingly. For five months, he'd been trying to encourage her to really join in and be one of them. "But not tonight."

Jake and Tom shared looks—as if they agreed their houseguest was impossibly difficult to deal with.

To change the subject to one she wanted to resolve, she asked, "When is Puss going to be allowed to come home to me?"

Even if it wasn't her home, and even though she stopped to visit him at the kennel every night after work, she wanted her fur ball curled up in her lap at night when she relaxed and read a book or watched TV, or to play with him with a flashlight beam as he tried to capture it, or to run her hand under the covers as he tried to tackle the hidden object. Sure, Doc Mitchell, the vet, let Puss have free rein over the clinic and kennel, but she wanted Puss home with her to cuddle and play with! She'd considered sneaking him home with her, hoping Darien would see how much her cat meant to her.

Her words met with silence, and then Lelandi and Darien walked in. He had his arm wrapped around his mate's waist, and they both looked perfectly satiated. Carol caught herself before she shook her head, wistfully wishing that she had someone in her life like that. They seemed perfect for each other, even though they had their disagreements. Carol would cheerfully suffer discord with a prospective mate if she could have the glow that Lelandi had worn ever since taking Darien on.

"Good morning, everyone," Lelandi said, giving Carol a big smile. With her long red hair curling over a navy-blue velour running set, Lelandi looked ready to compete in the festival games, although Carol had heard that Darien had suspended the tug-of-war competition. He wouldn't say why, and no one would even speculate, which she thought was odd.

Casting a cursory glance at Carol, Darien was back to his

business look, as usual. "Jake, I need you to make arrangements for a gathering tonight."

Jake turned his attention to Carol. *Great.* What now?

Could they be thinking of having her debut to polite society as if she'd just reached the age of maturity and was eligible to "court" like debutantes did in the Regency novels she loved? Some regions *still* held coming-out parties or balls for groups of well-connected young women. She supposed *she* was now well connected—if living with Darien and Lelandi was the wolf equivalent. Yet presenting her to "wolf society" at her age seemed preposterous.

"Did *you* have a coming-out?" she asked Lelandi. She'd learned Lelandi's mother and father had both come from pack-leader families, so she imagined they'd been high in wolf social circles.

"Oh, yes."

Carol fidgeted with the napkin in her lap. "But you mated with Darien," she said pointedly.

"Um, yes. I wasn't quite in the market for one of my pack members, not when the man of my dreams kept coming to me in my sleep." Lelandi glanced at Darien, who reached for her hand and squeezed.

Carol loved how the two of them looked at each other, as if the world stood still while they searched each other's souls in that powerful moment.

However, the point she was trying to make seemed to be lost, although she didn't figure it had any bearing anyway. Darien would have his way in this, no matter what.

As if reading her mind, he said, "It's our way, has been for centuries. Not all find mates this way, of course, but…" He shrugged.

What was left unsaid was more telling than anything else. Carol sat taller and tried not to frown too much. She had been doing a lot of that lately, and her mother had always said that if Carol continued with it, she'd have wrinkles permanently etched in her forehead. "*But* since I'm newly turned, I have no choice, right?"

"Oh, no," Lelandi said quickly. "The choice of who you want to see, date, and mate is up to you. Up to *both* of you." She gave Darien a look indicating he'd better agree.

Jake gave Carol an evil smile. "Mervin's invited, right?"

If the table leg hadn't been in the way, Carol would have kicked Jake.

"Sure, if he's interested." Darien carried plates to the table for Lelandi and himself, set them down, and then pulled her chair out for her as she brought their mugs of coffee.

"He's interested, all right. *Real* interested," Jake said.

"Guess that means I'm forgoing my romp in the woods tonight," Tom said with a sigh.

Avoiding a look at Carol, Darien sat at the table. "No need to. Jake can handle it."

"I'll help him out." Tom gave Jake a look like he'd better behave or else.

Why couldn't Tom be interested in her? She'd noticed that when Lelandi and Darien were together, or Sam and Silva, she smelled a distinct sexual attraction between them. She hadn't noticed that special scent whenever any male was near her. Which meant? She guessed no one was *that* interested. Heck, she hadn't had a real boyfriend since she'd started nursing school four years ago, and now that she was a wolf, she couldn't even excite a bunch of horny wolves who didn't have mates.

The way Lelandi was casting surreptitious looks, Carol knew she wanted to speak to her about something out of the guys' earshot. Probably sisterly wolf advice about meeting with a man alone in the woods. Even if he'd been a wolf. *At first.*

Darien quickly devoured his breakfast, kissed Lelandi's cheek, and then said to his brothers, "Come on. The celebration doesn't truly start until we show up."

She knew that included Lelandi, but...something was being left unsaid.

Jake and Tom glanced at Carol. Yep, the secret society of wolves, and she really wasn't part of it. The men hurried to leave while Lelandi began clearing away the dishes. Carol rose to help her.

"What did he want, Carol?" Lelandi asked casually, but Carol noted the disapproval in her tone of voice.

Trying to appear nonchalant, Carol asked, "Who?"

Lelandi turned and touched Carol's arm in an appeasing way, her eyes worried. "I can't imagine what it's like for you trying to adjust to our ways, but you have to realize Darien only does what's best for you and for our people.

"I hadn't wanted you to be changed against your will or to suffer as you did. But I thank God you survived the attack. You're like a sister to me now, always and forever." She hugged Carol and breathed in deeply. "Always know that."

A feeling of belonging washed over Carol briefly. She was glad to have a sister when both she and Lelandi had lost their own. She expected Lelandi to say something more about Ryan, to warn her off him, but for whatever reason, Lelandi continued to rinse the coffee mugs and put them in the dishwasher without saying another word. Maybe she figured Carol wouldn't listen anyway. And she had that right. Carol couldn't be a beta like most of the people in the pack. Most of the time, she wouldn't roll over and play the subservient wolf unless she felt she had no other choice.

The issue of the vision she'd had the day before kept plaguing her. She knew she had to tell Lelandi. Even though the more she considered it, the more she was afraid Lelandi wouldn't believe her.

Keeping her hands busy so speaking about the subject would be easier, Carol rinsed off a dirty dish and put it in the dishwasher.

"Lelandi...I...well, I know it's sometimes difficult for others to believe how I can see things that haven't happened yet. Until they can be proven. I mean, if I give a warning and then whatever I predicted actually occurs. Then it's perfectly verifiable. I know sometimes you feel that's true even when the vision hasn't come to pass, but sometimes..." She shrugged.

Lelandi set the washrag on the tile counter and stopped wiping off bread crumbs and coffee spills, her expression an attempt at neutral, but her jaw tightened marginally. "What's the matter?" Her voice was even but tinged with concern.

"It's...it's just that I saw Doc shift into a wolf and then, well, he couldn't shift back."

Lelandi's brows rose, and then she smiled. Any hint of concern vanished, and she went back to wiping the counter. "He changes back. We all do."

"That one time you couldn't."

Lelandi paused and looked thoughtful. "Yes, but that

only has to do with my strong feelings for certain people. It's only happened twice, each time when my brother nearly died. It took a couple of hours, maybe longer, to turn back into my human form. Then I was back to normal. No one that I've known during my long years of life has had trouble shifting form."

"Even newly turned wolves?"

"Did you see yourself in that predicament? Unable to shift back?"

Carol slowly shook her head. But she figured the only reason she didn't see that was because she refused to change and was able to fight it successfully. For how long, she wasn't certain. She also noted that Lelandi didn't exactly answer her question. "Have any newly turned wolves that you know of been unable to shift back?"

"Not that I've ever heard of. Besides, Doc's a royal red like me. No human influences in his roots for generations. So like me, he can change at will." Lelandi smiled and patted Carol's shoulder. "Doc Weber will be fine. You said your visions were brief glimpses of the future. So he shifts, and you just don't see him change back. He has to shift back eventually, only you don't see a vision of that. That's all.

"Really, Carol. I've explained how I was tied to my sister's and brother's stronger emotions whenever we were in close proximity to each other. That's all the problem was with my inability to shift back. Don't worry."

But Carol did worry. Lelandi was right that Carol couldn't see a lengthy video stream of what would occur, but just like Lelandi felt strong ties to her brother's emotions, Carol had strong feelings with her visions. And she knew something was horribly wrong. It had to be that Doc couldn't shift back. She couldn't imagine what else the matter could be.

She sighed. Until she could see something more that would convince Lelandi, she knew she'd never get anywhere on that front. Might as well talk to Lelandi about what Carol knew was bothering her. "In the woods last night...Ryan said he had something to ask me. That's all."

Lelandi stopped rinsing the sink out and turned to gape at Carol. "Ryan?"

"Um, Chester Ryan McKinley, but he asked me to call him Ryan."

"He changed from a wolf and stood naked in front of you to speak?"

Carol shrugged. "It was no big deal. I'd had a vision of him, and I needed to know who he was and what he wanted. He couldn't very well answer me as a wolf. And he was a perfect gentleman, just as he always was with you."

Her green eyes narrowed, Lelandi gave a ladylike snort and tucked her red curls behind her ears. "He was a gentleman with me because he knew he'd be a dead man if he was anything but. Men are wolves, no pun intended. Lusty wolves.

"If he's got any ideas about you—which he very well may have, now that you're one of us—you'd best stay clear of him. Darien and his brothers will make short work of him if he interferes in pack politics. He's not here by invitation, and last night, he trespassed in our territory without permission. Darien's quite incensed about it."

Her heart sinking, Carol glanced out the kitchen window. She was a healer by trade, and the last time she'd watched out the sunroom windows was when the pack gathered in the meadow to take down a murderer. She couldn't deal with this part of being a wolf. Maybe subconsciously that was another thing that bothered her about being a part-time wolf. If she changed, would she have the urge to kill?

With shaking hands, Carol put the last of the dirty silverware in the dishwasher. "I'll...I'll see you at the festival."

She rushed out of the kitchen to warn Ryan to leave right away if she caught sight of him first.

Lelandi called out to her, "Don't get in the way of Darien's handling of our pack, Carol."

Right. When she was already an outsider with so many strikes against her, what did another few matter?

Why did the men in Darien's pack still want her? Were they just desperate? She'd seen them smile as if they were interested. She guessed they hadn't approached her yet because of Darien's ruling. But still, she was bothered by the niggling thought that they would get a lot more than they bargained for if they pursued her. She didn't think any of the beta males could deal with her uniqueness.

She sighed and shoved the sunroom door open.

CHAPTER 4

LELANDI SMILED AFTER CAROL AS SHE BOLTED OUT OF the house. Lelandi could talk until she was blue in the face, trying to get Darien to listen to her about Carol's special circumstances, without making a difference. Either Carol's desire to save Chester's—rather, Ryan's—butt would change Jake's or Tom's interest in Carol, or maybe Ryan *was* her match.

Whatever Lelandi could do to help, she was ready. She was certain that the right man would work wonders in helping Carol accept what she was now. And time was running out. Soon, Carol would inevitably shift, and when it happened, Lelandi prayed that Carol was at home or with their own kind only. Lelandi had convinced Darien to continue to allow Carol to work at the hospital, but he'd nix that before long if she didn't shift soon.

Lelandi's best friend, Silva, sauntered into the kitchen, bottled water in one hand and a red ribbon in the other. Her dark curls piled on top of her head, she was wearing short shorts, a pair of thigh-high boots, and a short-waisted shirt that showed off her navel. Lelandi swallowed a grin.

Sam had better get off the fence about making a commitment to Silva, or he was going to have a lot of competition on the playing field today.

"I heard McKinley sneaked around the grounds last night to see Carol," Silva said, brows raised.

Lelandi shrugged.

Silva grinned. "He did!" Then she frowned. "Ohmigod, the bachelor males will be out for blood if he shows up at the festivities." Silva leaned over the kitchen sink and looked out the window. "You should be with her, don't you think? I mean, both of us. If we chaperone her, McKinley won't come near, and Darien and his brothers won't have to hurt him."

She turned to Lelandi. "So what *did* happen last night? I heard Carol was in the woods with him. *Alone.*"

Not about to tell anyone what Carol had shared with her in confidence, Lelandi sighed. "What about Sam? Is he going to protect you in the game of tag?"

Silva laughed. "Hell, if he doesn't, it's his problem, not mine."

But Lelandi knew Silva wanted Sam, and he truly wanted her. She wasn't sure how to get them to finally capitulate and become mates. Lelandi rubbed her stomach absently. She thought she'd gotten the two of them going in the right direction.

"Come on, Silva. Let's have some fun." And she prayed that fun was all they'd have—and no male battles of wills.

Carol backed up closer to the woods, where maybe Ryan could sneak out and talk to her while everyone was busy playing tag. But then she saw four men combing the woods. Ryan would never manage to talk with her alone again.

"Come on. Let's get a ribbon," Lelandi said, joining her and tugging at her arm to get her to move closer to a group of men and women, mostly men, who were dividing up ribbons. Blue for one team. Red for the other.

"Smile. The world isn't going to end. We play games like this all the time, both as wolves and as humans, although not in mixed forms. It's our nature to show solidarity, teamwork, and cooperation. It's who we are and how we survive. Besides, Darien's brothers will protect you from the big, bad wolves."

Carol wasn't worried about the game as much as she was worried about the battle that might ensue if Ryan showed up. And now she felt as though she was a pawn in the scheme of things—the much sought-after conquest of a bunch of mate-hungry bachelors.

Laughing at herself over that, she told herself she'd believe that when she saw it.

Lelandi motioned to Sam, Silver Town Tavern's bartender. "He'll watch that the males don't get too frisky with you."

At six four, Sam was a formidable foe. He stroked his black beard, his dark eyes surveying the crowd, the breeze tugging at his shoulder-length ebony hair. He looked more like a grizzly than a wolf in disguise.

Carol was actually hoping for a bit of friskiness. Anything to show she was still alive. She didn't think Sam would watch her as much as he would his waitress. Already, he was eyeing Silva with lustful interest as she joined Carol and Lelandi.

"Are we ready to play, ladies?" Silva winked at Carol. "Ryan McKinley is one determined wolf, so I'm betting he'll be here. Despite," Silva said, motioning to the woods, "Darien trying to ensure he doesn't come that way again." She waved her red ribbon. "What team are you all going to be on?"

Lelandi waited to say until Carol spoke. Carol let out her breath and took off toward the table. "Blue." She glanced over her shoulder at Silva. "Then I can steal *your* tag. Without getting myself into too much trouble." She smiled.

Silva laughed. "You'll be fine, sugar. Never doubt yourself."

His expression dark, Jake appeared out of nowhere. From the look on his face, Carol figured no one had seen any sign of Ryan yet. Jake headed in her direction, and she assumed that was the end of playing any game. But he gave her a small smile and took a blue ribbon from the ones piled on the table. "I'll watch your back."

That was when Darien showed up. He saw Jake with Carol and then chose a red tag. Lelandi smiled and then tied a blue tag around her belt at her back. Since Darien was making Carol attend some archaic gathering that evening, she changed her mind about going after Silva's tag and intended to target his instead.

Squeals from the kids—playing the same game but for junior-sized participants in another field—drifted to where Carol was, and then the signal came for the adult game to begin. Tom rushed to get a tag to join Carol's team. She should have known the two brothers would be her knights again.

At first, it was a mad race, with everyone running everywhere to grab tags. Some of the more beta bachelor males didn't look directly at Carol, but she had a sneaking suspicion they'd target her every bit as much as the ones who eyed her with a smile. That was when Sam joined her, and she gave the bachelors a devious smile. She had a whole team of alpha male bodyguards to watch her back.

Darien observed Lelandi, who was eyeing him with a challenge. But as soon as he ran for her, she darted to get a tag from one of the bachelor males who went after Carol. Carol forgot about Ryan, about Darien's desire to have her mated, about the bachelor males' interest in her. She forgot about the gathering tonight and about shifting. All she thought about was getting Darien's red ribbon while he attempted to get Lelandi's blue one.

Close enough for her to hear, Jake chuckled and said to his younger brother, "Normally, no one but Lelandi would have the nerve to go after Darien's tail. Except for you and me when the time is right."

Deep down, Carol wanted the pack leader's ribbon, if only to prove he wasn't as much in charge of her as he thought.

She believed she was free to grab his tag when two men appeared in her peripheral vision, heading straight for her. They were protecting not only their teammate but also their pack leader while taking the chance to get her tag.

Like a hefty football player, Sam tackled the one man, landing the guy flat on his back with an "oof." Jake went in for the kill, so to speak, with the other guy. Smiling, Jake winked at Carol in the interim, which gave her the go-ahead to try for Darien's tag again.

Lelandi whipped around and danced in front of Darien, keeping him distracted as he tried to get her ribbon so Carol could snag Darien's.

By accident, Carol groped his buttock, her face heating with embarrassment. Then she went for the ribbon prize with one last-ditch effort. And came away with...air.

Leaning against one of the tables piled high with ribbons, his arms folded across his chest, Ryan McKinley watched Carol glide and shift and dodge the brutes who went after her, her whole body in motion like a swiftly twirling exotic dancer. Exquisite and mesmerizing. He couldn't recall a time when he'd enjoyed watching a game this much. Normally he preferred playing. Spectator sports were not his thing.

Carol—not any of the other women playing the game—was the one who captured his imagination. Her cute little ass wiggled in her tight jeans as she leapt back and forth, her hands outstretched and ready to grab Darien's tag. Her agility, her quickness, and the laughter in her smile and eyes made her a pleasure to watch.

Her eagerness to go after the real prize, when no one else would dare, made Ryan smile. Too bad he was here just to clear up the matter of this psychic business. Although the mystery business with the red in the woods the previous night was another situation he needed to clear up by letting Darien know about it, if he didn't already.

A man tried to reach Carol, shoving at Sam to get by him, and every muscle in Ryan's body tightened. He fought against dashing out into the playing field to protect her. She already had such a force of bodyguards that she didn't need him. And he didn't want to dwell on why that bothered him.

He hadn't expected her to play the game so enthusiastically. More reserved, a nonparticipant, maybe. But not as a wildcat going for the gold. And that gold was Darien's ribbon. She had nerve, or maybe she didn't realize what taking on the male alpha leader meant. The fact that she doggedly went after him showed real strength of character. Ryan couldn't help being impressed. Damned impressed.

She ducked another man—an eligible bachelor, no doubt—and whipped around, stripping him of his ribbon instead. Already, she had three tucked in the front of her waistband, the vixen.

Lelandi caught Ryan's eye, raised her brow, and smiled. At least *she* wasn't against him being here. Her gaze shifted to where Carol was maneuvering again around Darien's backside.

Silva suddenly noticed Ryan and shook her head. Then a tall man wearing barbershop-quartet clothes attempted to approach Carol, but too many others blocked his path. The man danced around like a red-and-white barber's pole, minus the blue stripe, as he tried to reach her.

Jake saw Ryan, stopped playing the game, and stalked toward the outsider, his eyes narrowed and his jaw taut. Ryan figured Jake would tell him to leave. But instead, Jake joined him, leaned his backside against the table next to Ryan, and then folded his arms.

"What are you doing here?" Jake's voice was dispassionate, which surprised Ryan, as if Jake had half expected Ryan to show up and didn't care one way or another.

But Ryan didn't take Jake's tone for complacency. All three of the brothers could easily be provoked if they thought any of their pack members' welfare was in jeopardy.

"I'm here to finish my report. Couple of details I wanted to clear up with Carol."

"Nothing more than that?" Jake sounded skeptical and turned his attention back to Carol. "I never expected her to be like this…so spirited. Or to enjoy herself so much. I'm glad to see it finally."

Surprised she'd been unhappy with the pack, considering how cheerful she looked, Ryan frowned. His first thought was that Darien's pack members weren't treating her well. He quickly reconsidered, thinking it might have to do with her having been so recently turned.

"She's not content with being one of us?"

"She's learning to adjust."

That didn't bode well. When Jake didn't say anything more about the matter, Ryan asked, "What are the problems?"

"Everyone's different in how they handle being turned. Some embrace the changes. Some don't."

That didn't settle the unease Ryan felt about the situation. "And she's fighting it."

"You could say that."

Ryan had never considered that Carol might not like being a wolf, nor that anyone would be unhappy with his or her newfound abilities. Quicker healing properties, the ability to see at night, and heightened senses of smell, sight, and hearing. Increased longevity. Wolf's stamina. Of course, he'd been born a *lupus garou*, so it was hard imagining someone dealing with the changes overnight.

He rubbed his chin and watched her further, seeing the way she really was getting into the game. From his observations of her, he couldn't visualize her as a woman who was at odds with her wolf half. She looked like she was having the time of her life. Even last night when she had hunted him down, she had to have appreciated her wolf's nocturnal vision and enhanced sense of smell, which had helped her to locate him in the dark.

Carol went after Darien's ribbon again.

Ryan smiled at the determination she exhibited and the way Darien appeared not to mind and even seemed amused. "I didn't think Darien would look so pleased that she'd attempt to best him, even though he appears to be fighting against showing his feelings."

Jake laughed. "He wants to encourage her to be one of us. I believe if anyone else tried for his tag, other than Lelandi, you'd see some real aggression. Not that he's making it easy for Carol, mind you. It's not our way. If she grabs his tag, she'll have to earn it. But it's been difficult getting her to open up since she was turned. And Darien can't help but be relieved." He looked at Ryan. "Did you know that she hasn't shifted yet?"

Ryan schooled his look of disbelief. "Someone who's newly turned isn't able to fight the change for that long. Maybe for a couple of weeks at most, plus the time period when the new moon is out and only royals can change. But five months? She must be shifting when no one's around."

Jake shook his head and watched her again. "I don't believe so."

"In her room at night then?" Ryan asked. "You can't be watching her twenty-four seven." He folded his arms. "She's changing." No way could a newly turned wolf possess the inner strength to fight the moon's strong pull for that long.

Ryan watched the barber trying to skirt around Tom and a couple of other men on Carol's team, but the man was unable to make any headway. She deserved someone better than a man who dressed as if he were still living in the past.

Figuring he'd better address another concern that would interest Darien and his pack, Ryan said to Jake, "When I came by the house last night, I discovered a red wolf in the vicinity, male persuasion. He took off running west when he saw me. I tried to locate him to learn who he was and what he was doing in the area, but I lost track of him. Any relation of Lelandi's? One of her old pack members who might be trouble?"

Jake's expression showed raw disbelief. "We didn't catch wind of him. Just you. Trying to conjure up phantoms to explain your reason for skulking around the woods near the house last night?"

"Research." Ryan shrugged. "I like to tie up all loose ends before I close a case for good."

"Like?"

Ryan gave him a small smile. "A matter Carol can clear up for me."

Jake nodded. "You don't think she's psychic. No matter how much we want to believe otherwise, she knew things that should be impossible to know. Trust me on that. I wasn't sure I accepted her claims right away either, although Darien did. He was concerned that what she had envisioned could get herself and Lelandi killed."

"Everything can be explained scientifically. She overheard conversations, saw things she wasn't meant to have seen. But not as a future vision." Yet what if she truly had envisioned what she said she had?

"Have fun proving otherwise. So what happened with the red wolf? Lose him?" Jake's voice dripped with cynicism.

"Like you said, you couldn't detect his smell. Too many of our kind are beginning to use hunter concealment to prevent detection. Which can mean only one thing—he's up to no good."

"Not like you, eh?"

Ryan smiled broadly and straightened a bit. "Finding the bad guys is my business, whether they're cheating on their spouses—*humans mainly, of course*—or perpetuating insurance fraud or some other socially unacceptable deed. It's my job to expose them. I do happen to be one of the good guys."

"Come on, McKinley. Don't tell me you're not intrigued by the unmated red. She's unique, interesting, and easy on the eyes. But you'll never score with her if you don't believe in her abilities."

She was a hell of a lot more than easy on the eyes, and Ryan couldn't understand why Jake wasn't interested in having her for a mate. Unless he didn't want to deal with a woman who supposedly had second sight.

"So tell me the truth. What's keeping *you* from pursuing her?" Ryan asked.

Jake gave a sly smile.

What the hell did that mean?

CHAPTER 5

ON THE PLAYING FIELD, ANOTHER BRUISER OF A GUY ON Darien's team lunged after Carol with a wicked gleam in his eye as she again tried for Darien's tag. Perseverance had always been a way of life for her. Target what you want, and get it. Although getting a job at the hospital had meant becoming a wolf first, which wasn't quite what she'd thought she'd have to go through.

Sam was on his feet, intent on tackling the new threat to her, when Silva distracted him. Smiling, dodging around him, she tried to grab Sam's ribbon. The bartender grinned at her, but instead of attempting to get her ribbon, he mounted a full frontal assault and tackled Silva in a sexy way. Pinning her to the ground with his body, he nestled between her legs. Forget the tags. Their lips locked together, and they were busy with a new form of entertainment.

Carol sighed. One guard down. And what a way to go.

She lunged for Darien's ribbon. Her fingers latched onto the slip of silk. She tugged, sheer elation boosting her mood, and pulled the tag free.

In the same instant, Darien jerked Lelandi's ribbon off and tucked it into his belt with a satisfied wink at Lelandi, who smiled back at him and shook her head.

The whole crowd of players—and the older *lupus garous* cheering on the sidelines—ceased speaking and laughing and stood in shocked silence.

Carol grinned and, in triumph, raised Darien's tag, which fluttered in the breeze like a proud flag of honor. "Got one!"

But not just *anyone's*.

Darien gave her a small smile, looking pleased instead of annoyed that she'd managed to swipe his ribbon. That minor acknowledgment made her feel as though she was standing ten stories high. That, for an instant, he truly accepted her. And that meant everyone else would also. She hoped.

Everyone began clapping and cheering.

Darien fondly patted Lelandi's ribbon in his belt, but then without warning, he dodged after Jake's ribbon. His brother, already eyeing him warily, bolted away from him in time, and Darien headed for Tom with an evil glint in his eye, aggressively, no holds barred this time. Carol figured he was leaving her for the bachelor males instead of retaliating and taking her tag.

She went back to protecting her tail and targeting the guys who were out to get her, never having had so much fun in her life.

Six tags so far, and…

Bang! She was hit, shoved onto her back, taken down by…the red-and-white-striped fiend from her vision. Mervin, the barber?

He smelled of heavy hair tonics and sweat. She moaned, just thinking what being mated to him would be like. He was the only man in town who wore a costume year-round—a barbershop-quartet type of affair, complete with bow tie, red-and-white-striped sports coat, and dark pants, even for playing a rough-and-tumble game such as this. At some time or another during the game, he'd lost his white straw hat.

At least while he had her pinned on her back, he couldn't get to her tail. But then he wasn't trying very hard to get it, either, she belatedly realized. Keeping her pinned beneath him, he seemed to be enjoying another sport just fine.

She squirmed, trying to unsettle him, but her actions only brought a smile to Mervin's thin lips. His pale-yellow eyes smiled just as brightly. Great.

Without warning, Mervin flew aside, his eyes wide and mouth gaping. Her rescuer, Ryan McKinley, crouched next to her and rested his hand lightly on her shoulder, his brows knit in a deep frown, his eyes as dark as a stormy night.

"Are you okay?"

The entire playing field grew silent again, and her heart pounded in panic.

"You shouldn't be here," she whispered. "They've been looking for you."

"Carol's fine," Darien said, his voice terse as he drew close.

Darien offered his hand to help her to stand. She grabbed Ryan's knee instead and started to help herself up. Ryan quickly seized her hand and pulled her to her feet, keeping her close by his side in a protective mode, the heat of his body warming hers, his fingers still holding onto hers in a possessive way.

But she was more concerned about protecting him!

Darien gave Ryan a dark look, but not in the least bit cowed, Ryan squeezed Carol's hand reassuringly and tossed a sly smile to Darien. "Good game."

Lelandi quickly stepped forward and waved a handful of ribbons. "Blue team won!"

Still, everyone waited for Darien to respond, either

concerning the game or Ryan, or both. Darien looked at
one of his men, who lifted their team's captured ties, minus
Lelandi's that Darien still had tucked proudly in his belt. His
team was definitely short a few.

Darien gave Lelandi an evil smile. "Lelandi's team won.
Let's eat!" He wrapped his arm around her waist, offered
Ryan a warning look, and then nodded to Tom and headed
for the house.

Carol breathed a tentative sigh of relief. As uptight as
everyone was when waiting to see how their pack leader
dealt with issues, she couldn't shake loose of the tension
tightening her chest. She figured that the pressure wouldn't
go away until Ryan left the area for good.

Taking his brother's cue, Tom approached Ryan. "What
are you doing here?"

"Don't any of you talk to one another?" Ryan moved his
hand to Carol's back and stroked it once in a reassuring way.
"I told Jake I wished to speak to Carol about a matter concerning the murder investigation."

Tom's eyes widened a little. "Why? The case was solved.
All guilty parties were held accountable."

"Just a couple of questions concerning…investigative
techniques."

Carol's heart sank. *That* was what this was all about? Or
was Ryan just saying so as a cover? He still stood next to
her in protective wolf mode, their bodies lightly touching,
the heat curling through her. He sure seemed to want something more of her than to question her.

"Why were you here last night, skulking around?" Tom
asked.

Ryan didn't say anything, which made Carol wonder

again if he had an agenda he didn't wish to discuss with anyone else.

Tom cocked his head to the side, gave Ryan a look that said he didn't trust him, and then gave a short nod. "All right, ask your questions of her."

"Privately."

Frowning, Tom hesitated. Then he motioned to the side of the house. "Over there. That's as private as it's going to get."

People were milling about, most likely interested in what Tom was going to do to Ryan or what Ryan had in mind to do with Carol. Most of the onlookers were bachelor males, including one particularly sore-looking barber, who was brushing at yellow-green grass stains on his red-and-white-striped coat.

Ryan took Carol's arm and led her to the side of the house. His touch was gentle, caring, and protective, and every time he got close, a spark of interest seemed to ignite between them. She looked up at him, expecting...well, hoping he wanted to see more of her. Date her or court her, or whatever wolves did before they decided they were the right ones for each other and mated for a lifetime. Not that she was ready for a long-term commitment, but a couple of dates would be nice, just to see if he was even her type.

"Carol..." Ryan released her arm and shoved his hands in his pockets, his head bent to speak more privately with her. "Are you sure you didn't overhear conversations, which is how you came to the conclusions you did and were able to solve the case?"

Instantly, he stoked her ire. She folded her arms and narrowed her eyes at him. So he truly *wasn't* interested in her. "What are you inferring?"

He cleared his throat. "Darien and his brothers wouldn't let me speak with you concerning this matter when I was here before, at first because you had been injured so, and after that"—Ryan shrugged—"they were being protective, I suppose. But after giving your situation further thought—"

"For five months?" Her voice was rife with annoyance, yet she wondered why he'd truly thought about it for that long. Just a rabid need to learn the truth? Or was there more to the story than he was letting on?

Calmly, he ignored her outburst and continued. "Just that you may seem to have psychic powers or a sixth sense or something, but in truth..." He let his words fade, allowing her to draw her own conclusions, his gaze studying her eyes, observing her reaction. Like a PI and former cop would. Most likely jaded. Believing the worst in anyone they thought might have something to hide.

In truth, what did he believe?

She opened her mouth to speak but then clamped her lips shut. Hell, ever since her seventh birthday, after nearly drowning in a lake—well, technically she had drowned in the lake, been declared dead, and then revived—she'd had these unwelcome visions. She'd thought everyone else did, too, until she mentioned one to her mother.

She still remembered that day as if it were yesterday. She'd explained how she'd seen a man driving a pickup truck down the street from where they lived and running over one of her classmates. Except that the accident didn't happen until two days later. And the boy died. Night terrors followed, waking her, and she'd try to catch her breath, tears streaking down her cheeks, her pillow soggy.

Horrified and unable to deal with what she'd seen, she

finally told her parents. They'd immediately sent her to a *special doctor* to get rid of her *episodes*. After three years of visits, he gave up on her, declaring her utterly hopeless. Well…even worse than that. To mollify her parents, he'd said in an appeasing but not very sincere way that she'd probably grow out of it. The real reason he dropped her as a patient in such a hurry went deeper than that.

Waiting for her to respond, Ryan cleared his throat and shoved his hands in his pockets.

"Sorry. You had a question for me?" Carol tapped her fingers on her folded arm, an insincere smile playing on her lips. He hadn't asked her a question, but the way he spoke was definitely a ploy to get her to respond to his observations. And she wasn't biting.

"Don't you suppose you might have come by the information you did through some means other than a psychic connection?"

"Hmm, sure. That's what happened."

Ryan's mouth curved up ever so slightly, but she could tell he wasn't being taken in by her surrender.

Before she'd become caught up in the wolf culture, she'd kept her abilities secret. Now that those in this pack knew about her, she really didn't care if any were skeptical. As long as they didn't try to tell her that she didn't have a sixth sense because it wasn't possible. She supposed that was all because of Dr. Metzger and the way his icy-blue eyes would peer through his brass-rimmed glasses at her, while his big chin tilted down, condemning, judging.

If people didn't believe her in private, fine. Yet usually if people confronted her like this, she would smile disingenuously and tell them how right they were. She never felt the need to defend what she could see when others couldn't or what she could envision or perceive sometimes when she touched an object.

"But you truly believe otherwise," Ryan finally said.

This time, her smile was bright and true to her feelings. She couldn't help liking Ryan, despite his denial of her abilities. He had an easy but determined manner about him, not brusque like Darien or teasing like Jake or afraid to make waves like Tom. His determination was matched only by her own.

She glanced at the men standing about, including both Tom and Jake. Which made the situation worse. Why couldn't any of the alpha males show any real interest in her? She was not a beta kind of girl. She supposed that was because her father had become so downtrodden by her mother's treatment of him. She couldn't see being married, um, mated to someone like that.

"Carol?" Ryan said, his deep baritone voice again yanking her from her faraway thoughts.

She really needed to get more sleep. She turned her attention back to Ryan. He thought *she* wasn't being honest with him about her abilities, when *he* wasn't honest about why he had been lurking in the woods last night, watching her window. She didn't have to be psychic to know something more was going on between them. Time to turn the tables. Throw him off balance.

Trying to look like this was a perfectly natural way for her to act, she smiled, wrapped her arms around his neck, and leaned into the soft sweater covering his hard body, which instantly reminded her just how hard his body was when he wasn't wearing a stitch of clothes. She only meant to give him a slow kiss on the mouth, just to prove to him that he had another agenda that he wouldn't admit to. Or if not, then maybe Tom or Jake would finally show some interest in her. But more than anything, she wanted to get Ryan off the subject of her abilities before she said something in anger that she shouldn't.

To her surprise, he eagerly captured her mouth with his. Not cautiously, building up the desire in slow, careful increments, but judiciously, as if he had been starved for affection for a very long time. His hand cupped the back of her head, his free hand drifting lower on her back and holding her in place.

She hadn't meant to respond so fully to the kiss either, but his unbridled need fed into hers. Forgetting they had an audience, she parted her lips to accept him, to open an intimate path between them, their tongues dancing, touching, exploring. Her hands fisted in his soft sweater at the back of his neck and held him even tighter. She pressed her body against his hard muscles, and shamelessly, she wanted more.

But then he released her and unwrapped her arms from around his neck, his eyes smoky and dark, his expression otherwise unreadable, his hands still securely holding her wrists. Their breaths came quickly as their hearts thundered at a runner's pace. He opened his mouth as if he was going to say something, but she didn't want to hear the apology she figured he would offer or another word about her abilities, if that was what he had in mind.

She quickly spoke instead. "I accept. Come pick me up for a date at six o'clock. Promptly."

She'd show him he wasn't as much in control of the situation as he might think.

Then she winked, pulled free, and stalked off toward the house without a backward glance, her blood sizzling with arousal and irritation.

She harrumphed under her breath. All the idiotic romantic notions she had been harboring for Ryan McKinley...and all he really wanted was for her to confess she wasn't psychic?

She doubted Ryan would take her on a date, and she doubted even more that Darien would allow it. But if the date did come to pass, she would get out of the gathering of bachelor males tonight, and she'd give Ryan McKinley a piece of her mind.

───────────

Ryan stared after Carol as she stalked toward the house, sparing Jake and Tom a smile before disappearing inside. What the hell had just happened?

Did she think that if she kissed him, he'd forget why he'd come here to see her? Hell, if she had, he hated to admit that for a moment, it had worked. Never had a woman taken him by surprise like that. Never had one heated his blood to volcanic proportions with the way her body had pressed against his, her tongue slipping into his mouth and dancing in an erotic way with his.

The spark of electricity between them couldn't be denied. So what had gotten into him to kiss her back? Convention. If he was interested in a woman, he let her know it. But he sure as hell hadn't planned to go down that path. Not that she wasn't intriguing as hell, but she sure wouldn't be interested in someone like him who didn't believe in her special "abilities."

Would she tell him the truth tonight on a *date*?

Or would they get themselves into even hotter water if he spent any more time alone with her? He hadn't even *been* alone with her.

He breathed in the air and still smelled her sweet feminine scent, a mixture of jasmine and the fresh grass that she'd been lying in after Mervin knocked her flat on her back. He could still feel the way her body had pressed against him, her breasts and her thighs, soft and curvaceous and sensuous. If he didn't keep his distance from her, he *would* forget what he'd come here for. Was that her ploy? Sidetrack him with a siren's lure and keep her secrets to herself? The vixen.

All he wanted was to close the file on the murder case in Silver Town permanently. So why didn't that thought appeal to him? He should have been satisfied to return home and get on with his own business.

Tom and Jake glowered at him and then headed into the house. Ryan was beginning to think that this case wouldn't be cleared up easily, particularly if she employed her feminine wiles to tangle with him. Yet a deeper primal urge growled to be released, and he wasn't sure he wanted to keep it leashed—even though Carol was newly turned and probably didn't understand what she was getting herself into.

"What did Ryan McKinley want?" Lelandi asked Carol as she fixed a double cheeseburger for herself in the kitchen, where the aroma of seasoned burgers and cheesecake and lemon meringue pie filled the air.

Everyone else had already taken their food outside or into the dining area or sunroom, and laughter and conversation drifted through the house like the cool breeze through the open kitchen window.

Carol dished a hamburger onto a bun and topped it with slices of pickle and tomato. Although she was fuming inside, she smiled at Lelandi.

"He wanted a date. Isn't that nice?"

Lelandi fumbled with her plate and nearly dropped it. "You can't be serious. Darien will never allow it."

Silva, who Carol swore overheard conversations better than any wolf alive, sauntered into the kitchen. "My, my... sounds like McKinley is harboring a death wish—or he's one determined wolf. I heard he kissed you like there was no tomorrow."

Heard? Or had she seen something out one of the windows?

Silva chuckled. "Yep. The bachelors are ready for a showdown."

Eyes wide, Lelandi asked, "He kissed you and then asked for a date?" She shook her head. "He's got nerve." But her tone of voice reflected a trace of approval, and Carol noted a shadow of a smile in Lelandi's expression.

Carol almost laughed to think she had been the one to suggest the date and that if she hadn't pushed Ryan into proving something to the other guys, he would never have kissed her. How could he not believe her about her psychic abilities after all that had happened? Even Darien's people believed her.

In fact, she thought a couple of his people were a little afraid of her because of it. What if someone did something that he or she shouldn't, and then Carol envisioned it and shared their misdeeds with Darien? At least, that was what she thought might bother some of them. Beyond that, she really didn't think Ryan would come tonight.

Lelandi smiled and lifted her burger. "You know, when Darien told Ryan he didn't want him interfering in the investigation, Ryan stubbornly refused to take no for an answer." She shrugged. "I doubt he will this time either."

Carol didn't know that Ryan had been told he couldn't help with the investigation, just that Darien hadn't liked the idea. But she couldn't believe this issue of whether or not she was psychic was such a big deal that he'd butt heads with Darien over it.

"So what's the gathering all about?" she asked, figuring that was what she'd have to prepare herself for next. Forget Ryan and his agenda.

"You won't be alone with a bunch of men, Carol, if that's what you're worried about. I'll be there with Darien, presiding over the party. Silva will be there and Sam, too, serving refreshments. Two other women are coming from another wolf community. They like what we have here—where wolves run the town and not humans. One's a librarian who wants to start a library in town. And the other is a masseuse. I think she's going to be a real hit."

All of a sudden, Carol didn't feel so important. Not that she wanted to mate with someone for life whom she wasn't interested in...but to compete with a masseuse? Carol probably had the librarian beat. She shook her head at herself. This was still barbaric. And she wasn't going along with it.

Lelandi was rattling off a list of names of married couples who were going to attend, but Carol watched the way she rubbed her fingers over her stomach every once in a while, and Carol's mouth dropped open. "You're pregnant?"

Her gaze riveting from her cheeseburger to Carol, Lelandi's lips parted for a second, and then she smiled. "Four and a half months."

Silva immediately put her hand on Lelandi's belly. "Well, I'll be. Just how long were you going to hide this little secret from us, sugar?"

"At least until after the games today. If I'd mentioned it before then, Darien wouldn't have let me play. You know how he is."

That was why he was being so careful with her on the playing field and why Lelandi had been napping more lately. He had to have realized Lelandi was pregnant. Carol grinned.

"Wow, this is really a reason to celebrate. Triplets. Just like I had envisioned."

"Do you know what sex they are?" Silva asked Carol.

Three boys, but Carol looked at Lelandi to see if she wanted to know.

Lelandi shook her head. "No. If you know, don't tell me. And I don't want to mention that I'm expecting tonight. This is your coming-out. Not the other ladies' either. They've already been introduced to their wolf packs to court. And neither cared for their prospects. So that's why they're here." She took another bite of her burger.

"They were born *lupus garous*, weren't they?" Carol asked, hoping that at least one of them was newly turned like she was.

"Yes. And they don't get along. So I'm hoping one will stay and the other will look elsewhere. I've already inter-viewed them, and both seem pleasant enough by themselves.

But there's some hostility between them, having to do with families, I think."

Silva grabbed a plate with chips and a burger. "So what if a couple of the guys want the women, and they both end up staying here?"

"We'll have problems. Darien has already counseled the men and said that if matches are made, one of the couples will most likely have to move on. But finding a mate is so important that the men are willing."

Carol gave a short laugh. "Especially with a chance at a masseuse."

"I don't know, Carol. You're more of a known quantity, one of our own, and no one would have to leave the pack," Lelandi said.

"Hmm, nothing else then?"

Lelandi smiled. "I sure didn't put that right, did I? The guys have been talking about you. They shut up when I'm around, but they're intrigued."

"Same here." Silva waved a potato chip. "As soon as I hear your name mentioned at the tavern, I check on the table next to them, but the guys see me coming and end the conversation. So yep, they're interested."

"Sure are. For five months, they've been bugging Darien—or his brothers so they would relay the information to Darien—to let them date you," Lelandi said.

"And you've been the one to keep them from dating me." Carol felt relieved in a way. At least she was glad that they had not been avoiding her because they thought her too different.

Her green eyes flashing with humor, Lelandi laughed. "Not all my doing. Darien wanted you to adjust to being one of us, and he wants you to shift first. We never thought anyone who was newly turned could prevent the shift for this long though."

For the first time, Carol was glad for her psychic abilities, if that was what was keeping her from shifting. She just hoped she could put it off forever or that her visions of Doc being unable to shift back to human form were a mistake. That the worry about him was something benign.

But the event tonight was what she had to deal with now. She hoped that Ryan would come for her, that Darien would allow it, and she'd be able to skip the whole affair— even if it meant dealing with Ryan's inquisition.

CHAPTER 6

NORTH REDDING HAD AVOIDED BEING ANYWHERE NEAR the two women, both gray wolves from another pack and both newly sick from the bioengineered plague that Miller had concocted for them. The lure of money had worked. So from a distance, North observed the way Marilee and Becky looked. Sexy, he thought. Like sending the Trojan horse as a gift to Troy during the Trojan War, the women would attend the gathering and infect as many of Darien's damn people, and Darien himself, as they could. Payback was hell.

The only drawback was if Carol got sick. She was the one he wanted. A red, turned by his own cousin. She would be his, and being a nurse, she could counter the effects of the sickness, if Miller was lying about his intentions.

The women entered the house, and North briefly saw Lelandi smile and motion for them to follow her. Carol could also take care of Lelandi in the event she got sick. It wasn't Lelandi's fault she'd left their red pack. Damn their previous pack leader and his brutish ways!

North took a deep breath and slunk into the woods. The *package* had arrived.

His next mission was grabbing Carol before it was too late.

Normally, Ryan would dress casually on a fact-finding mission—in jeans and turtleneck or T-shirt, depending on the weather. So why the hell was he dressing up for this "affair"? He scoffed at himself for making such a big deal of this as he peered into the bathroom mirror of his room at the bed-and-breakfast. He ran his hand over the five-o'clock shadow that gave him more of a wolfish look and considered whether to shave again or not.

Hell, the first date he ever had, he took the girl to a swimming hole. It was an impromptu situation, and neither cared about what they were wearing—or not wearing as the night wore on. Of course, she'd been human, and his and her hormones had been running high. Over the years, he'd been just as spontaneous. He'd take a liking to a human girl, make it known and, if she was of like mind, have a one-night stand.

But with Carol, he knew deep down it wasn't the same. That she needed a mate. That one-night stands were out, and although he kept telling himself he had nothing to prove, damn if he couldn't shake loose of the need to show up the other males, if she was even interested in anyone else.

He pulled on his sports jacket, hoping to convince Darien that he needed to speak to Carol pronto so he could quit interfering in Darien's pack business and return home. At least that was what he told himself.

As soon as he reached the cozy sitting area for guests at the inn, Bertha Hastings greeted him with a smile and twinkle in her eye. "Your sister, Rosalind, called. Asked if you were all right, because you wouldn't answer your cell phone. I told her you were watching the games earlier and were going to the gathering tonight.

"She asked if you were seeing Carol. Since I hadn't been at the earlier event, I couldn't say. I did mention you were taking Carol on a date tonight. Your sister was real quiet after that, and then she quickly thanked me and said good-bye. But I must say you're looking really spiffy. Enjoy the gathering."

"Thanks. I'll ask Carol a few questions and be on my way." And have a word with Rosalind again. Hell, by the time he was finished with his business here, Rosalind would have everyone thinking he was chasing after Carol and soon would be mating her.

"Only one question is worth asking." Bertha grinned even broader and made her way to the kitchen. "If you young folk want something to snack on later, bring her here after your date. Plenty of food for everyone."

"Thanks." It wouldn't be necessary. As soon as he spoke with Carol, he was returning ASAP to Green Valley and the business he should have been conducting.

Shoulders straight, he stalked outside to his truck and took a deep breath of the chilly night air. He was ready to try to persuade Darien to allow him to see Carol one last time. And to end this obsession, he had to set the record straight with Carol.

When Carol came down from her bedroom before the gathering, men and women were already settling in the sun-room. She was wearing jeans, boots, and a soft pink cardigan, trying to look cool and casual instead of more nervous than she'd like to admit.

She'd been planning to go to the kitchen for a glass of wine to soothe her nerves when Ryan walked in the front door with Sam and Silva. Carol's heart skipped a beat.

Ryan was wearing a steel-blue sports coat and a pin-striped blue-and-silver shirt. He had left three of the buttons open from the collar down, giving the appearance he was ready to unfasten the others in a hurry in the call of duty. She couldn't decide if that meant shifting or sex, but he definitely looked ready for either.

Jeans gave his look more of a dressy casual, which she totally approved of, but then her gaze riveted to his face to see his expression. A shadow of a beard graced his angular face, roughening it a bit and making him appear more like an outdoorsman than someone who sat around an office all day.

He was studying her face, just like a wary investigator would, and observing her reaction to him being here. Instead of smiling, he raised a brow as if to say he was here at her request. *Let's get this over with.* She couldn't believe it. But promptly at six, here he was. Maybe Lelandi was right. When Ryan got something in his mind to do, he wouldn't be stopped. Wouldn't he be surprised if he stayed around long enough to discover she truly was psychic!

That could take a really long time, considering that her visions were so unpredictable and that he probably was quite stubborn about refusing to believe in the paranormal.

She let out her breath. She assumed Darien would be pissed that Ryan was here. Jake also, because he'd made all the arrangements for the gathering. And because this was her *coming-out*.

Darien and his brothers stalked into the foyer to meet Ryan, all of them looking stern and with firm resolve. "Your *date* will have to wait until after the gathering. Where do you plan to take Carol?" Darien asked.

Her heart thumped harder. Darien was allowing it?

But her second thought was that this was so much like when she was sixteen, going on her first real date with a boy and her dad had read him the riot act first! *No riding in vans, on motorcycles, or visiting homes when parents aren't there.* That was the only time her father had acted really alpha. She'd always suspected her mother had counseled him first as to what to say.

Carol was twenty-six now, for heaven's sake, and beyond needing fatherly lectures before a date!

Ryan smiled a little. "The movies."

Darien's response was terse. "We don't have a movie theater here."

Ryan had to have known that. *Cad.* Yet she loved his sense of humor and the way he challenged Darien. Darien's brothers supported him in just about every situation that arose. None of his people disagreed with Darien. She enjoyed seeing someone who would test him in a light-hearted way.

"We'll grab takeout and return to my room at the inn to watch something on TV then." Ryan gave Carol an elusive smile and winked.

Pure macho man and a lady-killer all rolled up in that one faint smile and sexy wink that promised a night of pure heated pleasure. After the way they'd kissed with an audience, being alone in his room didn't sound like a safe bet at all. She was certain Darien wouldn't think so either.

Every inch of her skin flushed with warmth, and if she hadn't known any better, she might have worried that the shift was coming. But the heat that signaled the impending transformation went much deeper, Lelandi had explained to her, as if it settled into the marrow of the bones and melted them. And she supposed it did, since the bones reshaped into a wolf's skeletal form or back again into a human's. What she was experiencing now was more of a surface heat, triggered by pure embarrassment.

Darien shook his head at Ryan's suggestion of taking a meal to his room and watching TV there. Darien tried to conceal the expression, but Carol had lived with him long enough to recognize he was fighting a smile. He admired alpha males, and she could tell that while it stuck in his craw that Ryan was an outsider intruding on his pack business, the gray was a challenge. And Darien enjoyed the game when someone had the audacity to oppose him in a non-threatening way from time to time. She wondered if Ryan reminded him of himself.

In good humor, Ryan folded his arms. "All right. What do you suggest?"

"The tavern. Have a couple of drinks. They're serving roast beef sandwiches tonight. You can enjoy the music. Best place in town for a date."

Also crowded with tons of pack members ready to observe their every move.

"All right. Agreeable, Carol?" Ryan asked with one raised brow.

"Sure, after the gathering," she grumbled. So much for getting out of *that* affair, although she appreciated that Ryan had asked if she was okay with the setup and hadn't just made the decision without her say.

"You'll bring her home by midnight," Darien added. Then he gave Jake and Tom a look.

Which meant they'd be Darien's eyes and ears at the tavern, along with everyone else's there.

Darien motioned to the sunroom. "Shall we?"

Carol wished she could have skipped the gathering altogether, dealt with Ryan, and settled this matter in private without delay. But as usual, Darien would have his way.

Lelandi came out of the kitchen and wrapped her arm around Carol's waist. "I should have told you earlier that the pack gathering is a throwback from ancient times and that even some humans adopted the notion after they learned our people were doing this. Although they hadn't a clue what we were. It then became fashionable in England and other locales to present women to society as acceptable to marry."

"*Wolves* started the trend?"

Lelandi smiled. "Yes. Only we stick to our traditions longer than most."

Carol envisioned the women's long gowns and other more restrictive articles of clothing and wondered how in the world they could have removed all those garments if the urge to turn hit them. Living back then would surely have been a disaster for her. For one, she'd have been considered a witch if she'd revealed her paranormal secrets. And a wolf on top of that? She would have been bonfire kindling for sure.

She glanced back to see where Ryan was, but he'd vanished. Had Darien or his brothers kicked him out of the house until he could return to pick her up for their date? She shouldn't have been disappointed that he was gone, considering the reason he wanted to see her further.

Still, she believed she'd prefer his company to that of the beta males in Darien's pack. She sighed and asked Lelandi, "Are drinks being served?"

Lelandi only smiled and guided her into the sunroom.

The room was bathed in warm lights, with the spring floral decorations giving off the sweetest scent of jasmine and roses. As soon as she walked in, Carol saw the two women from the other pack. Both were stunning, and Carol shriveled a little, feeling plain and unnoticeable. Yet something about the women gave her pause. She was awful about remembering names, but faces, especially as striking as those of the two women, stood out in her mind. She hadn't met these women, except maybe in passing. But where had she seen them before?

"Becky's the black-haired one, the librarian, over there by the leather sofa. And Marilee's the brunette, the masseuse, next to the fireplace," Lelandi whispered to Carol.

Both women looked to see who the new arrival was. Frowning, they didn't appear pleased, but Carol wondered why they were bothered. Becky was a black-haired and black-eyed beauty, her thick curls cascading over her shoulders. She was sophisticated and sultry looking, particularly wearing a shocking-pink sweater that dipped low at the bodice. Not at all how Carol pictured a librarian looking. The ones at the college where she went? Business suits, glasses, and buns. This babe didn't look like she read anything literary. Maybe she liked historical romances too.

Carol gave her a quick smile. The woman gave her a guarded smile back.

Marilee was a brunette with the same kind of luxuriously thick hair that caressed her shoulders, dark-brown eyes, and a plunging, silky orange neckline that also showed off ample cleavage.

Both wore black jeans and spiky black heels and looked

dressed to kill. And both towered over Carol by a good four inches. Which made her feel inadequately short—from her bobbed haircut to her petite height—and not half as sophisticatedly dressed or sexy. She'd describe herself as more casual sporty. Not a siren at all.

She glanced at Darien and his brothers, expecting someone to make a formal announcement, but no one did. The event appeared to be just a meet-and-greet affair where the guys would eventually garner the courage to speak to the women looking for mates. Although Carol was *not* in that category willingly.

None of the men were very alpha, and neither of the two women appeared to be, so no one made an effort to speak to anyone else.

Lelandi and Darien and the other mated couples talked freely among themselves about general news, but Carol felt that was more of a ploy to set everyone at ease. To make it appear that they were not chaperoning the women.

Dressed in a fresh red-and-white-striped jacket, no grass stains evident, Mervin walked across the room, headed in her direction, and gave someone a chilling glare. Carol turned to see who. *Ryan.* Where had he come from? But where he was going bothered her even more. He was headed straight for Marilee. *Of course.* The sexy masseuse.

"Sorry about earlier today," Mervin said, getting close—too close—to Carol and pulling her attention away from Ryan.

If her back hadn't already been up against a wall in a defensive wallflower mode, she would have stepped away from Mervin.

A cloying cologne clung to him like a cloud of heavy

allspice, when normally their kind didn't bother with heavy human fragrances.

"Are you all right?" he asked.

Thinking of the way he'd pinned her to the ground during the game and wouldn't let her up, Carol gave him a scornful look.

"It was supposed to be a game of tag, not a wrestling match."

She wouldn't let him get away with believing she thought his behavior acceptable. If she did, she was sure he'd continue to behave that way.

He didn't seem in the least bit remorseful and glanced at Ryan. "I don't know what he sees in Marilee."

Carol didn't mean to, but she nearly growled when she spoke. "Maybe he needs a good back rub."

Mervin snorted. "He shouldn't be here. This is a gathering for our pack, not for outsiders like him."

"I'm sure he doesn't have any intention of going after any of the women here tonight." Or maybe he did. What did she know?

Mervin gave Carol a look like she couldn't be serious. "He's an alpha male. They always go after available women and take their pick. I hear you have a date with him. Break it."

A short laugh tumbled from her lips. She doubted he'd say anything like that to Ryan, but he thought he could order her about, and she'd wilt and agree? "Why?"

"He's trying to make you jealous by talking to Marilee. But we all know you're the one he wants. Why else would he have sneaked around Darien's place last night? Why else would he have kissed you the way he did outside the house?"

She dismissed Mervin's concern and folded her arms in an annoyed fashion. Not for an instant did she think Ryan was talking to Marilee because he wanted to make Carol jealous. And he had only kissed Carol because he was trying to prove something to Mervin and the others who had been watching their interaction. She still wondered why Ryan had been sneaking around Darien's house.

She considered Ryan, who was standing relaxed and casual with Marilee. The woman's eyes flashed with intrigue. Her lips curved up in a smile. She might not be an alpha, but she had seduction down to an art. Hell, whatever he was saying to her, he'd sure gotten her number. She reached over and slid her hands over his shoulders. Instantly, Carol wanted to jerk her hands off him, as if he was hers. Where that unwelcome notion came from, she hadn't a clue.

Marilee fluttered her long lashes.

Which was another of Carol's shortcomings. Both of the women had thick, long lashes that fluttered beautifully. Carol's were pale blond and *short*. Even with mascara that claimed to make lashes longer and more noticeable, hers were not meant to flicker in a provocative way.

The woman was now looking adoringly into Ryan's eyes, her tongue sweeping over her already shimmering lips, which were coated in dusky-pink gloss. If the lout kissed her, the date was off.

Everyone seemed rabidly entranced with Ryan and Marilee's actions. Some of the bachelors appeared annoyed, frowns creasing their temples, arms folded or hands shoved in pockets. Some seemed in awe as they watched Ryan, small smiles on their faces. Maybe making mental notes of what worked when attempting to get a woman's attention?

"Let's go to the tavern and get a drink, Mervin." Carol had had enough of this fiasco. Even though she'd rather be anywhere with anyone else, at least Mervin had the guts to pursue her.

Mervin played with his bow tie and looked at Darien.

Oh, for heaven's sake. Did he have to get permission from Darien?

She headed for the great room, figuring everyone was so intrigued with Ryan and his conquest that no one would notice she'd left. As soon as she exited the sunroom, Mervin hurried after her. "We can't leave the gathering. Not without Darien's permission."

Grow some balls, she wanted to say. That was one thing she liked about Ryan. *He* stood up to Darien, no matter what the circumstances.

She strode through the great room toward the stairs.

Mervin hurried after her and roughly seized her arm. She clenched her teeth, her whole body taut with raw irritation.

Whipping around, she yanked her arm free. "Do *not* grab me like that again," she growled low, unable to curb her anger. Partly at being accosted and partly because the masseuse was fawning over Ryan—and he seemed to like it. With Carol, he was strictly business. Psychic business, and what she could do with it, was his only interest in her.

As soon as the fury at being waylaid had washed over her, heat swept through her, and she cringed. Oh hell... not...the...*change*.

CHAPTER 7

RUSHING THROUGH THE GREAT ROOM, CAROL HURRIED off toward the stairs to her bedroom before she did the unthinkable—got naked and shifted in front of Mervin. Heaven forbid! If he grabbed her again, she wouldn't be responsible for her actions.

"You can't leave the gathering," Mervin said half angrily, half pleading as he stalked after her.

Without giving him a backward glance, she ran up the stairs two at a time, praying she'd make it to her room and could concentrate on stopping the shift before it caught hold. And that Mervin wouldn't follow her.

As if instinct moved her, she tackled the buttons on her sweater before she reached the top of the stairs. Her heart was pounding so hard that the sound of Niagara Falls rushed in her ears, but at least Mervin must have paused at the foot of the stairs and didn't follow her up them. She imagined if it had been Ryan, he wouldn't have let her go. Then again, she didn't think he would have accosted her the way Mervin had, triggering the damnable shift in the first place.

"Carol!" Lelandi called out from the great room.

Hell. Carol raced to her room, sweater unbuttoned, her fingers struggling to undo her belt. Now she knew why more of their kind didn't wear accessories. Or blouses or sweaters with buttons either.

She dove into her bedroom, slammed the door, and locked it.

Lelandi's frenzied footsteps grew closer down the carpeted hallway, or at least Carol assumed that was who was coming after her.

Carol squeezed her eyes shut and stood still, hoping her second sight wouldn't fail her now. Anything that would thwart shifting.

"Carol?" Lelandi tapped lightly on the door, her voice soothing.

She tried to ignore Lelandi's entreaty, the heat still coursing through every muscle, through every vein.

"Carol, open up so we can talk." This time, Lelandi used a little more force in her words. A command, not a suggestion.

Go away, Carol wanted to shout. She *had* to concentrate.

"Did Mervin upset you? Darien wants to know. And Mervin's going to be ostracized from the whole pack if he did."

"No, Lelandi, I'm fine. Just...I'll be down in a second." Gritting her teeth, she stripped down to her bra and panties.

Then the room blurred into oblivion as a window into the future filled her mind.

"Come in, Carol," Lelandi said, her voice tinged with dread as she hurriedly motioned for Carol to enter her bedroom. Lelandi wrung her hands as she watched Darien in his wolf form pace back and forth. "What's happening? I don't understand what's happening. How can we stop this?" Her green eyes turned to Carol, and tears filled them. "He can't change back."

Darien. First the doc, now their pack leader? But what could Carol do? What could she ever do in a situation initially conjured up in her mind's eye? It was too late for Darien. Too late for the doc.

"Carol, you have to do something!" Lelandi pleaded, her voice strained, choked with emotion.

The feelings of inadequacy swamped Carol, as they often did when she had no control over future events. The fear of what could happen to her increased her resolve never to shift.

The door lock clicked open, instantly shattering Carol's vision. Lelandi had to have used a hairpin to unlock the bedroom door, damn it.

Her lips parted, Lelandi stared at Carol wearing only her peach lace bra and panties. "Oh, Carol." She quickly shut the door as more footsteps tromped their way down the hall. "Don't fight the change. It'll only make things worse."

How did Lelandi know?

A knock sounded, heavier, more masculine.

"We're all right," Lelandi called out in her most assertive way.

"Did Mervin upset Carol? I've got an outsider gray who's ready to tear him apart, not that I sure as hell won't take Mervin to task," Darien growled through the door.

Lelandi raised her brows at Carol.

She shook her head. "No." Although she thought Mervin grabbing her arm had resulted in the urge to change, he really hadn't done anything to her to warrant all the fuss. Oh hell, she had to find a way to control the compulsion to shift in case something like this happened again.

"Are you certain?" Darien asked, his control slipping.

Lelandi studied Carol, but she shook her head and frowned again.

"Nothing's wrong," she whispered.

Lelandi didn't look like she believed her. "I'll speak to you later, honey," Lelandi said to Darien, "but she says no."

"All right. But I want her returned to the party post-haste." Darien stomped off.

Carol was sure he didn't believe her either.

"What happened to trigger the need to shift?" Lelandi asked in a soothing way, as if Carol was fragile and would break if Lelandi wasn't gentle.

Carol clenched her teeth. If there was one thing she wasn't, fragile was it. "I wasn't getting ready to shift." She went to her closet and yanked out a sparkling peach dress with a low neckline and a gored skirt that caressed her legs when she walked. She slipped it on. "I just didn't feel dressy enough."

Lelandi gave her a slight smile. "The other women are not any real competition, you know. The men are much more intrigued with you, especially after you played so aggressively on the field this afternoon. And taking Darien's ribbon?" Lelandi gave a bright laugh. "They loved it."

"Everyone was shocked into silence."

"Well, all right. At first, sure. But once they saw how good-naturedly Darien took it, they loved how you stood up to him. No one would have dared. Although Silva does from time to time. As to the men, they still don't know about the other women. You're more of a known commodity."

"They don't like it that I haven't shifted." Suddenly, a thought occurred to Carol. Why couldn't she just pretend that she had shifted when she was alone? Then they'd quit worrying about her. "Not that I haven't shifted when no one is around to see it."

Lelandi tilted her head to the side and gave her a look that said: *Get real.* "I know you haven't shifted. If Darien learns you were having trouble with it tonight, he'll want to know what brought it about and how you managed to stop it."

Carol was dying to know how Lelandi suspected she had never shifted. Must have been a wolf thing. She zipped the low-cut back of her dress and slipped into a pair of slinky heels, still feeling underdressed but like she was on a manhunt.

"I love the dress, Carol. You should wear clothes like that more often."

"I bought it to go to a party held by one of the student nurses in one of my biology classes. Sat like a wallflower during the whole affair when I discovered the male medical staff in attendance had significant others, who were not at the party, but were looking for some extra nighttime entertainment. I didn't have a ride home or money to call a cab, so I stuck it out.

"But I loved the color." She ran her hand over the silky fabric. And the cut looked good on her, so she hadn't had the heart to get rid of the dress. Now she felt way overexposed for the current event, like she was trying to prove something to the other women or to the men, when she had no intention of doing so.

"Are you going to be all right?" Lelandi asked as Carol disappeared into the adjoining bathroom.

Carol touched up her lips with a shimmering peach gloss. "Yep, as right as can be." Under the circumstances.

"When you went into the woods with Ryan last night, did you see any sign of a red wolf?"

Frowning, Carol walked out of the bathroom. "No, why?"

"Have you had any premonitions that we've had trouble with a red wolf?"

"No." Lelandi's worried voice concerned Carol. What was up now?

Lelandi crossed the room to the door and opened it. "Ryan claims the wolf was skulking around the woods surrounding our home. Since there are only the two of us reds here, other than Doc..." Lelandi shrugged, but Carol could tell she was trying to hide her apprehension.

"Would it have been your cousin, Ural?"

"No, I called him, and he's still in my uncle's pack. Whoever it was, he was wearing some kind of hunter's spray," Lelandi said.

If it wasn't Ural, was it someone else from Lelandi's old pack? Someone who had survived the battle?

Carol opened her mouth to speak, but remembering how those who had attempted to kill Lelandi had worn hunter concealment sprays brought back a horrible flash of memory. She clamped her lips and eyes shut, the terror of the night she'd been bitten coming back to her in an instant. The red wolf's wicked canines primed to bite her, lips curled back, nose wrinkled, the growl, the sharp teeth sinking in, the stabbing pain, the numbing cold, and then blackness.

"Carol?"

Attempting to hide a shudder, Carol opened her eyes and gave a wan smile.

"What were you thinking of?"

"Being bitten."

Lelandi gave her a heartfelt hug and then pulled her to the door and into the hallway. "That's what I thought. But Sheriff Peter Jorgenson killed the wolf that bit you."

A deep frown marred Lelandi's forehead, and Carol got the impression she knew something else. "Was there someone from your old pack who was at the battle and survived?"

Lelandi stopped halfway down the hall and took a deep breath.

"Connor. Darien killed his twin brother. Connor appeared harmless enough to the others when he quit fighting to watch Darien battle with my former pack leader, so they let him go. But later, we had word that during the battle, another was downstairs called North, cousin of the one who bit you. Like Connor, he gave up the fight, and Jake let him leave."

A chill spiked up Carol's spine. "Would either of them want revenge for their kin's death?"

"Possibly."

But the way Lelandi said it as she headed down the stairs sounded more like she thought the red had some other agenda.

"What's another possibility?"

Lelandi looked over her shoulder at Carol, her expression worried. "Connor's brother turned you, but he died. Now either of the men, the brother or the cousin, might want to claim you, partly because you're a red and partly because in the old days when a man needed a woman, and sometimes a woman wanted a particular man, they bit and changed them. Then they took the newly turned wolf as a mate.

"In this case, their kin changed you, but you still don't have a mate, so Connor or North may feel you belong to the family. But also they might want you for revenge. Of course, I'm just guessing here. I have no idea if any of this is true."

Carol swallowed hard as uneasiness swept over her.

"Another possibility is that it's just a red wolf who smelled you or me in a gray territory and was curious about the two of us."

"Unlikely, right?" Carol asked. Just the inflection in Lelandi's voice told her Lelandi didn't believe it.

"You're right. The whole area is filled with gray *lupus garous*, which should be enough of a deterrent." Lelandi clasped Carol's hand and squeezed reassuringly. "Darien's put out the word you're to have a bodyguard at all times. The bachelor males have all eagerly signed up to take turns."

How could things get any worse?

Carol hesitated at the bottom of the stairs. Returning to the sunroom after her flight from the great room was a major feat. She wasn't shy, but she wasn't a stage personality either. She was sure she would be the center of attention when she returned, while she would have much rather blended in.

When she and Lelandi entered the great room, all eyes were upon them. Brows and lips lifted as the bachelors' interest was piqued by the sight of Carol in the dress. Ryan seemed to be grilling Mervin in a corner of the room, the poor barber's back to the wall and Ryan nearly nose to nose with him. Ryan's jaw dropped when he caught sight of Carol out of the corner of his eye, his fearsome expression instantly vaporizing. Now she wished she hadn't changed out of her more casual, conservative clothing to something that really got the guys' attention.

She stiffened her back and glanced at the two women, who were staring at her and exchanging words with each other, both of them giving her a chilly look. Hell, Carol wasn't going to be a wallflower any longer. The guys were single, and while she didn't think she'd really get interested enough in any of them to mate, she had to remind herself that if she just got to know one of them, she might find he truly was someone she could care for. Still for now, all she intended to do was have fun.

"Can we have some music?" she whispered to Lelandi.

Lelandi smiled back. "Silva, want to get the music going? Let's dance!"

That was all it took. One of the men hurried forth to grab Carol's arm, and she tried to tell herself she wanted this—*Do not* shift!

When he grasped her arm, she took a deep calming breath and concentrated on his flyaway dark-brown hair and intense air, his chocolate suit and matching tie at odds with his wild look, and attempted not to think of the force of his enthusiastic touch, which might trigger the shift.

"My name is Christian, and I couldn't have been more proud of you for stealing Darien's ribbon during the game today."

"Really," she said, holding him at arm's length as he moved her across the tile floor to dance. His darkened eyes looked at her as if he was fascinated with her, but his voice was a little too high-pitched to make her feel anything serious about him. "Everyone seemed shocked into silence."

He grinned. "Only until we saw how Darien would take it. I realize you don't understand everything about pack politics yet, but Darien's the pack leader, so what he says is the law. Not that we don't disagree with him sometimes, but we keep it to ourselves."

Betas. "And Lelandi?"

"She's the pack leader's mate, so sure, she has a lot of

say. But ultimately, it falls on Darien's shoulders to make sure that everyone follows the rules. His brothers help to enforce them also. So when someone does something that's contrary to those guidelines, there's a wait-and-see attitude. Does Darien find it acceptable or not? You might not think so, but the way he's taken you into his household means you're his ward, and no one wants to do anything to upset him concerning you."

She snorted. "Darien is protective. I'll give him that. But he's more annoyed with me than anything."

"That's because you're fighting the shift. It sets you apart from the rest of us, but worse than that, one of these days, you won't be able to control it. And you'll put us all in a bind."

Not liking the way he frowned at her and the sudden edge to his voice, she meant to pull away, but Christian tightened his hold. She was afraid that if she fought him, she might trigger the compulsion to shift again.

She could see it now—pulling her dress straps down, exposing her bra, yanking her dress the rest of the way off as fast as she could. Then before she knew it, she'd be standing naked in front of a crowd that was shocked or amused or interested. Definitely the entertainment for the night. And the talk for years of Carol's coming-out. She stifled a laugh. Yeah, coming out, all right.

Christian didn't seem to notice the tension in her body and continued to speak as if he hadn't upset her. "I'm your first bodyguard. And I'll take the job seriously. Anyone who tries to get to you will have to deal with me."

"Anyone?" she asked, curious if this meant he didn't intend to let any of the other bachelors get close to her either.

"Any red males," he said, smiling. "I'd keep any male

away, but not for that reason. Darien has sent some of the mated males out into the woods again tonight, looking for him. He won't get a chance to get near you. *Ever*."

Not wanting to think about being stalked, Carol switched topics. "What do you think of Marilee and Becky?"

Christian glanced at Becky, who was dancing with Mervin. Carol almost laughed when she saw them together. Becky was keeping her distance, and Mervin was watching Carol. Another bachelor clung to Marilee.

His expression fierce, Ryan was standing alone, arms crossed, watching Carol. She wondered why he looked so angry, so dangerous. Maybe because he was irritated that another bachelor male had stolen Marilee from him.

"Cute girls," Christian said. "They'll make some guys good mates."

Cute girls? Sexy as all get-out maybe, but cute? Not in this lifetime.

What she really wanted to hear was that Christian didn't think the women were worthy of consideration. Not that she was interested in him, especially the way he'd come across concerning her fighting the shift, but...

The music ended, and before he could dance with her again, Tom butted in. "Do you mind, Christian?"

Even if Christian had minded, and she was sure he did by the disgruntled look on his face, Darien's brothers had priority as subleaders in having their wishes met.

His mouth curved down, Christian bowed politely and then stepped away. She couldn't believe Tom had even asked her. He kept her separated from his body, very dignified, very respectful, but when he spoke, she knew Darien had prompted him to dance with her.

"Did Mervin upset you in any way?" Tom began.

She loved the way he was always protective of her. She wished he felt something romantic for her, but she assumed his feelings were more brotherly love for a sister who needed protection. "No, Tom. I just decided to change clothes."

Tom glanced down at her dress and smiled. "A different look for you. That's what the guys like so much about you. You're so...unpredictable."

"It also bothers them."

Tom, being the typical peacemaker, immediately changed the subject. "Did you see any red in the woods when you talked to McKinley there?"

"No. Lelandi already asked." She was surprised Lelandi wouldn't have already told Darien and his brothers.

"Are you sure?"

Carol frowned up at Tom. "I *said* I didn't see anyone. Just Ryan. Why do you think I would lie?"

Tom cleared his throat, his cheeks faintly flushing. "Darien's just...well, worried you'd had contact with a red male from another pack. Believe me, Darien wants the best for you. If there *is* something you're not telling us...we don't want to kill someone we think is stalking you when he's truly a love interest."

"Tom," Carol said, unable to hide her exasperation, "if someone's stalking me, I haven't encouraged it. First of all, none of you let me out of your sight long enough for me to have contact with anyone else. And second, if by some miracle I did have an encounter with someone outside the pack, don't you think that if I liked him, I'd tell you so you wouldn't terminate him?"

Tom didn't say anything right away, and as the music

stopped, he glided to a halt. "No. I think you'd be afraid to tell Darien if you were interested in leaving the pack. Look at what happened last night. You were with McKinley alone in the dark woods. Not a word to any of us. We didn't learn of it until we arrived home and Jake checked on you, finding your bedroom door wide open and no sign of you in the house. I found the back door unlocked, and you'd taken off into the forest."

He had her there. "Fair enough. Now that this has come up, I assure you I have no interest in any red male. No gray either." She smiled sweetly.

"All right." Tom released her to another man and gave him a look that meant he'd better keep his distance. Then he headed to speak to Darien.

"Name's Avery," the man said to Carol, taking her arm. His light-amber eyes matched his pale-brown suit, and compared to Christian, he had a much tamer look. His actions mirrored that, as his touch was light, not the least bit invasive.

"I've heard McKinley wants to talk to you later tonight about the investigation. Darien's not happy about it."

She shrugged. She wasn't happy about it either.

"And now McKinley seems to be targeting Marilee, like he can't make up his mind which of you he wants."

Carol looked around at the dancing couples and saw Ryan dancing with the masseuse. He was back for a return engagement. Carol attempted to hide a scowl. Ryan kept his distance with Marilee, but the woman attempted to snuggle closer. Wanting the alpha male? Had she learned he was an unmated pack leader? Or did returning to her show he truly was interested in her?

"Have you danced with her?" Carol tried for cheerful, not annoyed, when she shouldn't have cared in the least.

Avery stiffened. "She seems intent on making the move on McKinley more than she does with any of the rest of us."

Just as Carol suspected. Either she truly did find Ryan more appealing than the other men, or she was targeting him because of his position.

Becky was still dancing with Mervin, but he kept casting glances in Carol's direction. Poor Becky. Carol knew the feeling, having dated a guy on a blind date who had eyes only for the girlfriend who had double-dated with another man.

"So what do you think of Becky?" she asked Avery.

"I haven't had the opportunity to meet her. What happened between you and Mervin?"

"Nothing." Brother, she didn't think this was going to be so blown out of proportion. But then again, packs were close knit, she was learning, much more so than a human community, although juicy gossip often spread from social group to social group, no matter whether they were human or otherwise. She just hadn't expected all the questioning.

The song ended, and out of nowhere, Ryan stepped in to dance with Carol, like a silent predatory wolf closing in on its prey. She wasn't sure if that meant he wanted to dance with her or to rip Avery to shreds.

Instantly, everything changed between them. Avery scowled and hesitated to step aside. Ryan didn't let that stop him. He slid his hand around Carol's back and pulled her close and away from Avery. She couldn't quash the annoyance she felt toward Ryan not only because he planned to interrogate her later to try to prove her a fraud but also because he seemed so eager to get to know the masseuse better. That shouldn't have mattered, but irritatingly, it did.

She pushed away from him and held him apart, like she'd danced with the others, not wanting to go so far as to deny him a dance and then have to explain to Darien, his brothers, and Lelandi why she had said no to a dance. She was sure they'd all think he'd done something horribly scandalous. And then they'd send him away. Which bothered her more than she should have allowed.

Except for the music, everyone was quiet, and she feared they were watching every move she and Ryan made.

In perfect gentlemanly form, he moved with her across the floor, not saying a word, not pressing the issue. Then when she thought she couldn't stand the raw tension between them any longer, Ryan lowered his head and whispered in her ear, sending warm tendrils of fission cascading through her: "Want to leave?"

CHAPTER 8

DISAPPOINTMENT SLID THROUGH CAROL WHEN RYAN asked if she wanted to leave the gathering. He didn't want to hold her close and dance after all. He just wanted to get this charade over, question her to satisfy some stupid need, and leave Silver Town. Either that or he had wanted to dance with her but only close, and beyond that, no deal.

And she realized then just how much she desired being with a man like Ryan.

What the hell. At least Ryan had wanted to dance intimately with her, unlike the way he'd kept Marilee at arm's length. Carol let out her breath, pulled him close, and melted against his heated embrace, loving the way he felt.

She hadn't been with a guy who stirred her up like this since she was a nineteen-year-old in love with a twenty-one-year-old cad, who had used her and thrown her away for a much hotter number after a few months. Come to think of it, that hotter number had looked similar to Marilee, with darker hair and eyes and long lashes.

Carol sighed deeply. She didn't care if Ryan might be infatuated with someone who looked or acted like the masseuse. It was only a dance, after all.

Ryan didn't say anything about Carol holding him close at first. He just responded in kind, moving her across the floor slowly, his body pressed indecently against hers, heating her all the way from the crown of her head to the tips of her toes.

"Carol?" he finally queried, pressing the issue of leaving.

"Sure." She began pulling away, figuring she might as well get this over with, if Ryan really didn't want to dance with her. She'd show Darien she wasn't going to be part of the nonsense of this gathering any longer. At least she hoped she could. He might have words to say about it.

"*After* we finish this waltz. Breaking off the dance after we've barely begun would be inappropriate." His voice was husky and heated, and his eyes clouded with desire—or maybe just plain lust.

That was when she noted his growing arousal pressed heavily against her thigh. It hadn't been there when he'd first pulled her close. Maybe Marilee hadn't intrigued him like Carol had thought.

She slipped her leg in between his in a suggestive way, rubbing against his erection. Teach him to want to hold her close in the beginning and not face the consequences. A throaty growl escaped his lips. She bit back a smile and placed her head against his chest so he couldn't see the amusement on her face—and heard his heart beating at an increased tempo.

The smell of him—hot-blooded virile man, no fussy colognes covering up his delicious manly fragrance, just the woodsy scent of cedar, sage, and citrus—triggered an unexpected craving in her. And a reaction she didn't expect... her hormones tumbled wildly, and a musky fragrance of her own drifted to her nostrils.

Her lips parted in surprise. She still couldn't get used to being able to catch a whiff of smells so intimate that only wilder animals could normally sense them. She slipped one hand down his back and slid the other up his chest, feeling the muscles beneath the cottony fabric, every touch making them tense even harder.

His hands slid down her back, lower, until he was cupping her buttocks in a sexual way, leaning into her, making her wet for him. She almost laughed. So much for *her* attempt at enticing him to take notice. Ryan was an absolute wolf and well versed in the gift of seduction. Lelandi was right. With her, he was the perfect gentleman. With Carol, it was a whole different story.

If they hadn't both been wolves, she would have suggested they go to a hotel—in another town. Not that she'd ever felt that way about a man on a first date, but her wolf hormones must have had something to do with it. Or maybe it was just Ryan who brought out the desire in her. Except their kind didn't have casual sex. The act was a pledge to commit as mates for life.

Too bad. A romp with a macho wolf like him would have promised much pleasure, she was sure.

"Darien doesn't like it that we're dancing so close," Ryan whispered into her hair, but he didn't make a move to distance himself from her, for which she was grateful.

The touch of Ryan's heated breath on her scalp sent a new tingling sensation sweeping through her. "Hmm, I've never known you to care what he thinks."

"Not so," Ryan murmured huskily. "I respect another pack's territory."

She gave a short laugh. "Like you wouldn't give up trying to solve Larissa's murder, even though Darien didn't want you here getting into his family's business? You persisted until you had your man."

Ryan's hands moved to her lower back as if she'd hit a

nerve. Sure, she'd solved the case through her psychic talents. Was it that he didn't like that she, rather than he, had broken the case? Or was it strictly because of how she had been able to do so?

Fine, might as well take the conversation to something less sensitive. She didn't want him pushing her away in the middle of the dance and acting as though she was too repugnant to touch. Maybe he felt that way, but she sure as hell didn't want him to show that in front of all the others.

That was when she noticed how nearly everyone was watching them, even those dancing on the floor.

Lelandi smiled at her as she passed by with Darien, dancing nice and close also. He was scowling at Ryan, big time. Silva smiled at her as she and Sam waltzed by, while he was behaving as though he was as irritated with Ryan as Darien was. Ditto with Tom and Jake standing on the sidelines. Tom's hands were in his pockets, and he shook his head. Jake folded his arms and gave her the evil eye rather than Ryan.

Yes, she knew it was all her fault. She should have kept some distance from Ryan. She smiled and winked at Jake. His hard expression grew even harder still. Teach him to taunt her about Mervin being interested in her.

She didn't have to see what the bachelor males thought of the situation. She just hoped they wouldn't gang up on Ryan later and give him a rough time. Although as alpha as he was and as beta as they were, she figured they didn't stand a chance.

"So what did you think of Marilee?" she asked him, her question an attempt at light and unconcerned.

Immediately, Ryan's hands returned to Carol's rump

and he rested them there, the sensuous touch making her heartbeat quicken. So what did his reaction mean? He liked Marilee and wished he had his hands on her backside instead? Carol hated how she always overanalyzed people's behaviors.

"Hmm," Ryan said, and she didn't like the way he said it, thinking he enjoyed being with Marilee more, like some horny male, as he continued to dance with Carol crushed against his chest, his leg locked between hers and moving at intervals to brush her mound in an enticing caress.

She could imagine him closing his eyes and envisioning he had that hot, sultry number in his tight clutches instead—the long, curly hair, the luscious glistening lips, the fluttering long, dark lashes…all together tall, dark, and bosomy. Not short, pale and…well, Carol had nice-sized boobs, too, but that was about it.

"She's…not…my type," he said slowly.

Carol glided with him across the smooth tile floor, trying to let herself just soak up the moment, but she couldn't give up the gnawing notion that he liked the other women better. They were grays, had been born as such, and weren't an enigma like she was. Why wouldn't he prefer them to her?

When she didn't say anything in response, he sighed. "She's too…clingy, too…sweet, too…"

"Hot?"

He chuckled. "I'd be lying if I said she wasn't hot. But that doesn't mean I'm interested." He lifted Carol's chin and looked into her eyes. "You don't have to prove anything to anyone here tonight."

Which meant what? She wondered if he felt a connection

with her, maybe because of her solving the murder—not in the way he would, but that she could—like he did in his line of work. Like a fellow investigator, even though she hadn't investigated anything. Maybe he didn't really feel anything for the other women. Except that one was hot.

"Did you dance with Becky?" she asked, wondering what he thought of her. "She seems to need rescuing from Mervin."

Ryan's face turned dark. "What happened between you and Mervin?"

Not expecting him to question her about Mervin also, she pursed her lips in annoyance. And wished she hadn't brought Mervin's name up.

Carol shook her head. "Nothing happened between us."

"You make a lousy liar."

She stiffened her back. Didn't matter that he was right, but she didn't need him telling her so.

He immediately stroked her back as if attempting to placate her. "I'll learn one way or another, Carol. It's what I do." His voice was back to being darkly seductive.

She harrumphed, although she admired him for looking doggedly into a situation until he discovered the truth. She just wished *she* wasn't the focus of one of his bloodhound hunts.

"Didn't you already scare the truth out of him?" she asked.

"I always get confirmation. That way, I learn the *real* truth." He slid his hands down her bare arms with a sensuous sweep, caught her wrists, and turned them to consider her skin, his touch gentle, concerned. "He didn't bruise you."

Her lips parted in surprise. Did Ryan suspect what had happened? At this rate, she figured the truth would come out anyway. Except she wasn't mentioning the damned urge to shift. "He tried to stop me from leaving the house. That's all."

"All right. That's what he said. And then? You decided to change into this?" He slid his hands down her back again, skin against skin, then lower, caressing her body beneath the clinging silk and leaving a sizzling trail of desire. "Why?"

She was still absorbing the sensual feel of his touch as she fought to respond with an intelligent reply, no matter how much he unsettled her—both with his words and actions.

"You know, if you really want a chance to have me for your own, you'll have to quit questioning my motives all the time. And frankly, Chester Ryan McKinley, it is *none* of *your* business."

He whispered against her ear, "Why would you think I'm attempting to pursue you?"

She smiled just a hint. "It's your nature. You want what you can't have."

He gave her a husky laugh and moved his hands to her buttocks again. "If I wanted you, make no mistake, Carol, you would be mine."

She chuckled and rested her head against his chest again. "I love a man with a sense of humor."

"Hmm." He continued to dance slow with her, his arousal throbbing with need—that she'd happily created—and his hands treacherously sliding over her buttocks in a sensual caress. If he didn't want her, he sure was a master at deception.

She was beginning to think maybe he really was

interested in her, and her psychic business was what still bothered him. Then to her disappointment, the music ended, and another man stood at her elbow, ready to dance with her next. She hoped he didn't think she'd want to dance close with him too.

But would Ryan rescue her and take her to the tavern instead, like he'd wanted to, or give her up to the guy who was now tapping his foot on the floor, hands on his hips, an annoyed expression darkening his face?

"Sorry," Ryan said to the man. "She promised me two dances."

She was shocked speechless and quickly snapped her gaping mouth shut.

The guy scowled. "But…"

The music began again, and Ryan pulled Carol deeper into the group of dancing couples.

"I thought we were going on our *date* next," she said, amused that Ryan seemed reluctant to let her go.

"We are on our date. First here, then at the tavern."

"Yeah, but it's not a *real* date, and you're making a lot of men angry." She frowned up at him, really hoping he wouldn't have a fight with the other men over her. She laughed at herself. No one would have ever fought over her.

"They'll get over it when I'm gone."

Her heart hitched a little, when she shouldn't have cared one bit. She should have known. Maybe he already had his sights set on a woman in his pack.

As soon as the music stopped, Ryan hurried her to the great room, his hand clamped around her wrist, moving at double time. Thankfully, his touch didn't force the urge to shift.

She was afraid to see who would come after them—Darien, his brothers, Sam—all intending to put a stop to it. But all that happened was the sunroom remained really quiet. No music, no conversation, just Carol's heels clicking on the tile floor, headed toward the foyer as Ryan rushed her to the front door.

And then Darien's harsh holler came from the sunroom, "Remember what I said, McKinley! Bring her back by midnight."

Surprised Darien had allowed it, Carol wondered if Lelandi had convinced him to let her go with Ryan.

"I feel like we're eloping," Carol said, frowning at Ryan, barely able to keep up with his long stride while she teetered in high heels as he hauled her out of the house to his vehicle.

He raised his brows. "Just a meeting to set some things right."

That was what *he* thought.

"Hope you're not too disappointed when you go home alone to your bed tonight *without* the answers you are looking for." She gave him a sweet smile as he opened the pickup door for her, and she climbed into the passenger's seat.

His expression was noncommittal. "My conscience is clear, and I sleep well at night. What about you?"

She turned away and looked out the windshield as he still held her door, waiting for her response. She didn't sleep well at all. Certainly not last night after fighting the craving to shift half the evening. Her lack of sleep had nothing to do with having a bad conscience and all to do with the moon and a wolf named Ryan who had come to her in a vision. Mervin, too, wearing his red-and-white-striped jacket.

"I sleep wonderfully well." She gave Ryan a quick smile.

He smirked. "Right. That's why you have dark circles under your eyes. I *am* trained to observe people and objects. I notice things." He took a deep breath. "This won't take long."

Which suited her just fine. She folded her hands in her lap and nodded. "Let's get it over with. The sooner, the better." But she wanted to look in the visor mirror and see for herself if she had dark circles under her eyes. She hadn't noticed when she smoothed lipstick over her lips or applied makeup earlier.

He shut her door, skirted around his vehicle, and climbed into the driver's seat.

There was no figuring what was going on in Ryan McKinley's investigative mind, but why was she bothered by the notion that he'd be leaving soon?

He considered her for a moment and then nodded. But something was off in the way he acted. As though he had to finish this so he could get to more important business back home, yet he didn't want to let go of the business here so quickly either. What was that all about anyway?

Ryan circled the truck around the drive and then headed toward town.

No, it was something deeper than that. Something sexy, more primal, more wolf. If she shifted, would it help her to recognize better what was going on between them? Or was her usual cynicism about men blocking her ability to see what was really happening?

Giving up on psychoanalyzing the situation further, Carol leaned into the seat and smelled the fragrance of new leather. She noted the spotless dashboard and a medallion hanging from the rearview mirror as it swung with the movement of the truck. She tried to glimpse the words etched on the medallion, on a brass plate below the name *MacKinlay*.

"What does the motto mean?"

"'We force no friend; we fear no foe,' which was the motto for Clan Farquharson. But some say we were associated with the Buchanan clan instead. Others say a people named MacAnleighs might have been more related to our origin."

He didn't say anything further, and she prompted him, "Go on. Family roots fascinate me. Sometimes the meaning of a name gives a hint to a family's origins. Maybe something about their character that is passed down from generation to generation."

His mouth curved up a little. "Never know. Since we had more family in the area of Braemar, we go with Clan Farquharson's motto. McKinley is a variation of MacKinlay. Some say the name originated from the Gaelic 'Mac Fhionnlaoich,' meaning 'fair hero.'"

"Fair hero. Hmm. See? What did I say?"

"Yes, but another meaning is given. 'Son,' for Mac, 'of the white warrior.'" He waited for her response.

She smiled. "Seems, with the occupation you've chosen, you carry the gene that validates the claim for both the motto and the meaning of your name."

"I try to live up to the name, to make my ancestors proud."

She noticed the blanket lying on the seat between them, a predominantly blue-and-green plaid wool with black and red threads woven in, accentuating it. She ran her hand over the soft fabric.

"It's old," Ryan said.

"It represents the McKinley clan?"

"Yes. It was my grandfather's."

Chill bumps raced along her arms. Lelandi had explained to Carol how the *lupus garous* lived long lives, thirty years for every year after they reached puberty. So his grandfather could very well have fought in clan battles and been a clan chief even. Or not. He might have just been a sheepherder for all she knew. She'd read so many Highland romances that the idea she could be sitting next to the descendant of one of those brawny men—bare-legged, barefooted, and bare...she smiled...bare-assed men of the kilt—made her melt a little.

Ryan glanced at her and gave her a suggestion of a smile. Her cheeks instantly flushed with heat. He winked. "You may see visions of the future, but I wish I could read your mind."

Her face heated anew. She pushed some of her hair behind an ear and looked out the windshield. "What did your grandfather do as an occupation?"

"Fought for the clan, took a mate, raised a passel of kids, and whittled in his spare time."

"Whittled?"

Ryan chuckled. "That he did. Played the bagpipes too."

Carol sighed and touched the blanket on the seat, imagining what it would be like to fall into one of her romance novels and feel the soft plaid on a Highlander's hardened body until he slipped it off and settled it on the heather. Hand outstretched, he'd offer to take her into his world and show her just how hardy a Highlander could be.

Her lips dry, she was sweeping her tongue over them

when she caught Ryan glancing at her again. "Have you ever been to the Colorado Scottish Festival and Rocky Mountain Highland Games?" she asked wistfully. She had loved the place on the one chance she'd had to visit. All those Celts dressed in different tartans. The music. The games. The food.

"To listen to the pipes and drums, to step to the Celtic tunes, dance in the Highland competitions, participate in tug-of-war and the parade of clans? I've participated every year for the past four years."

"Do you win?"

"Every year."

"The truth?"

He smiled. "The truth is that a wolf's strength gives me a bit of an advantage." He shrugged. "I can't help it. Have you been?"

She sighed. "Once. All those men in kilts with great-looking legs nearly did me in."

He gave her another shadow of a smile. "Do you have a Scottish background?"

"MacDonald, on my mother's side of the family. Our motto: 'By sea and land.' We have an armored hand holding a cross for the clan's crest. After I went to that one festival, I went away to college, but I hope to go this summer again. Maybe I'll see you there."

And see Ryan in a kilt, his legs bare, naked biceps and back straining to pull at a rope as men on the other side fight to win the game. Darien probably wouldn't even let her go to the festivities, unless some of his people were willing to watch her.

Or if she had a mate already. And then her mate probably

wouldn't be interested in going there unless he had Celtic roots. She chewed on her bottom lip. She had to find other men who appealed like Ryan did, since she didn't think Jake or Tom would ever make a move in her direction.

Then a new thought came to her. The librarian and masseuse were from another pack. Why couldn't she go to their pack, or even Ryan's, and see if someone who suited her better was in one of those packs?

She patted Ryan's thigh, making him tense and speed up as he barreled down the road.

"I have an idea. When you have your next gathering, I'll come to Green Valley and check out the eligible bachelors there," she said. "Have any good, hardy Scots in the bunch?"

Ryan's mouth opened as if he was going to make a comment, but then he quickly snapped it shut. He tapped his thumbs on the steering wheel and finally said, "Darien wouldn't allow it."

She was a little surprised at his reaction. "Funny, I thought you might be less against it than he would be. I've heard that a pack leader who can encourage unmated females to accept bachelors in his pack earns brownie points."

Ryan's jaw tightened, and she assumed she'd hit another nerve. But she wasn't sure why this time, unless someone in his pack might truly be interested in her.

"In fact, I'll check into Becky and Marilee's pack while I'm at it. Surely, I'll find someone I'll be interested in. Don't you think?"

CHAPTER 9

HELL AND DAMNATION. RYAN COULDN'T BELIEVE HOW much the petite blond could get under his skin. One minute she was touching his plaid blanket, while he was wishing he was wearing his kilt of the same plaid right that moment and she was touching it instead, wondering when she'd ask the question most women asked. Did he wear anything under the kilt? Ha, what God gave him. The next minute, she was wanting to find a mate in *his* pack?

How Carol could think the other women were hot and she wasn't was beyond his comprehension. But the notion that she'd come to his pack and check out some of his bachelor males was unthinkable. Not that it wouldn't help his standing in the pack. But hell. Seeing her mated to one of his men—not any of whom would be right for her... He couldn't have it.

Even the notion that she'd check out the other women's pack didn't agree with him. Who knew what sort of men were in it? These women weren't interested in their own bachelors. Why would Carol be? Besides, she was a special case. With special needs, because she was newly turned. She had to have just the right man.

Ryan had no regrets about dancing close to her. He'd thought she might be feeling insecure about the way the other women looked because she'd changed into the clingy silk dress, and he'd wanted her to know she was just as hot an item in the soft pink sweater and jeans she'd worn earlier. He loved comfortable casual.

But he'd never expected her to turn his body into a raging inferno. Even now, he was still at half-mast, partly because of the way she'd danced with him, the heat and fragrance and softness of her body still lingering in his thoughts. And partly because of the way she had caressed his plaid blanket. Envisioning his body wrapped in it and her touching him made him harden even further.

He tried not to frown at her too much as he parked at the Silver Town Tavern, the lot fairly empty. He would speak to Darien about ensuring she didn't check out the other pack. *Or* his own.

"Ready?" he asked her as she stared out the window.

She snapped her head around to look at him, her expression startled, and he thought something was wrong.

"Carol?"

She smiled, but the expression was forced. "Sure. Let's get the interrogation over with. *Pronto.* I'm sure you have more important business to take care of back home."

She dropped the smile, and her look turned mutinous. Which appealed a hell of a lot more than when she was giving him a fake smile. Wondering about his own sanity, he shook his head and left the truck to get her door.

Ryan's question had yanked her out of a vision so fast that it startled Carol, but since he didn't believe she could see what she could, she hadn't any plan to enlighten him. Yet given the way he looked at her, she figured he'd question her about it anyway.

"What were you thinking when I drew your attention?" Ryan asked, helping her from his vehicle.

The biting cold…silky red hair floating over her face… male amber eyes narrowed, padded armor, and a tiredness she couldn't free herself from.

"Carol?" Ryan asked again, his hand firmly on her arm as he guided her toward the tavern.

"Nothing."

But the look he gave her told her he knew differently. He gave his head a slight shake. What did she care? He wouldn't believe she'd had another one of her visions. *Anyway*. And the meaning of the vision eluded her as before, so what was she supposed to say? Even if he had been more enlightened?

She walked at Ryan's quickened pace, observing the carved wooden wolves guarding the double doors of the bar. If she'd only known in the beginning what they had signified. Wolf territory.

Before she'd become a wolf, Carol had only been in Silver Town's tavern once during the fall festival when the doors were open to nonmembers as well as members. She hadn't realized that to obtain memberships, citizens had to be card-carrying wolves.

Ryan hurried to get the tavern door for Carol, the rusty hinges squealing as he pushed the heavy oak aside. Rustic fans circulating the air were probably new but looked antique enough to have been hanging from the time the place opened in the nineteenth century.

The smoky mirror behind the long, polished bar definitely had been there from the early days, and the counter was worn in spots where folks had leaned against it, drinking their choice of poison. She imagined the shadows of people from long ago reflected in the dingy glass. Silva swore she was going to make Sam replace it with new mirrors, but Sam was a rustic himself and wouldn't go along with it. Maybe because he was cheap too.

Amber glass lights hung on brass rods from the high ceiling, casting a soft light over the dark wood tables, some round for smaller groups, some long and rectangular for larger crowds. The place was fairly empty, with just a few older couples enjoying drinks and conversation. The talking died when Ryan and Carol walked inside.

Many of Darien's pack were still at the gathering. Sam and Silva had returned at some point and were preparing roast beef sandwiches and drinks, the aroma of the roasting beef filling the air. Silva hurried to greet them and directed them to a table in the center of the room surrounded by other tables.

A fishbowl.

"We'd prefer one over here, thanks." Ryan guided Carol to a table in a corner of the room where it was out of the traffic, half-hidden in shadows, quiet, and easier to talk privately. And unavailable.

"This is Darien's table," Carol whispered, her heartbeat accelerating, but she had a sneaking suspicion Ryan already knew that.

Silva tapped a pen on an order pad. "Boss man sits here with Lelandi and his brothers. I'll show you to another table."

"He's not coming here tonight," Ryan told her and pulled out a chair for Carol so self-assuredly that his move fed her own confidence.

His amber eyes steeled, Sam wiped the bar. "Darien might not be here tonight, but his brothers will be, guaranteed. And *they also* sit there."

"Not tonight." Ryan gave him a look that meant he would not be dissuaded. "Darien suggested we come here on our *date*. So I'm sure he won't mind if we take the most out-of-the-way, private spot."

Silva looked at Carol as if hoping she would make Ryan come to his senses. Carol only smiled, figuring what the heck, and took her seat. She'd already done enough to create a scene or two, so why not another?

"Yep. I figure capturing Darien's ribbon today entitles me to a reward."

Ryan gave her a small nod of approval and pulled his own chair out and sat down.

Sam poured a beer for a man at the bar and inclined his head briefly to Silva, giving his okay. She let out her breath.

"All right. It's on Sam's head if Darien shows up expecting his table and finds it occupied. What would you care to drink?"

"A strawberry daiquiri," Carol said.

Silva's brows shot up into her bangs. "You always get a Chablis. Are you sure?"

"Yep, tonight's a cause for celebration."

Ryan leaned back in his chair. "A beer for me, Silva. And a couple of hot roast beef sandwiches for the two of us."

Silva nodded. "You know, word is getting around that you're here to question Carol about the murder case and then you're leaving for good. Best be quick about it if that's all the business you have, because the bachelors are antsy about you being here. Rumors are circulating that it's more than that."

"They have a lot more to worry about than me being here."

Her face brightening, Silva said, "Oh?" Which meant she was delighted to share whatever the new gossip was around the tavern and the town.

"Some red male is running around here without Darien's permission, possibly targeting Carol or Lelandi, or both. That's who everyone should be more concerned about."

Silva gave Carol a worried look.

Trying to appear unconcerned, Carol shrugged. "The bachelors are all going to be my bodyguards, and Lelandi will also be well protected. Nothing to worry about."

"Ryan will be your bodyguard too?" Silva asked, sounding hopeful.

Carol attempted a nonchalant tone for her response, but it came out more annoyed than she had planned. "Ryan's going home as soon as he grills me."

Silva gave him a hard look. "You could at least guard her. Be nice while you question her. If you're not...well, Sam will take care of you. Believe me, you don't want that." She whipped around and headed to the bar to get their drinks.

Carol loved having Silva as a friend. "Ask your questions so you can return home."

He glanced at Silva as she spoke with Sam, ordering their drinks. "Don't you want to wait for your drink first, Carol?"

"Why? Think it'll make me tell the truth?"

Ryan gave her a hint of a smile.

"It won't."

His smile broadened.

"I mean that it won't get me drunk so that I'll tell the truth." She paused. "I mean..." she said, totally exasperated with herself, "I'm not telling you anything but the truth, no matter what. How do you suspect I learned about Larissa's murder?"

"You overheard something. I'm not saying you consciously have tried to hide anything. Just that—"

"Well, hell, that's nice to know." She didn't try to hide her annoyance. He might as well know that she didn't appreciate his questioning her as if she had something to hide. "The truth is that you don't believe in parapsychology. Right?" She lifted her chin a hair.

Ryan had to keep a stern face on that one. He didn't think he'd get anywhere with Carol if he smirked as though he thought she didn't have any abilities. He just didn't believe in anything that couldn't be proven 100 percent. What she claimed to be able to do wouldn't hold up under any kind of scrutiny and couldn't be used in a court of law.

"Just the facts, ma'am. Solid, hard, physical facts," he said.

"All right." She sat up straighter, and he loved her backbone. "Did you know that I was a prisoner of Darien's household before the battle between the reds and grays occurred?"

Not having known, Ryan frowned and pondered that. "Before you were turned?" He drummed his fingers on the table, then quit. "Of course. They feared for your safety because you'd discovered something about the murderer. They were afraid whoever it was would be sure to silence you also."

Looking like she was fighting to keep from showing her irritation, Carol clenched her teeth. Then she leaned forward and speared him with a hard look. But no matter how irritated she looked, he couldn't help thinking how attractive she was, her blue eyes heated and narrowed, her face lightly flushed.

"You're right, of course. The reason also was that if Lelandi was injured, I'd be her personal nurse. But the biggest reason?" she asked.

"Enlighten me."

Silva joined them with a tray of beers and one strawberry daiquiri. She leaned over the table and then deposited Carol's red frothy drink and his beer.

"Before she was changed, but way before she actually saw our kind frolicking in the woods, she had a premonition of it."

Ryan hadn't expected Silva to offer the explanation, and he really wished she'd butt out, but he nodded. The so-called premonition was certainly easy to explain away. "She could have seen it happen, but not as a premonition."

Silva smiled. "Tell him, Carol. Tell him how you saw us."

Carol looked as though she didn't think he would believe her, and he wasn't sure she was going to bother explaining. She took a strawberry from a tiny, plastic pink sword in her drink, wrapped her glossy lips around it, and then sucked for a moment. He swore it was the most erotic thing he'd seen in a long damn time. And that she did it on purpose to stir him up again.

Then she took a bite, chewed, and swallowed. "I saw men and women shifting in the woods near Darien's place. They stripped out of their clothes, and in a blink of an eye, they were wolves."

His gaze shifted to her dipping the strawberry back in her drink, and then he watched as she licked the sweet liquid off the remainder of the strawberry. It made him think of the way her tongue had touched and tasted and teased his earlier in such a seductive fashion when he had kissed her. And he was damn ready for a repeat performance. How appealing it would be to taste the sweet flavor of strawberries on her tongue!

Not intending to allow the vixen to distract him further, he cleared his throat. "I still say you could have seen this and then imagined that it had occurred as a vision. Dreamed it, whatever."

Carol licked her lips in such a sensuous way that he swore she was trying to make him hot all over again. Even if she wasn't doing so consciously, she sure had that effect on him. She dipped her strawberry back in the drink, pulled it out, slipped it into her mouth, and sighed.

Once she had finished the fruit, she pointed her tiny sword at him. "No, I saw everyone shift in the dark, and the night was foggy. As a human, I wouldn't have been able to see what you can."

He still didn't believe it. "The light from the house must have illuminated the forest some."

Carol gave a short laugh. "Yeah, right. Even you couldn't believe something so ludicrous. I'd envisioned following the others into the woods. I hadn't been turned yet. The vision was vague. I only knew Lelandi wasn't with the men and women there. But I recognized some of Darien's people and tried to warn Lelandi about what Darien and his people were.

"She wasn't from Silver Town, and because she was smaller, I thought she wasn't one of you. I thought she was like me and that Darien intended to change her. I'd never suspected anyone could be born as a wolf."

Silva leveled her gaze at Ryan. "Yep, so how do you explain that?"

Carol loved how Silva needled Ryan. She knew if Lelandi was here, she'd gang up on him too. Not that Carol couldn't hold her own, but it was nice to have the ladies backing her up. She'd never had friends like that before.

Ryan's forehead wrinkled as he considered Silva in a disgruntled way. "Aren't you supposed to be bringing us sandwiches?"

Silva smiled. "Yes sirree." She said to Carol, "He gives you any trouble, sugar, you just let me know." She sauntered off with the tray of beers for another table.

That was when the whole group from the gathering seemed to arrive at the tavern en masse. Darien walked in first with his arm possessively around Lelandi's shoulders. He looked straight at Ryan and Carol sitting at his table, but instead of making a fuss, he escorted Lelandi to a table nearer the restrooms.

Carol took a relieved breath, glad at least Darien didn't seem to be bothered about this. Maybe Ryan had been right in thinking that Darien had set this up, so he didn't mind giving up his table to them because of it.

As Jake followed them inside, he grumbled, although sounding more amused than truly annoyed, "Sam needs a talking-to if every time we come here, he's allowing some outsider to sit at our table."

Darien slipped his arm down lower, around Lelandi's waist, and leaned over and kissed her cheek. "Worked out well the last time."

Five men escorted Becky to a table. Marilee had several others falling all over her as they grabbed a table and stuck it against another farther away. Mervin was with the second group and gave Ryan another hard look.

Carol studied the women for a moment, still trying to remember where she'd seen them. At the hospital? As patients? But they weren't from around here. Then again, Lelandi had said she'd interviewed them, so maybe they'd been here for a couple of days prior to the gathering. Or maybe earlier to see what Silver Town had to offer before they even expressed an interest in attending the gathering.

"So where were we?" Carol asked Ryan, ready to end this. There was no convincing the stubborn man of science that what she could envision could really happen.

"You were saying you saw our kind shifting while you were still strictly human. Then Darien would have had to turn you if one of Lelandi's pack hadn't during the battle."

"Probably. But you missed my point. I didn't *physically* see them shift in the woods. I saw it in a vision of the future way before the battle commenced. When I eventually did see the scene for real, I had already been turned."

She could tell he didn't believe a word of it. No reaction, no expression to indicate what he was thinking. Trying to figure out the next question he'd ask her to see if he could tear her story into bits and prove it was all something made up from a way-too-vivid imagination?

She ought to tell him about the ghost she once saw. That was sure to go over really well. When she'd told some friends about it, the ones who believed in apparitions had known she was telling the truth. The others had had the same look as Ryan did now. Disbelief, not even a small smirk in amusement. No, he was not amused. He was too steeped in scientific fact to believe in ghosts or anything else in the supernatural realm.

"I bet you never read about fantasy worlds when you were young. Never believed in the Easter bunny or Santa Claus," she said.

He gave her a broad smile that made her wish she hadn't made the comment.

"What?" She let out her breath. "Don't tell me you and your kind don't believe in fantasy worlds. You're a living, breathing fantasy—all of you…well, us, if you want to really get technical."

"Fantasy is in the eye of the beholder. We are the stuff of legends, not fantasy exactly."

"Right, so I have psychic visions, and you think that's fantasy. But for me, it's real."

For an inkling, he appeared to consider her words as plausible. But then he said, "I believe we've established that fact." He shrugged. "Me believe in Santa Claus? Only if he wore a wolf suit sometimes." He smiled again. "Our versions of fairy tales might surprise you. 'Little Red Riding Hood'? The wolf, as caring about children as a good family dog might be, was trying to escort Little Red Riding Hood home safely to her grandmother. The woodcutter was the villain. He didn't give the wolf a chance to prove he was one of the good guys. The woodcutter took one look at the wolf and immediately labeled him as a beast of prey. Our kids, of course, read the original version also, so they know what others are talking about. But we feel we're a little more open-minded."

She raised her brows. "I take it the wolf is not the bad guy in 'The Three Little Pigs' either."

"Nope, he was totally framed." Ryan gave her that wolfish grin that suited him so well. He pulled out his credit card, tapped it on the table while watching her, and then finally asked, "Do you feel there's a reason for having the visions?"

She shrugged. "You don't believe anyway."

"If I did, why do you think you have them?"

"I have no idea why some people have a psychic connection and others don't. Probably just like no one knows why some have a photographic memory or can create music without any training or are geniuses in mathematics or quantum physics. Makes life more interesting when we're not all the same. Don't you agree?"

He studied her, and she swore he was mulling that over. Maybe he wasn't hopeless after all when it came to believing in something that wasn't exactly scientifically proven.

She sighed deeply. "No one in my family has any paranormal abilities. At least not that anyone is willing to speak about. No one wanted me to reveal my talents either. I even had nice little discussions with a psychiatrist, starting when I was seven.

"Dr. Metzger attempted to brainwash me for three years, trying to convince me I had an overactive imagination. That paranormal abilities weren't possible. That they couldn't be re-created in a scientific environment. In other words, those of us who have these abilities make mistakes like lab rats and don't get it 'right' all the time. So we're phonies. All of us."

Ryan's jaw tightened fractionally. She wasn't sure what the message was there.

"You know what made Dr. Metzger finally give up on me?" She raised her brows, waiting for Ryan to signal for her to continue. She'd never discussed the reason with anyone except her mother, because the psychiatrist had been so mad at Carol. She wouldn't have told Ryan, but for whatever reason, she wanted him to believe her. Not that telling him the story about the doctor would make any difference, but…

Ryan didn't say anything for a moment and then asked, "What made him give up on you, Carol?"

"I saw his wife and unborn child die in a car accident before it happened. At least I assumed it was going to happen. I didn't know anything about them. They might have died years earlier. But I saw his very pregnant wife driving the car, and she looked the same as the picture he had of her on his desk, probably taken shortly before the accident. I was sure it was a vision of some future happening.

"I wouldn't have told him about it, but I thought maybe, just maybe, he could stop her from driving into the city. We lived in Denver at the time, but he lived out of town. In my vision, it was winter, and the roads were icy. Their car skidded on the slick roads and crashed into a tree. He didn't believe me. Got really angry instead. Said I was creating the tale because I was mad at him for trying to help me. Help me! Ha!"

She silently fumed, remembering that day so well. Hot tears had filled her eyes, her throat closing.

"He said I was a horrible person for making such a story up."

No one had ever said anything like that about her. Not someone who was supposed to have her best interests at heart. Carol took a deep breath, the feelings of that day swamping her with regret. For years, she'd wished she'd never said a thing to him about his wife. At least she hadn't had to see him any further after that.

She looked at the table, fighting bitter tears. "He slammed his fist on the desk and cursed me. The frost giant and his icy-blue eyes turned darker and colder. Tears rolled down my face. I was only ten at the time. No one had ever gotten that angry with me over anything."

"Hell, Carol. His license should have been revoked."

Carol shook her head. "The worst was yet to come. When I left his office, he called my mother in, and behind his closed door, he told her he wouldn't see me any longer. That I was hopeless. That I was making up horrible stories. My mother asked what kind of stories, but he wouldn't elaborate. I heard him tell her through the door of his office that if I was committed, I'd quickly get over my need to make up these stories."

Ryan looked on the verge of getting up from his chair and coming around the table to comfort her, but she didn't need his comforting touch. She'd dealt with the issues, and they were in the past. At least that was what she kept telling herself. Yet the memory of Metzger's piercing eyes and the way he'd slammed his fist on the desk was forever imprinted on her brain.

"My mother kept asking me what I'd said to Dr. Metzger. I couldn't tell her, not until later that night. In the beginning, I really had hoped the 'special' doctor could help me sort out my abilities. Sometimes I wished I didn't have them. Sometimes I wished everyone else did so they knew what it felt like. But denying my 'talents' wasn't feasible. So I just didn't let on that I had them."

"Did Dr. Metzger's wife die?"

CHAPTER 10

CAROL SLUMPED A LITTLE IN HER CHAIR AT THE TAVERN as she became aware of Ryan's intense gaze on her. She had found no satisfaction in having been right where Dr. Metzger's wife was concerned. She only wished he'd saved her before Carol's vision had come true.

"Yes, his wife died. Not immediately. Three days later, she drove into Denver, or was on her way to Denver, when her SUV slid on ice and she hit a tree. She was in a coma for a couple of days, and then she and her unborn child died."

When Ryan didn't speak, she added, "It's not an exact science. I didn't know when it would occur. But usually when I get a vision, it's something that will happen pretty soon."

She gritted her teeth and swallowed the bitterness that came with knowing something bad was going to occur and that she couldn't do anything about it.

"Mom tried to keep it from me, not wanting to upset me. But I'd been looking for the news story, hoping that if it did come to pass, Mom would finally believe me. We never talked about it though. I guess I was always afraid she might think it would be a good idea to have me committed."

Ryan reached out and took hold of Carol's hand and squeezed. Although she thought she wouldn't appreciate it, she loved the way he gave her a little of the solace she could have used years earlier. Then again, as much as she tried to tell herself she could deal with it, maybe she still wasn't doing that great a job.

"Hell, Carol, I had no idea."

"Yeah, well, no one does who doesn't live with an early warning system in their heads."

"What happened to the doctor?"

"Dr. Metzger moved away from Denver, and I always wondered what he thought of my abilities then. Maybe if he had another patient who 'suffered' from my kind of delusions, he would treat them with more respect. Give them the benefit of the doubt. And maybe if he'd listened to me, he could have saved his wife and unborn child. I don't know. I wanted to save them in the worst way, but no one would have ever believed me."

Ryan frowned but didn't release her hand. "*Can* the future be altered?"

"I don't know for sure. My visions are hazy, not fully developed for the most part. So I suppose that in those cases, the truth of the matter hasn't really been revealed."

"Do you always foresee something bad?"

She ran her free hand over her chilled glass. "No. It causes problems with Christmas presents and keeping them secret. Especially from me."

"Because you can touch an object and know something about its contents?"

"Sometimes its history. I can see flashes of who had touched it and why. Sometimes a glimpse of the department where the item was purchased."

That brought a sexy smile to Ryan's lips, and his thumb stroked her hand with a gentle caress. That little stroke and the smile on his lips made butterflies flutter in her stomach.

"Wish I could read minds," she said.

He chuckled. "I can imagine you might sense some

impressions others wouldn't want you to know about." Then his expression turned dark and he changed topics. "Who is the red wolf who was skulking around Darien's house? Is he after you or Lelandi? Or something else entirely?"

At least he was done questioning her about her psychic abilities. "Lelandi thinks it might be the brother or a cousin of the one who bit me. The men are named Connor and North."

Ryan closed his gaping mouth and sat very still. "I thought they had all died. Hell, one of them wants *you* for revenge."

"Or Lelandi. Or maybe he just wants me. Not for revenge. Just as a mate." She shrugged like it didn't matter. Although it did. She definitely didn't want anything to do with Lelandi's old pack. She sure didn't want to be thought of as someone's possession because his brother or cousin had turned her.

Ryan glanced at Darien, who was still seated across the tavern with Lelandi and his brothers. "You said that Darien ordered the bachelor males to guard you?"

"Yep. Who else?"

Grinding his teeth, Ryan scowled. "They're not trained for this kind of work. Mervin's a damned barber. Avery? He sells gas at the local station."

"He owns the gas station and convenience store."

Ryan ignored the comment. "And Christian? He's a used car salesman."

"Manager and owner of previously loved cars. At least two of the cars he has for sale are new."

Ryan shook his head. "Right. Not one of them is qualified to protect you."

"I'll just have to take my chances. Besides, any of them just has to shift, and that takes care of that." At least she figured it did. They all had very wicked canines when needed.

"We're all hunters when in our wolf form, Carol. That's not what I'm referring to. In their human occupations, they don't normally hunt killers."

She reached over and patted his hand. "I'm sure I'll be fine."

"You'll have a premonition, and it will save you." He ground out the words, as if he couldn't believe she'd be that naive.

"Like I had about being one of you?" She raised her brows. "No. The premonitions are annoyingly unpredictable. So if I were to have one, it wouldn't mean it would help keep me safe."

His lips parted, and then he tilted his head to the side, a strange look on his face. "Have you had any lately?"

"Not that you would believe." She took a long sip of her drink to steady her nerves.

She wanted to tell someone who would believe her, because she knew something horrible was going to come to at least a few of the people in the pack, and they would have to figure out a way to stop it. But hell, if people who normally believed her wouldn't about this, no way would a PI trust her visions when he didn't think her capable of having such abilities.

She shook her head. No. Until she saw more of the dilemma, she couldn't solicit anyone's help.

Ryan had never considered that Carol would have been plagued by visions when she was young and that her parents would have sent her to a psychiatrist. Hell. The bastard should have had his license revoked for the way he'd treated Carol. Ryan hated seeing how much the experience had affected her, even though she had fought revealing her feelings.

If she was as young as seven when she began having visions, she might truly have abilities. He shook his head at himself. As an investigator, he had to look into this new lead before he began jumping to unsubstantiated conclusions.

He was also torn over the new information concerning the red who could be stalking the women. He really thought it was that cousin of Lelandi's, Ural, and no real problem. The guy was a nuisance but not a threat.

If it was the brother or cousin of the one who had bitten Carol, was he after her? Or Lelandi? Either would be a prime target for a disgruntled pack that had lost a battle with the grays. And both male reds could be dangerous.

Darien would ensure that Lelandi had the utmost security as the pack leader's mate, and he was with her all night, so no problem there. But Carol... Darien couldn't be serious about having the lame betas serve as her bodyguards. And the notion that any of the others would stay with Carol during the night... Hell, that got his blood pressure up.

But something more was troubling her. Something had been bothering her in the truck when they'd parked at the tavern. And she wasn't sleeping, although Ryan hadn't meant to upset her when he mentioned it. He couldn't help but notice the circles under her eyes, and he wanted to know what was disturbing her sleep so much. After he mentioned it, he figured he hadn't quite posed the question in a manner meant to solicit the truth. Instead, he'd antagonized her.

Might as well get this over with and ask what she thought she'd envisioned, while he tried to keep an open mind. He tilted his chin down slightly, and with his most—or at least what he hoped was his most—reassuring expression, he said, "I'm a reasonable man. Try me."

She studied him for a long moment, and he wondered what tale she'd come up with. She finally took a deep breath and seemed to come to the conclusion that she might as well talk. Humor him, maybe. "Darien shifts but can't shift back to his human form. Lelandi's worried sick about it, but I haven't a clue as to what to do."

What Carol thought she'd envisioned wasn't possible. Ryan didn't say anything, and the look on her face said she knew she'd wasted her breath on him.

"You've told them?" He wondered how the Silver clan's leaders had reacted to the news. Not that it would persuade him to believe in something he truly couldn't wrap his mind around.

"Of course not. I mean, not Darien. Lelandi, yes." But from the bleak expression on Carol's face, he assumed Lelandi hadn't believed her. He wished that she had, for Carol's sake.

"She didn't think what you had to say had any merit." Ryan folded his arms, suspecting Lelandi didn't believe her for the same reason he didn't. What Carol thought she saw just couldn't happen. Probably nightmares brought on by all the changes in her life recently.

She finished her drink and stared at the table, and he

figured he might have upset her, which he'd had no intention of doing, by bringing up the subject of recent visions.

Ryan let out a heavy sigh. "Carol, is this nightmare
you're having about Darien not being able to shift back
what's troubling you and keeping you from shifting? And
consequently keeping you from sleeping nights? Because
I've got to tell you that Lelandi's case, where she was afraid
her brother would die and she couldn't shift back, is the
only case I've ever heard of."

Carol smiled as if he was so off base it amused her in a
cynical way, and then she leaned back against her chair and
promptly changed the topic.

"So if I needed a bodyguard, since you've got the quali-
fications, could I hire you? Since you don't believe anyone
here is qualified. Although it depends on your going rate. I
can't be too frivolous with my hard-earned income."

He frowned at her, not liking that she switched the subject,
so he had no qualms about changing it again, thinking about
what Jake had confided in him about Carol not shifting yet.
He didn't believe she could fight the change for five months.

"You *have* shifted, haven't you? Without anyone being
aware of it. You've had to run as a wolf and haven't had time
to sleep to make up for it. Am I right?"

The corner of her mouth inched up. "Sure, I've shifted.
And you're right. I've been running around in the woods at
night, but I have to work at the hospital during the day and
haven't had any time to take a wolfish nap. You really are a
great detective. But then I'm sure you already knew that."

She was too coy and had switched too easily from being
indignant to being complacent. He gave her a small smile.
"You can't be fighting the shift."

"Nope, when you're right, you're right."

He'd rather she'd continue to be indignant. Like this, she was too agreeable and toying with him. He took another tack. "I found no sign of your wolf scent in the woods. You haven't been running through them as a wolf."

"Right again. I run around the guest room at night. Haven't howled yet though." She shrugged. "Not sure how to do that."

Ryan lifted a brow. "It comes with the shift. A natural part of who you are. Instinctively, if you're to howl to let others know where you are, to gather the pack, to warn others away, you howl. If not, you don't."

"Of course. I haven't needed to howl."

He rested his arms on the table and leaned closer, unable to shake loose of what he knew had to be the truth. "You can't be refusing to shift."

She smiled. "Refuse to shift? Of course I can't. That's impossible. Everyone keeps telling me that."

Hell. She couldn't be stopping the shift. But then again, the woman was unusual. Intriguing. Maybe she did have the inner strength to fight it. He tried another ploy.

"How does it feel when you shift?"

"Furry."

He chuckled and then grew serious again. "How are you keeping from shifting?"

She smiled just a little, her eyes, her lips. Something about that look made him think of a wayward wolf, full of mischief, impish, not to be trusted.

"Don't tell me. Your visions are keeping you from…" His mouth gaped as he recalled another incident. "When Mervin grabbed you in the great room, he triggered your need to shift, didn't he?"

Her expression froze, and she didn't say a word.

Which gave away what truly had happened. "You changed clothes but not to compete with the other women. That wouldn't be like you. Hell, you were stripping out of your clothes when Lelandi chased you down."

Ryan should have been there, not that lame Mervin. Although if he'd seen Carol fighting the shift, he wasn't sure what he would have done. Tried to convince her to shift, learned what he could about how she was fighting it, maybe.

"You didn't have a choice. Somehow you stopped the shift, and to cover up the fact that you were in trouble, at least to your way of thinking, you changed clothes. Did Lelandi recognize what you were up to?"

Carol shook her head. "I can't get anything past you, can I?"

Ryan rubbed his chin. No way could Carol stop shifting because of having so-called visions. Yet he'd never heard of anyone so newly turned being able to control that aspect of his or her new condition.

"You're a danger to yourself and others, Carol. You have to allow the shift to occur."

"You're right." Indignant, she rose from the table. "Tom can take me home, and I'll shift and run around the house for a while. Sorry I couldn't enlighten you further, but—"

The tavern grew deathly quiet.

Ryan rose to stand in front of her, towering over her. She looked up at him, and he swore her gaze pleaded with him to believe her. She looked so vulnerable, a little pale, and the dark under her eyes seemed to show even more now. She seemed tired—tired of the grilling, tired of being made to participate in wolf activities she wasn't used to—and now she had to be concerned that the red might be stalking her.

"What vision did you have that stopped the shift?"

"That Darien shifts to a wolf and can't change back," she whispered, tears in her eyes. "And I feel guilty because I believe I'll have more freedom if he is stuck as a wolf for a while, but Lelandi's so frightened, and I think of how it would be if all of our kind ended up in the same predicament. What then? If I shift, I'll be doomed to be a wolf forever." She bit her lower lip.

"It can't happen." He took her hand and squeezed. "Carol, you can't keep fighting this. It's part of who we are. It's our nature. Yours and mine."

She swallowed hard, pulled her hand free, and folded her arms tight around her waist. "What better way to learn the truth about my future visions than to hang around and protect me while being my personal bodyguard?"

Ryan pulled her back to her seat, watching her and pondering the notion. When she retook her seat, he took his, but the conversation in the room didn't begin again.

"You'll tell me every time you have the urge to shift. No matter when or where you are. And you'll let me know every time you have a vision? No matter what it's about?"

She tilted her chin up. "Gladly."

He smiled and finished his beer and then stretched his hand out so they could shake on it. She sighed and offered her hand. He gave it a firm shake, felt the heat and a spark of electricity, and saw the hope in her eyes, those large pools of liquid blue. He felt that if he looked into them much longer, he'd drown in them with pure pleasure. He released her, severing the connection. Somehow, touching her made him feel as though he might be able to coax her to shift when others in her pack hadn't had any success.

He scoffed at himself. She needed a mate who would encourage her to capitulate.

Silva immediately hurried over with another beer and their sandwiches. "Ohmigod, McKinley, you can't be planning to stay."

"You didn't hear our whole conversation, did you?" Carol asked, her voice a little shaky.

"Well, no, I *have* been waiting tables, and Darien, who is on the opposite side of the tavern, asked me a few questions. Despite what everyone says, I don't have hearing *that* sharp. But I did overhear you ask if Ryan would be your bodyguard.

"He hasn't gotten Darien's approval," Silva warned. "And you know how he is with outsiders interfering in pack business." She sighed. "You and Lelandi sure know how to stir up a pack. Did you need anything else to go with the sandwiches?"

Privacy. Ryan cleared his throat. "Looks good to me. Thanks, Silva."

Silva barely waited for Carol to answer, and when she shook her head, Silva stalked to the bar to grab another tray of drinks and sandwiches, and then hurried to drop them off at a table. After that, she rushed to Darien's table.

"If you want anyone to know your business, tell Silva. She'll spread the word," Carol said.

Ryan had already gotten that impression. He watched Darien's reaction as Silva spoke to him. Darien's eyes narrowed a bit.

Jake immediately looked in Ryan's direction and gave a knowing smile. He must have realized Ryan was up to the challenge. Tom flat-out frowned. Ryan had expected that. Lelandi smiled. Darien shook his head, gave Ryan a stern look, and then listened to something Lelandi said to him. He leaned over and kissed her lips.

"So what do you think? Was that a yes or a no?" Carol asked.

Ryan felt as if she was testing him, but he turned the tables on her. He wouldn't let up until he knew the truth. "You're the one with future visions. What do you see?"

She smiled at him. This was going to be a real test of wills. She lifted her sandwich. "Nothing in any future visions, but I'd say Lelandi convinced him to give you a chance."

"He'll allow it," Ryan confirmed, no hesitation in his response. "Either that or he's going to have to put one of his deputies or his brothers up to the task of protecting you. They'll be concentrating on Lelandi, in the event she's at risk. Because no matter what, he has to consider that someone from her old pack may want revenge. And stealing Darien's mate may be just the notion they have. So until it's proven otherwise—"

"I'm more expendable."

Ryan raised his brows, not believing she would think that. No one in a pack was expendable. "I'm very capable of protecting you." He took a deep breath. "What I was trying to say is that until it's proven otherwise, both of you need to be watched."

"All right." She took a bite of her sandwich, then set the rest of it down on the plate and eyed Ryan. "I wasn't sure why I'd seen you in a vision before. They're always important for some reason and have some connection to me. Maybe this is it."

He arched a brow. "You saw *me* in a vision?"

"Yeah, I mentioned it before, but you weren't paying attention."

"What was I doing?" He tried to sound like he believed her. He wondered if she was one of those people who told stories to get attention. He had a friend like that from Texas that he swore didn't even realize he was embellishing the truth because he believed in his own stories to such a degree.

"I envisioned you watching me from the woods as a wolf. That's why I went to the window and looked out. That's why I went outside when I saw you standing there and then followed you. I wanted to know who you were and what you wanted. Now I suppose it was because you spied the red wolf and are going to protect me from him." She smiled, the expression sweet and innocent, yet he was sure it was a facade.

She was cute and good. But he didn't believe it. Although he *had* wondered what had brought her to the window. And why she had come to see him in the woods. "You seemed irritated with me at first."

"You'd awakened me. I had worked a twelve-hour shift at the hospital, and I was *trying* to get some much-needed sleep." She didn't sound sincere, and she wouldn't look him in the eye. Something had kept her from sleeping.

"I'll try to be more considerate next time. But in the future, if you spy a wolf in the woods and don't know who he is, don't seek him out."

"In the future." The way she spoke indicated to him that

if she felt driven to do so, she'd take off into the woods again and check him out.

That made his gut wrench with concern. He'd prefer the damsel in distress to be agreeable. Made his work so much easier. He ate the last bite of the tender roast beef sandwich, the meat melting in his mouth. Then he wiped his fingers on the napkin and drew up taller.

"I'll have to return to Green Valley to get some clothes and other things. Darien and his brothers can keep you safe until then. At most, three hours, and I'll be back."

"Thank you."

Striving for professional, which he sure as hell had lost sight of when he'd first kissed her and then danced with her, Ryan said, "I have a job to do. No need to thank me."

Her lips curved up slightly. He had the sneaking suspicion she saw right through him. Damned if the more primitive side of him didn't want to haul her out of her chair and kiss her again. Forget professional.

She gave him a hard nod. "Right. Where will you sleep?"

"Close. No sense in being your bodyguard if I'm not nearby. And, Carol?"

"Hmm?"

"Wear something other than that silky nightgown you wore last night. I don't need the distraction." He smiled, winked, and rose. Then he slipped his credit card back in his wallet and deposited money on the table instead.

"I'll speak to Darien and then be on my way. Don't leave the tavern without Darien or his brothers' escort home."

She glanced at their table. "I'm sure they wouldn't think of me leaving without one of them accompanying me."

Watching Ryan and Carol, two of the bachelor males rose

from their seats. "Christ," Ryan swore under his breath and offered his hand. "Come on. We'll talk to Darien together, and you can sit at his table until you're ready to leave."

Hell, what was wrong with him to get so possessive with her when this was strictly business? But he couldn't help worrying that this was all turning into a real nightmare.

CHAPTER 11

AFTER GETTING DARIEN'S APPROVAL TO BE CAROL'S bodyguard, Ryan returned home to grab a few days' changes of clothes and called on his subleader to watch the pack and take over mayoral duties as his assistant mayor until he returned.

But his sister was giving him major heartburn. If he hadn't figured that she'd be more trouble if he took her with him, he'd have left her at the B and B in Silver Town so she would be close by and he could check on her periodically. But her nursery sales were skyrocketing with the advent of spring, and he knew she wouldn't want to leave her business for anything.

"Chester Ryan McKinley," Rosalind scolded as she continued to decorate the fireplace mantel in the living room with greenery, the fragrance of burning lilac candles scenting the air. "Don't you walk away from me when I'm trying to discuss this with you."

Ryan stopped in midstride and turned to frown at his sister, the only one in his pack who could get away with talking to him like that, but only in the privacy of his home—and she damn well knew it. "The *discussion* is over."

"Why? You speak about that woman constantly. You can't get over how she discovered who the murderer was, when you were investigating the crime just fine with your tried-and-true scientific methods. Why can't you believe she's psychic?

"According to Bertha, the owner of that bed-and-breakfast you stayed at, you not only went to the games to watch Carol but to the gathering *and* took her on a date. Now you're going to be her bodyguard? Admit that you feel something for her. Besides, you can use her on that case you can't solve."

"You remember the last time you insisted I use a psychic? What a disaster that was?"

Rosalind's lips and amber eyes smiled. "All right. So Madame Dulaney was a bona fide fraud. No big deal."

"No big deal?" His voice rose although he meant to curb his temper, but the false psychic could have cost him everything. "Hell, if I hadn't agreed to go out with Bennagin's spoiled-rotten daughter, he would have sued me for everything we own."

"Your business insurance would have covered it."

He gave her a scathing look.

She shrugged. "Besides, Miss Hoity-Toity-I'm-Owed-Everything-Under-the-Sun soon gave up on wanting to hang around you. Three dates, and she was glad to get rid of you. You sure know how to make a girl feel unappreciated. Well, in her case, loathed."

"What did you want me to do? Turn her and make her my mate?" He shook his head at the horrible notion.

Rosaline smiled a little. "No. Then she would have been related to me. But from everything you've told me about Carol Wood, this woman's the real deal."

"I explained to you that she most likely overheard conversations that led her to the evidence. Nothing to do with psychic predictions. Besides, I don't need a psychic to tell me that Eleanor's husband isn't seeing anyone behind her back. That the woman is paranoid as usual."

"What about when you get another case? Carol could assist you." Rosalind tied another pink satin bow on the cedar garland. "You could help me trim for spring, you know."

"I'm all thumbs when it comes to decorating," he said.

Her eyes were downcast, and Rosalind's playful expression had faded. Ryan let out his breath in defeat. He guessed Rosalind missed their mother helping her decorate for the different seasons. He stalked over to the table where cut flowers from her greenhouse sat in crystal vases and a single sprig of mistletoe sat among them. He raised a brow.

Rosalind tried to hide a smile. "Why, how'd that get in with my spring greenery? Carol's a red now. Rare red. Rare female at the right age for mating. Unless you aren't interested in her because she's newly turned. But having a newly turned mate offers advantages. You'd be in charge of her, show her the ways of our people, have someone you could mold to your own liking. Seems to me she'd suit your disposition perfectly."

Ryan snorted. "The woman is not in the least bit biddable."

That comment brought a real smile to his sister's lips. She'd like him having a cantankerous mate, he suspected. And hell, his sister and his mate would most likely bond in womanly fashion and gang up on him. Not that he couldn't deal with them, but he really didn't need the added aggravation.

He put the mistletoe down on the coffee table and then grabbed a frilly lace bow and fumbled to tie it to the garland. Decorating was a woman's job. He glanced at the fireplace. The flames blazed hot on this chilly spring night, and wood was already stacked to the hilt in a copper box nearby.

"You've chopped enough firewood to keep us warm for

the next three years. Which brings me to another point. You only split wood when something's bothering you. And lately only when Carol Wood's name comes up in the discussion. Suddenly you're out chopping down trees again." She raised a brow.

He ignored her and grabbed another frilly pink bow off the table. His sister was a gardener extraordinaire. When did she become a psychologist in her spare time?

Psychologist…hell, the psychiatrist. *Dr. Metzger.* The one who'd given Carol so much grief. As soon as he had a chance, he was doing a little research into her story. Problem was that he might not be able to verify that the doctor's wife had died after Carol had told the doctor her vision, unless Ryan spoke with the psychiatrist and could verify the date. Even then, the doctor probably wouldn't tell him anything about Carol's session because of patient confidentiality.

Her mother! But would her mother tell him anything? Only one way to find out.

"I've been talking to you, and you haven't heard a word I've said." Rosalind wove a string of pearls through the garland. "If you put off going after her—and I don't mean just being her babysitter—Darien Silver will surely convince her to mate with one of his eligible and *very* willing bachelors. I wouldn't wait too long. If you want her—"

"Enough, Rosalind! I have no idea where you've come up with such nonsense. When have I even hinted I was interested in the woman, except to learn the truth of how she came to know what she did?"

Rosalind pointed with her elbow at the coffee table and continued to wrap the string of pearls around the garland. "In that notebook, you have photos of her."

"I added photos of many of Darien's people while I was investigating who might have been involved in the crime."

Rosalind finished with the pearls, walked back over to the table, flipped open the notebook, and pointed accusingly at the picture of Carol sitting on top—just where he'd left it.

"Right, but why do you have *seven* photos of Carol? You've filed away all the rest of your papers concerning the case, so why are *her* pictures still out? You said from the start that you didn't believe she was a suspect."

"Hell," he muttered under his breath. Rosalind *would* be the one to make a mountain out of a ripple in the ground. "The case isn't closed until I learn how she knew of the evidence that confirmed the murderer's identity."

Her eyes round, Rosalind stared at him. "You think she's a coconspirator? Guilty of taking part in the murder?"

"No. Of course not. She was human at the time. They wouldn't have involved her. But she either wittingly or unwittingly overheard the conversation, and I'd like to know which, for the record."

"Hmm, then why don't you prove it once and for all? Have her work with you on a case, and let her help you solve it. What if she's not psychic but just very good at discovering leads, like you are? Maybe if you gave this woman half a chance..." His sister had a way of sounding facetious when it suited her.

"Even if I wanted to, I doubt her pack leader would agree with me mating her." That slipped out before he had a chance to stop his words. *Hell.* The truth of the matter was that if he wanted her and she was mutually agreeable, no one would be an obstacle in their match.

Rosalind's lips parted, and then she quickly smiled.

He let out his breath in exasperation. He refused to openly admit to Rosalind that the petite, blue-eyed blond was on his mind twenty-four seven. So much so that he couldn't concentrate on any PI case, nor could he keep a close handle on being mayor of Green Valley and pack leader. Ryan couldn't pinpoint what got to him about her the most. Yeah, she was a looker, but he wouldn't have noticed if not for all the attention she had received for solving the murder case through sharing her psychic knowledge.

That wasn't true either. Her looks had definitely caught his eye. But the way she tried to protect Lelandi from being turned, not knowing she was already a *lupus garou* from birth, and Carol's strength in not falling apart during the battle that could have killed her—that she didn't run away in stark terror—those attributes kept nagging at him.

"You won't know if Darien doesn't agree to you mating her until you try. You can't deny it, Ryan. You can't quit looking at those photos, and now you've offered to be her bodyguard? But of course she suggested it, which to me sounds like she's in as deep as you are in this…situation. You can't disagree with me that you're dying to be with her longer. Oh sure, you've tried to appear as though you are leisurely getting ready to leave, but I don't think I've ever seen you this seriously unsettled and distracted over anything. Or anyone."

Ryan shook his head and stalked toward the back door. The red who was skulking around Darien's place needed to be caught and confronted. In the meantime, Carol and Lelandi needed to be protected. That was all.

"If you cut any more wood, we will no longer have a forest," Rosalind teased.

Ryan shoved the door open and slammed it closed behind him, then stared at the pile of wood stacked as high as the two-story potting shed. Rosalind was right. As much as he hated admitting it. They had enough firewood for three winters at least.

Fine. He'd take a run on the wild side. Clear his thoughts on a long jog through the woods now shivering in a northerly breeze before he took off for Silver Town.

Ryan stalked to the shed. Inside, the aroma of wet peat filled the air, while flowers erupted from cold-hardy bulbs in rectangular planters and winter-tender plants snuggled close together on top of plant heating mats. The shed was Rosalind's "baby" nursery, and she defended the place with wolfish fierceness. Nothing could be changed without her permission.

Not that he minded. He was glad she had an occupation she so thoroughly enjoyed and that kept her out of his business—for the most part—and out of trouble. He quickly removed his shirt, boots, socks, and jeans, and then deposited them on a small wooden bench. The brisk cold chilled him to the bone. Which helped to freeze his thoughts of Carol Wood and her inquisitive blue eyes.

Then, his muscles heated with the change, stretching and accommodating the shift swiftly until he was standing on all four paws, the double coat of fur warming him better than any human-made coat could.

The shorter, fine fuzzy undercoat trapped a layer of warm air next to his skin, while the longer, coarse guard hairs repelled any hint of frost or snow or rain. Long tufts of hair growing between the pads of his feet gave him a good grip as he raced across the thin sheen of ice already covering the back patio while circling the place to make sure Rosalind would be all right. Although his deputy had told him he'd hang around to check on her two or three times a day.

Hell, Ryan had enough work to do here, and none of it included taking on the problems of a newly turned female. So why was he *really* bound for Darien Silver's territory after a quick run in his wolf coat?

Ryan cursed his unwanted desire to be with the woman again, but after taking a run on the wild side and ensuring that everything was quiet around his place, he didn't feel any more settled. He changed in the garden shed, returned to the house, and gave his sister a hug with a few choice words of instruction. She eagerly agreed to follow them, which made him suspect she wouldn't. Then he hurried to his truck.

Darien had dictated that he sleep in the sunroom on a sofa bed. How was Ryan going to protect Carol if he slept on the other side of the house?

He'd have to twist the rules. His job—his way.

"Just who's paying Ryan to be Carol's bodyguard?" Darien asked Lelandi as he paced across the master bedroom down the hall. Carol heard a hint of wry humor in his tone as she pulled off her clothes in the private bathroom adjoining her guest room.

Carol hated that her sense of hearing was so good that she could make out every word—muffled but still audible if they spoke loud enough. She figured most wolves tuned out conversations they didn't want to listen to. She wasn't able to do that yet, especially when the conversation was about her. That made her feel as though she was another Silva, overhearing exchanges that she wasn't meant to hear.

"Darien, Carol is willing to pay for his services, but it's our place to do so since the red in our territory most likely was from my old pack. So my responsibility, which means yours."

"We don't need an outsider bodyguard," Darien grouched. Now he sounded annoyed. "What is it with McKinley anyway? He's acting mayor of Green Valley, now full-time active pack leader, and he's still haunting our town."

"He's got a thing for Carol. Surely you see that as well as anyone here does."

Darien growled.

"What if he's the right one for her? I mean, Jake or Tom could be, but they haven't shown anything more than brotherly affection for her. Tom's more protective and Jake delights in teasing her, yet he'd protect her with his life. But Ryan...well, you saw the way he danced with her. And before that, the way he came to her rescue when Mervin tackled her. I didn't get to see it, but Silva said they shared *some* kiss outside by the house. You know how she is. She's an alpha. She needs someone who's strong of character like she is. Ryan would make a good match."

"We have plenty of pack members who would make her a good match. An alpha wolf doesn't have to have an alpha mate. For all we know, she might need a man who she can boss around." The floor creaked some more with his pacing. "All right, so McKinley comes here to fortify our forces, but it irritates the hell out of me that he thinks our men can't protect her. I'm only allowing this because you wish it."

No more words were spoken. No need to eavesdrop any longer.

Carol started the shower and turned on some New Age music. Next would come the lovemaking. At least the shower and music drowned out the moans and groans.

Carol climbed into the shower and closed her eyes as the hot water sluiced over her skin. Was Lelandi right in thinking Ryan was truly interested in her? The sexual interest was there, that was for sure. Every time she got close to him, her blood sizzled. Her heart pounded at an increased tempo.

But it wasn't just her response to him. His actions triggered her hormones to skip around in an excited frenzy. The way he observed her—although she had to remind herself he was probably trying to figure her out—and the way his gaze filled with admiration at times, lust at others, she knew she had more of an effect on him than he was letting on.

Even if they weren't a match, she was determined to prove to him, while he served as her bodyguard, that her psychic abilities were real. She shouldn't have cared if he believed her or not. She imagined that more than half the world's population didn't have faith in such things. But she *did* care that he believed. That he knew she had been honest with him.

She grabbed the container of liquid body soap and squeezed some into her hand. Then she slid the pearl-like soap over her shoulders, breasts, and stomach.

A distinctive thump sounded nearby, muffled by the water rushing in a heavy spray out of the showerhead. Darien dropping a boot on his bedroom floor? It sounded like it had come from her guest room though. She listened intently but didn't hear anything further except for the continued stream of water slushing out of the showerhead and the mystical New Age rhythm of drumbeats, flutes, and pipe whistles. Had to have been Darien or Lelandi making a noise. Or just her imagination.

She ran shampoo through her hair and over her face, the scent of peaches filling her nostrils with the sweet, refreshing fragrance. Her fingers swept the silky soap down her arms.

After that, everything happened so quickly that it was a blur. The rings of the shower curtain slid aside. The cooler air from the bathroom hit her wet skin. The smell of the onions and garlic the intruder had eaten permeated the air, right before a painful jab penetrated her arm. Her eyes and mouth shot open. Soap burned her eyes, tears forming instantly to wash away the stinging but further blurring her vision. A heavy hand clamped over her mouth to muffle her scream.

Heat quickly spread through her blood, and she felt as if she were slipping into nothingness. The hot water still ran over her, her eyes burning, and whispered words penetrating the darkness as someone held her tight. The smell of man and woods, of sweat and fear clouded her senses.

"Asleep. Let's get her out of here before we get caught," the man said in a rush, his voice hushed.

She didn't recognize his harsh and concerned voice. Her last thought was to wonder where her bodyguard was when she needed him so badly. Damn Darien for forcing Ryan to sleep in the sunroom on the other side of the house. If he'd even returned from Green Valley to watch over her yet. But she'd heard Lelandi arguing with Darien once they'd returned home from the tavern. Heard that Darien hadn't wanted Ryan in the same room with her. That it would stir up the other bachelor males. That it would encourage Ryan to want Carol for a mate.

Once they discovered she was missing, it would be too late.

She would have fought her kidnappers' confinement, if she could have oriented herself in this new world. But all she saw was blackness, no wolf's vision here. And all she felt was numbness spreading through every inch of her body. Huffing and puffing and grunting, not her own, filled her ears.

A jolt to her body and an abrupt change from cool air to frigid air startled her. Her wet, soapy body grew goose bumps as a chilly breeze whipped across her sticky, water-soaked hair, still coated in shampoo, and her naked skin. The biting cold encased her as silky red hair floated over her face. Her eyes filled with tears and soap, she briefly saw a blurry image of amber eyes narrowed as they looked down at her—a concerned-looking man with the start of a scraggly beard. Then she succumbed to a tiredness from which she couldn't free herself. Vaguely, it was as if she was seeing the vision she'd witnessed in Ryan's truck outside the tavern all over again. Only the cold was too real.

She floated, was jostled, and heard the crunching of footsteps in the dark and the heavy breathing and hard-charging heartbeats that revealed her kidnappers' panic. One of the men held her tight against his body, his chest covered in a padded vest that made him feel cuddly, not hard and strong. Clothed in flannel, his arms also felt soft.

She wanted to bury herself deeply in every part of him that felt warm wherever he touched her. His warmth helped to heat her body, but she felt as limp as a chilled, soaked noodle. She tried to open her eyes to get a better look at the man, but they stung from the soap and she barely opened them. Her eyes were too blurry with tears for her to see anything. Her head felt empty and floated separately from her body.

Then it hit her—although she wasn't sure whether it was a vision of something to come or a nightmare, or a little of both. She couldn't tell as her mind slipped into another reality induced by the drug.

Jake paced in his wolf form through the great room after a jaunt in the night with several others. Only he hadn't changed back. None of them had changed back. Carol watched helplessly. Lelandi's green eyes pleaded with her to do something. Anything. But what could Carol do? Just warn their kind not to shift. And look at how well that had worked! Damn it!

Then the world faded into something else. A room she'd never seen before came into view. A big-screen TV clung to the wall. And the walls: the upper half sunny and lighted with fan-shaped brass sconces to give the illusion of light, and the lower half covered in light oak paneling. The room had no windows. No windows, as if buried in the bowels of the earth.

Rich brown leather sofas and a light brown rug added to the earthy tones. A man's room, she thought. But something wasn't right. Bright lights from another room intruded on the soft lighting in this one. With the greatest apprehension, she moved without moving toward the doorway bathed in brilliant white.

Someone was in there. Shadows crossed the doorway briefly as someone moved about, blocking the light marginally. She had to see into the room. Had to see who the someone was.

Two shots rang out.

"Hey!" From a great distance, Sam shattered the future world Carol was in. Instantly, her thoughts became her own again, except that she couldn't remember what had happened, where she was, or what she was doing. Shots had been fired. Hadn't they?

The cold shook her from the fogginess—the shower, the soap, the kidnappers! She opened her mouth to speak, to call out, to get Sam's attention.

Shots rang out. Shots fired from close by. From the kidnappers. At Sam.

The acrid smell of gun smoke drifted to her.

Her mouth snapped shut. She couldn't be the cause of Sam's death. Best to let the villains take her away.

"Raise the alarm!" Sam shouted.

The man carrying her swore under his breath and tightened his hold on her, stumbling at a slightly faster pace.

"What the hell's happening?" Darien asked, growing closer to Sam's voice.

They were coming for her. The sensation that she was one of the pack gave her some peace of mind, but the danger the gunman posed if Sam and Darien caught up with her was too great to ignore. The bullets could kill Darien and Sam and any others who got too close. They couldn't risk it. *Don't risk it!*

"Three men running that way. They've got Carol!" Sam shouted back to him. "And they've got guns!"

Another shot rang out, and Carol tried to squirm, but not a muscle obeyed her.

"Carol!" Darien shouted.

She tried to speak, to shout, but she had no voice.

Suddenly, she felt herself falling, dropped like a sack of

cold groceries. She should have felt a hard impact, but her body didn't feel anything but a slight jolt. Now she was left in the sweet-smelling grass, crispy with frost, to freeze to death. She curled up into a fetal ball, trying to get warm, when a large hand gripped her shoulder and she shuddered. They weren't leaving her behind after all. At once, she felt an odd mix of reprieve and regret.

"You're alive," he said, his voice low and dark but comforting.

Ryan? A sense of overwhelming relief washed over her. And a fuzzy question surfaced. When had he returned from Green Valley? She envisioned him racing to the rescue on a white steed while he wore the McKinley plaid, the kilt reaching his knees, sword belted at his waist, a shirt open to his collarbone, his face frowning as he scooped her up from the cold ground and—

"I've got her!" Ryan wrapped her in something warm and soft that smelled of him, his distinctive male scent of fresh soap and heat. Of spices and the wind in the firs, of the wild. Was it his plaid? She imagined him now wearing only the long shirt that reached midthigh and sturdy leather boots that met his knees, his expression worried and stern.

"Are you all right?" he asked, lifting her off the cold ground. He jostled her as he ran, his arms so tight around her that she felt he was going to crush her. But the heat and his protectiveness comforted her.

And when they reached the laird's castle, he was going to kiss her and tell her how much he loved her, how he couldn't live without her. She would be a member of his clan as they would want her to join them. Despite her being a MacDonald. Did the McKinley clan fight with the MacDonalds? She didn't know but fervently hoped not.

"Carol, can you focus?" His darkened eyes studied her for a moment as he rushed toward their destination.

She parted her lips, couldn't get a word out, closed her eyes, and concentrated on him and the way he held her so... so possessively.

He squeezed her tight again and kissed her lips gently, which got her attention. As soon as she opened her eyes, even as blurry as her vision was, she saw his lips curve slightly upward, but his brow was still furrowed in a deep frown.

After what seemed like forever, his feet tromped on wooden steps—when she thought they should have been stone—and then inside. She felt the warmth of the castle keep and smelled the scent of apple pies coming from the kitchen far away.

"Ohmigod...Carol. Is she all right?" Lelandi asked. "What's happened?"

Lelandi? The Highland romance Carol was living instantly died, and she remembered the pies Lelandi, Silva, and she had made after returning from the tavern and her date with Ryan.

"I think she's been drugged. She's not said a word since I found her. She can barely open her eyes, and she is limp and unresponsive." Ryan rushed through the house.

Carol smelled the scent of the roses on the mantel as they passed them. Felt his legs lift, his thighs bumping her back as he ascended the stairs. What was she wrapped in, if not his plaid?

"Where were you when Sam raised the alarm?" Lelandi's

words were spoken close behind him, her footfalls on the carpeted stairs lighter but just as hurried.

"I was searching the woods out back when I heard gunfire and Sam's yelling. When I drew too close to her kidnappers, they must have heard me coming and dropped her."

"Oh, Carol." Lelandi's voice was clearly shaken. "Take her to her room. I'll call Doc."

Then the hazy world seemed to fade away. Carol was safe and home for the moment with the man of her dreams. And free.

CHAPTER 12

RYAN HUGGED CAROL TIGHTER AS HER SLIGHTLY TENSE body seemed to lose all strength again. He'd gotten Darien's approval to stay and guard her, but damn if Darien had said he'd stay in the sunroom, which was too far from Carol's guest bedroom to be any help. Although he'd planned to sit in the recliner in her room later that night anyway. If he couldn't serve as her bodyguard in the way he felt would offer her the right amount of protection, there was no sense in him being here.

If he hadn't been searching around the grounds outside before he retired for the evening, he'd never have heard the men take off with her on the other side of the rambling two-story house in time. And if he hadn't nearly reached them to identify them by sight, they wouldn't have dropped her and left her behind, he was fairly certain. For that, he was grateful.

"Carol, can you hear me? It's me, Ryan," he said, his voice soothing, wanting her to know it was him and not one of the men who had taken her hostage.

"Hmm," she said, stirring a little.

As little as it was, he was still glad to hear her response. "Until Doc gets over here with something to counteract the sedative they used on you, you're going to feel pretty out of it. Your skin and hair are caked with soap, and Lelandi doesn't have the strength to wash you in the shower. A bath would take too long to prepare, not the way you're shivering. I'll have to wash you in the shower."

"Hmm."

He took that as a yes, although they hadn't any other choice.

When he reached the bathroom, the shower had been turned off, but the room was thick with warm moisture, the mirrors steamed, the scent of sweet peaches still lingering in the air. He lay Carol down on a towel on the tiled floor, but as soon as he released her, she reached her hands slightly up to him.

"I'm right here, Carol," he coaxed, squeezing her hands, hating to have to leave her unattended for even a second when she didn't seem to understand what was going on.

Then he released her again and turned on the hot water. Once he had stripped out of everything but his boxers and when the water temperature felt right, he unwrapped her from his goose-down jacket and lifted her in his arms.

She shivered, and he squeezed her tightly against his body as he climbed into the tub.

"I'm going to set you down, wash the soap off, and then dry you and put you into bed. Doc will be here soon."

Lelandi hurried into the bathroom. "What will the other bachelors think?" Her tone was more amused than alarmed. She eyed him as he stood in only his boxers with a naked Carol in his arms. "Here, let me help," she said, reaching out to grab Carol's arm.

"I've got her," Ryan said, setting Carol down in the tub, not wanting Lelandi to do any heavy lifting.

Lelandi handed him the handheld showerhead, and he washed Carol's face and hair, the spray wetting him also. "She's probably got soap in her eyes. If I can't get her to open them, Doc will have to flush them."

"He's unable to come. He said the drug should wear off. Silva will pick up some medicine that will help counter the sedative. Doc's got three cases of swine flu and a human boy whose brother accidentally broke his nose playing basketball with him, and one of the pregnant humans is in labor now, so he has to remain at the hospital. Nurses Charlotte and Matthew are busy helping him."

"I should have been with her. Those bastards would have never gotten near her." Ryan lifted Carol's chin and applied a steady stream of water to her face.

Lelandi grabbed a towel from the nearby rack. "I'm sure Darien will agree now to allow you to stay close to her."

"A little late," Ryan muttered. From now on, he would do this his way.

"I feel the same way, but you know Darien. You're an outsider." Lelandi handed Ryan a warm, wet washcloth. "He still wanted one of his bachelor males to woo her. Now you're becoming a real obstacle to his plans."

His own feelings mixed on the subject, Ryan wasn't about to reveal his thoughts on the matter. "How do you feel about what he thinks?" When she didn't respond, Ryan looked back at Lelandi and noted the wry amusement on her face. He shook his head. "Jake or Tom would make tolerable mates for her but not the beta males."

"What about you?" Lelandi asked softly.

With the rush of the shower as he ran the water over Carol's hair, he almost didn't hear Lelandi's words. "I'm here to do a job. Serve as her bodyguard. That's all." Yet even as he spoke the words, he didn't feel sincere in the least.

He gently washed Carol's eyes, finished rinsing out her hair, and ran the water over her face again and down her body, where a sheen of soap still covered her skin and goose bumps raised. It would take a saint not to notice her soft feminine curves, her vulnerability, and her beauty.

But he was trying his damnedest to keep his wolfish thoughts at bay, just as he knew she had when she'd observed him after he'd shifted and remarked, *You look nice and healthy to me.* He'd seen the admiration in her gaze, noticed she'd taken a gander twice at his size, and wasn't fooled by her pretense. Not when he heard her heart beating rapidly and saw the faint blush tinge her cheeks beautifully.

Her eyes suddenly blinked, and she squinted.

His heart hammering, he lifted her chin gently. If he hadn't had an audience, he would have kissed her lips, maybe enticing her to open her eyes again.

"Can you do that again, Carol? Open your eyes so I can wash the soap out?"

She tried, but she could barely lift her lids, her face grimacing. Then she went completely limp again, deep in drug-induced sleep.

"You're very good with her," Lelandi said.

"I'm used to helping victims of crimes." Although he wasn't capable of feeling impersonal in this case. Not when Carol was naked and so defenseless. Crouching in front of her, he squeezed the water out of her hair with one hand, his other holding her shoulder to keep her from sliding.

"Ah, and the kiss you shared with her earlier before the gathering?"

What could he say about that? A mistake? Was dancing too damn close to her at the gathering also a mistake? No, none of it was. Just some errant need to get closer, to possess, to quash his compulsion to learn how she scrambled his thoughts to such a degree. To show her he thought she was much more intriguing than the other women at the gathering. Hell, maybe she did have psychic abilities. The kind that included mind control.

Many of his Scottish ancestors believed in witches in the old days, many of the women having practiced the healing arts in their unusual ways. Carol was a nurse and had ancestral ties to the Highlands of Scotland, so maybe some of her ancestors were among those healers and she had inherited their genes. He shook his head at himself for even going there.

"Want to turn off the water?" He didn't say anything in response to Lelandi's question, figuring she had already decided he was hooked on Little Miss Nightingale. Not that she wasn't desirable as hell, but she really needed someone who could completely believe in her.

Lelandi handed him an oversize fluffy white towel. The cloth contrasted sharply with Carol's skin, flushed from the heat of the shower, as he wrapped the towel around her.

"Can you get something for her to wear other than that silky see-through nightgown?" he asked.

Lelandi's brows shot up as she handed him a towel for Carol's hair. "How do you know what she wears at night?"

"She was standing in the window watching me in the woods. Hard not to notice."

Lelandi's lips parted. Then in silence, she shook her head and left the bathroom while Ryan wrapped Carol's hair in the second towel and then lifted her from the tub.

Carrying Carol into her guest room, he saw Lelandi holding up the shimmering translucent nightgown he'd seen Carol wear the night before. It reminded him of the silken goddess standing in the window, staring out at him, as beguiling as ever.

"Guess she's not used to sleeping naked like the rest of us yet. She's got some other nightgowns, but all are shorter and more revealing," Lelandi said.

Carol looked small and sleepy in his arms, and beautiful. But the idea of her lying naked or wearing that silken piece of nightwear or anything even shorter and more revealing as she slept next to him in bed tightened his groin even further.

"Does she have sweats? A long T-shirt?" Damn, considering anything she might wear made him think of her as sexy as hell.

Lelandi glanced down at Ryan's soaking-wet boxers. "Don't let Darien see you like that."

How could he help it if rinsing off Carol's naked body had left him hard as steel? Even though he'd done his damnedest to keep his efforts as professional as possible. He was only human and a lot wolf after all.

"What made Darien realize she'd been kidnapped?" he asked, resting Carol in the bed.

Lelandi held out a light-blue T-shirt. He helped Lelandi pull it over Carol's head. When they stretched it down Carol's body, it barely covered her feminine enticements.

Lelandi slid the comforter up to Carol's shoulders. "Jake was still up, editing his photos of wildflowers on his computer."

Ryan raised his brows.

"It's Jake's hobby. Sam was watching him work, but both thought they heard something bump against the side of the house. Sam ran outside while Jake tore up the stairs to check on Carol. He found her shower on and a trail of water leading to the window. The men had used a ladder and left it there. Outside the house, Sam smelled the reds and a perfumed soap that lingered in the air. The same shampoo that Carol uses. Jake alerted Darien, and I woke Tom. And here you are, her knight to the rescue."

Hell, if he'd been a true knight, he wouldn't have allowed her to be taken in the first place.

Ryan glanced at the bedroom door. He realized then that there was no sound of anyone else in the house, no evidence that the group chasing Carol's kidnappers had returned. Which wasn't good.

"I'll dry her hair. You get dressed."

"We're alone? Just you, Carol, and me?" he asked. "What if the men had tried to take you also while everyone left you alone?"

"I've got big teeth if anyone is of a mind to show up who doesn't belong here. I called the sheriff and his deputy, and they're on their way."

"Hell, that's not soon enough. And these guys have guns."

"I heard. What is the world coming to?" Lelandi sounded flippant, but her worried look belied her true feelings as she hooked up a blow-dryer and began running the hot air over Carol's hair.

Ryan watched Lelandi comb her fingers gently through the damp strands the way he had done when he rinsed the soap out. Silky blond curls turned from wet and dark to soft spun gold, and he thought of how it would feel to run his fingers through her hair when it was dry.

Shaking loose of the notion, he headed into the bathroom to strip out of his boxers. "At least three men were out there. Maybe four. See if you can recognize any of their scents tomorrow when it's daylight and you have plenty of protection."

"I'll do that."

Sam barged into the bedroom and gave Ryan a disparaging look. "Hell, what happened?"

"She was drugged." Ryan dried off and jerked on his jeans in the bathroom. "Did anyone catch any of the bastards?"

"Not yet. Darien and his brothers shifted and are tracking them. He sent me back to help you guard the women in case the men doubled back and returned to the house." Sam walked over to the bedroom window and peered out. "Reds wouldn't be a match for us grays." He turned around to look at Ryan and frowned. "Where were you that you got to Carol so quickly?"

Ryan grabbed his shirt. "Outside. I'd already circled the grounds once, and then I thought I heard whispered voices on the other side of the house headed for the woods. I came from a different direction than you and Darien. Since you were shouting and I was in stealth mode, they didn't hear me coming until it was almost too late. They dropped their precious cargo and hightailed it out of here."

"Damn good thing too."

The sound of footfalls coming into the house through the back door caught their attention. Sam stormed out of the bedroom.

"Lock the door," Ryan warned Lelandi. Ready to shift and take care of the threat, he dropped his shirt on the end of the bed and took off after Sam.

As soon as they made it down the stairs, they saw Darien and his brothers stalking into the great room. "They shifted and took off," Darien said, his brow furrowed, his face red. "Where are Carol and Lelandi?"

"Carol's sedated and sleeping in her room. Lelandi's with her," Ryan said. "I'm staying with Carol until we catch the bastards."

Jake growled, "You don't tell a pack leader what he's going to allow, not in his own territory, McKinley."

Ryan suspected Jake was angrier about them losing the men who had taken Carol than that Ryan was making the rules in his brother's territory. "I'm not budging on this."

Darien looked at how underdressed Ryan was, and his own scowl deepened. "Where the hell are the rest of your clothes? You didn't shift out there, did you?"

Ryan had only managed to get his jeans on. Boxers were soaking wet, lying in the tub. Boots, socks, and a soapy down jacket remained on the bathroom floor, while his shirt was draped across the foot of the bed. No time for anything else when he thought the bad guys were storming the house and he might have to shift to take care of the menace.

Sam motioned to the stairs. "He had to wash the soap off Carol. But Lelandi was with him the whole time."

Although Sam hadn't really known what had gone on, Ryan appreciated the backup. But Darien glowered at Ryan, waiting for him to give his version.

"Hell, Darien, soap caked Carol's hair and covered her body. She had soap in her eyes even. Lelandi couldn't have managed washing her. What did you expect me to do? Leave her like that until you returned? As for guarding her until we catch these bastards? I'm staying with her, and that's my final word."

Darien's scowl evaporated some. "As a bodyguard only.

You can sit in the recliner at night and nap during the day. I'll have others watch her while you catch up on your sleep." Darien marched off to the stairs.

Tom glowered at Ryan and then headed up the stairs after his brother.

Sam moved toward the kitchen. "I'm getting myself another cup of coffee, and I'll settle down here."

Jake eyed Ryan for a moment more and then said, "Darien doesn't like it that you want Carol for a mate. Bodyguard, my ass. Admit it, Ryan. You can't quit thinking about her. But you can't have her if you don't believe in her abilities. Just remember that. She deserves better."

He stalked off to join Sam in the kitchen.

Jake was right, of course. The thing of it was, no matter how much Ryan told himself psychics weren't for real, he couldn't help questioning *his* rigid beliefs. Hell, now he wanted to believe her more than he wanted to prove she didn't have second sight.

So when did that happen?

CHAPTER 13

CAROL DRIFTED IN AND OUT OF NIGHTMARE WORLDS of wolves fighting, teeth bared, growling and snarling, and of hackles raised, noses wrinkled, and amber eyes narrowed. Of the painful bite that had changed her life forever. And then as if that wasn't bad enough, she relived the pain jabbing her in the arm, the freezing cold and sticky wetness, her eyes burning, and exposure, naked to the spring chill.

A whimper escaped her lips, and strong arms pulled her to a hot, hard body. She tried to recall when she'd felt those arms wrapped around her last in her drug-induced foggy conscience. She remembered hurried footfalls, the aroma of apple pies still lingering in the air... Home. And...*Ryan*. That was who had taken her from the cold and held her close, heating her chilled skin with his warm clothing and with his even hotter body. And now?

She smelled his unique scent, his maleness, the wind in his hair, the peach soap on his skin. Her peach soap? Had he showered using her shampoo?

No. She vaguely remembered him trying to rinse the soap from her eyes. The burning misery. She'd tried to cooperate. *She really had tried.* But her eyes had stung too much to oblige. Her brain had turned to mush again, and she'd slipped into darkness with no way out.

Then Lelandi had spoken softly to her, the noisy hair dryer nearly drowning out her words as Carol had tried to hear them. *"You're a match, dear Carol. You just need to ensure Ryan sees it before it's too late."*

It was already too late. How could Carol love someone who didn't trust in her abilities? Who believed she was lying? Or was just too dumb to know the truth?

She recalled the onions and garlic, the smell of the man who had kidnapped her, the feeling of hopelessness, of wanting to fight him off but being unable to. She tried to wriggle free and whimpered softly, attempting to cry out, to tell Darien and his brothers and Sam where she was. But then the crackle of gunfire sounded, and she gasped.

"Shh, Carol, you're safe. In the guest room. With me, *Ryan*. You're safe. *Sleep.*" Ryan's words were sleepy, soothing, and masculine. His arms wrapped tighter around her, anchoring her to him, her lifeline, her protection.

She took a deep breath of him, blocking out all other memories and settling against his solid form. She felt a whisper of his warm breath against her hair and knew that if heaven existed, this was it. Maybe it wasn't too late. Maybe she could convince the stubborn man of science to open his mind to another world.

She cuddled with him, his solid chest pillowing her head, his heart thumping with a steady beat against her ear, the heat of his body warming hers. His hand stroked down her back, lightly, tenderly, in a comforting way. She purred like Puss, mesmerized with Ryan's gentle touch. And could have stayed like this forever.

Hell, Ryan really was trying to be a gentleman here, but the way Carol's fingers spread across his chest with a featherlight touch, the way she snuggled closer to him, one leg slipping over his, the way she softly purred like a kitten in ecstasy, he was having the damnedest time keeping their relationship strictly impersonal.

Her T-shirt had risen again, and her soft, naked belly was pressed against his hip, her bare leg touching his thigh. Was she still so out of it from the drug that she had no inhibitions? Or did she really want him, like he was dying to have her?

He let out his breath in a heavy sigh. His job was to guard her body, not ravish it. After what she'd been through last night and five months ago, she needed to feel secure and protected. So why the hell did he have to keep reminding himself of that?

Maybe because her silky smooth leg had slid up his thigh even further and was pressing lightly against his arousal. That was why.

"Carol?" he whispered.

She didn't respond. He figured she was asleep and wasn't even aware she was putting him through all this torture. He kissed the top of her head and closed his eyes, trying to will himself to sleep for what was left of the early morning hours. Like *that* was going to happen while he kept his arm wrapped around the half-naked siren and she clung intimately to him.

The issues of her psychic business were quickly taking a back seat to his desire to have her—as a wolf would have his mate.

But then, Carol's fingers teased his chest more than once, and he was sure she was waking up or already fully awake.

"Carol?" he whispered again.

"Hmm," she finally said and cuddled closer. "Do you ever wish you were human?" she asked softly, almost as if she was afraid to pose the question.

Ryan raised her face and gave her a dark smile. "I *am* human. What's on your mind?"

She looked at him with those beautiful blue eyes, questioning, enticing. "I just wondered if you ever wanted to have sex with a wolf but couldn't because then you'd be mated for life."

"If I wanted to have sex with her, I'd want her for life."

Carol's fingers swept across his heated skin again in a tantalizing caress, and now that she was awake and fully aware that he was with her nearly naked and not in the least bit bothered by their close proximity and intimacy—

"Well, if you were human—all the way—you could have a wolf lover with no consequences," she continued, her words still spoken in a hush, as if she didn't want the world to know she was awake or that she was speaking to Ryan or even what she was speaking about.

"True."

She rested against him in silence for some time as he stroked her soft hair, his body hardening, his desire for her growing, despite his efforts to keep his burgeoning craving to have her in check. She wasn't making it easy. Considering her quickening heartbeat and the subtle changes in the sweet scent of her, the hint of arousal—and even the way she touched him and stroked him softly, playing with him— she had to be feeling something for him also.

"I wonder how Sam and Silva do it," she said under her breath.

"Pardon?" He could guess where this was going, and he was instantly interested, as long as she knew what she was getting into and was just as willing.

"Nothing."

"Do what, Carol? You brought it up," he pressed, hoping he wouldn't scare her off with his enthusiasm.

She cleared her throat and whispered, "As hot and heavy as the petting is getting between them even in public, I wonder how they can hold back."

"Maybe they aren't."

"You mean that they've already done it? Consummated the relationship? Are secretly mated?"

His fingers paused on her hair. "They'd let everyone know if they'd mated. No, I'd say they haven't quite gotten there yet."

"Oh." She had to have gotten the picture.

"It's perfectly acceptable." He wanted to push her onto her back to demonstrate just how far wolves could go with one another before being committed as mates, but he was still afraid she wasn't ready. "We aren't talking about Sam and Silva here, are we?"

Her face flushed with color, and her fingers grew still.

"I have to admit I'm a bit surprised. But not in the least bit...unwilling." When she didn't respond, he thought he'd scared her off, that she hadn't had that in mind, that she was only curious about Sam and Silva's situation. He had to admit that because she was newly turned, wolf relationships might still be a mystery to her. And he felt a bit of a cad, believing she had wanted him.

She didn't say anything for so long and was so still—barely breathing, her heart still beating at an increased cadence—that he wasn't sure how to rectify the situation.

Before he could speak, she whispered, "Someone might hear us."

If he could have, he would have whisked her away to somewhere private, away from Darien, his own family, and the world. But if she was willing... Hell, who was he not to satisfy her cravings?

That was when he rolled her onto her back and captured her mouth with his, intending to kiss her so thoroughly that she wouldn't be able to make a sound. The only thing he regretted was that they didn't have time to luxuriate in the feel of each other, to make the experience last.

But she seemed to be of like mind and parted her lips for him, opening to the curl of his tongue as he seduced hers with his, her fingers sifting through his hair, his hands holding her face in place, his thumbs stroking her cheeks. A soft moan escaped her throat, spurring him on.

Feral and ardent, from the moment their lips and tongues touched, he felt his blood sizzle with heat and desire. His arousal pressed against her waist, and she released his hair and swept her hands down his naked back, skin to skin, her touch leaving a fiery wake in their path. With his mouth greedy on hers and her response just as fiercely passionate, he felt her nipples beneath her cotton T-shirt bud against his chest, hard, tantalizing, aroused.

He meant to move aside her so he could cup a breast and feel the delectable nipple, but she spread her legs, and he found himself resting between them, a dangerous invitation to sex and consummation and mating.

And for the first time, he truly wanted it. With her. For all time. But she wasn't ready. Not yet. Maybe never.

Her lithe body arched beneath him, pressing against

him to solicit him touching that most intimate of all spots. He swallowed a deep-seated groan and tried to keep his thoughts intact. No consummation. Just pleasure, even if it killed him.

He moved over so he could pull off her shirt, straddling her soft leg, still trapping her. And when he'd freed her of the fabric, he caressed her now swollen breasts, which were flushed, the nipples like dark cherries begging for a kiss. His tongue teased one, and she closed her eyes and clamped her teeth shut against another moan.

And then his fingers dipped into her sweet sheath, hot, wet, erotic, but he quickly silenced another of her moans with a deepening kiss. Her fingers dug into his buttocks still covered in boxer briefs, her body writhing against his fingers, arching, pleading for resolution. His fingers continued to ply her with caresses, stroking, then thrusting inside her, while he watched her shuttered gaze and parted lips, heard her shallow breaths, and felt her fingers clinging to him.

Unable to help himself, he rubbed the erection straining in his boxers against her soft naked thigh. Bone-hard, wanting, thrusting, he felt burned to the core by white-hot heat as he pressed for deliverance.

Carol absorbed every feel of him, from the way his fingers worked miracles on her nub to his erection thrusting against her thigh. God, she wanted him inside her where everything had turned to aching, molten lava. She craved release and begged for it, pushed him to hurry and finish it before she died an exquisite death from wanting. Without being able to hold onto the rising tide of pleasure, she came, the climax filling her with a rush of satisfaction, her breath ragged, her body hot and flushed and sweaty—and sweetly satiated.

Ryan's face was dark and flushed, his breath hurried, his eyes smoky brown, and his heart beating as if he'd run for miles as a wolf. She exhilarated in the feel of his touch, his wildness, yet gentleness, too, the fact that he wanted to plea-sure her and would keep it quiet.

He was the hero of her dreams, the fantasy in the novels she so loved to read, the kilted warrior who'd somehow lost his kilt and wore instead a pair of boxer briefs. Which wasn't right. A Highlander went without. She slipped her fingers down his backside and underneath his waistband and squeezed his buttocks, soliciting a groan from his lips.

But then she tugged at his boxer briefs, and he hurried to slide them off. Then he was all hers. She ran her hand over his rigid length and felt it jump in her hands, tightened and stroked and smiled as he reached up to kiss her lips. But he was already so primed that he couldn't last. With another stroke, she sent him reeling, and he came. She continued to stroke and marvel in the way he reacted, his eyes clouded with lust, his body jerking with completion, him calling her name in a husky whisper as if she was the one sent to save him.

He kissed her as if he never wanted to stop, his tongue again stroking hers, his hand caressing her jaw, her throat, her breastbone, her breast.

And then he groaned one last time, collapsed beside her on his back, and pulled her into his arms. They lay together in perfect bliss for what seemed like an eternity, floating, satiated, and warm in each other's embrace.

"Have fresh sheets?" he finally whispered hoarsely.

She frowned. Getting sheets out of the linen closet in the hallway adjoining the other bedrooms would be difficult to do without alerting anyone.

"In the hallway," she whispered back.

He smiled, kissed the tip of her nose, and yanked the covers aside. "I'll get them."

She prayed no one would question him if he got caught.

———————————

"He was sleeping with her last night," Tom said, his tone angry as he talked to someone downstairs in the great room of Darien's home.

Ryan smiled and held onto Carol tighter in the bed in her guest room. After a long night of whimpers and struggling against unseen forces and the most wondrous sex, Carol had finally settled down into a deeper sleep.

And yeah, he was sleeping with her—or trying to anyway. He wondered now if the way she'd whimpered, half waking from nightmares, had occurred on other occasions. Was that what had been keeping her awake nights? But every time he had tightened his hold on her, she had relaxed and fallen into a more restful sleep. He didn't need to stay up all night sitting in the recliner, not when he was able to wake at the slightest indication of trouble and shift quickly.

The nightmares she was experiencing gave him even more of a reason to stay with her like this, wrapped around her like a cocoon surrounding an awakening butterfly. A nearly naked butterfly, her T-shirt drawn midway up her waist, although he'd pulled it down for her a couple of times during the night. Until they'd pleasured each other in wild, abandoned, almost consummated sex. If she'd given him the go-ahead, he might have let his other head rule his actions. But now she again wore her T-shirt, and he his boxer briefs, in case anyone dropped in to check on them.

"Hell, Tom, what did you expect from an alpha male leader? That he'd sit in the recliner dutifully? On the other side of the room?" Jake responded finally.

"Darien said—"

"Our brother can boss around our own people just fine. Others also. But Ryan, if you haven't noticed, doesn't take no for an answer. And he plays by his own rules."

Ryan could almost hear the smile in Jake's response. And for the first time, he noted Jake had called him Ryan, not McKinley. Even though alphas might not like having to butt heads with others, they still respected one another for having the gumption to stand up for what they felt was right. Had Ryan felt that Carol would have been more comfortable alone in bed, he would have sat in the recliner all night long. But he knew better.

She'd needed someone's comforting touch. If not his, someone else's. And he sure as hell hadn't wanted it to be anyone else's. If any of the beta males had stayed with her and insisted she consummate a relationship while she was half drugged, she might be a mated wolf by now. Not that he had any ready knowledge about what the bachelors were like deep down, but he didn't trust any of them where Carol was concerned.

He ran his fingers through her soft hair, luxuriating in the silkiness. Until last night, when she had talked about the ordeal she'd been through with the psychiatrist—and even her own family not believing her—he hadn't realized how having psychic abilities could have been a problem for her growing up. Now that she was also one of the wolf kind, she had new problems and more adjustments to make. Neither of which he could comprehend like someone who was forced to live like this.

"He's not right for her," Tom persisted. "He doesn't believe in her abilities. Hell, she deserves someone who knows just how special she is."

That, Ryan could agree with. She was special all right.

"Did you see the way he kissed her? Danced with her? If you want a chance at her, you'd better make your move."

Tom responded, "I haven't had dreams of her."

Silence followed.

Dreams? That was another thing Ryan hadn't believed in. The notion that someone dreamed about mating with the one who fate had chosen for them. Dream mating was something that Darien and some of his family had supposedly been cursed or gifted with. So now Tom thought that dreams would reveal the one for him also?

Pure nonsense.

"Darien might have had the ability, Tom. You can't believe you will too." Jake's tone was conciliatory, which surprised Ryan.

He hadn't heard Jake speak like that to his brother since he'd been around the two of them. But he'd heard Jake didn't believe in dream mating either, at least as far as it would involve him.

Someone paced. Then Tom said, "So why don't you make known how you feel about Carol?"

Jake gave a short laugh, but it sounded forced, unnatural. "Seems I'm too late."

"You can't mean Ryan. Carol needs to stay here. For Lelandi. Carol's one of our pack. She belongs here with us."

Jake countered with, "She needs to have a mate first and foremost. If Ryan turns out to be the one, so be it. Maybe he can convince her to shift before it's too late. None of us has had an ounce of luck with her. You know how dangerous it is for her not to get some control over her shifting."

That was another thing Ryan wholeheartedly agreed with. Carol needed to embrace her wolf half without delay.

The brothers quit speaking, and their footfalls died away as they headed in the direction of the kitchen.

Ryan kissed the top of Carol's head in a protective, consoling way, unwrapped his body from hers, and began to leave the bed. She'd be getting ready for work at the hospital soon, and he intended to be with her every step of the way.

She tossed and turned, her hands searching for something. Him? Hell. Maybe she didn't have to work today. He crawled back under the covers and pulled her into his heated embrace, vowing this time to control his sexual urges.

Being a bodyguard had never felt quite this...pleasurable. He suspected it would never feel the same way again.

Later that morning, after he had breakfast with Darien, Ryan intended to call Carol's mother about the situation with the psychiatrist. But he didn't want Darien, his brothers, or Lelandi to know about it and get the wrong idea. If they heard he was calling to verify that Carol truly had had an early vision, he was sure that would put him in the doghouse. His investigative skills dictated that he ask Carol's mother about the episode with the psychiatrist to learn how he'd treated her and if her mother believed in Carol's abilities now.

"I've got to make an important call," he said to Darien as he finished the last of his eggs and another slice of ham, the sun streaming in through the kitchen window and warming the room. Lelandi had relieved him a half hour earlier to sit in the recliner and watch over Carol while she still slept. Lelandi was using the time to catch up on her studies on behavioral psychology.

Tom and Jake planned to hang around the house guarding the ladies today. The brothers had taken up positions in the sunroom and in the den, so they would be safe for the moment.

Darien raised a brow and sipped his coffee. "I understand you slept with Carol last night."

Alpha leader. Protective of his pack member. No beating around the bush. "She was experiencing night terrors."

"Anything occur between you two that I should know about?"

Again, to the point.

"If you mean did we mate, no. She was drugged and consequently asleep for the most part, although her nightmares partly woke her half the night." Darien didn't need to know about the rest.

The doorbell rang, and Tom hurried from the sunroom to get it, passing the kitchen on the way to the front door and giving Ryan a reproachful look. Darien smiled wryly.

A couple of minutes later, Tom carried a vase of roses to the sunroom.

Darien motioned to Ryan's phone. "Go, make your call. We're all here to watch over Carol until you return."

"Take only a minute." Ryan headed for the great room and then made his way to the back patio. Outside, he called information, got Carol's parents' home phone number, and punched it in.

"Hello?" a woman asked, sounding like Carol, only a little older, but with a voice a little sharper.

"Hello, Mrs. Wood. This is Ryan McKinley."

Silence.

"I'm a private investigator out of Green Valley."

"I know who you are," she growled.

He paused. Hell, had Carol told her mother about him?

"I was calling about..." He rephrased the comment. "Carol told me about her ordeal with that psychiatrist, Dr. Metzger. About how—" The phone clicked dead in his ear.

Carol woke to the turning of pages in the guest room and felt her legs pinned beneath the comforter, but Ryan was gone. Disappointment vanished when she glanced down and saw what was wedged between her legs. Her heart lifted. Puss. Her tabby: soft, happy, and sound asleep. She couldn't believe Darien had allowed her cat to leave the kennel so he could stay with her.

A warm, fuzzy feeling instantly filled her with serenity. She smiled, pulled Puss into her arms, and cuddled him soundly. Then she looked at Lelandi, who was seated in the recliner reading one of her psychology books. Lelandi was determined to become a psychologist. Darien backed her, but he had lots of stipulations about her work. For example, he'd prefer she only counsel females. But knowing Lelandi, if anyone made an appointment with her to discuss their problems, she'd see them. With or without Darien's approval.

Even though Carol had had a bad experience with a psychiatrist, she knew Lelandi would be perfect as a psychologist. She was a lot more open-minded, for one thing.

Carol wished Ryan was still with her, although she was afraid things might have heated up between them again. And this time, they might have gotten caught.

On the other hand, maybe he regretted what they had done. She tried not to think of it, but still, a little irksome worry fluttered around in the pit of her stomach. Seeing him this morning without letting on was not going to be easy.

Puss's little motor began to rumble. He stretched a little and then continued to sleep, rolled up in a ball, eyes shut, breathing slight. Carol was thrilled to have Puss back. Sighing, she gave him another gentle squeeze.

What had changed Darien's mind?

Lelandi looked up from her book and gave her a bright smile. "You're awake. How do you feel?"

"Fine. Except for my arm." The skin was bruised and the muscle sore. Carol thought what a lousy nurse the man would have made.

"One of the men gave you a shot. The bruise should fade soon. Do you remember what happened?"

"Someone grabbed me from the shower. Stuck the needle in my arm first, though, and I felt drugged. Then he dropped me on the grass, I guess. I must have been slowing them down once Sam and Darien were in hot pursuit. Ryan found me, I think. And carried me back to the house. I recall him rinsing out my eyes, and then that's about it."

"Hmm. He stayed with you last night. Did anything… happen between the two of you?"

Carol raised her brows. "You think we had sex last night?"

Lelandi smiled a hint. "If you're mated, Darien has to let the bachelors know you're no longer available."

"We didn't do anything last night." Not that Carol would admit to, but Lelandi was observing her closely, like a psychologist might observe a subject. She hoped she didn't look as guilty as she felt. "He slept with me?" Wondering how anyone might have known. Had they heard their moans and groans while having sex?

"That's what Tom said. He peeked in on you sometime in the night to see if Ryan needed to be relieved from guard duty and found him with his arms wrapped tightly around you, his back naked. After Darien questioned Tom about every detail for what seemed an eternity—suspecting Tom was leaving some of the story out—Tom finally admitted he'd heard you whimpering and poked his head in to make sure Ryan was being honorable."

Carol's heart nearly stopped. Had Tom seen them in the throes of sexual frenzy? "Ryan was being honorable. Just helping to calm my night terrors."

"About being kidnapped? Or something else? More visions?"

"Don't remember." Carol yawned. Then she sat up abruptly. "What time is it? I need to get to work."

"Matthew and Charlotte are working extra half days to cover for you. Darien doesn't want you working today after what happened last night. Take a break, and you can go back to the hospital tomorrow."

Carol slid out from under her sleeping cat, who stretched a little but didn't bother opening an eye. She crossed the floor to the antique dresser, jerked the drawer open, and yanked out a bra and panties.

"I'm fine. And no way am I making Charlotte and Matthew work my hours." She'd fought hard to get a job at the hospital. She wasn't going to shirk her responsibilities now. "Why is Puss here?"

Lelandi hesitated to say.

"Lelandi?"

"Unofficially, and just between you and me, I believe Darien felt badly that he told Ryan he couldn't stay with you and then you were kidnapped. But officially, he thinks that if you mostly have your life back the way it was before you were changed, you may accept our ways and shift."

To have her life back, she'd be living in her own apartment again. Instead, Darien had insisted she put her things in storage and close up her apartment. Her life as she had known it was over. Yet she'd become accustomed to being with others—with Lelandi, with Darien, with his brothers. The thought of returning alone to her apartment and only having Puss to talk to didn't appeal either.

Carol shook her head and grabbed a pair of kitty-cat scrubs from another drawer. "If I shift, I won't be able to shift back. Simple as that." She entered the bathroom and shut the door.

"Did you see this in a vision?" Lelandi asked from the recliner.

"No, but that doesn't mean it won't happen."

"You say Doc shifts and can't change back. Is he the only one?"

"Darien also. Jake is in the same predicament as well. You're really upset and want me to do something about it. But I can't. I have no idea what's happening. If everyone chooses to ignore me, I can't help anyone."

"We love to shift, Carol. It's part of who we are." But this time, Lelandi didn't sound quite so sure of herself.

Carol dressed, brushed her hair, and applied a little makeup.

When she opened the bathroom door, Lelandi smiled at her. "Ready for some breakfast? With Sam and Ryan chowing down with Darien and his brothers, there may not be anything left. Mervin's down there also, but he eats like a bird."

"I can grab a bagel and green tea at the hospital."

"Nonsense. If you want just tea and a bagel, the guys probably haven't touched those. But the bacon and sausages? I'm sure Tom will have to make another trip to the store." Lelandi opened the door to the guest room and walked into the hallway. "So you've seen Darien, Doc, and Jake unable to shift and me agitated. Do you see me change and unable to shift back?"

"Not yet. But maybe you're beginning to believe me." Carol studied Lelandi's petite frame as she walked down the stairs, wondering how long it would be before she began to show. Soon, she imagined, with triplets on the way.

"Did you tell Darien about the babies?" Then it dawned on Carol: maybe that was why Lelandi was cautious about Carol's warning visions. Lelandi had more than herself to think of now.

"He guessed before we had the games. He wasn't happy that I had tried to keep it secret from him. He'd worried that if someone had tackled me, I might have been hurt. Or the babies would have been. So he told all the guys in a special meeting that if they as much as made a hint of a move in my direction, he'd oust them from the pack. That's why he didn't have the tug-of-war game. Afraid I'd want to participate and might injure myself."

Carol had suspected as much.

Lelandi glanced back at her. "During the game, I figured everyone would be afraid of touching me because I'm Darien's mate. I didn't know that he'd warned them away." Then she gave Carol another award-winning smile. "Alphas are like that." She turned around and headed across the great room as Carol hurried to catch up. "I imagine Ryan will be the same."

"He doesn't believe in my second sight." Carol shrugged. "Things wouldn't work out between us." Then she frowned. "Who else knows that Ryan slept with me last night?"

"I imagine at least half the pack. Maybe more. Tom was pretty incensed about it. When he talked to Jake, he didn't get the support he wanted, so he spoke to Darien and Sam. Sam told Silva, and you know how that goes. She means well though. She wanted to warn the wolves of our pack that if they desired having you for a mate, they'd better do something about it. If Ryan wants you, same thing. He'd better stop resting on his laurels."

Incredulously, Carol shook her head.

"I'm serious." Lelandi pointed to the sunroom. "You have a dozen glass or ceramic vases, brass pots, and baskets filled with flowers. Rosie, at the flower shop? She called and gave me a list of names. Silva wanted to know who hadn't sent you flowers and wangled it out of her."

Carol sighed. "Isn't anything sacred?"

"Rarely, in a pack. You know who didn't send you flowers?"

"Tom, Jake, and Ryan."

"Two of the three did. I have to tell you, I was pretty darned amused."

Carol pulled Lelandi to a stop outside the kitchen where the men's conversation had died. She'd made out Darien and his brothers, Ryan, Sam, and even that lame Mervin talking in the room before they heard Lelandi and Carol's conversation.

Lelandi's expression brightened. "Everyone but Ryan sent you flowers. Sure sign he's in love. Darien did the same with me when I was injured."

Ryan and everyone else in the kitchen had to have heard what was said. Every inch of Carol's skin heated with morti-fication. But then she concentrated not on who *hadn't* given her flowers—she figured Ryan wasn't a romantic—but who had...Tom and Jake.

Lelandi leaned over and whispered to Carol, "Jake didn't give me flowers either, when everyone else did. I figured he was too cheap." She straightened. "So there might be some-thing to it, you think?"

Lelandi gave her a conspiratorial wink, and Carol real-ized Lelandi was doing her matchmaking business with her, just as she was always doing with Silva and Sam.

But what if Ryan and she were already a match? Or maybe this was just a test on his part. See if the female wolf is right for the alpha male leader. She was reminded once again that she really didn't understand this wolf business as much as she needed to if she was going to make the right decisions from now on. With her head held high and her stomach flittering with unwanted jitters, she walked into the kitchen.

Ryan instantly caught her eye, and as hot as her face was, she had to have flushed crimson.

CHAPTER 14

WELL, THAT WAS ONE MESSED-UP OPERATION, NORTH thought to himself as he and two of his men stood in the forest miles from Silver Town, trying to come up with an alternative plan.

"Hell, North. You said that it would be a piece of cake. That no one would even miss the red. Shows what you know." Galahad—so named because he thought of himself as a knight who had been concerned about their pack's direction while Bruin had run it—motioned to the ground and a rough-hewn map he was drawing in the soil. "Here's the new plan. We grab her at the hospital. When she's in the break room. Or when she's coming or going. Maybe when she's in with a patient."

North shook his head. "Miller won't like it."

"Hell, I don't trust him. He's renovated the basement of that old place, turned it into his own private quarters, lab and all, and I swear it's like a bunker. No telling what all he's doing down in his lab with all that bioengineering crap. He's quiet and thoughtful, *too* thoughtful. Something's going on in that mind of his. He might be a genius, but I swear he's a borderline nutcase too." Galahad gave North a hard look, emphasizing his dislike of Miller.

"One of us can be a patient," Hank said. He was Galahad's brother, a nice enough red but a little too preoccupied with computer role-playing games for North's liking. Hank seemed to have missed the whole point of Galahad's tirade.

Or maybe it was that they'd heard it before, and Hank didn't believe anything was wrong with Miller, then or now.

"If we wear the hunter's scent, no one would be the wiser. As long as Lelandi doesn't show up at the hospital and spot any of us. She's the only one who knows us from the pack," Hank added.

Galahad pointed a stick at North. "*He* was in the house when the fight was going on. Darien and others in his pack may very well recognize him. But the rest of us…" He shrugged. "We weren't there, and as long as they can't make us out to be reds, we could pull it off."

North didn't like it. The whole thing had been his plan— and it would have worked if that damned gray pack leader from Green Valley, McKinley, hadn't spied Hank snooping around the forest surrounding Darien's home. Now North was left out of the whole deal. "I don't want Carol Wood hurt."

Hank grinned at Galahad. "I told you he wants her for his own." Then he scowled. "You shouldn't have dropped her and left her for the grays."

North gave him a look like he'd better watch his words. No one was exactly the pack leader yet. North wanted to be, but he was still butting heads with his cousin Connor. Because of that, no one in their newly formed pack took North as seriously as he thought they should. Then again, he suspected, the bioengineer in their renegade group of wolves had some loftier plans of his own in mind.

Miller Redford liked to work behind the scenes. North felt as though the rest of the bachelor males would take all the risk, and then Miller would step out of his lab bunker and end up with the prize and maybe even the pack. He was sneaky and smart. He didn't outwardly act as though he were the take-charge type, sticking more to his lab and his scientific studies. But Miller had a way of smiling and shifting his eyes when North questioned his intentions that made North leery.

"She's a red, turned by my cousin, and since Connor is sick and out of the picture for now, it's up to me to bring her home," North said to Hank and his brother. "She belongs to us. As far as what happened? Hell, they were catching up to me. And would have if I hadn't left her behind. I doubt they would have gone easy on me after we took Carol the way we did."

Galahad poked his stick at the square drawn into the dirt that represented the hospital. "Hank's right. Admit it, North. You want her. But she has to be agreeable. Any of us," he said, motioning with a sweep of his stick, "might turn her head. So it's up to the little lady."

"She won't agree to it." Hank sat down on his haunches. "The grays have already brainwashed her about staying with them. Look at Lelandi. That Darien Silver did the same thing to her."

North glanced in the direction of Silver Town. "Bruin and his two brothers were the reason for Lelandi leaving our pack. We should have killed the three of them when we had the chance."

"That was the thing. We never had the chance. Hell, even your cousin who died was in thick with them." Galahad slapped North on the shoulder. "What's done is done. If we could have, we would have eliminated our leaders and then brought her home. But now?" He shrugged his broad shoulders. "The nine of us have a pact. Start anew. The three of us need mates. Carol Wood's a red. And unmated."

"What about the two women we paid off to attend their gathering?" Hank asked.

"They're grays, and except for an interest in our money, that was it. We need Carol Wood. She belongs to us." North looked back in the direction of Silver Town. "My cousin and the rest of us need her, and hopefully, soon she'll have a solution to our problem. We just can't let Miller know what we have in mind when we get hold of her."

Carol and Lelandi joined Darien and his brothers, Sam, Ryan, and Mervin for a bite of breakfast. The men appeared to have finished theirs already, with dirty plates remaining, but they were all sipping fresh cups of coffee. The worst thing was that Carol's and Ryan's gazes instantly caught— and held—and she knew everyone was watching their actions. Which made it even worse when her skin flushed with heat as if she'd just stepped into a sauna.

Ryan looked like he felt her pain, yet he wouldn't release her gaze, as if he wanted her to know he felt no remorse for what had occurred between them. She didn't either, except that she had had an audience as witnesses, and she was certain she had given her and Ryan's activities away.

She hurried over to the teakettle and heated water for a cup of tea.

"You've had a traumatic experience and need to stay here with…that cat of yours," Darien said grudgingly as she toasted a half a bagel.

At least he wasn't talking about Ryan and her. She raised a brow.

"Puss. Thanks so much for allowing him to stay with me. He'll contentedly sleep until he wants to roam in the room, and then he'll go back to sleep. He'll be fine." But that clinched the deal that Darien wasn't fond of cats. Probably a canine thing.

"I won't make Matthew and Charlotte put in longer shifts because I've failed to report to work. Besides, Doc Weber said another four patients have shown up with cases of the flu. Not the swine flu, thankfully, so no one needed overnight admittance, but the staff is getting swamped."

"I'll go with you," Lelandi said. "Just to hang around for a while until you're through."

Carol buttered her bagel. "Absolutely not. I don't want you coming down with anything." She turned off the teakettle, figuring it was going to take too long to make a cup of tea if Darien was making an issue about her staying home. Headed for the doorway with bagel in hand, she brushed past Jake, who shook his head.

"What?" she asked him.

"When the boss—that's Darien—" Jake said in a sarcastic way, jerking his thumb in Darien's direction, "wants something, he gets it. If he says you're to stay home, it's not open for debate." Jake picked up his plate and took it to the dishwasher.

Darien gave a hint of a smile.

Carol smiled broadly and grabbed Ryan's hand, while he stood in anticipation of her departure for the hospital.

"I have my bodyguard. Unless you or Tom want the job."

Ryan's hand tightened on hers as if he wasn't giving her up to anyone else's protection. She glanced up to see his expression. He gave her lifted brows and a small smile in response. But the smile indicated something way more than anything to do with guarding her, as if he was thinking about what *she* was thinking about—and if she didn't quit thinking about him and his slick moves in that way, he was going to do something about it.

"I want the job," Mervin said, sounding peeved and pulling her attention away from Ryan.

"I'm paying for Ryan to serve in that capacity." Darien cast a hard look at Mervin.

Mervin appeared to still be in the doghouse over accosting her the night before at the gathering.

"So see? This way, Ryan will earn his pay. If he got to loaf around your house, it would be like paying him for vacation time," Carol said, squeezing Ryan's hand. She wasn't letting him go. And his smile hinted at a darker secret and desire.

"You stay with her even when she's seeing a patient," Darien warned Ryan.

He gave Darien a mock salute. "Hadn't planned on doing anything differently."

Carol frowned, not believing Darien would suggest that. "Patient privacy issues come into play here. Policy dictates that Ryan can't be in an exam room when I'm seeing a patient."

"Make up your mind, Carol," Darien said, not willing to be challenged in the matter. "Either he stays with you at all times, or you remain home. Your choice."

She let out her breath hard.

"Doc can put you on wolf cases only. There won't be any privacy issues then," Lelandi said, trying to smooth things over. "Darien's right. You can't be alone at any time."

Carol didn't intend to be. She planned to make up a

syringe full of the same cocktail she figured the red had given her. And she'd give it right back if any of them tried to grab her again.

"That should work," she said cheerfully, although if the workload was mostly human, she'd help out, and Ryan could wait beyond the exam-room door, despite what everyone else said.

"Ready?" she asked Ryan, tugging on his hand.

He yanked out his keys. "Let's take care of your patients."

Jake pulled out the keys to his truck. "I'll follow, just in case."

"I'll go with you." Tom tucked his phone into its pocket at his belt.

Mervin hurried to join them.

At least she felt safe with her entourage of bodyguards, although she really didn't think the reds would be bold enough to try to take her at the hospital anyway. She hurried to eat her bagel as Ryan walked her to his truck.

Movement in her bedroom window caught her eye, and she looked up to see Puss watching her through the glass, his tail twitching and his ears perked. She had a twinge of regret that she couldn't have cuddled with him longer.

"You were having nightmares last night. What about?" Ryan asked, pulling her from her thoughts.

She had thought he might talk about their nighttime moves. She sighed and climbed into Ryan's truck and tilted her chin up slightly. "I have one better than that. A vision. At least I think it was. I was kind of doped up at the time. But I saw Jake become a wolf, and then he was unable to shift back."

Ryan didn't say anything as he climbed into his truck

and then pulled onto the road toward town. "Did you have a vision of your kidnapping?"

He still didn't believe that the men in the pack had turned into wolves and couldn't return to their human forms. "No. I told you the visions can be irritatingly unpredictable. It would have been nice to see it happen beforehand...to at least prepare myself, but it doesn't work that way." She stared out the window, watching the firs whiz by. But then an uneasy feeling crept through her when she recalled something else. "Oh, no..."

"Oh, no...what?"

She rubbed her temple, trying to recall the exact details. "I...I had a vision before we went into the tavern yesterday."

Ryan stared at her. "About?"

"A man with long, red hair. It dangled in my face when he bent over me. He wore a padded vest. And I felt so tired, so incredibly tired."

"A vision?"

"How else do you explain it?" she asked quietly, studying his taut profile as he continued to watch the road as he drove toward town. "You pulled me out of it when you said something to me in the truck after we arrived at the tavern. I had no idea what the vision meant."

His jaw clenched, and his eyes narrowed.

She looked back out the window.

"Why didn't you tell me then?"

"We didn't have a pact back then that I would tell you if I had any visions—and you wouldn't have believed me anyway. Besides, it didn't seem important. And I didn't think about it when we were in the tavern."

Ryan grunted. "You said you didn't have them unless

they were important to you. So it seems this would have been important. And you said that they were premonitions of something that would occur pretty soon. You should have said something to me. Did you recognize him? See a face?"

"My...my eyes burned. I remember how blurry my sight was when I tried to see him. I thought it was the vision, but I think now it was because my eyes were filled with soap."

Ryan mulled that over, not saying anything for about a mile, and then shook his head. "Great."

"Great, what?"

"How does this work, Carol? Do you conjure up the visions? Something trigger them? Or do they just happen?"

She studied his stern face. "They just happen."

"You can't force one?" He glanced at her, his eyes trying to read her like a wolf's would.

She looked back out the window.

He didn't say anything for some time, but then he pulled over to the side of the road. Startled, she glanced at Ryan, wondering what was up now.

Jake drove up behind them and parked. Ryan's cell phone rang, and he jerked it off his belt and answered. "Yeah, we're okay, Tom. We just have to discuss a little matter." He ended the call and pocketed his phone. "Can you force a vision?"

She frowned at Ryan. "Not exactly."

"Define *not exactly*."

"It's not normal for me to be able to force a vision."

"But?"

She took a deep breath. "Maybe it's the changes in me. Being a wolf. Or maybe as I grow older, I have a little more control. I don't know. Sometimes I can do so now. Not any particular one, but of something that is close to happening."

"Like?"

"Darien not being able to shift back."

"Wishful thinking?" Ryan asked.

She cast him her chilliest look, one that could have frozen the nearby lake despite it being spring. "The night before last, I envisioned someone in a red-and-white-striped jacket tackling me. The feeling I had wasn't fear but annoyance, so I knew it couldn't be too bad."

Ryan swore under his breath, reached out and took Carol's hand, and squeezed. "Mervin at the game."

"Yeah. He's the one who kept me awake half the night with the stupid visions of him."

Ryan sighed. "All right." He pulled back onto the road and headed the rest of the way into town.

All right? Now he believed her?

"How about a vision of anything else? Foresee any problems at work, perhaps?"

"No. I'll let you know about any visions I have. I said I would."

He drove in silence for a while and then said, "Why did you conjure up the vision of Darien?"

She sighed under her breath. What difference would it make if Ryan knew? She looked out the window and said softly, "To keep from shifting."

Ryan remained so quiet that she glanced back at him. He snapped his mouth shut. Then he said, "Hell, Carol. You're a ticking time bomb."

She smiled. "Really hot stuff you mean?"

"You're hot, all right. And you'll work with only wolf patients, like Darien ordered." Ryan glanced at Carol, his expression all business. She would obey him, or else.

She smiled back. "Of course. Unless we're swamped with human patients."

Ryan ran his hands over the steering wheel. "That's not the deal, and I won't go along with it. You're one dangerous lady. So about these nightmares you're having…"

She sighed loudly. "They're about the visions, about being bitten and changed, and they haunt me. Probably brought about by the drug the reds used on me." She wondered if the drug had inhibited the need to shift last night. She took a deep breath, relieved she hadn't tried to shift while Ryan was sleeping with her. Or doing anything else. A chill cascaded down her spine. Could having sex trigger a shift?

"Do you…believe in dream mating?" he asked out of the blue.

CHAPTER 15

HER STOMACH CLENCHING WHEN RYAN QUERIED HER about dream mating as he drove her to the hospital, Carol worried that maybe he believed in such a thing and was searching for the woman of his dreams. And she wasn't it.

Still startled, she stared at him in disbelief. "Do you?"

"Of course not. But I wondered if you did."

"Oh." Her stomach unclenched several degrees. She thought about the stories Lelandi had told her and nodded. "Sure. Lelandi and Darien were dream mated. I didn't know such a thing could exist until I heard of their case. Why bring it up?"

Ryan remained silent, and Carol huffed. "You tantalize me with some tidbit of news and then don't share it with me? What if I were to do that with you? Say that you wouldn't believe the vision I had this morning, but then not tell you what it was."

"Did you?"

She paused and then let out her breath. "I'm not sure if it was the drug or what, but I saw a golden room and brilliant lights spilling into it from another room. I was drawn to the lights, as if I didn't have any choice. And then shots were fired, and I heard..." She thought for a moment. Ryan glanced at her. She continued, "I heard Sam shouting. Then more shots rang out. So what brought on this dream-mating query all of a sudden?"

Frowning, Ryan tapped his thumbs on the steering

wheel and didn't answer her for some time. Then he said, "Was the golden room a premonition of something to come, Carol?"

"It might have been nothing more than the effect of the drug."

"Think carefully. You heard shots in the vision? Before Sam shouted?"

"The gunfire might have been outside of the vision. I might have heard it as I was envisioning the room."

"No," he said, his voice dark. "Shots rang out *after* Sam hollered. That's why they fired in his direction. At the sound of his voice. No gunfire sounded before that."

Carol considered the implications. Not good. She would be in a room headed toward another filled with bright lights where someone was shooting. Why would she do that?

"What are you thinking, Carol?" Ryan reached over to squeeze her ice-cold hand. His hand felt warm and large and secure.

"The room means danger."

"Then you're not going there." He glanced at her and continued to hold her hand.

"Right."

He didn't say anything for half a mile and then let out his breath. "Okay, so what happens in the room?"

"I don't know. That's what's so frustrating about my visions. I don't know what happens. What about your dream-mating inquiry?" Carol watched him, chewing her lower lip. Had he dreamed of her? She was fairly sure she hadn't dreamed of him, and she was certain she would have remembered.

"Tom said he was waiting for the woman who would

reach out to him in his dreams." Ryan glanced at her. "I thought you should know."

"Ah." Which meant that if Ryan wasn't the one for her, she'd have to scratch Tom off her list too. She sighed with disappointment. "That's good to know. But a dream woman is no match for the real thing." She folded her arms around her waist.

"Meaning?"

"Meaning that if the right woman came along, whether she was in his dream or not, I'm sure he'd want her." She looked out the window. It appeared to be the start of another sunny day, not a cloud in the sky...too bad she had to work. After the terror of last night, it would have been nice to curl up on Darien's porch with Puss sleeping on her lap, a cup of hot cocoa, and a good time-travel romance set in Scotland to read. Or if the house had been empty, she could have taken a nap with Ryan, although she might not have gotten any sleep.

Then again, she wouldn't have taken that much enjoyment in either, knowing Matthew and Charlotte had to work longer hours to make up for her not being there.

"Jake doesn't believe in dream mating," Ryan said as if that would make her feel better.

"Yeah. I don't blame him really. I'm sure I'd never conjure up my soul mate that way either. Still, it's an interesting way to satisfy some needs before they can be truly met. Don't you agree?"

Ryan pulled into the hospital parking lot, and Jake parked right alongside him on the passenger's side. "I think any substitute for the *real* thing wouldn't be half as satisfying." He gave her a slow, predatory grin.

Her body felt like she'd been roasting in the sun all day, but she managed a shake of her head and a small smile. "Lelandi warned me you were a wolf."

He chuckled, but before he could say anything further, her door opened. She turned to see Jake holding it open for her, waiting for her to exit the truck.

"Thanks, Jake." She cast Tom a sideways glance. "I hear you're waiting for a dream mate to appear for you. Hope you don't have to wait long." She smiled, even though she was disappointed. She'd have to scratch him off her list of hopeful mates, which looked as though that left her only with Jake. She hurried inside the hospital as Tom turned to his brother and scowled.

"You told her that?" Tom asked his brother.

"Hell, no. I don't even believe in that nonsense." Jake looked at Ryan, who raised his brows as if he didn't know what they were talking about.

Ryan stalked after Little Miss Nightingale. What part of he was her protector at all times did she not get?

"Who the hell else knows?" Tom asked Jake, following them into the hospital as Mervin brought up the rear.

"I swear I didn't tell anyone about our conversation. I don't know how Carol found out."

Ryan wasn't one to eavesdrop normally, unless it suited his purpose in his PI work. But if Tom wasn't truly interested in Carol, and she had hopes he might be, Ryan hadn't wanted her to be disappointed. He stalked after her as she headed down the hall of the clinic, while Tom, Jake, and Mervin trailed behind them.

The place smelled of disinfectant and fresh floor wax, rubbing alcohol, and, in the staff lounge, harsh coffee brewing. Ryan couldn't imagine working in a hospital environment, day after day. He much preferred the fresh out-of-doors, where he met with the residents and businessmen as mayor while coming up with plans for improving the city; the fragrance of new leather in his truck while he was in his PI surveillance mode; and the aroma of cocoa java bubbling at his office, compliments of his administrative assistant. Ingrid dutifully kept the business going whenever he was on an assignment elsewhere.

A tall nurse named Matthew approached them, wearing blue scrubs and carrying a chart. He looked official as he headed toward Ryan and Carol in the wide hall washed in light. With dark hair and eyes and a build that was a little scrawny and wiry, he looked like most of the other grays in Darien's pack. The guy cast Carol a harried smile, and *that* bugged Ryan more than he wanted to admit. Matthew pinned Ryan with a look that meant he didn't like Ryan following Carol so closely.

"He's her bodyguard," Jake said, explaining the relationship.

Matthew's expression remained hard, and he said to Carol, "I'm sorry I didn't make it to the gathering. Work, you know. But if you'd like to go out tonight…"

He let his words trail off. If Ryan had been Matthew, he would have scheduled the date, not left it up in the air like that. The other thing that bugged Ryan was that the rest of the pack knew about Carol's abduction already, so this clown had to. Otherwise, he was certain Matthew would have asked why she needed a bodyguard. So why didn't Matthew say anything about her being kidnapped and offer her consolation, protection, or anything? The guy was a total loser when it came to winning a woman over—that was why.

"Where did you want to go?" Ryan asked Matthew. "On a date?"

Matthew's jaw dropped. Carol looked like she was fighting a smile. Jake grinned. Tom shook his head. Mervin stared at Ryan as if he had lost his mind.

Ryan folded his arms. "I go where Carol does. So…" He shrugged. "Where did you have in mind?"

Matthew stiffened and spoke again to Carol as if Ryan hadn't just addressed him. "I'll talk to you later. Have to see a patient. Another case of the flu, I'm afraid. I've heard she came to the gathering last night."

"The gathering?" Carol glanced in the direction of the waiting area and saw Marilee reading a magazine. "The masseuse?"

"Yeah. The other, Becky? The librarian? She was already in here earlier."

Carol frowned. "Diagnosis?"

"Flu."

"Great. Then they exposed Lelandi."

"Yeah, well, I'm sure Darien's not going to like it, but then again, they probably didn't know they were coming down with it," Matthew said.

"Marilee could have known," Ryan argued. "She began coughing when I danced with her. She said it was allergies. If she's got the flu, she could very well have suspected that's what she had. She may have been worried that Darien wouldn't let her come to the gathering."

Matthew clenched his medical chart, his neck muscles tightening. "That's the problem with a private dick. Everyone's guilty until proven innocent."

"Have anything in your past you're afraid to share with the pack, Matthew? I understand you came here after your brother and his family and you had difficulties in a former pack. Anything that could create problems for you here if your past came under scrutiny? I'd be happy to look into it for Darien as a favor to the family."

Matthew's face reddened, and Ryan wondered what the nurse might have to hide. Carol looked like she didn't appreciate Ryan bringing it up here in front of Jake. But if the guy was going to attack Ryan's business ethics, he was fair game.

"We'll get together another time for a date." Matthew gave her another hint of a smile, cast a deadly look at Ryan, and hurried off.

Satisfied that he'd chased off a potential suitor who wasn't good enough for Carol, Ryan waited for her to go about her nursing business.

"Being in charge of my social calendar is not what you're paid to do," she said with mock indignation.

"I'm getting paid to guard you wherever you go and no matter who you're with, Carol. That's the deal." Ryan smiled.

Carol did not look too disappointed that he had put a damper on the date with the nurse, however, Ryan noted.

Jake smiled at the exchange and then grew serious and started giving orders. "Mervin, take a chair and sit by the back door so you can make sure no one we don't know goes in or out of there. Tom, you can watch the entryway and waiting room. I'll check out the exam rooms and the perimeter of the place while Carol sees her patients. And, Ryan, let either of us know if you need a break, and we'll stick close to Carol then."

Ryan offered a single nod.

Jake gave Carol a last command also. "You see *only*

special patients, not any of the others, Carol. One of us has to be with you at all times."

Exasperated, she sighed. "Fine. I have work to do." She headed into an exam room and busied herself with something nursing in nature, Ryan assumed, while he watched her back. Afterward, she went to her station, took the first patient's chart, and then returned to the waiting area.

Ryan wanted to speak with her about what had happened between them earlier that morning. But he knew he shouldn't, or he'd find himself sunk even deeper into a quagmire of trouble. The way she had looked at him in the kitchen that morning, flushed with awkwardness, had endeared her even more to him.

He figured everyone in the room—Darien, his brothers, Lelandi, even that lame Mervin—suspected more had gone on between Carol and him during the night than they'd admitted. And he regretted he'd have to be more…guardlike tonight. Sitting in the recliner would have to do.

His attention on Carol, Ryan felt like a puppy following his master around as Carol called out, "Miss Silverpenny?" But he didn't mind, as long as Carol remained safe.

Silverpenny was a good gray name, and when the petite elderly woman stood up from a chair in the waiting area, Ryan relaxed a little. She appraised Ryan as she joined them and smiled at Carol. "How was the gathering, dear?"

"Great," Carol said, walking at the woman's slower pace to her nurse's station and casting a look at Ryan as if she didn't want him to contradict her.

But hell, he hadn't danced with anyone in eons who'd made him feel like a randy teen like Carol had. And he would have remained on the dance floor, holding her close, swaying to a new song, if he hadn't known he'd have to give her up to the other bachelor males after a dance or two. More than that though. He hadn't wanted her to dance with Jake or Tom, not close like he'd danced with her, and he'd been afraid Jake might have tried to butt in.

Folding his arms, Ryan leaned against the wall across the hall and out of the way as Carol helped the woman stand on a scale.

"I swear I shrank another inch and gained two more pounds," Miss Silverpenny grumbled, her slim figure on the frail side.

Carol smiled.

The woman cast a glance over her shoulder at Ryan. "When she measures my height, she makes me remove my shoes." She motioned to the thick wedge-soled shoes she wore, which would add an inch and a half to anyone's height. She pointed an accusing finger at Carol, although her eyes twinkled with mirth. "And when she takes just my weight, she won't let me remove my shoes." They had to have weighed at least five pounds.

The woman reminded him of his cantankerous old aunt Tilda, good-natured and harmless.

"Are you her boyfriend?" the woman asked, her tone serious now.

Ryan opened his mouth to reply in the negative, but Carol beat him to it, which bothered him to a degree. Not that he minded her telling the truth but that she seemed so anxious to ensure no one thought he might be the one for her. What was wrong with him as a prospective mate anyway?

"No," Carol quickly said to her patient, shaking her head as if her word wasn't enough to convince her.

The woman looked back at Ryan, raised her brows, and smiled a little.

"You might have heard I had some trouble last night, and, well, Ryan's watching over me to make sure there's not another…incident," Carol continued as she readied a thermometer to take Miss Silverpenny's temperature.

The woman's kindly eyes widened, and then she nodded firmly. "Yes, you know how it is here in Silver Town. Everyone was alerted to the problem with the reds, and should anyone see any sign of them, they're to be reported." She waved her hand at Ryan.

"As for Ryan, I *thought* he was your boyfriend." She said it as if she hadn't heard Carol say he wasn't. "You can tell by looking at a man if he's good or good-for-nothing. Ryan has nice smile lines beneath his eyes. Not much in the line of wrinkles between his brows, which would indicate he frowns a lot."

Then she directed her comment to Ryan. "Welcome to the…" She stopped speaking when a human man walked into an exam room across the hall with Nurse Matthew. "…to the neighborhood."

"Thank you, Miss Silverpenny, but I'm just here for a short stay."

"You're taking our pretty little nurse away with you? Oh my, whatever will we do without you, Carol? She hasn't been with us for very long, but we adore her. Anyone who steals Darien's ribbon in a game of tag—other than Lelandi, of course—is someone to be admired." She seized Carol's hand and squeezed. "We'll miss you."

Carol's cheeks flooded with color. Ryan loved the blush on her cheeks. She didn't try to explain any further that she wasn't going anywhere and instead took the woman's temperature and then her blood pressure. Afterward, Carol escorted her down the hall, led her into an exam room, and sat her in the chair across from Doc's while Ryan closed the door for privacy.

"Is he going to stay with you all day?" Miss Silverpenny asked. "Night too?" She smiled broadly.

Yeah, she was just like Ryan's aunt Tilda. If his aunt knew he was staying with Carol, she'd have him mated to her already, at least as far as gossip went.

With her pen poised over the patient's chart, Carol cleared her throat and asked, "What are you having trouble with today?"

"Allergies. Doesn't matter if I'm a wolf"—she glanced at Ryan—"or running around as an old lady. I can't quit sneezing. If it's not that, my skin's itching to high heaven. But if I took that darned allergy medicine the doc gave me, I'd be sleeping my life away."

"Omega-3 fatty acids found in fish oil from salmon, herring, and sardines can help as natural anti-inflammatory agents," Ryan said, trying to be helpful.

Carol opened her mouth to speak, but Ryan kept talking. "My aunt Tilda had trouble with grass, ragweed, and mold. You name it, she was allergic to it. We didn't want her shifting into the wolf because her feet and legs itched so much from walking through tall grass. She'd chew on her exposed skin incessantly until she turned back into her human form."

"Ryan," Carol said, her tone indignant. "You are my bodyguard. Not the doctor and not a trained nurse."

"Sorry," he said to Carol. He turned to Miss Silverpenny. "My apologies, ma'am. But if you try some of that fish oil, you never know. Good for your heart and whatever else ails you. And also, although it's not been proven scientifically, my aunt's allergies are better when she has a little home-grown honey daily."

The old woman smiled at him. "Thank you, Ryan."

"Is there anything else that is bothering you, Miss Silverpenny?" Carol asked, her tone clipped.

"Oh no, dear. Since I'm already here, I might as well see Doc while I'm at it, but my goodness, you ought to hire your boyfriend at the hospital."

"The doctor will be here any minute." Carol seized Ryan's arm with one hand and the doorknob with the other, opened the door and pulled him out, and then shut the door behind them.

A woman had never accosted Ryan in such a rough manner, and while he didn't think he'd like it if most anyone else did, Carol was another story. Hell, the woman was a tinderbox ready to ignite, and her firm touch was stirring up his libido all over again. Too bad they couldn't put all that fire to good use.

Scowling, she guided him against a wall and released him, hands on her hips, brows furrowed in a cute little frown, standing so close to him to keep the conversation private that he could feel the heat from her sweet body. He wanted to pull her into a full-body embrace, kiss her lips, draw the venom out of her bite, and prove to her that as much as he had irritated her, she couldn't stay annoyed for long.

Drawing him from his wayward thoughts, she said, "Let's get this straight. You are *not* a doctor *or* a nurse, and you're *not* to give patients any medical advice."

Jake approached from down the hall, wearing a big-headed smirk that Ryan interpreted to mean he'd been the subject of her ire before. Or maybe he was just amused at seeing Carol pinning Ryan to the wall with her verbal assault.

"In the exam room, you stand against the door and look like a bodyguard. Not my boyfriend. Not medical counsel. A bodyguard. Period," she said to Ryan, her body so close to him that he could breathe in her peach scent, remembering vividly how he'd rinsed the soap from her skin the night before, every inch silky and soft. And later, when he'd kissed her soundly, his senses had filled with the delicious fragrance of her, the sweetness, the arousal, the heat of the moment.

The way her chest rose and fell with her hurried breathing and the flush of her cheeks stimulated some deeper need in him. Even the way she berated him appealed to him. He knew she was doing her job, making sure her patients got the best advice, although his advice came from his local doctor, so he knew it was sound. He loved the way she stood up for her patients, even though she had to know he was giving good information.

He wanted her. Wanted to take her all over again. To share the intimacy. To feel the heat burning between them and escalating.

A smile tugged at his lips as he bowed his head slightly in agreement, his face nearly touching hers. He wanted to kiss her in the worst way. He was sure his smile led to her reiterating her point.

"I'm serious," she said, a little breathless and a lot flushed. He could tell she was as affected by their close proximity as he was. She motioned to Jake. "If you can't be quiet, Jake can take your place."

Jake lost the smirk and cleared his throat as he neared them. "Didn't find anyone in the unoccupied exam rooms who shouldn't be here. Outside the hospital is clear. Deputy Trevor's watching things out front now. So far, no problems with anyone coming in through the front door, and no one trying to slip in or out through the back door. How are the two of you getting along? Need a break, Ryan?" Jake's expression was again amused.

"Maybe a little later," Ryan said, never taking his eyes off Carol's sharp blue ones. "I'll practice being a bodyguard a while longer." Hell, forget the recliner. He was guarding her body in bed again tonight. He smiled.

Carol turned away from him, whipped out the next patient's chart, and stalked down the hall to the waiting area.

Jake chuckled. "She's a spitfire when she's angered. What did you say to rile her?"

"Told the patient she could use fish oil to help with her allergies. I also would have mentioned a dehumidifier if she was having trouble with mold. Worked for my aunt."

"And you have a degree in?"

"Life." Ryan headed after his charge.

Jake laughed behind him.

At first, Ryan couldn't see Carol in the waiting area from his location in the hallway, and his heart pounded faster as he increased his pace. But when he reached the sitting area, he saw her waiting for a man whose whole expression brightened when he saw her. He was about Ryan's age, limping toward her and smiling with a look that was an attempt at "Woe is me—give me sympathy."

"Robert, did you need a wheelchair?" she sweetly asked.

She didn't sound as professional as Ryan would have liked. Not as serious. More good-natured and, well, way too sweet.

As Ryan approached, the man's amber eyes, piglike in appearance, switched from Carol to Ryan, and he swore Robert looked like he was about to have a heart attack.

"The nurse asked if you needed a wheelchair," Ryan said, his voice verging on a growl as he advanced toward the muscular man.

Carol's mouth dropped open as she stared at Ryan. "Ryan McKinley, whatever is wrong? Mr. Grayce has lived in the area forever."

Ryan glowered at the man and folded his arms. "You sure?"

After forgetting all about Tom, Ryan finally noticed him leaning against the check-in counter. Tom nodded to confirm Carol's statement, his expression bemused.

Carol cast Ryan an annoyed look and then took Robert's arm and helped him back to an exam room. Her hip pressed against the man's as she eased him down the hall at a crawl, and Ryan swore the patient leaned into her more than necessary. She should have gotten him a wheelchair or, at the very least, crutches or something. She didn't need to use her body to hold him up!

"Where are the wheelchairs?" Ryan growled.

Continuing down the hall with her charge without a backward glance, Carol ignored Ryan.

Half hiding a smile, Tom pointed to a storage room. Ryan stalked inside, grabbed a wheelchair, and hurried it after the limping man. Just in case the man was truly hurting, Ryan couldn't slam the chair into the back of Robert's legs like he wanted to, but he'd give the poor guy a seat so he wouldn't have to limp all the way to the exam room.

Ryan stopped the wheelchair and seized the man's arm, assisting him into the seat, and then grabbed hold of the handles. He gave Carol a smile as her mouth gaped wide again. Then she snapped it shut.

"The least I can do as your bodyguard, Carol, is help with your patient."

As red as her face was, he was certain that at the first opportunity, she would attempt to replace him as her bodyguard with anyone else. Mervin even.

He sighed heavily and wheeled Robert into the room Carol motioned to. He had never suspected that guarding the woman would be this difficult.

And this was only the first hour.

CHAPTER 16

"HE'S IMPOSSIBLE," CAROL SAID OVER HER CELL PHONE to Lelandi and then took another sip of her bottled water to finish it off. She was making the call from the hospital staff lounge during her break. Although as annoyed as she was with Ryan, Carol hated to admit she'd miss him when he no longer had to guard her during her patient visits.

Ryan stood with his legs apart, arms folded, staring out the break-room window, still playing bodyguard and listening in on her conversation. Small break room. Wolf's hearing.

Coffee bubbled in a pot nearby, the aroma mixing with someone's beef-in-wine-sauce lunch that was hastily heating in the staff microwave.

"Impossible," she repeated and cast Ryan an annoyed look, but his back was to her, so he didn't get the full benefit of her irritation.

"What did he do that was so wrong, Carol? He's supposed to be there protecting you. You have to make allowances. I know it's hard to have someone watching your every move. But he's only trying to help." Lelandi was her usual reassuring self, as if she was practicing her psychology lessons on Carol.

Feeling worn out from her experience in the woods the previous night and Ryan's and her early morning romp into sated bliss, Carol propped her cheek on her hand as she rested her elbow on one of the lounge tables.

"He gave medical advice to six of my patients! Six! From allergy remedies to how to relieve tension headaches. Even gave them all kinds of dietary advice. And where did all this medical wisdom come from? Dealing with his aunt Tilda, who has every ailment known to man and wolf kind."

"Was any of his advice dangerous?"

"Well, no, of course not. But he shouldn't be offering it!"

"Do you want Jake to stay with you instead? He said he would. Or Tom for that matter."

Carol lifted her head and watched Ryan. His whole body had tensed. Something she had said? Or did something he was watching out of the window catch his attention?

He jerked his phone off his belt and then hesitated. She parted her lips to speak with him, but he punched a couple of buttons, and said, "Jake, south of the hospital, three men met across the street and then hurried down an alley. Yes, of course they should be checked out. I would, but I have to watch Carol. All three were wearing blue jeans and sweatshirts, real casual. They were taking a lot of interest in the hospital. Yet they didn't make any move to approach it. One even motioned to your truck and then mine."

"Carol?" Lelandi said over the phone, breaking into Carol's concern about Ryan's conversation with Jake. "Did you hear me? Did you want Jake to watch you instead?"

"Jake's got another mission." Carol sighed. "After Ryan's finished guarding me here, I'm going to recommend he go to medical school."

Ryan folded his arms again and continued to watch out the window.

Even though she didn't want to believe that the men Ryan saw were the same ones who had grabbed her, she couldn't help the shiver trailing down her spine. The best medicine for what ailed her was work though. She glanced at her watch. "Break time's up, Lelandi."

"I'll have dinner on when you get home."

"Can't wait. See you later." She ended the call and said to Ryan, "Ready to go back to work?"

He turned around and nodded, his face a mask of indifference.

"Do you think it was them?" she asked, rising from the chair and hoping she didn't sound nervous. But hell, they'd shot her full of dope, taken her out into the cold naked, and dumped her when they thought they might get caught. No wonder it bothered her that they might try something like that again! She shoved her hand in her pocket and felt the syringe, her defensive weapon if she needed one.

"Could have been. Or not."

She wasn't sure what Ryan's response meant. He kept any hint of emotion out of his words so they were not reassuring but not alarming either. She threw her empty water bottle in the trash and headed for her nurse's station.

"It's not that I don't appreciate you being here for me, Ryan. I really do. But you could get yourself, me, and the hospital into a lot of trouble if you keep giving medical advice to patients."

He opened his mouth to speak but then frowned and yanked his phone off his belt. He walked her back to her station.

"Yeah, Jake? Same ones?" He rubbed his chin, studying her.

Another tremor stole up her spine. Ryan was trying to keep his expression neutral, but she could tell he was worried by the way a small crease appeared between his brows and his eyes slightly tightened.

Hell. She'd hoped that after Ryan and Darien and the others had kept those men away the night before, that would be the last of it. That today they were being way over-cautious. And that tomorrow she wouldn't need Ryan or anyone else staying in the exam room with her.

"All right, Jake. Tom will watch over her. Be right there." Ryan raised a brow at her. "Same rules as before. No seeing any humans. Tom will stay with you this time. Christian is going to watch the waiting room. Mervin's got the back door. I'll see you tonight."

"You're going to try and track them down?" She hated how worried she sounded.

"It's what I do, Carol. I'm a damn good PI." He motioned to Tom, who was already headed down the hall toward them. "Did your brother call you?"

Tom joined them and stood near Carol in guard stance. "Yeah. Jake said for me to stay with her."

"She's only to see special patients."

She rolled her eyes at him, perturbed that he didn't think she could handle this.

Ryan half hid a smile. "Is Christian in place?"

"Yeah, he hurried over here and is sitting in the waiting room, pretending to be a patient, but he wanted to be the one in the room with Carol instead."

Ryan shook his head. "He can want all he likes, but Carol needs one of *us* to watch over her."

The unspoken words were that she needed an alpha for protection. And Mervin and Christian were definitely not alphas.

"I agree," Tom said. "Ready to get your next patient, Carol?"

Ryan hesitated to leave. Did he think Tom couldn't handle it?

"I'll be all right." Carol shoved her hand in her pocket and ran her fingers over the syringe.

To her shock, Ryan stepped close to her, his gaze remaining on hers as he slipped his hand in her pocket, sliding his fingers over the inner-pocket fabric covering her thigh in a much too sensuous caress before he pulled out the syringe.

Tom's eyes grew even bigger when he saw the syringe. "What's that for?"

"A weapon," Ryan said. He handed it back to her. "You won't need it, but if it makes you feel safer...keep it with you. I'll be back." Then he stalked off down the hall.

All of a sudden, she didn't feel so safe. Sure, Tom was an alpha, but Ryan was truly someone to be reckoned with if anyone got on his bad side. Hell, she had been afraid he might have given Robert Grayce a stroke, and here the poor guy had torn tendons from a bad fall at the river. She thought Robert might have even asked her out if Ryan hadn't been hovering over him until Doc came to examine the man's leg. But she felt incredibly safe when Ryan was with her.

Now, she felt apprehensive again, and while she thought Ryan might be more successful than someone else trying to hunt the men down because of his PI and former police training, she still wished he hadn't gone.

"You okay, Carol? Want to go home?" Tom asked, concern etched in his expression.

"No, I can't leave the others to work here alone. I'll be fine." She patted his chest. "I have you." And the hypodermic with the tranquilizer cocktail in her pocket.

Ryan was torn between wanting to stay and protect Carol and locating the bastards who had taken her from her shower. He hated that she felt she still wasn't safe, so much so that she had to keep a weapon—syringe, nurse style—with her for protection. On the other hand, he admired her for having the foresight to protect herself, and he knew she had the fortitude to carry out her plan, as long as a would-be kidnapper didn't get the upper hand.

If he could catch them, he'd make sure they'd never mess with Carol again—or Lelandi either, if they had a mind to go after her next. He met Jake and Darien, their expressions hard and determined, near the woods where the reds had taken off.

"None of us can shift this close to town," Ryan said.

Darien raised his brows at him.

Jake shook his head.

Well, hell, Ryan was used to being a leader and not used to giving up command, even in another wolf's territory, at least not in a case like this where it was a dangerous situation. Darien motioned for them to get a move on. "We've got several coming to aid in the search."

"We…you want us to split up?" Ryan asked, trying to be more amenable and not so much in charge, even if it killed him.

"Ryan, you're good at tracking. Probably better than most of my people. Sam and I will team up. Jake will go with you. Just watch out if they're shooting bullets again."

Appreciating Darien's comments, Ryan nodded and headed out while Jake ran to catch up to him.

Trudging alongside Ryan, Jake shook his head. "I never

in a millennium would have thought Darien would say that about you. But you know, I think he's kind of taken a liking to you. So do you believe in Carol's sixth sense now?"

Ryan bent down to check out a broken branch and then headed west. "She had a premonition about being taken."

"Hell," Jake said.

"I wonder if she thought she had the vision earlier, but she really had nightmares about it after the fact when she was still half doped up." Not that Ryan didn't believe her, but in his business, he always looked at all possible sides of an issue.

Yet that didn't explain what she'd been thinking of when she was sitting in his truck with a faraway look, like she was not really there. Just like when he'd be deeply contemplating a case and Rosalind would interrupt his meditation with a question. He suspected Carol was telling the truth, that she'd had a vision and that she truly had other psychic abilities.

"Keep thinking she doesn't have psychic connections, and I'll have to mate her," Jake said.

Ryan glanced at him. He looked damn serious. "Then why the hell don't you?"

"Annoyingly, she's got a thing for you."

Ryan almost smiled.

"In this premonition of hers… She didn't tell you that someone might steal her away?"

Glancing up from a footprint, Ryan gave him a look of exasperation. "Are you going to help me search for these guys or just talk your fool head off?"

"Did she?"

"No. She said her visions are too vague. That she didn't know what this one meant."

"Trouble. Every time she's had a vision, it's been trouble." Jake sniffed the air. "This way."

"Always?"

"Since I've known her, yeah. So she'll always be a handful, I suspect."

Which supported Ryan's opinion that Carol needed someone uniquely qualified in her life. Someone who could deal with the dangerous situations she found herself in. She wasn't a police officer or trained in military tactics. Yet if she envisioned a crime being committed and she tried to stop it, or if the perp learned she knew about his or her commission of a crime, she could put herself in a world of jeopardy. Beyond that, she needed to learn how to control shifting. From what she had admitted to him, she needed someone to help her through the transition.

Ryan paused to examine scattered leaves. "They ran through here." He quickened his pace. "She needs an alpha, Jake." But not just any alpha.

"Yeah, I know. So that means you, me, or Tom, unless we let her go to another pack."

"But Tom thinks he'll find his dream mate."

"Yeah, and who the hell told Carol that?" Jake frowned at Ryan, in protective brother mode.

Ryan hid a scowl. "She needed to know the truth. She was harboring some notion that Tom might be interested in her."

"Oh."

Ryan glanced at Jake. "And you too."

"But she practically melted in your arms during the dance. And the way she kissed you…" Jake shook his head. "Guess that means I'll have to call you out."

"Call me out?"

"Yeah, see who wins the little lady."

Ryan chuckled under his breath. "I'm sure she'd love that. Probably decide to mate with Mervin instead and give the rest of us up."

"About what you said to Nurse Matthew. Do you really think he was in trouble in his previous pack?" Jake asked.

Ryan smiled a little. "Only as far as he fought with his pack leader's brother over a woman a number of times. That didn't set well with either the pack leader or his second-in-command."

Jake looked surprised.

"I investigated everyone—those in your pack and those who were joining—just as a courtesy to Darien in the event anything was important."

"Did you tell Darien?"

"No need to. The woman chose Matthew's competition. He came here to lick his wounds. Figure that's why he hadn't hit on Carol yet. Probably still feels something for the woman who didn't choose him."

"But you made it sound like he had something to hide."

Ryan sniffed the air. "His own failure." He suddenly stopped and pointed at the path the three reds had taken this time. "There. This way."

"Darien said to take them any way we had to. If they fight us, so be it."

Ryan nodded. If he'd gotten hold of the man who'd stolen Carol away before, the man would have been dead—no argument.

He and Jake quickly stripped off their clothes and shifted. The showdown would be between two grays and three reds, if Ryan had any say about it. Then he bolted through the woods in hot pursuit as Jake skirted around the trees a few yards away.

At least this way, the reds they were hunting would be far away from Carol, and he figured she'd be safe, no matter who was watching over her.

For over an hour, they pursued the reds, who were surprisingly speedy. Expecting their next move, the three separated, and Jake chased one while Ryan targeted another. Even if they took only two of them to task, it would show the grays' strength and possibly stop the reds from trying anything further.

That was when Ryan discovered a campsite, tents, a smoldering fire, and tuna cans and cracker wrappers littering the ground. What caught his eye next was that the man he'd been chasing was no longer running as a wolf. Half-dressed in a pair of jeans, hairy chest naked, boots unlaced, his face covered in a scruffy red beard and amber eyes narrowed, he pointed a gun at Ryan while he hovered near a pickup, his getaway vehicle.

Shit. Split-second decision time: lunge at the armed man, or make a hasty turn, try to avoid getting shot in the back of the head, and run in the direction of Silver Town. Tucking tail was not Ryan's way.

Before he could leap, he heard the sound of gunfire. The bullet ricocheted off a tree and grazed Ryan's left foreleg before he reached the bastard. Panicked, the guy fired again twice without aiming. And Ryan darted behind a Douglas fir.

The bullets struck the tree next to him with a *whap...* *whap*! When Ryan came around the tree to take the man down, the red dove into the pickup, slammed the door, charged up the engine, and tore off with the truck leaving a trail of dust in its wake.

Hell. Ryan's foreleg burned even though the bullet wound was superficial, as far as he could tell. He licked the injury, knowing that his wolf saliva could reduce some kinds of bacterial infection and that studies had shown that it could actually aid cell regeneration because of saliva's epidermal growth factors.

He howled for Jake, letting him know he had lost his prey and was headed in, but then Ryan caught the whiff of the other man who'd split off from the three and took off after him. Taking care of the flesh wound could wait.

Jake howled to Ryan in response. A chorus of other wolves let him know where they were and that they'd gotten the message. If the reds weren't already scared shitless, the sound of all the grays in the woods probably would do the trick.

Unable to keep up the faster pace he'd used getting there, Ryan finally slowed to a trot for a good long while, his leg bleeding some and the wound still burning, while searching for clues of the third man.

Jake soon joined him, sniffed his foreleg, and trotted beside him. Ryan couldn't help but envy Darien and his two brothers. Ryan's sister meant everything in the world to him, but having someone who acted like a brother to watch his back when they were on the warpath was a unique experience. And welcome.

From the looks of it, Jake must have lost his prey also.

While Ryan continued to look for clues of the other man, Jake seemed more concerned about Ryan's health, glancing back in the direction of the hospital, circling as though he wanted to return. Maybe because Ryan kept limping, although he was trying hard not to. Unable to locate the red, Ryan finally gave up and motioned with his head toward town. Looking relieved, Jake dipped his head once in agreement. The two took off for their stash of clothes.

When they reached them and then shifted, Ryan fumbled with his shirt. Jake looked like he was about to offer to help him, but Ryan finally managed. "What happened to your guy?"

"You were wounded."

"Hell, Jake, I would have been fine. You lost him, didn't you?"

"Carol wouldn't have forgiven me if I'd left you to your injuries and you died. I didn't know if your wound was superficial or something more serious."

Ryan shook his head. "I didn't say I was wounded when I let everyone know what I was going to do."

"Gunshots had been fired in the vicinity from which you howled. You said you had lost your prey and were headed in. Not that you were helping me search for the one I was after or the other, but returning to where we'd left our clothes. Which meant you were wounded. Except I didn't think you'd be trying to track down the third guy anyway."

Struggling with his belt, Ryan smiled a little. "You'd make a good detective."

"Just an observation of your nature," Jake said matter-of-factly, although the way his mouth lifted slightly at the corners, he looked like he appreciated the comment. "Still, you shouldn't have gone after the other guy." He yanked on his shirt. "Being a wounded hero always impresses a lady. Why didn't I think of that first?"

"You'd take a bullet just to make points with Carol? I doubt she'd be overjoyed with the prospect." Ryan snorted. "Besides, a hero solves the crime and saves the damsel in distress. I just managed to get myself shot. Where are the heroics in that?"

"It's the thought that counts."

Not feeling the least bit heroic, Ryan shook his head. "Besides, I don't need looking after. It's just a graze."

"Which means?"

"They're not trying to kill us." Shooting a tree hadn't been the red's plan, Ryan didn't think. "But if they keep trying to take Carol…" Ryan lifted his good shoulder with a slight shrug. "I won't be responsible for my actions."

"You and me both," Jake growled. "Darien or Tom either, believe me."

———————

After some of the more alpha men had left the hospital to chase after North's men, North attempted to sneak in as a patient to see Carol. He knew for a fact that Lelandi wasn't there, so she wouldn't be on the premises to ID him. For a few minutes, he'd be alone with Carol in an exam room before Doc Weber, who also could identify him, showed up. North patted the hypodermic in his pocket, this time with a much lower tranquilizer dose so that he could sneak Carol out the window. She'd still be on her feet but drowsy and unable to fight him.

His clammy hands planted in his windbreaker pockets, he tried to look calm instead of on edge as he waited his turn for the nurse to call him. Thankfully, the woman at the desk didn't seem to think anything of the fact that he specifically had asked for Carol. While he studied a magazine, feigning interest in an article, his focus remained on the receptionist. He was listening to her phone conversations to make sure she didn't alert anyone about him.

He figured one of the men sitting in the waiting area was here to guard Carol. Other than him, an elderly balding man in a running suit, two women, one with a small boy, all human, were waiting to be called. North was a walk-in, but the women were, too, so he fit right in.

His hair unruly, the younger man turned his gaze in the direction of the hall, never once looking at North. *Idiot.* If he was a guard, he sure would be easy to slip by. The man didn't seem sick and was definitely a gray. He'd been here before the woman and her little boy arrived, and still he sat without being called.

The nurse motioned for the elderly man. "Mr. Howard?" The man got up stiffly, grumbled about moving to Florida and the warmer temperatures, and followed the nurse down the hall.

The guard had been here before the old guy too. North knew because he'd been watching the place for a good two hours from across the street, away from where his men had been stationed. His men's ploy had worked, drawing the alphas to chase after them. Hopefully, none of them would get caught, and he'd be successful in his mission this time. Even though they'd grumbled about him taking the inside job. They could grouse all they wanted. Carol would be his.

He swallowed hard. Damn, his throat was raw. A tickle started low in his throat, and without being able to quell it, he coughed. Which led to another hacking spell. Hell, he didn't need to fake being sick, and he figured he was destined for his cousin's fate soon. Then Carol came down the hall, this time dressed in cat scrubs, her blond hair bouncing with her step, the memory of her naked in his arms making him hard all over again. He'd almost had her. No way would any of his men have the chance to convince her they suited her better.

"Mr. Graylink?" Carol called out.

North concealed a sinister smile.

CHAPTER 17

THE GUARD IN THE HOSPITAL WAITING AREA WAS EYEING Carol until she mentioned North's made-up name. That was when he looked over at North and seemed to realize that North might be someone to watch. But the guard didn't make a move to do anything, and Carol smiled as North stood and walked in her direction, coughing for effect, although the urge to do so was there anyway.

"How are we doing, Mr. Graylink?" she asked, walking with him toward the weighing station.

"Been sick. Running a fever. Coughing. All stuffed up." He hated to admit any of it. As a wolf, usually he just shifted. If it was a human viral condition, his wolf side would knock it out, since the flu was nontransferable. Same thing if he had a canine bout of flu. But this time, it was different. His cousin was the proof of that.

North nearly had a heart seizure when he saw Darien's youngest brother, Tom, watching Carol from the station. Not good. He didn't realize Tom was here. The alpha male was eyeing him with suspicion. North was too short to be a gray and wearing the hunter's spray, so Tom couldn't smell that he was a wolf. North had been afraid that if he didn't use a gray name, he might not get in to see Carol, since she was newly turned. Now he was afraid that hiding his scent would create the same problem.

Tom drew closer, took a deep breath, analyzing the air, and held up his hand. "Carol, you have another patient waiting for you."

North coughed again, only this time, he couldn't help it. The damned tickling in his throat wouldn't stop, yet it was so sore he was ready to rip it out. He cursed Connor for hiring the bioengineer and the man himself for what he had done to their renegade pack.

"Just this once, Tom." She smiled at North. "You don't mind if Tom Silver stays in the exam room with us, do you?" She shrugged. "Stalker boyfriend. Have to have a bodyguard around the clock until they catch him."

North smiled, hoping his expression didn't look too evil. Stalker boyfriend. That was about right. But then he looked serious and nodded, even though this was not what he'd had in mind. An exam room alone with Carol, that was what he'd planned for. He figured he didn't have much of a choice. Hell. He'd have to knock out Tom and then grab Carol. Hopefully, they wouldn't make too much of a ruckus and he'd manage to pull this off.

Tom shook his head. "Darien said only special cases."

"Special" as in *lupus garou* only because she didn't have her shifting under control, North assumed.

"Matthew is seeing a patient," Carol said, sounding exasperated. "I'll only be with Mr. Graylink a moment. You'll be with me. Then Doc will see to him."

"No, Carol. Darien would have my head on this." He said to North, "Sorry. Please take a seat again in the waiting area. Matthew will be with you in a minute."

North cleared his phlegm-filled throat. "Probably nothing the doc can do but order me to get bed rest. Unless I have a sinus infection. Might as well go home."

"What are your symptoms?" Carol asked. He loved the caring way she spoke to him.

"Carol," Tom said, exasperated.

"If he has a sinus infection, he needs to be on antibiotics," she said firmly.

"And Matthew can take care of it." Tom wouldn't back down, but neither would Carol.

North waited, sweat beading on his forehead.

Carol's gaze shifted, her brows furrowing. "Have you had a fever?"

"One hundred and one," North lied. He'd had a fever, but it was low grade and had vanished by the previous morning. "But that was last night. I didn't have one this morning. And my teeth have been aching, headache, earache." Which was true.

"Come over here, and I'll get your blood pressure and temperature."

Tom folded his arms and glowered at North. In response, North attempted to look demurely sick and unthreatening. Despite feeling lousy, he could still manage a good fight.

"No fever," Carol said reassuringly. "Come with me, and you can wait in the exam room for Doc."

Tom gave her a look like he could throttle her. She ignored him. North hid a smile.

When they entered the room, she motioned for him to sit in a chair and held up a chart, waiting to question him about his symptoms. Tom watched him like a predator would, and North wasn't sure he could overcome Tom and Carol before the alarm was shouted.

Hell, he was here, and it was his show. Without further hesitation and with a well-aimed swing, he hit Tom with a hard-knuckle fist in the cheek. Tom stumbled back, crashed into the exam table, and swore.

Carol screamed, and North knew he had no chance to take her now. Still, he jerked a syringe out of his coat pocket, but to his amazement, she pulled one from her scrubs pocket too. For a moment, they stared at each other, hypodermics readied like two swordsmen in battle. He smiled. The woman was worth having.

Then he dodged out of the room, shoved aside the nurse headed for the room, tore down the hall past a startled Dr. Weber, and dove through the back door before a guy in a red-and-white-striped jacket could even get up from his chair. *Beta wolf.*

"Are you all right, Tom?" Carol asked, touching his shoulder and feeling horrible about the whole affair.

He tossed her an angry look.

"I'll…get an ice pack."

When she returned to the exam room, Doc was shaking his head.

Appearing sheepish, Christian, who had abandoned his guard post in the waiting area too late to have been of any service, and Mervin stood in the doorway watching them and not saying a word, probably thinking that Darien was going to be pissed at the lot of them for letting one of the reds get so close to Carol and then letting him get away.

Tom glowered at her. "He wasn't human."

"I know that now," Carol said, annoyed but also regretful.

Doc cleared his throat. "That was North, a red from my old pack. Must have been wearing hunter's scent. I didn't smell him as he raced by me. Where the hell is Ryan? I thought he was supposed to be watching you." The inference was that he wouldn't have let anyone near Carol like Tom and the rest had.

She felt bad too. If she hadn't insisted on seeing to the patient, wanting to prove that she could still see humans without any threat of shifting so that they would allow her to be a nurse like she should be, Tom wouldn't have been hurt and in trouble with his eldest brother. Jake would be just as annoyed with him, she figured. And Ryan also.

Matthew poked his head in. "Got a case where the boy probably needs to be referred to an orthopedic surgeon in Denver, Doc."

Doc gave Carol a hard look that reminded her she was one of the pack and had to obey rules. "I'll see to him," he said to Matthew.

Tom took charge of the guards. "Mervin, return to your post. Christian, stay outside the exam room until Carol leaves for the day."

Feeling like a *lupus garou* failure, Carol worked for three more hours, seeing to one sick patient after another, but she couldn't help worrying about Ryan and about Tom—knowing she'd caused trouble for him.

After finishing with another gray female who had the flu, she thought again about Ryan. Even though she didn't want him getting himself or anyone on the staff in trouble by offering medical advice, she missed his antidotes, all given in the spirit of wanting to help others in need.

She realized then that he was similar to her in wanting to help others. As a PI looking into missing persons or wayward spouses or insurance fraud. As the mayor, trying to provide his people with a better way of life.

She glanced out the window between patients as Christian sat outside her exam room and served as a guard, while inside the room, Tom watched her. He'd finally given up scowling at her and was resigned to his fate, but she hated seeing where the red had struck him, a reminder to her that not everyone could be trusted, sick or not.

"Ryan will be all right," Tom finally said.

At the moment, she was worried about how Ryan, Darien, and Jake would react when they learned North had tried to take her again, this time from the hospital, and Tom had gotten clobbered for it.

"Ryan's been shot three times—an unhappy husband caught in an adulterous affair, one fire insurance fraud case, and a robbery attempt at the bank next door to his PI business. He always comes out on top," Tom continued.

Carol closed her gaping mouth. "How—"

"Darien checked up on him. You don't think he hired him to be your bodyguard without seeing if he had the fortitude to do the job, do you?"

"But…if he's been shot that many times, wasn't Darien afraid he wouldn't do the job right?"

"He's had hundreds of cases over the many years he's lived. So proportionately, he's done damn well."

"You don't really seem to like him," she said, although Tom had surprised her this time, sounding less harsh concerning Ryan than before when the two were butting heads.

"I think Jake should be the one for you. Then we'd keep you in the family."

For the first time, Carol saw that he really did act like a protective brother. She smiled. "That's sweet of you. But he's not shown any real interest."

Tom shook his head and winced. "He's coming a little too late to the party, I'm afraid."

Her cell phone rang, and she glanced at the caller ID. Her mother. She'd been so irate every time she and Carol had had a visit recently because someone from the pack always accompanied them. Lelandi, Silva, one of Darien's brothers. Carol imagined her mother was mad about it again, but Carol couldn't tell her why Darien always wanted her chaperoned—that she was a newly turned wolf and might let her "condition" slip.

Now with her having been kidnapped, pack members were watching her to an even greater degree. Hopefully her mother did not want to get together again soon, although she had loved to go shopping with Carol or to share a lunch. But how could she explain to her mother that she was being guarded more than usual again?

"Hello, Mom. What's up?"

"Ryan McKinley called me."

Carol's brain turned to mush. Not in a million years did she think Ryan would call her parents. "He called you? What about?" Her dad was always a real beta in wolf terms, even though he was human like her mother. Her mother definitely wore the pants in the family.

Her mother hesitated to say what McKinley had called her about, and Carol didn't know what to think. "Mom?"

"Did you tell him that I sent you to see that psychiatrist?"

Crap. So was he trying to figure out if she was telling the truth concerning Dr. Metzger's wife's death? Ryan was an investigator, she had to remind herself. It was his business to investigate, and he wouldn't get the truth from Dr. Metzger, not with patient confidentiality issues. But to call her mother...

"What did he ask you, Mom?"

"I didn't tell him anything. I hung up on him. That's what I did. He had no business calling me. He's the one who doesn't believe in your abilities. Isn't that what you said? I have no time for people like that. I don't care if he's interested in dating you. He can't. And that's my final word."

Carol raised her brows. "I *am* twenty-six, Mom."

"*Are* you dating him?"

"Well…"

"Oh, Carol. You can't be serious. Your relationships never work out. You need someone who at least believes in what you can do, like your father and I do."

"I've only had one real relationship. And that was just out of high school." There was a significant pause, and Carol glanced at the patient's record again.

Her mother said, "I want grandkids."

Carol bit her lip and looked back at Tom. He was watching out the exam-room window, but she knew he was mentally taking notes of everything she said to her mother. Speaking to any pack member was acceptable. But talking to a human alone, even when that person happened to be her mother? Wouldn't be allowed. Which was ridiculous. If she made a slip about being a wolf, would anyone believe her? They'd think she was joking.

Well, maybe not, since Carol was psychic and her parents had finally had to embrace the fact. What if she spilled the beans to them? They'd be destined to be just like her. Or terminated. According to Lelandi, anyone who learned that *lupus garous* existed had two choices—become one of them or die.

That seemed cruel, but it was the only way their kind

had survived for a millennium or two. Carol could just imagine what would happen if wolves were found to be real. They'd be treated differently—like outcasts—and most likely examined ruthlessly.

The worst of it? They were virtual fountains of youth, living much longer than their human counterparts. What if humans could manufacture whatever anomaly gave wolves their increased longevity and bottle it? What if everyone wanted to be wolves?

Hmm, that could be a good thing, she supposed. No more hiding what they were.

"Carol? Did you hear me? I want grandkids," her mother repeated over the phone.

Carol took a deep breath. How could she tell her mother that grandkids were out? That they'd be were-kids—and who knew what kind of trouble they could get into? How could she raise little *lupus garous* when she hadn't grown up as one and was still fumbling around with her own identity?

"Mom, I'm working at the hospital and need to go."

"You do plan to have children, don't you? You're the only daughter we have left now."

The guilt trip again. "I need a guy in my life first."

"I shouldn't have hung up on Ryan, should I have?" Her mother sounded really sorry for what she'd done.

Carol smiled. "Probably served him right. Got to go. Talk to you later."

"Next time you visit, bring Ryan along. I haven't met him, and I want to make sure he's all right for you. That is if you're hell-bent on dating him. I'll give him a talking-to about your uniqueness."

Uniqueness. Even now, her mother couldn't bring herself to say Carol had psychic abilities. "He lives in Green Valley."

"I know, I know. He told me. Just bring him by sometime. Soon."

"All right. Bye, Mom."

"Ask him if he wants kids. It's important to discuss such things with a guy you're interested in."

"All right, if I get interested."

"He's interested, Carol, or he wouldn't have called me."

Her mom might not have psychic connections, but she was fairly intuitive when it came to understanding people. Still, Carol figured Ryan had only had one thing on his mind when he called her mother.

"You don't think he was just going to ask if I truly had a vision about the doctor's wife?"

"Of course he was. That's what made me mad. He shouldn't have to ask. But he wouldn't have bothered calling me if he wasn't intrigued with you. And I loved his sexy voice."

Even though her mother didn't like that Darien had moved Carol into his home or that he or his brothers or Lelandi were always watching her, her mother loved Darien and his brothers' sexy voices also. There was something about alpha males' voices that made everyone take notice.

Call waiting warned Carol that she had someone else on the line. "I have another incoming call, Mom. We'll have to talk later."

"All right, dear. Goodbye."

"Bye, Mom. Thanks for giving me a ring."

Carol hung up and then stared at the caller ID. Rosalind

McKinley? Was she Ryan's sister? It seemed to Carol as though she truly was dating Ryan, the way everyone was calling her about him. At least, that was what she suspected his sister wanted to talk to her about, since Carol had never met Rosalind…or spoken with her before. The day just got weirder and weirder.

"Hello, this is Carol Wood. How may I help you?"

"Hi, Carol, this is Rosalind McKinley, Ryan's sister. I wonder if Ryan has told you how much he wants you."

Carol glanced at Tom, who was trying to listen to her conversation. He set the ice pack down on the counter and folded his arms, his look annoyed. He didn't budge from the room.

"What makes you think that?" Carol asked Rosalind. She already liked the woman for having the gumption to call her. But she wondered if Ryan's sister really knew what she was talking about or just *thought* she knew her brother that well.

"Oh, Carol. I can call you Carol, can't I?"

"Sure."

"Well, Ryan hasn't been able to think of anything since he met you five months ago. It was Carol this and Carol that, and dark brooding looks, chopping wood, pacing back and forth, wearing out our carpeting, impossibly distracted whenever I tried to talk with him."

"He said nice things about me then?" Carol felt a warm glow.

"Oh, no…not at all."

That hit Carol like she'd just been sprayed with a cold shower, dousing the warm, fuzzy feeling at once. "No? What then?"

"My brother was obsessed with you. Still is. Mate the poor fool and put him out of his misery. I can't wait to meet you. No other woman has had this kind of effect on him. It's wonderful."

"But what did he say exactly to you about me?"

"He had taken tons of pictures of you. He keeps them in the top of the folder, and despite the case being closed, he keeps the file out for handy reference. Not to study the case but to get another look at you. You know what that means, don't you?"

"Not exactly." Carol noted that Rosalind did not exactly say what Ryan had told her about Carol either.

"He's in love. I've never seen him fall so hard for a woman. But I was worried he might not get the message across to you, so I thought I'd better call and let you know how he feels. Just in case."

"Um, thanks." *I think.* Carol could just imagine telling Ryan that she understood he loved her and was thrilled he felt that way. He'd look at her like she'd lost her mind.

"Don't thank me! I'm getting a sister!"

Her comment made Carol smile.

A commotion ensued in the lobby, garnering Carol's attention, and Tom moved into the hall to check it out. "We'll have to have this conversation later, Rosalind. Thanks so much for calling me."

"Can we have lunch soon?"

Carol already really liked Rosalind, her friendliness, enthusiasm, camaraderie. She seemed like someone who'd be in Carol's court if she needed her. "Lunch sounds great."

"Hell, I'm fine, damn it," Ryan growled in the waiting area down the hall.

Carol furrowed her brows and glanced back at the hall, but she was unable to see Ryan. The thrill of seeing him back without a scratch was tempered by worry that he'd be angry with Tom…or her…for letting North into the exam room with her.

Jake said in a scolding tone, "Don't tell me you're one of those people who is a horrible patient. If you won't go peaceably, I'll have to send you to Matthew to check you out instead of Carol. And you definitely won't make brownie points there. Guaranteed. Your choice."

Her heart tripping, Carol looked at Tom.

He gave her a wry smile. "Guess that makes four times. Unless he was wounded in some other fashion."

"Is that my brother growling about something?" Rosalind asked.

"It's him. But I'm not sure what about. I've got to go. Trouble at the hospital." *Concerning your brother*, but Carol wasn't about to tell his sister that in the event it wasn't anything. "I'll call you later."

"Look forward to it." They disconnected.

Her blood running cold, Carol shoved the next patient record into the holder. If Ryan had been shot because he was trying to protect her, she didn't want to even think about it.

She hurried in the direction of the waiting room.

CHAPTER 18

WHEN CAROL SAW RYAN'S SHIRTSLEEVE BLOODIED, SHE frowned and quickened her pace toward the hospital waiting area. "Let's get you into an exam room."

"I'm fine. It's just a graze, for Chr—"

She gave him a look to curb his tongue. He noted the two small girls in the waiting area and snorted. Then he wordlessly went with her down the hall as she held his arm, his whole body tensing. Touching him made her feel so much more secure. Although she was afraid that once he saw Tom and the goose egg he was sporting, Ryan would be more than furious with the both of them.

"What happened?" she asked.

"I was chasing one of the reds as a wolf, and when I located him, he shifted and held a gun on me."

They approached the exam room as Jake followed behind. "And then he fired a shot at you?"

"A couple, but he missed all three times, dove into his pickup, and vamoosed."

"Missed all three times?" She touched the sleeve of his shirt, blood spotting the blue and white print.

"He got lucky. One ricocheted off a tree, or he would never have hit me."

She frowned at him. "You went after him even when you learned he had a gun, didn't you?" Not surprising, but she didn't like that he took such risks either. "You shouldn't have."

Ryan gave her a hard scowl back, his hands clenched into fists. She felt his muscle tighten beneath her fingertips. "By lunging at him, I threw him off guard. If I hadn't, he could have fired several steady shots at my retreating backside."

"I hope you didn't continue to chase him," she scolded.

"While he was driving a pickup? Not likely."

"I would have thought you might continue to look for clues of the other guys. At least you came straight away here to be treated."

He didn't say anything.

She looked back at Jake. "You did come straight here, right?"

Jake shook his head.

Ryan said, "If Jake hadn't insisted, I wouldn't be here to be examined by you or Doc. I have a job to do, and being a patient is not on the schedule."

"Were you this bad the other times?"

His expression puzzled, he frowned at her. "What do you mean?"

"When you were shot the three other times. Did you behave as unruly as a patient before?"

"I was unconscious for two of them."

Shocked, she parted her lips.

That was when Ryan noticed Tom in the exam room and his swollen, red cheek. "Hell, what happened?"

"North tried to take her. My fault." Tom looked guiltily at Jake.

Jake cursed under his breath and motioned to the break room. "Tell me what happened."

Silence stretched between Ryan and Carol. She figured he was mad at her already, not even knowing what had happened. She led him into the exam room and shut the door. He still didn't say anything, which made her more self-conscious than before. "It was all my fault," she finally admitted. "Not Tom's. He insisted Matthew see to the patient. But the man was truly sick."

"He was a red," Ryan growled.

"Yes, but we couldn't smell him. For that reason, Tom wasn't going to let him see me, thinking he was human." She guided Ryan across the room and held onto his good arm to help him up on the exam table. Once he was settled, she released him, but she remained standing next to him.

"Hell, Carol. If you couldn't smell he was a red or a gray, Matthew *should* have seen him."

"I know. I know. It was my fault," she reiterated. "I...I just wanted to prove that I could continue to see patients, human or *lupus garou*, without getting anyone in any trouble."

Ryan didn't say anything for a moment, as if he was really considering why this was so important to her.

"He got away." Ryan sounded resigned and a little weary as he tucked a curl of hair behind her ear. "A guy could get used to a woman fawning over him."

The way he'd been acting so reluctant to be examined, she expected him to keep up the resistance. This business with North and the way he'd dropped the subject... Well, the change in his attitude totally threw her. Maybe in front of Tom and Jake or anyone like Christian who was within earshot, Ryan felt he had to put on a show. Mostly, she was glad he wasn't angry with her about her seeing North and putting both Tom and herself at risk.

"I'll be more careful next time," she said softly, hating to acquiesce but not willing to get anyone hurt on account of her being so stubborn.

She pressed against his knees to unbutton his shirt, but he spread his thighs, pulled her between his legs, and lifted a brow. "Easier to get to the buttons." He looked like he was attempting to contain a smile. Devilish, desirous, rakish.

She tried to be professional about this while his legs caged her in, his inner thighs touching her flesh, heating her skin through her scrubs, making her nipples tingle. She should have pushed away, moved to the side of him, but she didn't imagine standing next to his thigh on the outside would feel any less...erotic.

All at once, she was reminded of the way he'd touched her earlier that morning in the canopied bed, the way his hands and mouth and body had teased her into submission. Left her body flaming with desire. Even now with their close proximity, the way his hard inner thighs touched her, his face leaning closer to hers, she was growing wet with need.

Her mind warred with her heart. She wanted to lift her chin and kiss his lips, to wrap her arms around his waist, to hold him close and know he was safe. But Doc would be coming soon.

She meant to reach up and unbutton Ryan's shirt and take care of him like a nurse was supposed to, but his hand cupped her chin, and his mouth lowered to hers. A quick kiss, she thought. A really...quick...kiss.

As soon as she tilted her lips up to meet his, as soon as she closed her eyes to savor the really quick kiss, she was lost. Lost in the way his hands held her hips, keeping her from bolting, lost in the way his alluring mouth firmly pressed against hers, increasing the pressure and gliding over hers, his mouth coaxing hers open. Creating an intimate path between them.

She moaned and swore he echoed her sentiment, his hands drawing lower and over her buttocks, pulling her against his groin. Despite being wounded, he was hard and wanting all over again. Somehow in her lust-filled thoughts, she heard someone coming as Ryan's tongue tangled with hers. She paused, momentarily still, rashly wanting to carry on with reckless abandon but knowing she couldn't.

Ryan released her with a curse under his breath, maybe at himself for losing control, maybe at whoever was headed their way. Maybe at her for getting him all stirred up again.

As quickly as she could manage, she unfastened his buttons, feeling aroused and needy and desperate to finish what they'd started. Then she gently tugged the shirt off his shoulders, her hands brushing against his heated skin. She glanced up at him, hoping he was ignoring her. But he wasn't. His gaze still smoldered with lusty fascination. She cleared her throat and slid the shirt down his arms, trying not to hurt his injured arm.

He sucked in his breath. "Somehow, I don't see the nurse removing the patient's clothes on a regular basis unless the guy's half-dead."

Her face flushed when it shouldn't have, but she wasn't going to let him stop her from doing her job. "You're wounded, Ryan McKinley. It would be too difficult for you to unbutton your shirt with one hand. What am I supposed to do? Watch you struggle in pain? Besides I'm *not* taking off your trousers."

He chuckled wolfishly. Hell, the way they'd been going, she might have done just that!

"What is transpiring between us is strictly business." At least that had been the plan before he pulled her between his legs and began kissing her.

Whoever was walking toward the room had already passed by, and Carol took a relieved breath. Attempting to ignore the way Ryan heated her to the core and to do her duty as a trained nurse, she wiped away the blood on his arm, glad to see that the bullet had only grazed him like he'd said. Given wolves' advanced healing capabilities, the wound should heal sufficiently by morning.

Ryan took hold of her free hand and looked into her eyes as if he was ready to analyze her every reaction.

"Did you see any visions of this or of anything else?" he asked.

Unsure whether he still didn't believe her, she sighed. "No. If I had, I would have warned you." She pulled away from him and cleansed the wound. She thought of Rosalind's call to her, but before that, her mother's and planned to ask him about both.

"By the way, why did you call my mother?"

Ryan didn't look in the least bit sheepish, which surprised her. "I called to see if she believed you had psychic abilities after she had sent you to that damned psychiatrist."

"And if she didn't believe in my talents?"

"I'd tell her what a marvel you are."

She stared at him, her lips parted. "Seriously?"

"Seriously. Only she hung up on me, which didn't bode well."

"What difference does it make if she believes me or not?"

He rested his hands on her hips and pulled her close to his body. "Because we're dating. Remember?"

She gave him a ladylike snort. "Right." Yet it gave her hope he truly did believe her, and her whole spirit lifted.

Before she could ruin the feeling and ask him what he'd said to his sister about her that was not complimentary, Doc Weber opened the door. The doctor raised his brows to see Ryan on the exam table and Carol standing between his legs, ministering to him. She was grateful Doc hadn't seen them kissing earlier.

She noticed how tired Doc looked, with dark circles under his eyes and his shoulders stooped. He was a red from Lelandi's former pack, here to doctor the patients until they could find a gray. But he planned to stay until Lelandi had her babies. He'd taken Carol under his wing because she was a nurse, newly turned, and a red like him.

Because she'd been turned by one of his former pack, Doc considered Carol like one of his family. Since he'd never had a mate and no offspring, she and Lelandi were like the daughters he'd never had. That meant he kept giving them fatherly lectures. Since Lelandi was mated, though, she didn't receive as many as Carol did.

Carol moved a respectable distance from Ryan while Doc examined his wound. "I thought you were posted here as her bodyguard. What happened?" His tone was accusatory. What good would Ryan be if he didn't stay and watch over her?

"Tom was keeping an eye on her while I took off after the men. By the looks of it, I should have stayed. They're intent on shooting anyone who tries to stop their mission, but they don't have the nerve to fight wolf to wolf. You probably know them. Three reds from Lelandi's and your former pack?"

The doc peered closely at the wound and shook his

head. "The men who were left behind were decent sorts. None of them would do a thing like this."

Except North? And the others with him had to be from the same pack.

Ryan pursed his lips tight and didn't say anything to Doc, but Carol thought he wanted to. How could the men be "decent sorts" when they had taken Carol from the house like they did? And they had to be from Lelandi's pack. No other red pack lived in the area. And what about this latest clash with North and Tom?

A flash of memory of the shooting she'd witnessed at the hospital the previous fall suddenly swamped her with regret. The doctor had lain dead on the exam-room floor, his nurse just as unresponsive. She wasn't sure what had brought the memory back. The attack on Tom maybe. Or the one on Ryan since he'd been shot, or both. Or the idea that it would happen again and be fatal this time?

Carol turned away quickly as tears filled her eyes, not wanting Doc and Ryan to see her like this—unable to control her emotions. Everyone expected her to be strong, both in the workplace and around family. She was the one who held up through any crisis. When her sister died, she had helped her parents get through it. She had to be resilient when others needed her.

Doc cleared his throat. "Just apply some of that salve and bandage it, and he should be back to doing his job."

"Yes, Dr. Weber." Carol tried to hide the hitch in her voice. She hated when she got emotional on the job.

"Carol," Doc said, his voice soft and consoling.

Unable to look him directly in the eye, she fought to hold back the burning tears. "Yes, Doctor?"

He looked sympathetically at her and then patted her shoulder. "Got another case of the flu to look after." He walked out of the room, his movement slower and stiffer than usual.

She wanted to tell him *he* needed to take care of himself. That he should get more rest, but she knew it would be futile. She wondered, though, what he'd intended to say. That the other doctor and nurse dying hadn't been her fault?

No, it wasn't her mistake, she tried to convince herself. The miner who killed them was the one responsible. But if she'd only raised the alarm somehow before he shot them...

Still, maybe that was why the memory haunted her again. That it had been her fault, just like Tom having been attacked was too. And if the reds hadn't been trying to take her hostage, Ryan wouldn't have been harmed either.

"Carol?" Ryan said, drawing her from her mental self-bashing. He left the exam table and touched her arm. "Are you all right?"

"They died because of me." She pulled away from him and stood in front of a supply drawer, staring at it but not seeing it.

"The former doctor and that nurse?" His voice was gentle, and no matter how badly she felt, his tone was like a mental salve. He ran his hand over her back in a gentle caress.

Carol let out her breath. "Yes."

"I've been there, done that, Carol."

She turned around and stared at him in disbelief.

"Yeah. Only it was my job to protect those who ended up dying. In this case, you were an innocent bystander."

"Not an innocent bystander at all. I knew they'd come to harm. I didn't…" She shook her head. "I didn't save them. Even after they had been shot. I didn't remove the bullets fast enough."

He pulled her into his arms and held her tight. The patient comforting the nurse. It was wrong. Everything about this was wrong. But she couldn't push him away. She needed this. She needed him. The warmth. The security. No pressure. Just concerned friendship. For the moment.

His hand swept down her back, massaging the tension from her stiff spine. "You didn't know what they were, what we were. The injuries they had received were fatal. Even with our healing abilities, they couldn't have been saved. You reacted the way your nurse's training had prepared you. You did the best you could under the circumstances."

She looked up at him through tears and saw his face frowning with concern. "I wish my visions had told me that part of the equation. But they're irritatingly scant and…" She shook her head. "It's a curse I have to bear." Just like having to shift against her will was now. And damn, if she could keep it at bay, she would. She turned, opened the drawer, and retrieved antibiotics and a bandage.

She motioned to the exam table. "Do you want to sit up there?"

"I normally hate anything to do with hospitals," Ryan said, his tone lighthearted, as if he was trying to change the somber mood. He sat on the table and smiled. "I've changed my mind."

She shook her head, trying for professionalism again. "Here I thought you were going to be a difficult patient."

"With you tending to me?"

With as light a touch as she could manage, she dressed his wound with the antibiotic and then wrapped the bandage around his arm. He stiffened, but when she looked up to see if he was hurting, he cast her an elusive smile. "On the scale of one to ten, the pain is nonexistent. Your hands are cold."

She frowned at him and secured the bandage. "I didn't touch you with my cold hands. You don't have to be macho for me. I know it has to hurt." She handed him his shirt.

He pulled it on while she watched, ready to help him if he needed further assistance.

"Do you know why Darien and the others shift in the visions but can't shift back?" he asked, surprising her.

She thought he already believed her. She folded her arms, unable to avoid feeling defensive. "I don't know. That's why it's so frustrating. I thought you believed me now."

"Let's just say I normally don't put much stock in psychic abilities. Not in supernatural entities, ghosts, or any of that stuff."

Just as she suspected. "Then if I told you I've had a ghostly experience, you wouldn't believe me?"

His mouth curved up a hint, his eyes sparkling with amusement. "My aunt Tilda sees them all the time."

"Ahh, and you don't put much stock in your aunt Tilda."

"Quite the contrary. I find her about the most well-grounded of my family."

"Except for the ghostly visits."

He shrugged and winced and then began buttoning his shirt. "She needs lots of attention. I imagine she conjures them up when she's lonely."

Carol leaned in between his legs to fasten a couple of buttons on his shirt. "And me?"

He touched her hair in a loving way. "You've just had the one experience?"

"Three, but who's counting?"

"I do have faith in your abilities, by the way."

She closed her gaping mouth. She had hoped, but…she hadn't realized he thought she'd told the truth. Tears filled her eyes again. "You really do?"

He pulled her close, rubbing her shoulders in a gentle manner. "Yeah, Carol. I really do."

"Thanks." She sighed deeply. "You don't know how much that means to me."

"I imagine I do." He leaned down to kiss her lips, but she pulled away before they got too involved again.

"I've got another patient to see, last one of the day. Another case of the sniffles. Everyone thinks they have the deadly flu when most of the cases are colds or allergies. I'll see to him while you finish dressing."

His expression hardening, Ryan went back to buttoning his shirt and followed her into the hall. "How am I going to guard you if I'm not with you?"

She harrumphed. "And just how did you get that?" She pointed at his bloody sleeve.

"I was trying to protect you *away* from your workplace."

"Admit it. You'd rather chase down the bad guys than play the wait-and-see game."

He smiled darkly.

When she called out the name from the chart and Ryan saw who her next patient was, his dark expression lightened up a lot.

The gray-haired old man shuffled toward Carol and gave her a small smile. "You brighten an old man's day, young'un."

"Hmm, Luciso, you always make my day."

Luciso glanced at Ryan, took in his bloody shirtsleeve, and shook his head. "Is *he* the one everyone's saying is hitting on you?"

"My bodyguard," she corrected.

Luciso snorted. "Looks like this business with the reds is going to get real nasty. You tell Darien if he needs an old guy to help out, I'm ready and willing."

"Thanks, Luciso. I'm sure he'll appreciate the offer." She heard the doc coughing and glanced down the hall. "Are you all right, Dr. Weber?"

"Going home to get some rest, Carol. Pulled an all-nighter."

"Sleep well," she said, but then a sickening feeling washed over her as she envisioned the doctor shifting into the wolf to knock out his illness. She hurried after him, leaving her patient behind in her haste, figuring Ryan would catch up to her. But she had to warn Doc not to shift. He'd think she was crazy, but she just had to warn him.

"Wait, Dr. Weber! I need a word with you!" she said as the door slammed shut.

CHAPTER 19

"HELL, NORTH, ALL YOU DID WAS GET US INTO DEEPER guano by stirring them up at the hospital," Galahad said, pacing across the meadow, at least thirty miles from Silver Town.

"At least I got a shot off at that outsider gray. Once that happened, the majority of them turned around and high-tailed it out of there," Hank said grinning. "We might not be as good in a fight with them wolf to wolf, but they can't argue with bullets."

North shook his head. "If it hadn't been for Darien's brother watching over Carol, I would have had her. The others guarding her were clueless."

"Well," Hank said, "I didn't want to injure the gray that badly. I just want to get Carol. Hell, they've got the damned hospital watched, every entryway inside and outside. No grabbing her there from now on, it looks like."

"Yeah, unless some of them start having the same trouble we're having," Galahad said. "Both Marilee and Becky went in today since they're feeling so poorly. At least they shared the flu at the gathering last night, although they should have arrived earlier to expose more folks. If nothing else, when Darien's people get sick, they'll have to try to find a cure. Damn that Miller anyway. He promised the vaccine he gave us beforehand would keep us from getting sick and be a cure for those who already have the virus."

"I blame Connor for paying the guy to create the virus

in the first place. I wonder if Miller lied to us about staying isolated from the rest of us while he tries to find a vaccine that works this time. Hell, what if he already has one and inoculated only himself against the virus?" North asked. He'd kill the guy.

"What good would it do him if all of us came down with it but him?" Galahad asked.

"Yeah," North reluctantly admitted, shoving his hands in his pockets. "You're right. Unless he figures he'll rescue those of us he wants to when the time is right and leave the rest of us to deal with the condition. As wolves, except for trying to kill him, we wouldn't have any way to resolve this issue. What if Carol ends up having the same problem?" He scowled in the direction of Silver Town.

Galahad threw his hands up in an aggravated posture. "What about Doc? Surely he'll know we weren't trouble-makers and he'll help us out."

"Yeah," Hank agreed with his brother. "He'll probably help us."

"After I took a swing at Tom, I doubt Doc will be very agreeable. He's there because the other doctor died. The town needs a doctor right now. He's not going to leave his responsibilities behind."

Hank cleared his throat. "Not for long, North. But maybe he'd have some ideas. What can it hurt? We can just call him."

"All right. But as soon as we do, he'll know who we all are and who's been trying to grab Carol. Just remember that. His loyalty is to Lelandi and her family, not to us." North brought out his phone and punched in Doc's number.

Mervin jumped up from his chair at the back door of the hospital. He prevented Carol from leaving by blocking the door with his body as she tried to reach Doc Weber before he took off in his car. Luckily, Mervin didn't grab her this time.

She scowled at him. "Let me through, Mervin. I have to speak to Doc."

Ryan joined her and shook his head. "What part of 'I'm to protect you at all times' don't you remember, Carol?"

"Tell him to let me out of the building so I can talk to Doc!"

Ryan opened the door and stepped outside. "His car's gone. He's already headed for home. What did you want to speak with him about?"

"It's personal." She headed back down the hall. "I'll see my last patient and then call Doc."

"What is it about?" Ryan appeared concerned.

"What I envisioned would happen to him. All right? He might not believe me either, but I have to warn him."

"Why now? Why not before?"

She appreciated that Ryan really wanted to know how this early warning system worked. "Because I feel like it's going to come to pass soon. Sometimes I have this impending feeling of doom, and all of a sudden, the scene I've envisioned becomes a reality. That's why."

Trying to hide her frustration, she finished working with her last patient and grabbed the work phone as soon as he left the exam room. When she autodialed Doc's number, all she got was his answering machine. Discouraged, she put the receiver back on the base.

"He looked exhausted," Ryan offered, running his hand over Carol's arm in a consoling way, but she couldn't relax. He rested his hands on her shoulders and considered her glum expression. "He needed to sleep. And that's probably just what he's doing. You do also, after you get a good meal."

She was wired, and no amount of consolation was going to change that. She had to warn Doc. "I want to run by his place before we go home."

Jake and Tom joined them in the waiting room, while Mervin reluctantly went with Christian, who was dropping him off at his place.

"Ready to go?" Jake asked, noting the tension between Ryan and Carol, she thought.

"Carol's worried about Doc," Ryan said, his hand lightly rubbing her back.

"He appeared not to be feeling well. I want to check on him." Carol gave Ryan a look like he'd better not say one word about her warning Doc about shifting. Even though she didn't think Doc would believe her, she had to tell him anyway. Just in case.

"He worked all night. He'll be sleeping. You know how he is," Jake said.

Carol frowned at Jake. "He was coughing."

"He's a doctor. He'll know to take care of himself," Jake countered. "Besides, with our faster wolf healing ability, he'll be fine in no time. And if he has the flu, he can shift and that will take care of it."

Which was precisely what she was afraid would happen!

Carol stalked off for the hospital entrance. She continued to be plagued by the overwhelming fear that Doc could be in trouble. "In your PI business, you get hunches, don't you, Ryan?"

"Sure."

Jake and Tom followed behind, and she knew they were listening to her conversation, even though she kept her voice low for Ryan's hearing and not for anyone else's. But their hearing was too darned good. And when she was upset, they took notice. Probably figured she might all of a sudden shift into a wolf.

She slowed her walk. Hell, what if being highly distressed, more than the physical manhandling she'd had to endure when Mervin roughly grabbed her, *could* trigger the change? She took an unsteady breath and said to Ryan, "Think of my premonitions as a hunch."

"Carol."

"I'm serious."

They exited the building, and Tom and Jake paused to see Carol safely to Ryan's truck. She climbed inside and folded her arms, not about to be stopped from completing her mission.

"Drive me to Doc's place. It'll only take a moment. I've got a key to his house because I care for his houseplants when he visits Lelandi's old pack on occasion."

"Carol."

"I'll only use it to make sure he's okay."

In a humorous way, Ryan arched a brow. "What if he's got a girlfriend over?"

Carol rolled her eyes.

He smiled. "Never know. Can never judge a person's sex life by their age."

"Well, he won't." Although she wished he had, but as haggard as Doc had looked, she was sure he'd be alone.

Ryan started the engine. "All right, give me directions."

She breathed a sigh of relief, although she wasn't sure she was going to make any headway with Doc. He'd never said one way or another if he believed in her abilities. She figured he'd be like Ryan—a man of science, having to see it to believe it, which made her wonder why Ryan finally believed her without proof positive.

As soon as Ryan parked the truck at Doc's rental house, a neat little clapboard house with a white picket fence surrounding it, she noted the sign hanging above the door. The sign welcomed visitors, which was just like Doc. If patients needed him when he wasn't on duty, they were welcome to come to see him at any time.

Carol jumped out of the truck before Ryan could exit the vehicle. She hurried to Doc's door, afraid Jake would try to stop her. Ryan stalked after her, his footfalls getting closer. After knocking and not getting a response, she unlocked the door. She saw Jake park behind Ryan's vehicle as she hurried inside, hoping she could speak with Doc before he might decide to shift and it would be too late.

To forestall any disagreement, Ryan waited on the porch to talk to Jake and Tom, who were hurrying up the walk. "She's just checking on him."

"She has his key? Hell, what if the old guy has a girlfriend?" Jake shook his head and folded his arms while both of them stared into the dark house.

Tom watched in the other direction, making sure no one visited the house who shouldn't be there, just like they shouldn't.

Jake suddenly turned to Ryan, his eyes widening. "She had a premonition?"

"No. Well, just a feeling, from what I understand." At

least he didn't think she'd had a new vision. And he wasn't giving away the vision she'd had of several of them shifting and not turning back. Not unless she wanted him to.

When she didn't appear right away, they walked into the living room. Carol hurried down the hallway, waving for them to leave.

"He's sleeping soundly," she whispered, looking vastly relieved.

Ryan took her comment to mean that Doc was still in his human form.

In the kitchen, the phone rang. Carol instinctively ran to get it, but Ryan grabbed her hand. "You're not supposed to be here," he said, his voice hushed.

"I don't want the phone to wake Doc." She paused as the answering machine came on.

"Hey, Doc. I called earlier but didn't leave a message. This is North Redding, and we've got a bit of trouble here."

Carol trembled, and Ryan put his arm around her shoulders and pulled her close as if he was protecting her from the menace.

"We really could use your help. We're no longer with Lelandi's pack but started our own. If you could see your way to helping us out, we'd sure appreciate it. I'll call back later to see if you're agreeable."

The connection disconnected.

Ryan rubbed Carol's arm. "Was that one of the men who took you hostage?"

She nodded. "The one who carried me. He'd spoken to the others when he took me hostage the first time. I'd recognize his voice anywhere. He's the same one who hit Tom when we were in the exam room. Doc identified him by name."

Jake said to Tom, "I want you to stay here and watch over Doc. I'll send others to help look after him in case North tries to take him hostage. Can you manage it?"

Tom nodded. "Hell, yeah."

"North was sick, and maybe others in his pack are also. If they need our help…" Carol said, letting her words trail off.

"Why go after Carol and the doc? Why not contact either of the other nurses?" Tom asked.

"North and his men are reds," Ryan reasoned. "Even though Doc is, too, I imagine they went after Carol first because they wanted to keep her in their pack. Then when they figured it was going to be too difficult to try for her again, they decided to solicit Doc's help."

"I'll keep him safe," Tom said. "Just let any of them try to break in."

Jake slapped him on the back. "I'll send Deputy Trevor and a couple of other men over to watch the outside. Let us know at once if anything happens."

Ryan headed out to the truck with Carol and Jake, leaving Doc under Tom's protection. "You might have someone posted to watch out for the other two nurses, just in case North and his men go after them, figuring they can't wait for Doc's help," Ryan said to Jake.

"Hell." Jake brought out his phone and punched in a number. "Darien, we've got a new situation."

"See you at the house," Ryan said to Jake. Jake gave him the thumbs-up, and Ryan led Carol to his own truck.

When they were on their way to Darien's home, Ryan asked, "Doc was all right, correct?"

"Yes." Carol rubbed her arms and still appeared unsettled.

"Good thing you wanted to check on him. If we hadn't

learned of North's interest in him, we might not have discovered what they were up to until it was too late. Whoever's
sick can be brought here. And none of the medical staff is
going to them. Certainly not after what they pulled with
you. Are you sure you didn't have a premonition of the
phone call? It seems odd that you were so desperate to go
there, and we find he's just sleeping, but then we learn of
North's interest in the doc."

"I didn't have a vision of anything. Just a strong feeling.
And since the last vision I had was of Doc not being able to
shift back, that's what I feared this was all about."

"I thought we established that you don't see lengthy
visions, that he could very well shift later on."

"In his wolf form, he's agitated. I can't see where he is,
but it's like he's caged in. Like he's stuck."

Ryan could allow that she "felt" something. She was correct in assuming that he'd have a hunch about a situation
and know danger was present or that someone was lying to
cover their illicit deeds. Nothing that he could prove in a
court of law. Just that elusive feeling.

But he couldn't help feeling that something more had
triggered her need to be at Doc's house at the right moment.
Something that was a little more than a hunch. Something
like a sixth sense that went beyond what he normally
believed in.

Silence filled the air as he thought about Doc being in
his wolf form, pacing and anxious, and what could bring
that about. "Maybe he just does that normally, Carol."

She turned to stare at him. "What?"

"Doc. Maybe he turns into the wolf and paces when he's
agitated sometimes. All of us handle situations differently.

My aunt Tilda likes to take a nap as a wolf. As a human, she feels she isn't allowed. To her way of thinking, only children take naps. But as a wolf, she feels it's acceptable. So maybe when Doc Weber is stressed, he shifts. To an extent, it does change who we are for a while. It's a different sort of freedom."

"Maybe he does shift for that reason," she said quietly, "but I wouldn't have a vision of something that is perfectly normal for him."

Silence stretched between them as Ryan mulled that over. "Do you see more pieces of the vision later on?"

"Sometimes. Mostly it's just the same spot in time, the same image. Like with Mervin tackling me."

Despite not having any confirmation that what she envisioned could come to pass, Ryan was beginning to worry for Doc too.

CHAPTER 20

TWENTY MINUTES LATER, RYAN PULLED INTO DARIEN'S drive, unable to let go of Carol's concern over Doc or his own worry that she might be right. He turned off the ignition and spoke to Carol as Jake pulled in behind him and parked.

"You sure you didn't have another premonition about Doc that triggered your concern?"

"I'm certain. Why do you keep asking?"

He shook his head and opened his door. "I don't know. Maybe your premonitions have...gotten me to thinking."

"You felt something too?" Her eyes were wide. "A hunch that maybe something wasn't right?"

Or maybe her worry was feeding into his psyche. Almost as if her concern for a future unknown event had sensitized him to the possibility that it existed. He shook his head at himself, she sighed, and he closed his door. Before he could reach hers, Jake was already there again, helping her out.

Darien headed outside to speak to them. "I don't want Lelandi to know about this latest development concerning North and his men. She's to be under guard as usual until we settle this. But it appears that the hospital staff are most likely the targets this time. Tom called and said Doc woke to find him there, was coughing his head off, and decided to shift."

"No," Carol said, her voice hushed as her hand flew to her breast.

Ryan caught her free arm as she wobbled on her feet.

Darien frowned. "He thought he'd feel better. Sometimes our wolf halves can handle colds or allergies better. If it's the flu, canines can't catch the human variety. So it would knock it out. Anyway, if it's any of the more common stuff, sometimes shifting will lessen the symptoms. He'll know before long and can change back if need be."

Carol looked pale and distraught.

"Let's go inside," Darien said, studying her. "Lelandi's got supper on."

His arm around her waist, Ryan walked Carol into the house and whispered to her, "You all right?"

"Sure...sure, I'm all right."

"Is Tom staying the night with Doc?" Ryan asked Darien.

"Yeah. The sheriff is running by there to watch the area, too, and a couple of other men also. He's well safeguarded." Darien motioned for Jake to take Carol into the dining room. "I want a word with you, Ryan." He walked Ryan back outside as Jake led a reluctant Carol into the dining room. "Have you learned how Carol is stopping the shift?"

"Visions."

Darien raised his brows. "*Really.*" He said the word with awe, but then he frowned. "Can she always control it?"

"If her panic in attempting to reach her bedroom after Mervin accosted her is any indication, I'd say no. She stopped the shift, but I think she was awfully close to changing until she was able to control the urge."

Looking thoughtful, Darien rubbed the dark stubble on his chin. "Not good. If she doesn't have any real power over it—which would be expected since she's newly turned, although some have better control than others—she's going to be real trouble. Can you convince her to shift?"

"No. I believe she'll continue to try and avoid it through her visions. I don't think there's any way that I can convince her to accept that part of our wolf nature. At least for now."

"You have faith in her visions now?"

As much as Ryan had a hard time trusting in anything of the sort, he did. "Yeah, I do. Even though it goes against everything I've ever believed in. I did try a psychic once in my line of work, but she turned out to be a fraud."

"I know," Darien said, his lips curving up slightly.

"You knew?" Ryan was used to doing the investigations, not being investigated.

"When someone gets interested in joining the pack or shows interest in one of my pack members, I have him or her checked out. I owe it to my people."

"And you discovered?"

"All about your faux psychic. If that had happened to any of my pack members, the man who threatened you with libel and the woman who was a phony psychic would have been leaving town for good."

"That's the problem with Green Valley being a human-run town for the most part. We want more of what you have here in Silver Town, where you and your brothers run things."

Darien nodded. He didn't say anything for several lengthy moments, studying Ryan the whole time, and then he asked, "What if you mated her?"

Darien could have knocked Ryan over with the question, it surprised him so. He observed the Douglas firs shuddering in the breeze. He hadn't planned on taking a mate. Hadn't been looking for one. Yet ever since he'd met the determined woman five months ago and had seen her heroics, her determination to help save others in need, no matter the consequences to her own life, he couldn't deny that he'd been thinking along those lines.

The way Carol reacted to him physically was a sure indication that the wolf side of them was well aware of the interest they had in each other. After Carol had caressed his plaid in the truck and he envisioned himself wearing it while she continued to touch the fabric so intimately, he'd again envisioned her being his mate. They'd partake in the Celtic festivities, even if he was a McKinley and she was a MacDonald. He'd wrap her in his plaid and show her just what a Highlander of old was capable of.

He looked back to see Darien waiting for a response. Would Ryan be able to convince her to shift if he mated her?

"I'm not sure she'd shift if I mated her. She's pretty stubborn."

Darien snorted. "Tell me about it. Come on. I know Carol's concerned about something, and I want to find out what." He slapped Ryan on the back. "Let's get something to eat before we upset Lelandi by letting the food get cold."

When they entered the dining room, Darien said to Carol, "You seemed concerned that Doc had shifted. What's wrong?"

She gave a heavy sigh as he watched her, his brows furrowed. Ryan was sure that if she told Darien what she'd envisioned, he wouldn't believe her. Even if he might believe her about her other premonitions. Then again, Ryan wasn't sure she'd even tell him what she'd seen.

With an expression that bordered on insubordination, she straightened her shoulders, looked Darien in the eye, and said, "I see Doc, you, and Jake shift into your wolf forms, but none of you can shift back."

"Oh." Darien's whole expression lightened several degrees. "Can't happen. Sometimes we stay in our wolf persona for hours or days. Depends on the circumstances. But your visions are only fragments of time, so I wouldn't worry about it."

"I won't." She sat in the chair Ryan pulled out for her as Jake brought in a platter of hickory-smoked brisket. "And I won't even tell you I told you so when it happens." She shrugged. "The point will be moot."

The aroma of brisket and dark-brown gravy filled the air. Broccoli and cauliflower sat in a separate serving dish. Mashed potatoes were piled high on another, and Ryan's stomach growled.

Smiling, Lelandi pulled off an apron, looking very domestic for a change. Ryan helped bring in a platter of bread while Jake hurried to carry in the other dishes.

"Poor Tom doesn't know what he's missing," Jake said a little too evilly. "Guess there will be more for me."

"Where *is* Tom?" Lelandi asked casually.

Darien's expression darkened, but then he put his hand around Lelandi's shoulders and guided her to the table.

"Doc's got a cold, and Carol was worried about him. Tom is staying the night to make sure he doesn't get worse."

Carol and Lelandi shared looks. Lelandi had to know that wasn't what Carol was concerned about. Then Carol opened up her phone, punched in a number, and said, "Hey, Tom? Tell me the minute Doc shifts back into his human form, okay?"

Lelandi hesitated to sit at the table.

"Thanks." Carol hung up her phone and gave Lelandi a wilted smile. "The meal looks terrific. Wish I could cook like this."

Lelandi managed a laugh. "Don't believe her. She's a great cook."

Everyone took their seats.

Jake scooped a pile of mashed potatoes onto his plate from a large bowl. "Yep, except she's very nutrition conscious. Makes us eat the right amounts of veggies and fruits with all our meals."

"I shouldn't be the one who has to tell you to eat right, Jake." Carol forked some beef onto her plate and then handed the platter to Lelandi.

Ryan could feel the tension between the two women, the unspoken words, the shuttered looks. With Darien and his brother, the tension vibrated between them also, but for a different reason. He was sure they didn't take Carol seriously on this issue and were more concerned about North's message to Doc. And the possibility the reds were targeting more of the medical staff than they had first bargained on.

"I'll be moving into our grandfather's house in a couple of months," Jake announced, stirring gravy into his potatoes and trying to change the subject, no doubt. "Should be livable by then."

Lelandi sighed. "You don't have to move."

Darien took her hand and squeezed. "Believe me, he has to. Once three new babies are in the house, he'll have to find his solitude elsewhere."

Jake nodded. "The old place needs another coat of paint, some new plumbing, and some other minor repairs. But after that, it should be ready to move in. Tom and I've taken care of updating all the electrical wiring, and the chimney is cleaned out and ready to use. He said he'll live with me for the time being."

"Sounds good." Darien sipped a beer.

Lelandi took another deep breath. "I'd hoped you would be our babysitter when we went out nights."

Jake laughed. "Silva's already put her name on the long list of babysitters. Even got Sam rooked into it. And I know for a fact the list is growing daily."

Carol sipped some of her wine but didn't say a word. She looked consumed with worry, although she tried to smile at the conversation.

Darien's phone rang, and he lifted it off his belt. "Yeah, Tom?" His brow pinched together in a frown. "Tom, what's... Tom!" He quickly rose from his chair and headed for the door.

Jake hurried after him.

"Call the alert roster. North and his men approached Doc's house. Tom's cell phone went dead after that. You stay here with Ryan to protect the women," Darien said to Jake.

Lelandi sat frozen to her chair. Carol joined her and rubbed her shoulder. Ryan checked out the front window, looking for anyone who shouldn't be there, while Jake called someone. "Call the alert roster. Tom's in trouble at Doc's house."

His voice trailed off as he left the dining room and checked the sunroom's and great room's back doors.

"I guess I should put the food away," Lelandi said, her voice small and disconcerted.

"No," Ryan said. "Eat. You're not feeding just one now. And, Carol, you've been on your feet all day. Go ahead and eat."

Jake returned to the dining room. "Ryan's right. Everything's locked up. Lelandi's made a delightful meal. I, for one, am not letting it go to waste."

"Several in their red pack have to be sick," Carol said softly.

"Then they can damn well come here for treatment. Not take off with you like a bunch of thieves in the night," Ryan growled.

Lelandi gave him a small smile and ate more of her potatoes. Then she attempted to change the volatile subject. "So, Ryan, do you have any brothers or sisters?"

"A sister. She lives with me. Owns a successful nursery that keeps her out of trouble most of the time." And he hoped to hell she was staying out of trouble while he was away.

"Is she unmated?" Lelandi asked, her brows elevating with intrigue.

"Cantankerous."

Lelandi's gaze settled on Jake.

He snorted. "Your psychology courses don't include Matchmaking 101, do they?"

This time, she smiled broadly and again turned her attention to Ryan. "How do you feel about cats?"

"Cats?" He was a dog kind of guy. Cats were too independent to his way of thinking. Dogs knew he was the alpha in the situation whenever he'd encountered them. Cats? Hell. The cats thought *they* ruled.

"Yeah, fuzzy little felines," Lelandi continued as if he didn't know what they were.

"Most of us don't have pets." Which was the truth. Ryan could just imagine what would happen if he had a Tweety bird and then turned into a wolf. On the other hand, even wild animals that were normally predator and prey could be raised together and become best of friends. Still, he didn't even see himself as a dog owner—and certainly not a cat owner.

The mischievous look on Lelandi's face said she had some reason for bringing the subject up. Carol didn't show any expression one way or another, so he couldn't tell if she liked pets or not.

"Why?" he finally asked.

Lelandi forked up some more brisket. "Just wondered."

Ryan glanced at Carol. She quickly focused on her meal.

Hell, Carol must have a cat. Jake was right. Whenever Lelandi had an opportunity to play matchmaker, she worked hard at it.

"I have a cat," Carol finally said and waited for him to show his distaste for the idea. Instead he just grunted. She shrugged. "He's good-natured, loving, and won't catch mice, although he loves to tackle my feet when I'm wearing a long robe or play with my shoelaces."

The long robe made him think of Carol in nothing but satiny skin underneath. "But when you shift? Then what?"

"Puss loves dogs. I'm sure he'll love me just the same."

Lelandi cleared her throat and directed her comment to Carol. "Rose took him over to her flower shop for the day to show him off, if that's all right with you. She's been missing her own cat since he died a few weeks ago. I tried calling you to ask if it was okay, but you must have been with a patient. She thought he wouldn't be so lonely when you're working your nursing shifts."

Carol smiled. "He loves people, so I'm sure he'll enjoy visiting with her and her customers."

"She'll drop him by after the shop closes in a couple of hours."

Jake's cell phone rang. "Yeah, Darien?" Jake was on edge, which showed in both his voice and the way his body tensed. He frowned and looked at Carol.

"Okay. Everything's fine here. See you in a little while." He hung up his phone. "The sheriff and Deputy Trevor were knocked out. Nurse Matthew is looking after them. Tom fought off North and a couple of men until they retreated. Matthew is looking after our injured men. Doc's still at the house."

"In his wolf form," Carol whispered, hating that what she thought would come to pass had. She was certain he would still be in his wolf form.

"Yeah, but not to worry," Jake said.

Carol frowned. "As a wolf, he couldn't tell anyone what had happened."

"Darien said he smelled that North and the others had been there."

"Why didn't Doc change back, Jake? Why wouldn't he talk to Darien?"

"He'll change when he feels the urge." But this time, Jake didn't look so sure of that, and Lelandi's face paled.

"Why didn't they take Doc with him? Was it because he couldn't help them? That he couldn't change into his human form? Call Darien back. Tell him to order Doc to change back. He has to comply with Darien's wishes, right?" Carol said.

Jake let out his breath in a huff. "All right, all right." He punched a number and said, "Hey, Darien, Carol wants you to order Doc to shift back to his human form." His brows pinched into a dark frown. "And?" He looked at Carol and shook his head slowly.

"Have him brought here so we can watch him. And Puss's favorite bed is still at Doc Mitchell's vet clinic. Can he have someone run by there and get it for him?" Carol asked.

Jake passed on the information. "Anything else, Carol?"

"Don't you or Darien shift again until we can figure out what happened to Doc."

"Darien, Tom, and I aren't royals. We have to change sometime during the phases of the moon, except for the new moon. We don't have a choice."

"Try not to," she reiterated. "Please."

Jake passed the information along to Darien and then signed off and stared at the uneaten portion of his meal. "What happens that makes you think I can't change back?"

"In the vision, you're agitated, and Lelandi says Darien can't change back. It's not a nightmare. It's a vision."

"Hell, Carol, you didn't say that Lelandi said so. That makes a world of difference," Jake scolded her. "I mean, with the other version, I just figured you couldn't see that I'd changed back."

"Yeah, well, I told Lelandi."

"Sorry, Carol. I just couldn't believe it myself." Lelandi rubbed her arms covered with goose bumps.

"What's causing the trouble?" Ryan asked.

"Well, if Doc doesn't change back, maybe it has to do with the cold he got. Or flu virus." Carol chewed on her lip. "Since he's a wolf now, he'll have all wolf genetics. Have Darien call Doc Mitchell and run some tests on Doc Weber's blood. See if he can discover if he's still sick. If he isn't, the change probably knocked out the illness like you said it might."

"You're sure about this?" Jake asked. "I doubt Doc

Weber will appreciate it if the vet starts testing his blood without his permission."

"It's the only correlation I can see for now. Besides, if there isn't a problem, Doc Weber can shift and tell the vet where to go. If there is a problem, I'm sure he'll be grateful we're trying to learn the cause and do something about it."

"All right." Jake called Darien. "Carol needs one more thing done."

CHAPTER 21

HELL, EVERYTHING IS GOING FURTHER DOWNHILL, RYAN thought when Darien called an hour after dinner with news from the vet clinic. Doc Mitchell was missing.

"I have to return to the hospital and take blood samples from Doc Weber," Carol said, sitting at the dining table and looking ready to leap from her seat and do something, anything.

"Not without Darien's approval." Jake stared out the window. "And besides, Matthew said he'd do it. We've got men looking for the vet. Some others are watching Doc Weber in case anyone tries to take him, and some are watching Nurse Matthew and Nurse Charlotte. Seven men are here guarding the house from the outside, and others searching for North and his men. For now, Darien doesn't want anyone to move from his assigned job. Not until he knows what we're up against."

Lelandi, who had been on the go every minute the last time Ryan was here, looked tired again, slumped in her chair and quiet, with her eyes half-closed. And as restless as Carol had been throughout the night, she looked exhausted. If she had to go back to the hospital in an hour or so, she needed some rest.

"The ladies look like they need to lie down for a while," Ryan said to Jake.

He frowned at Ryan, looked at Lelandi, and then switched his attention to Carol. "All right. Come on. I'll watch Lelandi, and you guard Carol while they get some sleep."

Ryan and Carol walked up the stairs, following Jake and Lelandi. This time, Ryan intended to sit in the recliner and watch over Carol like a dutiful bodyguard.

Both women were moving so slowly that he wanted to carry Carol and tell Jake to do the same with Lelandi. But he assumed Jake didn't want to push his luck by overstepping his boundaries with Darien's mate unless it was absolutely necessary.

Ryan wrapped his arm around Carol's waist and helped her up the stairs. She slumped against him, cuddling with him. Instantly, the notion of sitting in the recliner seemed not as likely.

As Jake passed Carol's bedroom door, he gave Ryan a stern look that warned him to behave himself with Carol. Ryan told himself that he would behave himself as long as that was what Carol wanted. He wasn't so sure she wanted him to control his sexual urges with regard to her, not after the way she'd kissed him back at the clinic. Maybe it was damned wishful thinking on his part.

He followed her into the bedroom and closed the door as she sat on the bed and then pulled off her tennis shoes. He walked over to the recliner and sat, hoping for an invitation to lie down with her. Dog tired, he hadn't gotten much sleep the previous night either. But she needed to sleep more than he did if her medical services might be required later that night. Unless she needed his comfort if she experienced any more night terrors, she was probably just as well off sleeping alone. Maybe even better off. Although he hated to admit it.

For a moment, Carol sat on the bed, staring at the floor and not saying a word.

"What is it? Another vision?" Ryan was ready to leave the chair and sit next to her, to coax the truth from her if need be.

She shook her head and took a deep breath. "It's like when you deal with one of your cases, I'm sure. Just trying to sort out what's going on." She pulled her scrub's shirt over her head, exposing a silky sheer bra. Her darkened dusty-pink nipples pressed against the fabric like two perfect jewels. Did she even realize how sexy she looked?

"Your sister said you talked about me to her." Carol stood, grabbed her waistband, and pulled her scrub pants down her hips. She let the pants slide to her feet and then stepped out of them.

His gaze latched onto the thatch of golden curls showing through the silk bikini panties.

"Ryan?"

His gaze lifted to see her brows raised. She pulled the eyelet cover aside, climbed under it, and then situated the top of it under her chin.

"What did you say to your sister about me?"

"What did I say to her?" His mind was in a fog. His thoughts were still centered on the way Carol looked in her sheer underwear—sexy, tantalizing, and inviting more than just his gaze.

"Yes. She said you kept talking about me."

He frowned. "She called you?" The notion finally sank into his lust-filled brain. He didn't recall the conversations he'd had with Rosalind about Carol during the investigation. He supposed he'd said he thought Carol's psychic abilities weren't for real.

"Not sure. Most likely about what you'd envisioned."

"That I'd lied then?" She didn't sound angry, just sleepy and inquisitive.

"Not lied. Just overheard conversations and incorporated them into dreams and thought you'd had a vision."

"That's all?"

He couldn't believe Rosalind would bring it up. If she wanted Carol to like him, why cause a rift between them? "I honestly don't recall anything else I discussed with her. Except maybe about another case."

"I'll have to ask her then."

He ground his teeth, not liking that Rosalind intended to stir things up. Even though he'd planned on remaining on the chair and only joining Carol if night terrors revisited her, he changed his mind and began unbuttoning his shirt.

"Whatever was said before was the past. It's not important. The future is what concerns me."

She watched him unbutton his shirt, and he swore she was undressing him with her eyes before he could even get to his pants. Which made him work faster on his belt. He divested himself of the rest of his clothes, except for his boxers, and climbed into the canopy bed. He motioned to the eyelet canopy overhead. "I feel I've entered the bed-chambers of a cloistered princess."

"Hmm, as a Highland warrior of an opposing clan? This is not exactly a Highland bed or setting." She moved closer to him and snuggled against his body, the warmth of her silky soft curves heating his blood.

He kissed the top of her head, wanting from the bottom of his heart to make her fantasies come to life. He told himself that was because of all the years of wanting and never fulfilling his own destiny. Carol, Little Miss Nightingale, and one sexy witch rolled up in one was the only woman who'd ever be right for him. Not that they didn't have a lot of things to work out—shifting and coming to grips with her wolf half were at the top of the list.

"Do you want me to get my plaid blanket out of the truck and toss it over us?"

"You mean you'd run outside like you're dressed now? Wearing only your boxer briefs? What would the men guarding the house think?"

"If this were my castle, they'd cheer me on. At Darien's, they wouldn't like it much."

She chuckled, the sensuous sound teasing his senses. "It doesn't matter as long as the Highlander is part of the setting." She smiled up at him, and for a moment, he thought she didn't look all that sleepy—instead, sultry and decadently wicked in her seductive lingerie.

But being honorable—or as honorable as he could be when he wanted something less than honorable—he said, "Get some sleep in case Darien calls and wants you to return to the hospital."

With her gaze focused on Ryan's chest, she stroked his belly with the tips of her fingers, softly tantalizing and as erotic as anything he'd ever experienced. Already his blood was running south, preparing him for a much more vigorous workout. He wanted to move her onto her back, take her as her mate would, and claim her for his own, but he assumed she wasn't ready for that.

He cleared his throat and ran his hand through her hair, luxuriating in the silky golden strands. He hated to ask, hated to ruin the moment, but he had to know how far she was willing to take this before he did something she wasn't prepared for.

Before he could question how far she wanted to go, she murmured, "Hmm," and slid her fingers lower, past his navel, lower still until she slipped them underneath his waistband and gingerly caressed the skin beneath the elastic.

He sucked in a breath, waiting for her to move her fingers even lower, where his erection had curled upward, begging for her touch.

Then a horrible thought occurred to him. They didn't have much time. What if Darien called and wanted Carol to go to the hospital pronto? Yet Ryan couldn't move, the anticipation of her touch suspending him in time.

Her fingers surged deeper into his briefs, sweeping across the tip of his penis, which jumped at her touch.

He still wanted to know how far she was willing to go. Oh, hell. Forget words. He couldn't come up with the right ones. And he assumed she wanted what he did at this point anyway. He rolled her over on her back and straddled her leg so he could slide his fingers under *her* waistband. He didn't take as long to find her sweets, slipping his fingers through her curly hairs and then lower until he found her warm wetness and began to stroke the jewel that made her arch slightly against his fingers.

He knew then that she had to be his. Or he would never have taken it this far with one of his own kind. But he also knew he had to take this slowly until she was ready to accept him all the way. After all, she was newly turned and probably still didn't completely understand what taking a mate meant.

She barely breathed, her fingers touching his chest but

not moving, just frozen in place as she concentrated on how he stroked her hard little nub, her body undulating with fever. He leaned down to kiss her gently, to savor the wine on her lips. To his surprise and delight, she devoured him as if she'd been starved for affection forever, her lips caressing his, her tongue darting around his mouth, tasting, memorizing, and tangling with his.

She drugged him with her sensuous urgency. She might not have been born a *lupus garou*, but she knew how to stir up the wolf in him. He plunged his tongue into her open mouth, and she sucked on it, her fingers groping for his erection. He almost forgot what he was doing, considering the way she fueled a fire deep inside him, until she gave a soft moan and writhed under his fingertips. He stroked her willing, hot little nub as her fingers dug into his arms, her eyes closed, her lips parted. A soft moan escaped, and her body trembled with orgasm. He smiled, loving how willingly she'd responded to his touch.

But no sooner had he had those thoughts than she worked his erection, coaxing and stroking up and down with the right firmness. He couldn't last. Before he could begin to draw the sensation out, he felt as though he were free-falling from an airplane without a parachute—free, on top of the world. Her hand on him kept up the pressure until he came. He groaned her name, wishing that he could have been inside her as she milked him, with her eyes half-lidded and her tongue sweeping over her well-kissed lips.

He pressed his mouth against hers again, savoring the softness, the sweetness, moving down to her throat and then to her silky sheer bra. Pushing her bra down with frantic urgency until he exposed a breast, he sucked on one of her firm, eager nipples that was greedy for his touch.

"Did you envision this?" he asked, his voice still husky with need, his hands cupping her other breast, fondling, and drawing his thumb over the nipple still confined in silk and loving the different textures.

She gave him a tender smile and swept her hands over his bare shoulders. "Envision, yes, when I saw you shift and standing as such a healthy specimen of a man in the woods nearby. And again, when I imagined you wearing your plaid. But a premonition of the actual act? No. If I had, Ryan McKinley, I probably wouldn't have told you. Some things are just not meant to be said."

"Yet we agreed you would tell me everything you perceived. Everything." He smiled at her and removed her bra and panties and his boxer briefs. Then he drew her out of the bed, swept her up in his arms, and carried her to the bathroom.

"Lelandi will hear the shower running and suspect something isn't quite right," she whispered.

"She already knows I've claimed you for my mate."

She raised a brow as Ryan set her on the bathroom floor. "I didn't think wolves were considered mated unless they truly consummated the relationship."

"That doesn't mean you're not mine," he said, not caring how possessive he sounded as he turned on the shower. "It just means we only have one more hurdle to cross."

"Hurdle."

He lifted her and set her in the tub under the pulsating showerhead. "Yeah, hurdle. You're no longer available, even if we haven't consummated the relationship. Once that's done, we've overcome the last barrier." He smiled down at her as she rolled her eyes.

"Darien or the others won't go along with that."

"He and the others will know better than to challenge me in this. I know this isn't the time, but on a lighter subject, we have another difficulty."

"And that is?"

"Jake's ready to have a showdown with me."

She frowned. "What are the two of you in disagreement over now?"

"You."

"You guys are funny…you know that? He's never shown any real interest in me. You're the one who came sneaking around Darien's house in the middle of the night, hoping to catch a glimpse of me. Only my hair wasn't long enough to let down out of the window to give you a way up to rescue me."

"Rescue you?"

"From Darien's ruling that I have to have a mate—soon."

"If I'd known how you felt, I would have brought a ladder."

"Hmm," she said, reaching out to grab his hand and pulling him into the shower with her, her heated gaze raking over him in a seductive pass. "You would have been naked."

His hands molded to her shoulders, and he caressed them with his thumb, remembering how she'd taunted him with her scandalous nightgown. He reached down and softly pulled on one of her erect nipples. "Why did you go to the window in such a see-through gown? Hell, what if I'd been bad news?"

"Ryan McKinley, you *are* bad news."

He slyly smiled, and she slid her arms around his neck

and leaned into his body, rubbing a little to stir him up. And hell, it did. She was arousing him with the way she touched him, pressing, demanding more.

The hot water ran over her shoulders in a silky stream and slipped down between their chests. She raised her chin and offered her tantalizing mouth. Despite not wanting to appear overzealous, he couldn't help the way he wanted her. *Again.*

Quickly succumbing to her seduction, he realized he hadn't the strength to show restraint and kissed her hard with uncontrolled yearning, his tongue deeply penetrating her mouth, tasting her, wanting her. As if of their own volition, his hands slid down her back, with the water sluicing over her skin, and firmly cupped her buttocks.

She moaned and tightened her hold around his neck, leaning against him further. Then she sighed and released him. He thought she meant to stop him in his quest for fulfillment, dashing his hopes, and for a second, he was annoyed with himself for pushing her so fast. But she separated from him only enough to squeeze some soap out of her lavender body-wash container. Then her fingers were all over him again as she ran the pearly substance over his chest, the sensuous touch making him groan with want.

Making a special stop, first on one nipple and then the other, she teased just around the edges and then rubbed the tip with a soft thumb. *She was killing him softly*, came to mind as his hands returned to her tantalizing behind.

He desired her more than he'd ever wanted anyone in his life. And he was so close to having her for good. But patience, he reminded himself. For her sake, he had to let her get used to the idea.

Shifting his hands to her wet hair, he gently combed his fingers through the silky strands, mesmerized with the feel of her slippery body pressed against his and the way she licked her lips and watched him with eyes filled with desire.

She broke the spell by running soap down his penis, which reacted instantly and eagerly to her touch. He captured her mouth in a hungry kiss with no holds barred, urgent, passionate, needy. God, he was needy. Forget having the strength to let her get used to the notion of being his mate. He wanted her now, fully and forever.

He slid his fingers between her legs and began stroking where he found her wet from her own needs and from the shower. She moaned with pleasure and clenched her hands around his waist, demanding that he finish what he'd started. But he wanted to finish so much more than what he'd begun.

He stroked her sex, and his touch took her by storm, judging from the way her knees weakened and how tightly she clutched at him.

He wanted to trap her against the tile shower wall and claim her, but he continued to stroke her, watching her eyes close as she clung fiercely to him, her breath shallow, her heart beating fast and furious. Arching against his questing fingers, she let out a little cry, right before he captured her mouth to silence her sounds of exultation. She trembled and sagged against him as the orgasm rippled through her, looking as though she wasn't up for much more.

Her lips curved up in a wicked little grin as her eyes opened, her gaze capturing his. She huskily whispered, "Your turn."

Only this time, he wanted her snug little feminine

chamber holding him tight. Then again, her hand on his erection—sliding, touching, and tightening—held him hostage, a very willing hostage, and he was grateful to have this intimacy between them any way he could. His hands were on her hips now, his cheek against hers, his body soaring with her strokes.

Carol felt drained and, at the same time, as if she'd soared on an eagle's wings across the world and back. She wanted to collapse in bed with Ryan and sleep the rest of the day, tight in his embrace. She loved to see his reaction when she stroked his needs, just as she could see how much pleasure he got from seeing how much she loved his touch. She knew he wanted to be inside her. She wasn't ready. Or at least she wouldn't admit to herself that she was. Not yet.

This touching—the sexual play between them, intimate and satisfying—was enough for her now. She hoped he would understand. Although from the way his heart was pounding and his hands were gripping her hips harder, he was having a difficult time holding on. He seemed all right about wanting just this for now.

She had claimed him, held power over him, and seen his eyes swimming with lust. He was beautiful and sexy. Hard all over, but tender of heart. She loved that he was a wolf and a man, all wrapped up in one.

Her hand squeezed his arousal just a little more as she stroked him, and he groaned and even appeared a bit weak-kneed. Then he came with a more soulful groan, which she hurriedly tried to silence with a deep kiss. He responded desperately to her kiss with the same passionate tongue strokes.

"You're killing me, Carol," he whispered against her ear as he hugged her tight against his chest.

If the water hadn't begun to cool and she hadn't shivered, she was sure he would have held her there longer in his hard embrace.

"I'm the one for you. All your patients say so. The bachelor males in the pack already know so. Tom's out of the picture since he's looking for a dream mate. And Jake's too late. Even my sister informed me you would be perfect for me, nice and pliable," Ryan said in a hushed voice, as if making a last-ditch effort to ensure she knew he wasn't giving her up to anyone.

Carol's brows arched at the reference to her being pliable.

"I told Rosalind you weren't the least bit biddable."

"What do I have to say about this? Anything?" Carol pinched his nipples lightly.

"Just agree." He quickly rinsed them both off before the water could turn from cool to cold. "You need to learn our ways," he added, whispering against her ear.

She backed away, but he stopped her with his hand on her wrist before she could leave the tub.

"Absolutely no way am I shifting. Not in light of what's going on. And besides, I won't take a mate just because..." Her eyes narrowed, and she stiffened. "Don't tell me that it's okay to mate with me now that you believe I'm psychic."

"That's not the reason at all. But you're going to be my mate."

She laughed, which made him frown.

"I'm serious," he said, feigning bruised pride.

"Well, of course you are. I've told you all along that you want me. But more is at stake here than your needs." She left the tub and grabbed a towel.

By the time he'd finished rinsing off and towel dried, she had dressed and left the bedroom. He should know that this business of shifting would be a sticking point with her.

When Carol reached the bar in the den in search of a good stiff drink, she found Jake drinking hot cocoa as he leaned back on a recliner and watched her. "I thought you were supposed to be in Lelandi's room, watching her."

"She didn't want me sitting there. She said I could guard just as well from downstairs and Ryan was upstairs anyway."

Carol frowned at him, whipped around, and headed for the kitchen, the cocoa sounding a lot better on this chilly night. Besides, chocolate always did her a world of good.

"Problems?" Jake asked, following her into the kitchen.

She really didn't need Jake pestering her right now.

Jake took a sip of his cocoa and then set the mug down and pulled one out of the cupboard for her. "What did he say or do to upset you?"

"Nothing, Jake."

"Your face is flushed. You're breathing hard. If you were a wolf…"

"I'm not, damn it." She stared at the counter, her eyes blurring with tears. She brushed away a couple that dared to slide down her cheeks.

Looking uncomfortable, Jake didn't say anything further. He just poured her a mug of hot chocolate. She heard

Ryan coming before he entered the kitchen and wished they'd both leave her alone.

When Ryan walked inside, he didn't speak to either of them, but she knew they were exchanging knowing looks. Two men, both born *lupus garous*, both on the same side of the issue. She wouldn't gain anyone's sympathy here. She muttered a thank-you to Jake for the hot chocolate and then escaped to the solitude of the sunroom, hoping that neither of them would follow her.

Carol's phone rang and she saw it was from Rosalind and answered it.

"Hey, I hope you're not busy, but I wanted to tell you about the time I encouraged Ryan to get a psychic to help him with a case." Rosalind told her all about what had happened and then Carol understood more where Ryan was coming from when it came to her psychic abilities.

Rosalind finally said she had to go, but Carol was glad she had talked to her.

The room was cold: the fire was untended, and the massive windows let in the chilly air now that the sun had disappeared for the night.

She sat on one of the sofas and threw a wool afghan over her lap and took a long sip of the hot chocolate, wishing she and Ryan were just two ordinary people who had found each other and fallen in love. Everything was so complicated with them being wolves. Did Ryan think he could order her around because he had been born a wolf? Because he would be her mate? She was not shifting!

She gazed out the window at the darkness and saw Mervin staring off into the woods. Serving as one of their guards, no doubt. She sighed. No matter how much she wanted to avoid her wolf side, she also wanted Ryan. Unfortunately, having one meant having the other.

The room was so cold that she slipped off her shoes and tucked her feet underneath her on the velour sofa. But she still shivered as she looked out the window where she observed the growing moon, beautiful and white like a huge, exquisite pearl against the black velvet night.

She drank more of her chocolate, trying to shake the chill. The heat from the chocolate and the blanket were beginning to warm her. Warm her... *no.* The moon. She gritted her teeth, feeling the urge to shift, the craving to ditch her clothes, and tried to summon a vision. But nothing came to her.

She hurriedly set the mug on the coffee table and jerked the afghan aside. Her movement caught Mervin's eye, and he smiled at her and waved.

No, no, no! She jerked off her scrubs shirt, exposing her bra-clad breasts, and felt the heat deepening as it worked its way through her bloodstream.

See something, Carol. Envision something. Make it stop!

Mervin watched her from his distant post, his mouth agape. She couldn't leave now, couldn't head for her bedroom, or Ryan and Jake would catch her in her current state of alarm as she made her way through the great room to the stairs. And follow her. Probably try to make her accept what she couldn't accept.

She jerked off her socks and yanked down her scrubs pants. Oh, God, no. She couldn't do it. The heat invaded her bones, and her skin perspired lightly. She was going to shift.

Jake didn't say anything as Ryan fixed himself a cup of coffee, but Ryan knew he wanted to hear what had upset Carol. He'd probably figured out what it was all about anyway. Ryan didn't owe Jake an explanation, but he offered it anyway.

"She's mine."

"That goes without saying." Jake poured himself another cup of hot chocolate.

Ryan looked in the direction of the entryway to the kitchen. "I upset her when I told her she needed to learn our ways."

Jake gave a conceited smile. "Figured that was what was bothering her. I could have told you that Darien and I have gone round and round with her over it. Tom is more subtle about it. Lelandi's tried in a sisterly way." He shrugged. "Her mate will have to take care of it."

Lelandi smiled as she walked into the kitchen, looking much revived.

"Hmm, the aroma of hot cocoa. You knew what would stir me from a nice spring nap, didn't you, Jake? So whose mate will have to take care of what?" She pulled out a mug from the cupboard, and Jake poured her a cup of chocolate.

Neither Ryan nor Jake said, but they shared looks with each other.

"Oh, Carol," Lelandi whispered and then frowned. "Did you…you know…finalize things?"

Ryan shook his head.

"They haven't mated. But he's declared she's his," Jake said with a smile. "Better let Silva know so she can spread the word via the grapevine. But there are problems in paradise already. Carol doesn't like him telling her she's got to learn our ways any more than she likes us telling her."

"Where is Carol now?" Lelandi asked, her voice low.

"Sunroom," Ryan said. "I was giving her a minute to be by herself. I'll see to her."

The door to the sunroom slammed open, and Ryan said, "Shit. She couldn't have run off by herself. What the hell is she thinking?" He tore off for the sunroom with Jake and Lelandi on his heels.

When they reached the sunroom, Mervin raced inside to meet them. "She, Carol...hell, she..." He motioned to her clothes piled up on the sunroom floor next to the couch.

"Shifted?" Ryan couldn't believe it.

"Yeah and went out the electric wolf door. I don't have permission to leave my guard post."

"She's one of the ones we're guarding!" Ryan squashed the urge to call Mervin an idiot. Instead, he began ripping off his clothes.

"I'll call Darien," Lelandi said. "Jake, you go with Ryan."

"I have to stay and protect you. I'll call in more help."

Ryan didn't wait to hear what else Jake decided. Instead, Ryan shifted and raced out the door. Mervin ran outside after him and pointed in the direction she had run. But Ryan could smell her just fine and took off after the footpad scent she was leaving behind.

He hoped the hell North and his men were nowhere about and that Carol wasn't too traumatized by what she was experiencing. He had no idea how she might cope with this aspect of her life, but he wished she'd let him be a part of it.

He'd run for about a mile when he heard the sound of gunfire. Hell. And then more. A wolf yelped in the distance. Then another.

He paused. Carol's scent headed in a different direction

from the sounds of the injured wolves. Ryan lifted his head and howled. He was met with silence. He howled again, long and deep and low.

Except for the rustle of the breeze stirring the tree branches, nothing.

He took off after Carol's trail again. He had to find her and then locate the other wolves. Just as he ran down toward the river, he saw her, a beautiful red wolf snarling, her nose wrinkled, teeth bared, ears and tail held high, as she stood backed up against the water's edge, while three men taunted her with a fishing net.

It was North and two of his men, one of whom had grazed Ryan with a bullet.

CHAPTER 22

THEIR BACKS TO RYAN, NORTH AND HIS MEN READIED A fishing net that was aimed at Carol. Her wolf posture indicated she was ready to bolt, and the men's bodies steeled with tension as they shouted to one another, "Don't miss her this time, damn it!"

"Hell, I'm not a fisherman, North!"

"Yeah," another man said. "If we fish, it's with our teeth!"

Her red fur bristling and fluffed out to the max, Carol appeared larger and more threatening, yet she had the sense to skitter out of the way of the net. But she wouldn't go into the water where she could have easily escaped capture. Seeing this, the men kept her corralled with her back against the stream. As soon as the net landed on the ground, missing her, the men scurried to retrieve it while watching her to make sure she didn't attack. Why didn't she just jump into the water and swim away?

At least none of them seemed inclined to shoot her.

Ryan kept running toward them. Concentrating hard on Carol, not one of the men realized the threat swiftly approaching at their backs. Ryan could have growled to warn them before he attacked. But he was worried that they might have guns and shoot him, and then he couldn't protect Carol. He targeted the man in charge, North. Even now, Ryan could see red, remembering how the bastard had left Carol wet and naked, shivering on the frosty grass near Darien's house.

Carol glanced over at Ryan, her eyes widening, her ears flattening a little, her snarl vanishing. The men turned around to see what had caught her attention.

"Holy shit!" one of the men said, dropping the net and running for dear life.

North and the other man ran in a different direction. His wolf urges dictating his actions, Ryan fought the craving to chase any of them down and end their sorry lives, which would mean leaving Carol alone. He couldn't abandon her. Not with the possibility that the person shooting wolves might come upon her. Or that North or his other men might come back for her.

Mostly, he wasn't sure how she'd react now that she was wearing her wolf coat, and he had to be here for her more than ever.

Her ears perked up again, and she studied him. He loped toward her, hoping she wouldn't run off. He had no idea if she could understand their ways in wolf form. Not unless she'd grown up and learned their nuances. He grew close. Still, she didn't take flight. He stepped nearer, nudged the side of her muzzle with his nose, and then licked her face. *Come home*, he wanted to say to her. *Come with me.* But she seemed frozen in place.

He heard a couple of people running toward them and looked back over his shoulder. Christian and Jake, neither of whom had shifted.

"What the hell's going on?" Jake said to Carol. "We're glad you shifted, Carol, but you need to return to the house now! Lelandi's going to have those babies early if she gets any more upset about this."

Carol looked toward the house and then filled her

lungs with air. Making up her mind, she loped toward the house, to Ryan's relief. He joined her and ran alongside her, his body lightly touching hers, trying to console her if she needed his support. He was sure she needed someone's.

Jake and Christian ran behind them, but at a human's speed, they'd never catch up. Jake was talking on his phone, giving Darien an update on Carol and the wolf shootings.

"All right, we'll hang tight until we get word from you. Yeah, she'll be all right. You know Carol. She always perseveres."

Ryan was glad to hear the admiration in Jake's voice instead of condemnation. Carol needed encouragement more than anything else, and he planned to be her uncritically enthusiastic supporter, helping her through the changes in her life.

When Ryan and Carol reached the house, Mervin was inside with Avery and Lelandi.

"Thank God, you're all right," Lelandi said to Carol. "We heard shooting." She rubbed her stomach in a worried way. "I put your clothes in your room." She bit her lip. "And yours also, Ryan."

He would have smiled at Lelandi's thoughtfulness, except for the seriousness of the situation. Instead, he followed Carol out of the sunroom, through the great room, and then up the stairs to her bedroom. He didn't even give a thought to the possibility that he might not be able to shift back or that she couldn't. When they reached her bedroom and he shifted, she didn't. He closed the door and dressed while she paced like a caged beast.

Shifting was so natural to someone born a wolf that he didn't know how to explain what she should do. He thought the process would be innate, but apparently not. Or...

He didn't want to think about the doc. She couldn't be stuck in her wolf form!

He walked over and touched her neck. She stopped and waited. He wrapped his arms around her neck and hugged her, leaning his face against hers.

"You can shift back, Carol. Just will it. You're so distraught that you're not thinking clearly." At least that was what he hoped the matter was.

For at least another ten minutes, which seemed an eternity, she stood there and breathed in hard breaths, her eyes gazing at him briefly. Then she focused on the dresser. It felt like she would stand there for the rest of eternity, just staring at the furniture, unable to do anything else.

"You can do it," he encouraged and rubbed her head between her ears. Then he ran his hand over her back, attempting to console her. If she hadn't liked it, she would have growled or moved away, but she didn't seem to mind.

Still, when he stopped petting her to see what would happen, she didn't nudge his hand to encourage him to continue. And then she began to pace again.

Hell. "Carol, you can do it. You can shift back. Close your eyes and see the change. Feel the heat, the swift transformation. Feel it."

She suddenly ran into the bathroom and pushed the door closed with her nose.

She didn't want him to see her shifting? "Carol, shifting is a natural occurrence for us. It's a beautiful process, something to be cherished."

Minutes later, she jerked the door open and scowled at him, naked and beautiful, her expression heated as she stalked toward her clothes laid out on the bed.

"For you, maybe, damn it, but not for me."

He grasped her wrist to stop her from avoiding him and folded his arms around her silky body, holding her tight. Her armor instantly slipped.

"I thought I was lost to the wolf," she sobbed.

He swallowed hard, kissed her on the top of her head, and held her close until the sobs died down. "You're all right, honey. You're going to be fine."

"I'll never be fine again," she said through the tears.

"You will. Together, we'll do this. I'll always be there for you."

She looked up at him, her eyes shimmering with unspent tears. "You want me? Even as much of a mess as I am? You're a pack leader. You need a mate who can help you lead. Not someone who is totally clueless and doesn't even know how to howl or shift back. Or control when she's going to shift in the first place."

"You'll be fine, Carol. What brought about the shift this time? Mervin came running to tell us you'd taken off. Did he accost you again?" Ryan tried to control the growl in his voice, but if Mervin had grabbed her again…

She quickly shook her head. "I was just sitting in the cold sunroom, trying to get warm while I drank the hot cocoa. I saw Mervin guarding the place and then glanced up at the growing moon. The damnable moon."

"The moon has something to do with the change as it continues to wax. But the cold can too. If we're in a really cold environment, we can shift into our wolf half so we can be warm."

"Yeah, but you do it when you choose to. Not when the wolf chooses to." She sighed deeply. "Ryan, I couldn't fight them. North and the others. The natural ability to defend myself came into play, the growling and snarling, the baring of teeth, but I couldn't attack them."

"There were three of them, and they had a net. If you'd attempted to attack, they could have easily captured you with the net. Instinct warned you that using a defensive posture was the only way to deal with the situation."

"I couldn't have killed them. Not any of them."

"If one had tried to kill you or someone else, you might have seen it differently. That's not important. What *is* important is that you get the shifting under control. You could have escaped by swimming across the river though."

"I can't swim."

He raised his brows. "Swimming is a natural ability for wolves."

She frowned up at him. "Yeah, well, shifting is supposed to be a natural ability for us too. And so is howling. Why couldn't I howl to let you know the three men were trying to catch me in a damned fishing net?"

He smiled. "You could have swum. Later, when things are more settled, I'll teach you how as a human. As for howling, you probably were too busy concentrating on the men and their net. If I had been in your fur coat, that's what I would have been doing."

Jake hollered up the stairs, "Everything all right up there?"

Ryan rubbed Carol's bare arms and kissed her cheek. "You all right?"

She nodded and pulled away from him to dress.

"We'll be down in a minute. Everything's fine up here." But Ryan had a new worry, and he was certain that was some of what was still bothering Carol. When would she next shift? And why hadn't she been able to conjure up any visions this time to block the need to shift?

Not wanting to see anyone in the pack ever again because of having turned into a wolf, Carol reluctantly went downstairs with Ryan to join Jake and Lelandi. She knew Lelandi had to be worried about her. Jake also. But she didn't want to face them. She'd lost what little control she'd had over her shifting ability, and now Darien was sure to ban her from working at the hospital.

Jake eyed Carol with too much concern.

"I'm okay," she said, rubbing her arms and glowering at him. But she didn't feel okay. She felt that any little thing could trigger the shift again.

Lelandi crossed the floor, gave her a big hug, and rubbed her back. "You'll be fine, Carol. It's just the beginning. I swear you'll get used to it."

Jake's phone rang. He whipped it off his belt and said, "Yeah, Darien?" His gaze shifted to Carol. "Shit. All right. I'll take her to the hospital now. What about Lelandi?" He glanced in her direction. "All right, she stays here with her guard detail. I'm on my way."

He hung up and called someone else. "Deputy Trevor, three of our men have been shot—in their wolf forms. Not by North's men. By human townsfolk. Get the word out pronto that anyone who shoots a wolf gets mandatory jail time. The sheriff's tracking the shooters down now, so he needs you to spread the word. I've got to get Carol to the hospital to help with the victims. Talk later."

Jake motioned for Carol and Ryan to come with him as he called someone else.

"Sam, I want you to take care of the guard detail watching Lelandi. Silva can come and stay with her. I've got to get Carol and Ryan to the hospital. Some of our men have been shot in their wolf forms, and Doc Mitchell has disappeared. Yeah, I know. Talk about a hell of a mess. We'll leave as soon as you get here."

Carol couldn't believe it. Then again, she'd felt deep in her bones that Doc's shifting into the wolf and not being able to shift back was only the beginning of the nightmare.

Lelandi rubbed her arms as she followed them into the great room. "You can go and help our men. I've got a guard detail already."

"No," Jake and Ryan said at the same time. "They're all betas," Jake added. "Sam will be here as soon as he can."

"I could run Carol over to the hospital until Sam relieves you, Jake," Ryan offered, figuring this time, they wouldn't have any trouble.

"No," Lelandi said. "What if North and his men try to ambush you?"

"I need to take care of the men who've been injured," Carol said, her voice resolute. "It'll take Sam an hour to pick up Silva and get here."

"Ryan?" Jake asked.

On the one hand, Ryan wanted more protection for Carol. On the other, he knew she needed to get to the men and minister to them. He pulled out a gun.

"I can manage. Besides, North and his men are probably still running through the woods."

Jake considered the gun.

"It'll slow them down if they try to take Carol hostage again. It's unlikely they'll be out here watching what we are doing after the last fiasco—fishing for a wolf with a net. Are you all right with this, Carol?"

She was already headed for the door. He swore she would have been the first one on the scene to take care of the wounded on a battlefield, no matter what the threat to her own safety, and he couldn't help admiring her for the quality.

He strode after her, glancing over his shoulder at Jake. "We'll let you know if we encounter any trouble or, if not, when we reach the hospital."

Jake gave him a stiff nod.

"Be careful," Lelandi said to Carol.

"You take care of yourself," Carol said, her look worried. Then she headed out of doors.

As soon as Ryan and Carol were secure in the truck, he tore off for town. "Had any more visions? Anything about you shifting or the men and the net? The men who were shot?"

She leaned against the seat and ran her hand over his plaid. "No. If I'd had a vision, I might have been able to stop the shift."

"I know you don't believe it now, but the sooner you embrace our ways, the easier it will be for you to adjust."

"Thanks for having faith in my other abilities anyway."

"If you'd danced any longer with me at the gathering the way that you'd done, I would have believed in *anything*."

She chuckled and then grew serious. "Believing in my sixth sense scares you."

He cast a wry smile at her. He didn't scare easily, but

yeah, knowing a person could have glimpses of future trouble was a bit unnerving. Not only that, but the fact that she could touch an object and gain insight about it seemed too surreal to be true.

She let out her breath. "I thought you ought to know that your sister called me back and talked to me further about you."

His neck muscles tensed. God only knew what Rosalind had told Carol. That he'd kept a portfolio of pictures of her? That he wanted her to be his mate even before he realized that was the issue? His sister had already stirred up enough trouble.

"She said you used a fake psychic once who got you into real hot water over a case of slander. So I understand how you would feel that we're all frauds."

"I didn't think you were a fraud exactly."

"Right. I just make up stuff because I'm such a great storyteller."

He rubbed his temple, getting himself deeper into this. "I had to know that you were for real, Carol. From the time we met, I've tried to debunk your 'visions,' at least in my own mind. It didn't work. Either you had hearing like Silva, which you couldn't have had as a human, or you just happened to be at all the wrong places at the right time. And that was too much of a coincidence. Unless you were seeking to learn the truth about the murder."

"And you suspected I might be?"

"No. You're a healer. First and foremost. If you investigate anything, it's related to helping others to heal. Murder cases are not your forte."

"Hmm." She unsnapped her seat belt to slide across the

bench seat, snapped on the belt in the middle of the seat, and snuggled up next to him.

He wrapped his arm around her and held her close as he steered the truck with one hand. "About the night you saw some of our kind shifting, I agree with you. You couldn't have witnessed such a thing in the dark. Not without our wolf's vision."

"You've never sounded like you believed me. Well, maybe an inkling. Yet you continued to question me and offer other reasons why I thought I had visions."

He shook his head. "I was grasping at straws, and all of them vanished before I could grab hold. No, I believe you're the real deal. And I need your help."

She looked up at him with a surprised expression. "My help?"

"In case I'm investigating a situation and you may be able to *see* something I can't."

"So *that's* what this is all about. You want me to be your mate so I can solve all your cases for you."

Loving her sense of humor, he chuckled darkly. "Yeah, devious of me, isn't it?"

She sighed. "I'll help if I can. My visions aren't always predictable. I can't force..."

He looked down at her, his expression warning her he knew better.

"...*always* force them."

"Only when you're fighting the shift. And that was the other thing. You couldn't fight the shift unless you were somehow special."

"Special," she murmured. "No one's ever called me that. Crazy, yes. Well, not so much that word exactly, but Dr. Metzger inferred it."

"Crazy, eh? You're about the sanest person I know." He gave her a warm squeeze. "For five months, I've been thinking about you. Did Rosalind tell you that? That I've been fiercely distracted? She's a gardener at heart, but she was doing some investigative work of her own, trying to discover what ailed me."

"She said you have pictures of me. Were they good shots?"

"I figured she'd mention them. I took photos of many of Darien's pack members."

"Hmm-hmm, and I wasn't under suspicion. Not really, according to Rosalind. So why the pictures? And why so many? Fess up, Ryan. You've always wanted me." She rested her hand high on his thigh, the heat sizzling through his denims and arousing him instantly. "But now if you want me badly enough, you'll have to deal with Darien."

"I told you that if I'd wanted you, nothing would stand in my way."

"Just a little psychic business."

He sighed. "*That* wouldn't have stopped me. See anything in regard to us being together?"

CHAPTER 23

CAROL LIGHTLY RUBBED RYAN'S THIGH UP AND DOWN, nearly touching his package on the upsweep. He was ready to pull the truck over and take her for his own before they even reached the hospital, but it was too dangerous with North and his men still unaccounted for.

"Hmm," she murmured in a sultry way, "I dreamt you came dressed in your kilt to rescue me on a white steed. It was the night North and his men took me hostage. You yanked off your plaid, wearing only your shirt and boots, and wrapped the fabric around me. Then you carried me off to the castle."

Prophetic that she should dream of him in that way? Or some deep-down desire to be with him that cast her into a fantasy world where he was her knight? He'd dreamed of her, too, only she was wearing the silky translucent gown that he'd seen her in when she had stood gazing out the window at him.

"Castle? I was the laird, no doubt." And he would have been, had his family kept the drafty old keep. But sometime or another, they'd lost it to taxes and moved to Prince Edward Island first, and then eventually to North Carolina, where many Scots ended up. Wolf or otherwise. Some of his family settled in Colorado, and there they'd stayed.

"And your clansmen were glad to see you'd finally found a lady to tame your wild ways," Carol said, her hand still stroking his thigh with a light touch.

"Sowing my wild oats, you mean." He winked at her.

"Do that often?"

He laughed. She chuckled. "But I'm worried about being a MacDonald. What if the McKinleys had fought the MacDonalds?"

"In the old days, who knows? Now, it doesn't matter. You know what this means?"

"What?" Her hand paused on his thigh.

"We're moving the engagement date up."

She stroked his leg some more, and he gritted his teeth against the rising tide of need. "If we have time before Doc and the other men arrive…" he said.

She stilled her hand on his lap. "What about Darien?"

"He'll understand. Believe me. Know anyplace private where we can…sort things out?" He didn't want to tell her that he had already made Jake aware Carol was his, that Silva would be the next to know, or that Darien already asked if he'd take her as a mate."

Chuckling, she squeezed his thigh. "You get right down to business, don't you?"

"You saw me rescue you and whisk you away from the villains to the safety of yon castle, so it seems you had a pre-monition. Since you can't change fate, we seem destined for this. So is there any place private where we can go?" he asked again.

Smiling, she shook her head.

"I thought you were an adventurous sort. More than that, I'll barely be able to move in the direction of the hospital if you keep manhandling me."

She laughed. "An exam table? Stirrups?"

"No-hands examination?" He grinned. "Now that's an idea."

"The basement has a lounge area, a testing lab, a laundry room, and a snack room. Couches, clean laundry, snacks."

"Getting better."

"The nurses' office and the doctor's office have beds for when we have to stay on call overnight."

"Can we lock the basement facilities?"

"Yes, all of the rooms will lock. It just depends on what you're in the mood for. When I was in training in Denver, I once found a nurse and a doctor fooling around in a linen closet. But linen closets have never appealed to me. Unless, of course, I got locked in one with a hunk of a guy and had to while away the time."

"With just any guy?"

She patted his thigh. "Not with just anyone. Twice, I've also discovered patients having sex with lovers in their rooms. Once I'd even knocked, waited for a response, and figured the patient was asleep when no one answered."

Ryan laughed. "So what did you do?"

"Turned around and muttered something about coming back later. I was embarrassed the first time I caught a middle-aged married couple at it. By the second time, I was getting the hang of it."

"Sounds like the patients didn't need to be in the hospital. Is an unoccupied patient's bed another choice then?"

She shook her head. "Not unless I'm one of the patients and feeling frisky and the visitor looked a whole lot like you."

"Sounds like you're an adventurous sort after all." But this meant a whole lot more to Ryan than the sex. Mating was the selfless commitment between a man and woman that promised a partnership through the rough times and cherishing the good, a way to carry their genes forward through their offspring, a companion for life. No matter what, his being with her for the long term felt better than right.

He just hoped the problems she was having with transitioning could be resolved once they were mated.

———————————

When they arrived at the hospital, the place was quiet. Nurse Matthew met them in the waiting area, gave Ryan a hard look, and then said to Carol, "I bandaged Tom and the others that North and his men had attacked earlier. Sam dropped by to pick up Tom and take him to Darien's house, and Silva's gone with him to stay with Lelandi. The others had someone pick them up and take them home. We've got six guards around the outside of the hospital. The place is quiet with no overnight patients tonight.

"The three men who were shot are being transported here. Should be another hour before they arrive though. They have to be carried to where a vehicle can reach them and then brought here.

"Doc's sleeping in his room off his office, still in his wolf form. I took blood samples, and the medical technologist has performed routine and some highly specialized tests on them. He went home for the night, if you want to take a look at the results down in the lab.

"You'd know more about them than I would, since you were training in that field before you decided to become a nurse. With Dr. Mitchell and Dr. Weber both unable to look at them, I don't know who else to send them to. I'm wiped out. Until the wounded men arrive to be patched up, I'm going to lie down in one of the staff rooms."

"Thanks, Matthew. I'll look at the blood samples in the basement. As soon as the wounded men arrive, I'll be back up here to help you treat them. Just let me know when they're here."

Matthew nodded and headed for the nurses' room.

Ryan followed Carol down the stairs to the basement, knowing he could never undo what he was about to do—and not regretting that in the least.

"You sure you want to do this?" he asked, just in case she wasn't ready for a full commitment. As they reached the bottom step, he opened the door for her. He had to be certain she wanted this as much as he did. "No last-minute change of mind?" He was afraid she'd settle for less than a mating again. Although getting hot with her like that again was appealing, he wanted more—to claim her, to make the commitment, to settle down with her.

She gave him a quick smile. "You have to ask? You're not getting cold feet, are you? You promised to help me through what I'm going through. 'Together,' you said." She raised a brow.

Just what he wanted to hear. He pulled her close and kissed her, ready to show her just how much he wanted her. Her fingers gripped him tight against her body, and her mouth softened against his kiss. Her body was stiff at first but then melted. His body felt tormented from her touch already, but he knew then that she wanted him just as much as he wanted her.

Her breathing shallow, she suddenly broke free from their kiss and motioned to the door. "Might want to lock it."

Hating to break the spell of the raw sexual energy spiraling between them, he stalked over to the door and locked it with a click.

The water heater in the next room thrummed as warm heat filtered out of the vents above. Ryan turned off half the lights, cloaking the lounge in darkness. They could still see, but it was a lot more romantic, he thought.

She took his hand and pulled him close again. "You're a romantic at heart, Ryan McKinley. But somehow I'd envisioned you being a little wilder than that."

He couldn't help smiling broadly at that.

She ran her fingers over his cheek as he rested his hands on her hips.

"You didn't send me flowers like all the other men did."

"See how well it worked?" he said, raising her face to his.

Her eyes were shadowed pools of blue, filled with anticipation, liquid with desire. Her lips parted, and he kissed the fullness, the softness that was all Carol, while feeling her arms go around his neck as she anchored her body against him.

"Besides," he said, whispering the words against her lips, his hands shifting lower on her back, "I don't follow trends."

He reached for her waistband and slid her scrub pants down her legs, bending lower to slip them off completely and kissing her belly down to her waistband. She pressed against the heel of her tennis shoe to remove it, but he crouched to take off that one and then the other. Then he slid his hands up her bare leg, kissing her on the inside of the knee.

She shivered.

"Cold?" he asked, rising, his hand sweeping up her thigh

and touching her intimately between her legs. The only thing stopping him was her sheer silk panties, like a see-through chastity belt protecting the treasure. But not for long.

He slid the panties down her legs, pressing his mouth against the inside of her knees and pushing them apart to gain entrance. Then with her legs spread, he slipped his fingers into her wet, hot cleft, and she immediately arched against him. Her body already screamed for release, the earlier unconsummated sex having been only the beginning.

"Hot," he said, describing the way she looked and felt.

"Exquisitely hot." She reached for his belt and struggled to unfasten it while he ran his hands up under her scrubs shirt and massaged her breasts, which were covered in the sheer silk bra without an ounce of padding. The pads of his thumbs stroked her erect nipples, and she closed her eyes, her fingers hesitating at his belt, her full lips parted in wonderment. She moaned softly and then quickly opened her eyes and jerked his belt open. After she slid his zipper down, she trailed her fingers along his rigid length, making it jump to her touch.

He pulled her scrubs top over her head, dropped it on the back of the couch, and then stared at her bra. It was better than lace or opaque material or anything else she might have worn. Her lingerie was sheer delight with her darkened nipples peaked against the fabric. He grasped her waist and licked the tantalizing peaks, first one through the silky fabric, and then the other as she speared her fingers through his hair, none too gently. Another soft moan from her lips spurred him on.

Fully aroused, he wanted her now before anything

stopped him from taking her as his mate. She was playing with his buttons, so he quickly kicked off his shoes, his tongue still teasing a nipple. Then she had his shirt off and on the floor, and his trousers went the way of his shirt.

He attempted to unfasten her bra but couldn't manage, so she grabbed for the fastener while he lifted her and carried her to the couch.

"Do you want to be on top or underneath?" he asked.

"The couch is scratchy. I have very delicate skin."

"I'll say." Ryan nuzzled her soft cheek.

"Besides, I'm a take-charge kind of girl."

He grinned broadly at that. She might think she was, but he had other plans.

Carol loved the way Ryan listened to her wants. With him, the ritual went so much deeper than mere sex. It was a commitment to cherish, to protect, to stand together forever—and forever was a very long time, given the life span of a wolf.

She was ready for the commitment, to be with the man who would risk his neck for her, who embraced her psychic quirks and patiently understood her reluctance to shift. She knew he was the one for her. She only hoped she wouldn't disappoint him as she struggled to accept the changes.

He set her next to the couch before he lay down on it. Naked, muscular, and ready, he smiled with lusty fascination. She crouched next to the sofa, brushing the light hair on his chest and moving lower, down the trail that led to his erection. The edge of her hand touched the velvet tip, already wet with anticipation and fully aroused. Now he shuddered with expectation as his erection pulsed with craving.

The smile still lit his face, although his eyes were dark with desire. She slipped her leg over his and moved until she was straddling his thigh. He placed his hands on her thighs, stroking and waiting to see what she'd do next.

She felt driven to take charge of her life. To choose Ryan for her own. For once in her life, she wanted to feel in control. Maybe not of her shifting problems or her psychic abilities. But right now, she was in charge of a hunky alpha male who she'd be committed to for the rest of her life. And that felt good.

She moved her hand down his arousal, gliding over the stiff rod, memorizing the feel of every velvet ridge, and only stopping when his erection moved under her light touch. She reached her leg across his other one, spreading herself for him, her belly brushing gently against his heavy arousal.

He moaned. "Carol…" She swore that if he didn't have such a husky, rushed voice, he might begin to beg. Begging was good.

Paused in a partial crouch, hovering over him with her hands planted on either side of his body against the soft couch, she held herself aloft, planning to sit and take hold of his sex and stroke until he was unable to stand the sheer pleasure another second. Until the back of his fingers swept up her inner thigh and she bit her lip, his touch sending a tremor of need through her. And then his fingers chafed against her thigh again, whisper soft, heating her core and making her blood burn for him. His hand touched the short curly hairs at the juncture of her thighs and paused there.

She leaned against his hand, pressing her mound against

his tormenting fingers. Her arms were giving out, so she decided to forgo stroking him and situated herself over his arousal to take the plunge. She also wanted to draw out the experience, so she lowered herself against his hand again, stirring him into action. His fingers slipped into the wet folds, and she nearly died—a wonderfully exquisite death.

Every fiber of her being, wolf and human, craved having the alpha male. Nothing else mattered. She was beginning to move higher, to line herself up with his arousal, when his hands grasped her inner thighs, and she swallowed a gasp. He wasn't going to let her take control.

He pulled her closer, his thumbs directed toward her woman's core, and then reached up and began to stroke her. Her whole body felt like vanilla pudding in his hands, and she didn't think she could stay like this for very long without collapsing on him. His smile said he knew it too. His strokes became faster, bringing her to the edge and stirring her passion until…she felt the sun and moon collide—and she cried out at the first time she'd ever felt so wildly intoxicated, her body still quivering with the rush of adrenaline.

Ryan should have warned her that if she thought to entice him with her feminine wiles, she'd better be prepared to accept the consequences.

———————————

The smell of her sweet arousal and the way her legs straddled his, opening herself to him, were driving him mad. Holding onto his sanity, attempting control while she touched him, had to be the hardest thing he'd ever done. Hell, as soon as she climbed on top of him, leaving herself ripe for penetration? He'd wanted to take the plunge right then and there. He sighed. The little red wolf would be the death of him.

He released her thighs and reached up to take hold of her waist. She gasped as he lifted her away from him and switched places so that she was on her back, her sweetness bared to him. Alpha male on top, in control, he slid his hands up her arms, lifting them above her head so her breasts were ready again for his tongue.

She was beautiful and sweet in a spicy way, and all his.

She smiled at him and licked her lips with a slow slide meant to prime him. But he had been ready to finish this before they'd even shed one article of clothing. He slid his leg over hers and pinned her to the couch. Her lids lowered, and he gently touched her lips with his. He craved her more than he'd ever desired anyone.

As soon as he kissed her, she ran her hands over his arms, her touch tantalizingly sensual. Then she lifted her leg between his, gently pressing against his stiff erection. He groaned, and her lips twitched upward slightly. But he wouldn't be pushed into a quick resolution.

He lowered his head and latched his mouth onto one of her nipples again, the bud puckered for his enjoyment. She moaned and ran her hands through his hair, her fingertips massaging his scalp with such finesse that he wanted to rest his head against her breast and give in to the sensual feel. He couldn't decide which gave him more pleasure, hearing her light moans as his fingers stroked her swollen nub, or the way she caressed him—as if he was as precious to her as he felt she was to him.

With her orgasm still fluttering deep inside her, he

slipped his erection into her and thrust again and again, deeper, harder, primal with wanting, as he claimed his mate forever.

"Ryan," she cried out when he couldn't hold onto the moment any longer and filled her with his seed.

He had meant to build up slowly, to make her enjoy the pleasure of him touching her last, but she arched against his fingers, her breathing shallow, her heartbeat pounding wildly, her eyes closed as her tongue wetted her lips, and he knew she couldn't last much longer. She was the most beautiful woman he'd ever been with—from the golden-blond hair framing her alabaster skin to nicely rounded breasts that made his mouth water for another taste, and nipples dusky pink and fully extended for his pleasure.

"Ah, Ryan," she whispered, her heated little body arching one last time. She sighed and licked her lips again, the orgasm rippling through her in another cascade of waves.

No one had ever said his name with such eroticism, longing, and need.

For a minute, he lay snuggled together with Carol, loving the feel of her silky warmth, the vitality of her beating heart, the sweet scent that was unique to a red female and even more special because of Carol's alluring fragrance. He had spent five months obsessing over her, and now she truly was his.

Teaching her the way of the wolf was next on the agenda. That trial had only begun.

CHAPTER 24

Snuggled against Ryan's hot, muscled frame, Carol needed a moment to realize that someone was at the basement door trying to get in, shattering her blissful contentment.

"Carol and that gray outsider have locked the damn door to the basement. I've tried to reach her, but there's no answer on her cell phone. Are you sure that you have the key to the facilities down here?" Nurse Matthew asked outside the door to the lab, lounge, and laundry area.

"Oh, hell," Carol said, scrambling to untangle herself from Ryan on the staff-lounge sofa. "We must have fallen asleep." She searched for her bra and frowned.

Naked, his body a chiseled wonder, Ryan put his arms behind his head and watched her.

Her face heated as he eyed her breasts. If she and Ryan had been someplace else, someplace more private, and had the circumstances been different, she would have told the intruders to go away.

"Later, Ryan," she said, her voice still hushed. "We've got to get dressed."

He got up off the couch slowly like a wolf, took her shoulders, and then kissed her mouth leisurely and with meaning. He had claimed her; she was his, and everyone had better get used to the idea.

All right, all right, so she was his. And he was all hers too. But this was not the time to prove it.

She nipped his mouth. "Help me find my bra." She hurried to pull on her panties, her scrub pants, and then her tennis shoes.

He searched under the couch and around his pile of clothes. "Don't see it."

She gave him a dark look. "Fine. Get dressed. Hurry."

"I've got the janitor's keys, and one should unlock the door," Jake said, his voice a little louder than necessary, as if he was warning Ryan and Carol to get ready for the incoming invasion. One key, then another was inserted in the lock, metal against metal.

"Jake," Carol whispered.

"Hurry it up," Matthew said.

"There are at least fifty keys on this ring. You know which one it is?"

Silence.

Ryan dragged his shirt on and slipped into his pants. Carol ran her fingers through her hair, trying to put it in some kind of order. Then she hurried over to the lab and retrieved the lab tech's report and blood samples from Doc Weber in his wolf form.

"Where's Doc Weber?" Jake asked Matthew conversationally, still playing with the keys in the lock.

Thank you, Jake, Carol said silently.

"He's wolf napping again in his office on a dog pad they brought over from the vet's kennel after Doc refused to lie on his bed. As fastidious as he is, he probably didn't want to shed fur on the linens. He's still running a fever and coughing. The shift didn't knock out the virus like it should have. So he can't have had human flu."

Carol examined the blood sample under an electron

microscope, observing roughly spherical shapes that were covered in rigid spikes like a halo. *Some halo.*

She glanced back at Ryan to see if he was dressed yet. He had finished buttoning his shirt and shoving the tails into his pants and was giving her a devilish wink and a little smile when the door lock clicked open. She shook her head at him. In his macho way, he just had to prove to Darien's pack that she was his. Not that she minded. At least no other male would think she was fair game any longer.

Ryan zipped up his zipper and buckled his belt as Jake and Matthew walked into the room.

"The men who were shot are here," Matthew said to Carol, giving Ryan a scathing look. "Why did you lock the damn door?"

"For protection," Ryan said as Carol's face grew hot with embarrassment. "In case North or his gang happened to break into the place."

"The men who were shot?" Matthew reiterated. "Darien had to send some folks over to Doc Mitchell's place to care for the animals in his kennel until they can locate the vet. It's not like the doc to disappear without a word to anyone, especially when a lot of pets needed his care and no one was scheduled to take care of them in his absence."

"He's got canine influenza," Carol said finally. "Doc Weber does. The respiratory illness causes coughing, runny nose, and fever," she added for Jake and Ryan's benefit. "We can medicate him, make sure he has plenty of fluids, and help him through this. If any of you don't know, the virus was first found in horses, but then it transferred to greyhounds. But it doesn't transfer to humans."

She looked up at the men, her expression worried. "He could get pneumonia."

Matthew frowned at her. "But that doesn't make any sense, since the canine virus doesn't transfer to humans. He was sick before he shifted."

"The virus he has can't transfer to humans. I'm sure he had a human flu virus before the shift, but we don't have a blood test from him while he was human to prove it. If so, the virus he had before he shifted might not be one that can't transfer to canines.

"I believe what we have here is a novel virus. One that is an offshoot of another. Maybe. I don't know for sure. But the virus appears to affect the wolf kind. This inability to shift back has to have something to do with the virus. Don't you think?"

Ryan nodded. "Sounds like that could be the case."

"You haven't had any flu-like symptoms, have any of you?" she asked them.

Impressed at the logical way Carol dealt with a medical mystery, just like he would in a PI investigation, Ryan peered over her shoulder at the lab results.

"No. I think you might be right. Everyone in the pack needs to be warned not to shift if they can avoid it. Especially if there's any indication they're coming down with a bout of the flu. Hell, I need to notify my pack and my sister."

He lifted his phone off his belt, hoping no one in Green Valley had been infected with the virus, if that was what it was. He called his sister first.

"Rosalind?"

"Well? Did you finally see the light with Carol?" She sounded like she knew he had, even before he told her so.

"Listen, we've got problems here."

His sister remained silent. She knew that when his voice took on that dark tone, he meant business. "At least one of the people in Carol's pack has come down sick with something. A flu-like virus, it appears. It seems that if a person with this virus shifts into the wolf, he or she can't shift back into human form."

"You can't be serious!" Her voice was more than concerned.

"I *am* serious about this. I'll call my second-in-command, but I don't want you to be exposed to anyone until we can sort this out."

"Ha! This is the biggest season for my nursery business, Ryan."

"Rosalind." He only had to say her name once for her to know how grave this was.

"All right," she said tightly. "Carol discovered it, didn't she?"

He glanced at Carol. "Yeah, Carol's the one who discovered the sickness and the results."

"Through her visions, right?"

He sighed. "Yeah."

"Didn't I tell you so?"

"Yeah, so you've said already, and I've finally... Well, hell, she's got really good hunches." He gave Carol an elusive smile as she raised a brow at him.

"Not just hunches."

"She's the real deal." His voice turned more commanding. "Don't shift, all right?"

"All right already. I said I wouldn't."

He let out his breath. "I've got to call my subleader. I'll be home soon. Keep yourself isolated from the others. All right?"

"I will."

"I'll call you when I know anything new."

"Good luck, Ryan. She'll do it. She'll find a cure."

"Now you can see the future?"

Silence. Then his sister said, "Yeah, just like I know that if you haven't taken her for your mate already, you will soon."

"Bye, Rosalind." He wasn't about to say anything to her about mating Carol while Jake and Matthew were listening in on the conversation. He clicked off the phone.

"Hunches, huh?" Carol asked Ryan.

"Yeah, damn good ones. It's going to take a while to get used to you knowing things before I do…in an unscientific way, but…" He shrugged, punched in another number, and said, "Granbury, it's McKinley. Find out who all in our pack might be sick with a flu-like virus. Upper respiratory ailments. Make sure you warn them not to shift. That has dire consequences."

He looked over at Carol and found her observing him, a frown knitting her brow.

"They can't shift back if they turn into the wolf. I know it sounds crazy, but I've got an expert on the case. No one else who can help it should shift either. But especially those with the flu."

"Your administrative assistant was sick this morning."

"Hell. Has she shifted?"

"Not that I know of. She called in sick today. I'll call her, and if I don't get an answer, I'll run by her place and warn her."

"All right. Make sure she gets plenty of fluids. The canine flu isn't supposed to transfer to humans, but the way this is affecting our people, we're not sure of the effects with the shift. I'll give you an update as soon as I can. And let me know what's going on with Ingrid." He put his phone away.

Carol gave Ryan a weary smile. "Thank you."

"I'm sorry, Carol. I guess I was just too set in my ways before."

Jake raised his brows when Carol looked at him. He was studying her way too much. His gaze shifted from her to Ryan.

She rose from the chair and headed for the stairs. "How are the wounded men doing?" she asked Matthew.

"They'll be fine. They're still in their wolf form. The men lost some blood, and all three are sick with whatever Doc probably has. Three of them suffered hind leg wounds. One was hit in the rump," Matthew said, leading the way up the stairs, Carol following behind. "If we could have found Doc Mitchell, he could have performed the surgery at his vet clinic."

Ryan watched as Carol disappeared and then turned to see what Jake was doing in the staff lounge.

Jake glanced at the couch and drew closer. Then he bent over it and poked around. Hell. Jake pulled the silk bra out from between the back and seat cushions and took a deep breath. He shook his head and tossed the bra to Ryan.

"Looks like you two took the plunge." He gave Ryan a dark smile. "About time. But Darien will not be pleased."

Ryan tucked the incriminating evidence into his pocket. Carol would not be pleased to know Jake had found her bra, and while he didn't like to keep secrets from his mate, he had no plans to tell her about this.

He took off for the stairs, and Jake followed him. As soon as Carol finished treating the injured men, Ryan had every intention of transporting her home. To his home. His bed. He had people who could keep her safe just like Darien did. Now she belonged to his pack, not Darien's. And if his own people could suffer the same trouble as Darien's, Ryan needed to be there for them. He rubbed his chin in thought. As long as she could do her research in Green Valley. He'd have to make sure she could.

After they arrived at the operating room, Jake and Ryan served as guards and waited inside by the door. While Matthew assisted, Carol removed the bullet from the first of the patients. Ryan admired Carol for her dedication to the patient's care. She worked efficiently with steady hands, her deportment self-assured. Matthew aided her, his expression one of deep admiration, as if he had every confidence in her abilities. When she stitched the man's wound closed, she looked as though she could work like this all night. She had to be tired, but she didn't let on.

"I keep telling you that you ought to be a doctor, Carol," Matthew said. "Before Doc Weber arrived here, you'd removed how many bullets from pack members?"

"Three men wounded in that bank robbery. We heal faster, as long as the bullets don't hit anything vital that would make them bleed out. Rifle bullets can do a lot of permanent damage to humans, but our bodies will heal from the injury, given time. So it's not the same."

"You have the smarts and the skill to do it, Carol," Matthew argued.

She might believe she wasn't capable of doing the job, but with her determination, Ryan thought differently. If she wanted further medical training, he'd back her all the way. But one thing was certain: his Green Valley pack needed a *lupus garou* who had the medical skills she did. He needed to arrange for a wolf doctor to start a clinic, and she could attend him. If she wanted further training after that, Ryan was all for it.

Matthew bound the man's injured leg, and then they moved on to the next man.

Avery. Hell, he was sick now. And he'd danced with Carol. She'd been around Doc all day too. Ryan had danced with Marilee, and she also was ill. He wondered how long the rest of them had before they shifted with no way to change back.

Ryan turned to Jake. "Where are Marilee and Becky now? They're both sick with this crud. If they've got it, we don't want them returning to their pack and carrying the virus there."

"What if they brought it from their pack?" Jake jerked his phone out of its pouch and punched in a number. "Bertha? This is Jake. Marilee and Becky were staying at your bed-and-breakfast, right?" He frowned and then stared at Ryan. "Hell. All right. I'll tell Darien and give Ryan the word."

Jake hung up and punched another button.

"Darien," he sighed. "We've got more trouble."

Carol finished removing the bullet from the third wounded man, although concentrating had become an effort as soon as Ryan and Jake left the operating room to discuss some new trouble with Darien in private.

Matthew said, "Wonder what else is going on."

Carol took a deep breath. "Nothing good, we can be sure."

"You did it with him, didn't you?"

She glanced up from stitching the man's wound closed. Matthew looked slightly annoyed, eyes narrowed, lips pursed. "If you mean Ryan and I are mated, yes."

"He'll expect you to leave right away. To move to Green Valley. To take care of his people."

"I'm staying here until we resolve this." Beyond that, she hadn't really thought of leaving. Just that she'd be Ryan's mate. Why hadn't she even considered it? Did they have a hospital in Green Valley? Certainly not one that was run by wolves, she imagined. Would she be able to get a position? Should she even try, considering her shifting problem?

She ground her teeth and sighed. "Like you heard Jake say, if we're all infected because we've been exposed to this, we can't go spreading it to other packs." She figured that went without saying.

"He won't think that, Carol. He's a pack leader. His place is with his pack. He'll want to be there in case this hits his people. His sister and his aunt are there. Family takes priority. You wait. If one case of this sickness hits Green Valley, he'll want to drag you back there pronto."

She finished with her patient and was about to reply that Ryan wouldn't be that way when Nurse Charlotte came in for her work shift. Jake accompanied her, but Ryan wasn't with them.

Carol had a bad feeling about that.

Charlotte sighed heavily. "Looks like we have an epidemic of our kind getting sick and then not being able to shift back to their human forms. Now the humans think the wolves are invading Silver Town and the surrounding area. So they're taking up guns to get rid of the menace."

Jake shook his head. "Five men have already been arrested and thrown in the slammer. One said something about Darien being a wolf lover, and Darien just smiled in a sinister way. None have lawyers, so the court will appoint them." Jake gave an evil smile.

"All wolf lawyers. They'll get the maximum fine— $20,000—five years suspended hunting license, and sixty days in jail for harassing wildlife on private property, carrying loaded weapons in a vehicle without a permit, firing across a road, and anything else witnesses will attest to."

"*Lupus garou* witnesses," Carol said, half commenting, half questioning.

"Exactly. Silver Town is wolf run, and we plan to keep it that way."

Carol chewed on her bottom lip and rubbed her arms. "Someone needs to take care of Doc Weber and watch him around the clock."

"I'll do it," Charlotte said. "You run along now. My shift. You've already worked yours and more hours than you ought to have."

"Thanks, Charlotte. Hopefully you'll have a quiet night." Carol left the hospital with Jake, flanked by Mervin and Christian. She expected Ryan to be waiting outside the operating room, but he wasn't.

"Where's Ryan?"

"He and the sheriff had to question Marilee and Becky at the bed-and-breakfast," Jake said as he walked her to his truck. "When I called Bertha to learn if the women's pack members were sick, she said a man named Miller is behind all of this and had infected the two women to get back at Darien. Only now Miller won't give them the cure. This isn't just a normal virus."

"It's not just a mutation of some sort that affects our people?" Carol's head spun with the ramifications. "Some sick bastard bioengineered this?"

"Yeah, and then Miller gave it to them to infect our pack. Connor paid the *lupus garou* scientist to come up with the plague. Darien killed Connor's twin brother during the fight at the house and North is Connor's cousin. They feel that you belong to one of them since Connor's brother bit and turned you. Becky and Marilee wanted to start their own businesses, and Connor was going to give them a hefty sum for carrying the plague to our gathering. The only satisfaction any of us have is that Connor and some of his pack have come down with it. The women will have the same trouble dealing with it."

Ryan drove into the parking lot, parked next to Jake's vehicle, and hurried out of his truck. His jaw was hard, his eyes dark. The news wasn't good.

"Did the scientist make a vaccine?" Carol asked both Jake and Ryan.

"That's what we're trying to learn." Ryan hauled her close and held her tight as if he'd been away for eons. He brushed her cheek with his lips and then said to Jake, "We're headed back to the house."

Jake had an odd look on his face and didn't move toward his own truck to follow them.

"Jake?" Carol said.

He frowned at her. "You saw me shift and not be able to change back."

He finally seemed to believe her. "Maybe I'm wrong," Carol said. "Maybe I just see you shift, but like everyone keeps reminding me, I don't see the end result. That you shift back."

Jake's expression remained dark.

She patted his arm. "We'll find a vaccine. And a cure."

"And this damned Miller," Ryan said, hauling Carol into the truck. "See you at Darien's place."

"I'll be right behind you," Jake said.

As soon as they were on the road, Carol said to Ryan, "I wish I hadn't told Jake what I'd seen."

Ryan shook his head and tugged her close. "We'll get this under control."

But behind his words, she was certain she heard the worry that they might not.

"Darien's going to be pissed about us mating when we didn't say anything to him about it beforehand."

Ryan let out his breath, wanting Carol away from this nightmare immediately. "Even more so when I tell him that you're coming home with me tonight."

She looked up at Ryan as if he'd lost his mind, and he knew as soon as she did that she wasn't going to agree with his plan. But he had his own pack and his own place. Staying as a guest at Darien's wasn't in the plans. He had to investigate Connor and Miller's hideout, but he thought that if Carol was with his pack, Connor and North and the rest of them would never learn of her whereabouts and she'd be safer.

"I want to take you home with me," he said, a little more

amenable this time. He hadn't even considered she might object.

"I have to stay and figure out a way to cure this. Unless you have a doctor in Green Valley who might have some idea of what to do."

He sure wished he did. If the doctor had been a *lupus garou*, he might have helped. But as a human, he couldn't.

"No, Carol, he's human."

"Human?" She said it like the man was an alien just arrived from another planet when she'd been strictly human herself not that long ago.

"We can't allow him to learn what we are." Ryan was unsure why the fact that the doctor was human distressed her. Unless she'd had high hopes he could help with this.

"You didn't see Doc Mitchell change in a premonition, did you, Carol?"

CHAPTER 25

CAROL SIGHED DEEPLY AND RESTED HER HEAD AGAINST Ryan's shoulder as the truck rumbled toward Darien's house. She was tired, but this virus had to be stopped and the effects counteracted.

"No, I haven't seen any visions of Doc Mitchell." Carol wished she had—anything to know what had happened to him. She snuggled closer to Ryan, feeling more chilled by the situation they were in than by the weather.

"But the way the doc disappeared makes me surmise that either North and his men kidnapped him, thinking that he might be able to help with their medical problem, or he shifted, ran off, and was unable to change back. If North and his newly formed pack came down with this before we did, I need to interview them."

Ryan stiffened beside her. "You can learn what you have to over the phone. You're not meeting any of North's people face-to-face. I'll be leading a force to learn their where-abouts, the lab they've been using—and hopefully find a vaccine."

She tapped her fingers on her lap. "It's remotely possible our people could *eventually* change back on their own."

"That most likely would mean only a few like Lelandi, who is a royal, could avoid shifting during any phase of the moon."

"What if..." Carol's eyes brightened. "What if when the new moon appears, the condition vanishes? Those of us who aren't royals can't maintain our wolf forms. So what if the condition ceased to exist?"

"Maybe. But the first full moon made its appearance this morning. The three-quarter moon appears in the morning nine days later, and the new moon eight days after that in the evening. That's a long time to wait to see if we make it out of this on our own."

Surprised he'd know the exact timing of the phases of the moon, she raised her brows.

He shrugged. "I'd considered the moon's phases might knock out this anomaly, so I checked the timing of the phases for Colorado for this month."

"Hmph, you could have told me you'd already thought of it."

He rubbed her arm. "You haven't been a wolf long enough to think in those terms all the time. So what happens if half our pack or more can't keep from shifting while we wait about seventeen days for the new moon to appear? What if the town is no longer run by the wolf kind? And humans decide to take over? Worse, what if those who are stuck in their wolf shapes are still unable to shift back when the new moon appears?"

Ryan's phone rang, and he saw it was his assistant mayor. "Yeah, Granbury?"

"Your admin assistant is fine. Ingrid had already shifted and changed back. She knocked out whatever ailed her— she suspected food poisoning and that whatever she ate could be more easily tolerated by her wolf's stomach—and she returned to work. She didn't want me to tell you in case she shouldn't have shifted, per your orders. But she didn't get word until it was too late."

"Thanks. I'll check on her shortly." Vastly relieved, Ryan put away his cell phone. "My admin assistant was sick, shifted, knocked out what appeared to be food poisoning, and shifted back to her human self," he told Carol.

She relaxed against him.

"We may have an isolated case of this virus here in Silver Town. Which probably means that Connor and his bunch did engineer this sickness and brought it specifically to Darien's people."

"Thank goodness. If we can immunize enough people in the area—it's called 'herd immunity,' though in our case, the term 'pack immunity' suits us better—we could stop the spread of the virus. But letting other packs know about a vaccine wouldn't be easy, would it? Lelandi said that the packs are not very open about where they're located."

"Let's worry later about other packs contracting it."

"All right. So we need to know who was sick in our pack first."

"When they were dancing, Mervin said Becky told him she was worried about shifting and not being able to change back. He thought it was a strange thing to say and just figured she'd had some weird nightmares. But the word has spread through the pack that Doc Weber can't shift back due to this virus, and now she's really scared."

"She should be." Carol frowned and then shook her head. "A virus can be contagious from a day before a person becomes aware of having it to five days after.

"I've checked," Ryan said. She admired the way he could put his investigative skills to use and was one step ahead of her. He continued, "Their pack is clean. But it doesn't matter."

"Why not?" Carol asked.

"Becky and Marilee haven't been with the pack for a couple of weeks. I suspect they've been with Connor's people all this time."

Carol swore under her breath. "And you danced with Marilee."

"Only because she was acting nervous."

"So you danced with her out of concern for her?"

He chuckled darkly. "*No*, because she seemed unduly nervous. Like she'd set an explosive device in the house and wanted to leave. It made me curious, but when I tried to learn what the matter was, I didn't get anywhere with her. I assumed she was just anxious about finding the right mate. Now it seems she was even hotter than I suspected—germ warfare."

Carol pressed her lips tighter together. "I can't imagine anyone doing anything so despicable."

"Offer money and a lot of people will do something they'd never do otherwise."

A frisson of dread suddenly worked its way up Carol's spine. Before she could analyze what was making her feel so antsy, her vision blurred and she closed her eyes, not welcoming the vision and what it might foretell but having no choice. Ryan's words faded into the background like a conversation in the distance as the vision clarified.

As a wolf, Darien paced, panting, his teeth and lips bloodied. Wounded, he limped. A dead wolf lay near the bed on the blue carpet in his and Lelandi's bedroom. Carol felt Darien's satisfaction that the wolf was dead—and his frustration and dread because he couldn't change. He was stuck as a wolf.

Lelandi looked miserable, tears streaking her cheeks as she wrung her hands. Carol wanted to help and console her.

But then Lelandi grabbed her phone off the bedside table and punched a button.

Carol's phone rang and nearly gave her a heart attack, yanking her from the vision. Perspiration trickled between her breasts, and her heart rate accelerated as she pulled her phone out of her pocket and looked at the caller ID. "Lelandi?"

"Come home quick. I need to see you. But no one else."

"All right." Lelandi didn't have to tell Carol what had happened, that Darien had been victorious in a wolf fight, but he couldn't shift back. It was too late for Darien, too late for Doc.

"Not a word to the others," Lelandi made Carol promise.

"All right. We're nearly there." Carol hung up her phone, trying not to shake. Everyone would have to know their pack leader was in a real bind. Jake and Tom would have to take over until Darien could change back.

"What's wrong?" Ryan asked, pulling into the drive and parking in front of Darien's home.

"Nothing."

"Your face has lost every ounce of color, Carol. Your voice shook when you spoke with Lelandi. You're not a good liar."

She ground her teeth and looked at Ryan. Lelandi didn't want her to tell, but everyone would know before long anyway.

"Darien's shifted. And he can't change back."

"Hell."

Jake parked his truck next to Ryan's vehicle and hurried out. "Lelandi just called me. Told me the news." He gave Carol an anxious look.

Lelandi must have realized she couldn't hide the fact

that Darien couldn't shift back. Did Jake worry he would be next?

"We've got to find the lab where these men made the virus and destroy it, Jake," Ryan said, taking Carol's arm and guiding her toward the house.

Wolves in motion, Tom and Sam bolted from around the side of the house, and Carol jumped. Her heart took a dive. They shouldn't have shifted.

"Hell," Jake said to his brother and Sam. "You better be able to shift back." He opened the door to the house, and the wolves dashed inside and up the stairs, tails straight out, indicating both were tense.

"I should go with you, Ryan. To identify the vaccine, if they have one." Carol figured Ryan would say no because he'd worry about her safety, but she really thought it was the best way to handle this. "If they have a lab that produced the virus, they may have created a vaccine."

"Lelandi wants to see you," Jake said to Carol, motioning to the stairs.

"Don't you *dare* go anywhere without me, Ryan McKinley." She gave him a hard look, hoping that he wouldn't take off to search for the lab and leave her behind. Then she ran up the stairs.

"I see who's in charge in your family already," Jake said with a smirk.

Ryan folded his arms and watched her disappear upstairs. "I *would* leave her behind for her own safety. But she's got a valid point. We need her with us. You need to stay with Lelandi. I'll take Tom and Sam with me." As an afterthought, he added, "If that works well for you."

Jake shook his head. "Can't give up being a natural born leader, can you, Ryan?"

"Nope, it's in the blood." He just hoped he wasn't making a grave mistake by taking Carol into the enemy's territory.

Carol knocked on Lelandi's bedroom door, not wanting to intrude on her and Darien and their new dilemma. She felt terrible. If she couldn't solve this situation, Lelandi's children would never know their father as a human.

"Come in, Carol," Lelandi said, opening the door, her voice tinged with alarm as she waited for Carol to enter the bedroom. Lelandi wrung her hands and watched Darien pace back and forth in his wolf form. Thankfully, someone had removed the dead wolf's body.

"What's happening? I don't understand what's happening. How can we stop this?" Lelandi asked. Her green eyes turned to Carol, and tears filled them. "He can't change back. You have to do something!" Lelandi pleaded, her voice strained and choked with emotion.

Carol took Lelandi's hands and guided her to sit down on the bed.

"Take a deep breath. Calm yourself. We'll figure this out and reverse the effects."

At least she hoped so. What if they could only vaccinate against the virus before someone contracted it, but there was no hope for those poor souls who already had it? "Do you know who Darien just killed?"

"Yeah, Connor. Darien killed his brother after the guy bit you. During the initial battle, Connor had given up the fight, so Darien had let him live. Not this time."

Carol rubbed Lelandi's arm. "So he came here to avenge his brother's death, I suppose. His plan to make us all sick hadn't worked out the way he wanted, so he'd decided to kill Darien. I wonder if they thought they could take over Silver Town if all of us had gotten sick and couldn't change back."

"Possibly. The renegade reds left their pack. What better way to start over than to come into a town already run by wolves, eliminate the leadership through the use of the virus, and take over."

"Except that it backfired, because now they're getting sick too. What happened to the men who were protecting you?"

"They chased the other three reds off. Connor stayed to fight Darien."

Carol nodded, figuring this was one thing she'd never get used to, fighting among wolves. "Where's Silva? She was supposed to be staying with you."

"Downstairs making me hot cocoa."

"All right. I'm going to leave with Ryan and some others to try to find the reds' lab. In the meantime, Darien and Jake can protect you."

"Be careful."

"I will be." Carol gave Lelandi a hug, fought the urge to pat Darien on the head—figuring he probably would not appreciate it—and hurried out of the master bedroom. When she reached her room, she ditched her scrubs and changed into jeans and a sweater, and then joined Jake and Ryan downstairs in the great room. To her profound relief, she watched Tom and Sam exit the kitchen, tall and dressed and very human.

Ryan asked, "Ready to go?"

A big gray wolf loped out of the kitchen, headed straight for her, and her mouth gaped. "Doc Mitchell?"

"Some of the men found him on his way to the house to see Darien. He's been trying to tell us something, but we're not sure what. We think he may have been searching for these guys long before we were aware of what was going on," Jake said.

"All right, let's go." Ryan took hold of Carol's arm and hurried her out to the truck. Doc Mitchell loped alongside them.

"Guess he thinks he can help," Carol said, and she prayed he could.

Driving south from Darien's place, Carol and Ryan were quiet as Doc Mitchell rode in the back seat of the truck while Tom and Sam followed in Tom's truck. Carol watched Doc Mitchell's antics and interpreted them. He wagged his tail when they took the right roads and growled when they didn't.

If Carol hadn't been worried about how they might all become just like him, stuck forever as wolves with human brains, she would have admired his ability to guide them in the right direction. Even more, she worried that she might not be able to find the cure.

She took a deep breath, tried to give up thoughts of failure, and considered another situation that concerned her—bringing were-kids into the world, where they had to live in secret. She didn't think she could cope with taking care of them, not when she hadn't been raised as one. She thought about her mother's comment that she should talk with Ryan about children before they were married, or in this case, mated. Better late than never.

"I don't want children," she blurted out before she thought better of it. Now really wasn't the time to discuss this.

Ryan's hands tightened a little on the steering wheel as he continued to watch the road. "It's a little late to consider that now." He didn't sound mad, just a little concerned.

"I'm on birth control." She hadn't needed it for a long time, but she always wanted to be prepared—just in case. At least she'd been careful and not reckless.

She couldn't read his expression at first, but his pause made her think he wasn't happy with the idea.

"Pills?" he asked.

"Yep. Not that I've needed them, but…" She shrugged.

"Doc give them to you?"

She didn't like the way he asked, as if he was investigating one of his cases. She folded her arms. "No. I had enough of a supply before he came to work here."

"So…no one told you they won't work for us."

She stared at him in disbelief.

"They don't work for all women," he said.

She knew that from personal experience, because a friend of hers had gotten pregnant while on the pill—but at least her friend had been married. Her friend's sister also had gotten pregnant on the pill, only she was in love with the guy, not married. The day she learned she was pregnant, she also discovered her lover had a wife and two daughters. *Bastard.* And he had no intention of leaving his wife, because her dad was a rich man and would have ruined him.

"Yeah, I know," she said, annoyed.

"Well, our women are like that. We normally don't use birth control. Like humans, some of us can have children without any problem. Others never do. But as with any pack mentality, procreation of our species is important, and most of us want children. As a pack leader, it's essential. Are you afraid they'll have your psychic talents? And be ostracized?"

She frowned at him. "I hadn't thought of that."

"Oh." He sounded like he regretted mentioning it. "Then what?"

"How in the world can I teach my own were-children anything about growing up wolf when I never did?"

He smiled. "You'll learn, and that's what a pack is for. All pack members care for one another's kids."

She sighed. "A mother is supposed to know these things and be in charge. I'll be like the child."

He chuckled. "Not on your life. You'll be fine. Unless"—he glanced at her—"you want to abstain from sex."

"Like that's really an option." No way was she abstaining from anything of the kind with Ryan.

"Other forms of birth control work reasonably well."

She leaned against him. "It's not that I don't want kids. I always planned to have a couple. It's just this...were-issue." She guessed this was one more aspect she wouldn't have any control over. At least her mother would be happy. *If* she never learned what Carol's children's secrets were.

The tension left Ryan's body, and he wrapped his arm around her. "If we're meant to have children, we will. If not, so be it. But you'll be the best mother a litter can have, Carol. Don't you worry."

She smiled, thinking of raising more McKinleys and

attending the Scottish games, just like having their own little clan.

The thought of having a couple of sons who would help their dad in a game of tug-of-war, or a couple of daughters who danced to the Celtic tunes and captured the boys' attention, made her forget for the moment the potential danger that lay ahead.

About an hour and a half from Darien's home, Doc Mitchell began to pace in the back seat, make little woofing sounds, and growl. Her thoughts quickly shifted to the peril they could all be in.

"Must be close," Carol warned, feeling Ryan's whole body tense. She was fairly certain that another wolf fight would ensue. These guys never seemed to resolve anything between them in a nice, conversational way. She tried to relax and not be uptight, but as soon as Ryan drove toward a single-family dwelling surrounded by woods, the tension returned to every muscle, and she prayed she wouldn't shift again.

CHAPTER 26

"I wish you hadn't come," Ryan said. He kissed the side of her temple as they drove down the dirt road, closing in on what they thought was the location of the lab. His hand held hers as if he never wanted to let go.

"I know. You want to keep me safe." She tried to force her voice to remain even and not sound like she was having second thoughts. She wasn't a warrior at heart. But she had the courage to overcome her failings when the circumstances warranted it. And these definitely did. She certainly didn't want Ryan to think he'd made a mistake in bringing her.

Ryan drove down the bumpy, rutted road where tree limbs stretched into the lane, scraping the sides of the truck. He grumbled something under his breath about needing a new paint job after this operation. She figured his edginess probably had more to do with her being with him on one of his more dangerous investigative missions than with the paint job on his truck, especially the way he kept a tight grip on her fingers.

She couldn't complain. It felt good to have a man care about her the way he did. She was ready to move to Green Valley and start a life with him there.

When they came into a small clearing, she saw the house more clearly. It had three rooms, if that, with tall grass brushing against the bottom frames of the windows. Blue paint was peeling off the exterior clapboards, while the weathered shutters bordering the windows were missing slats. A rickety fireplace made of rough stone stuck to one side of the house with a couple of the corner stones missing. The house looked abandoned, except for the smoke trickling out of the chimney. Movement in one of the three windows caught Carol's eye.

"Someone's home," Ryan said glumly.

"How will you get in?" Carol asked.

"Most *lupus garous* carry lockpicks."

She raised her brows in question.

He shrugged. "If we're in a city and have an uncontrollable urge to shift, finding an unoccupied house could be our only salvation. Lockpicks are preferable to breaking windows."

She stared at him in disbelief. She hadn't thought of being in a city without a place to hide in the event of shifting. She could just envision herself in that dilemma. What a disaster.

"No one gave *me* a set."

He patted her thigh. "No one's letting you out of their sight either."

She sighed, realizing just how good she had it living in a wolf-run town. How would it be for her living with Ryan in Green Valley where humans ran the place for the most part?

Ryan pulled up to the front porch, breaking into her mounting concern. He turned off the truck, saying at the same time, "Stay here until we secure the place. Lock the doors. Doc, you want to stay and guard Carol?" He posed the comment as a question, but the intonation was more of a command.

Doc Mitchell gave a little woof. She took it as a yes. But

she wanted Ryan and the others to have the doc's added protection since they were facing unknown perils.

"Take him with you," Carol said. "He can help."

Ryan shook his head, his gaze studying her in a worried way. "He stays with you."

He leaned over and gave her a meaningful kiss that briefly chased away the chill in her bones. He squeezed her hand one last time. He let out his breath in a sigh of resignation and climbed out of the truck. Then he let out Doc Mitchell, who raced around to sit in wolf-guarding mode next to Carol's door.

She watched Ryan, her stomach bunched in tight knots, her skin icy with trepidation, praying that he wouldn't get himself killed.

Tom pulled up next to her passenger door, and he and Sam hurried out of the truck to join Ryan. Tom tilted his chin down, also giving Carol the silent order to stay put. They didn't have to tell her that she most likely would cause more problems if she entered the house before they checked it out. She folded her arms and glowered at Tom. His mouth lifted slightly, and he gave her a short nod.

Then he turned, and Ryan, Sam, and Tom stalked toward the house, backs straight, postures determined, like the Three Musketeers, except without the plumed hats and sharp steel swords. And that gave Carol another shiver of worry.

She barely breathed as Tom used his lock-picking tools to unlock the front door. Doc Mitchell's ears twitched with alertness, his body stiff with tension, making her more concerned that the three men were headed into danger.

When the front door opened. Ryan rushed in first, while Tom and Sam followed. The door remained wide open, and

Doc Mitchell stood, his attention focused on the doorway, his hackles raised. Every hair on Doc's body stood on end, making him appear bigger and more ferocious.

Snarling erupted inside the house, and Doc Mitchell growled softly in response, his ears positioned to hear the sounds inside.

Carol's muscles were so tense that her leg cramped. She was pressing her foot against the truck's floorboard to work out the painful kink when Doc Mitchell started forward. Maybe he just wanted to assist Ryan and the others. Or maybe he was anxious to see what the others had found.

She wanted him to join the others in case they needed his help. She thought she'd be safe enough in the vehicle. Yet the idea she'd be alone without any kind of protection made her spine stiffen with dread.

The way he stood, muscles taut, wired to the max, Doc Mitchell seemed ready to bolt. Then, as if he'd remembered his duty, he glanced back at Carol.

For a long moment, their gazes held. His amber eyes asked her a wealth of questions. Did she want him to stay? Did she want him to watch the men's backs? What did she want him to do?

"Go," she said, motioning toward the house with tears in her eyes. She'd never forgive herself if anything bad happened to Ryan, Tom, or Sam and she'd denied Doc Mitchell the chance to help.

Doc hesitated, his head riveting back on the house.

She again said, "Go. Help them! I'll be all right."

He looked at her again, bowed his head, turned, and dashed around the back side of the place.

Her mouth gaped. Why hadn't he gone inside? The

doorway still stood wide open, as if daring her to come inside. She took a deep, unsettling breath and prayed the men would all be okay. That whoever was inside wouldn't attack them. That they would find a vaccine.

Ryan had barely entered the old, rickety house, its wooden floors creaking as they walked inside, when he heard low growls coming from a hallway past the living room. The place smelled of mold and dust. In the main living room, where faded floral wallpaper peeled off the walls in sheets, three sofas with sagging cushions were covered with wolf fur and reeked with the odor of wet wolves. A little wolf bark emanated from a room with a closed door off to the right of the living room.

Tom motioned to the room, wanting to check it out. Dealing with a she-wolf and her pups could be a dangerous proposition, especially while the three of them were all in human form. The wolf could easily tear into them. But more of the pack might be hiding in the room too. Ryan agreed with Tom and gave him the go-ahead.

They walked down the short hall, and when they reached the room, Tom turned the doorknob. Locked. Sam watched their backs while Tom used his lockpick on the door. The lock clicked open. He glanced at Ryan, waiting for his approval. Ryan nodded.

Tom turned the handle slowly and it moved with a rusty, grinding squeak.

A low growl came from the other side of the door. An adult female growl.

As humans, Ryan and the others had no chance against a wolf's teeth. If it was a she-wolf and her pups, he had no intention of shooting her. But he couldn't risk Tom's life if the female attacked or if others were in the room that might.

"Shift first," Ryan whispered to Tom.

Tom's mouth gaped.

"If she attacks, you can pin her down. I'll do the talking."

Tom agreed and quickly stripped out of his clothes. After shifting, he butted the door open with his nose before Ryan could push it aside and stood in the entryway. Ryan was at Tom's side, gun in hand, to deliver the message that he'd shoot if anyone attacked, but only if he had no other choice.

A mother wolf stood with three little ones trying to reach her teats for supper. Another female growled low as she stood nearby in a protective stance, her belly bulging with pups. She was due to birth her own litter soon.

Ryan holstered his gun. "We're not here to hurt anyone."

The nursing mother sat, the tension draining from her, and her pups scrambled over each other, vying for a meal. The other mother remained standing, wary and protective. As a gray male wolf, Tom was still a threat to a couple of red females.

"Can you shift back?" Ryan asked the females. The nursing mother shook her head. Just as Ryan had suspected. That meant either they had shifted after they locked the door, or someone had locked them in.

"We've got movement in another room," Sam warned.

"We'll be back for you," Ryan said. He motioned for Tom to come with him. Once he was out of the room, Ryan shut the door so that the females couldn't try to rescue their mates if a confrontation resulted.

Ryan, Tom, and Sam went through the living area and then a kitchen. Surprisingly, the kitchen was spotless, although coffee and tea stained much of the counter near a teakettle, and part of the backdrop was coming unglued. But the fragrance of orange cleanser wafted in the air, the counters were clean with no dishes, and the porcelain sink sparkled. He wondered if the females had recently shifted.

Another short hall led to two more rooms. The door was unlocked and yielded to show a bedroom furnished with a queen-sized bed that was richly cloaked in a velvet comforter and velvet decorator pillows, all dark brown. The walls were freshly painted, and the place appeared to be under renovation. No pictures hung on the walls, and new carpet covered the floor.

A red male had slept here, but Ryan didn't detect any scent he'd smelled before.

They moved to the next door and found it locked. Ryan pulled out his set of lockpicks, as Sam said in a hushed voice, "I smell the reds here who have been causing all the trouble."

Ryan nodded. Then as the door lock clicked open, he hesitated.

He envisioned North or his men holding guns on him and firing as soon as he opened the door. Or standing as wolves, ready to lunge and rip their throats out. This was their territory, and Ryan, Sam, and Tom were the intruders, no matter how they justified being here.

"We'll work with you to cure this curse you cast upon all of us," Ryan said, his voice softly threatening, *play the game or die*, "and you can live. Your females and your pups need to live with a pack. One that offers more than what you have here—filth and no protection. Hell, the place ought to be condemned. More than that, if you want to be human again…" Ryan let them draw their own conclusions.

"This isn't where we normally live!" a male shouted from inside the room, his voice angry but shaky too.

Ryan suspected he was holding a gun.

"I'm armed. And I know how to use the gun," Ryan warned, in case this was the guy who'd shot him, via a ricocheted bullet off a tree.

Silence.

"Give it up, and you'll live. Right now, you don't have any other alternative. Do you?"

A low growl emitted from the room. Either the man had shifted, or…

"Hell, North. He's right. Your cousin's most likely dead. My sister's ready to have her kids any minute. Sascha and her pups need to be in a thriving pack with decent leadership. No offense, but this isn't the life any of us would have chosen," the man in the room said.

"North, we need to know where the lab is," Ryan said. "We'll find a vaccine, develop an antidote, and take care of your people. If Lelandi's uncle is agreeable, you can join his red pack south of here."

Another low growl. North wasn't going for it.

"Hell, North, that weasel of a scientist, Miller, is holding all of us hostage with this virus," the man in the room said. "Once he learns of our bank account holdings, he'll clean us all out. You know he will."

Ryan waited. Sam looked like he was done waiting, his fists and teeth clenched. "Want me to shift?" he asked.

Tom's ears were perked, his tail straight out, his posture

showing his eagerness to enter the room and take care of business.

"Agreed, North?" Ryan asked. "Connor is dead. Darien was protecting his mate. Either you help us to help you, or you clear out of the area for good and figure it out for yourselves while we find the solution for our people."

"Come on, North. I can't hold out much longer without shifting. Maybe through the night. Maybe not that long. Then I'll shift, and all that's left of us is my brother, Galahad," the man said. "Who knows how long he'll last."

Ryan didn't wait any further. "Sam, call Jake with the location, the number of wolves, who's left in the pack—"

Someone yelled from in back of the house.

"Galahad!" the guy in the room shouted. "Deal's off if that wolf kills him."

"The wolf won't injure Galahad if he doesn't fight back." Hell, what was going on now? Then a sickening notion swamped Ryan. If the wolf was Doc Mitchell, he'd left Carol unprotected.

———

Hating the wait and not knowing what was going on in the house, Carol clenched and unclenched her hands, watching the front door, the windows...the windows. She saw movement in one of them. A red wolf. The smaller head indicated a female. She looked like she needed help and implored Carol to come to her. And then she disappeared beneath the window.

Was it a trick? Was Carol naive to think the wolf needed her help?

She stayed put, waiting and observing the window. The wolf didn't appear again, and Carol couldn't stand the wait any longer. She wouldn't go in the house, just peek through the window.

After a few minutes, she'd traversed the yard, reached the house, and peered in. A mother wolf nursed her pups, and another due to have hers any day now was sitting nearby. Sucking in her breath, Carol turned to look at the front door, still open. The door to the room was shut, and the she-wolves were confined. She was a nurse. She could aid them if they needed her help.

The she-wolves saw her, eyes widening. The one with the nursing pups remained relaxed on the floor. The other was panting hard. Was she going into labor?

She needed someone to be with her.

Carol walked carefully to the front door, not making a sound. Then she peered inside. Nothing—no voices, no footfalls, silent as a ghost house.

She stepped inside the house and listened again. One of the she-wolves whimpered. The mournful sound of her voice spurred Carol to action. She hurried to the room and gingerly opened the door. The she-wolf that was heavy with pups rushed toward her, and Carol had the sinking feeling she'd just made one of the biggest mistakes of her life.

Ryan shoved the door to the cramped bedroom open as the man climbed out the window, and North jumped through the same opening in his wolf form. Ryan and Sam raced to the window as Tom ran beside them. A hundred yards from the house, Doc Mitchell had pinned Galahad to the ground. The man's hands held onto the scruff of the wolf's neck. Galahad's eyes widened in terror as Doc pulled his lips back in a snarl and exposed his sharp teeth even more.

"Doc won't hurt him, but this ends now. Drop the gun," Ryan ordered Galahad's brother.

As a wolf, Tom leapt through the open window, joining Ryan and eyeing North, who couldn't seem able to decide what to do. The two reds found themselves facing a bigger gray wolf and Doc Mitchell, too, as he moved off Galahad and positioned himself to attack North. The other man finally seemed resigned and dropped his gun in the tall grass.

Something moved behind them, and Ryan whipped around to see Carol walking toward them, on the phone and with the very pregnant wolf and the nursing mother and her pups.

"Everything's going to be fine, Lelandi, once we find the lab. Can your uncle take in some wayward reds? They have a couple of females, one with pups and another soon to have a litter. We need to have them transported to the vet clinic."

Ryan shook his head at Carol. He didn't think she'd ever mind him while he was trying to do his duty as her protector.

"What happened to sitting in the truck and waiting for us?"

"Two females needed my help. I never decline helping those who need it, you know. The female's ready to have her pups. We need to get them to some place clean and safe."

Galahad rose from the ground, and Doc Mitchell eyed him warily. Galahad turned to his brother with a look of regret.

"It's over, Hank. It was a harebrained scheme to begin with."

He spoke to Ryan. "The scientist's name is Miller Redford, a red wolf who was turned a decade ago and joined our pack a year ago. He gives the impression he's a mad scientist, but he's very sane."

Sam grunted.

"That's debatable, considering what his meddling could cost our kind," Ryan said. "Where is he?"

"In the basement," Galahad replied, motioning to the house.

"Hell. Everyone stay put."

Ryan headed for the open bedroom window, ready to end this now.

———————————

Ryan held his gun at the ready as he located a door off the kitchen that he'd assumed was a pantry. Without bothering with the light switch, he moved in the dark down the creaking stairs to the basement, where the walls smelled slightly moldy.

Light came from around the edges of a door, but when Ryan reached it, he found it locked. The blood thundering in his ears, he holstered his gun and used his lockpicks. Once he heard the soft click, he put away his lockpicks, pulled his gun out, steeled himself for trouble, and then twisted the door handle.

He expected to face a man armed with a syringe or a gun, but instead he saw a room exactly as Carol had described to him from the earlier vision. The wide-screen TV hanging on the wall was dark. Sconces hung on the walls and shot soft light upward toward the ceiling, showing off the gold walls. Leather chairs were companions to a leather sofa, and all were brand new, their leather fragrance permeating the air. Brown carpeting smelled new too. No moldy odor down here, and the paint was fresh.

If he'd had any doubts about Carol's psychic talents, this was proof she had them. The analytical part of his brain still fought with him, reminding him that she might have been here once before. But he shoved the notion aside. The chances she would ever have been here were minuscule at best. She truly was psychic.

A door off the living area was shut, and soft country-western music played overhead. Ryan moved quickly across the carpeted floor. He twisted the handle. No resistance. Miller wasn't expecting the troops. Or he was just plain crazy, despite what Hank had said.

Slowly, Ryan opened the door. Definitely a lab with tables and a couple of stools, a microscope, beakers, some jars filled with liquids, and others filled with powdery substances, as well as all-white, sterile-looking cabinets. The smell of disinfectant lingered in the air.

Something clinked in an adjoining room, and Ryan rushed through the open doorway. This room was smaller, set up like an office with books on shelves against one wall, a neat desk with all the papers stacked in a tray, and a toilet visible in another small room off this one. Next to a fridge, a coffee maker, coffee mugs, and a microwave oven sat on a counter, and the aroma of cinnamon rolls permeated the air.

Miller hovered over the coffee pot, pouring himself a cup. He wore a lab coat, black pants, and brown slippers.

He was a husky man, a little over six feet tall and much taller than most reds.

Ryan had hoped he'd catch Miller off guard. And he had, but only for an instant. Miller whipped around, his bearded jaw dropping, his yellow eyes narrowed, and blond hair sweeping his shoulders. Miller threw the hot cup of coffee at Ryan, yanked off his lab coat to reveal his bare chest, and then kicked off his slippers and jerked off his pants.

Ignoring the burning-hot coffee soaking his shirt and chest, Ryan fired two rounds as Miller shifted and lunged at him. The bullets both struck the wolf's chest, but because of his hefty size and the shot of adrenaline that had to be running through his system, the hits didn't stop him for long.

Ryan holstered his gun and yanked off his clothes as quickly as he could, but Miller knocked him to the tile floor before he could shift. Miller growled, his teeth bared.

"You're a dead man…" Ryan said with authority—although the wolf bearing down on his chest made his breathing labored—as he gripped Miller's neck with every ounce of strength he possessed, "…unless you give us the vaccine."

Considering the fate they all faced, Ryan was sure Miller wouldn't be allowed to live. He was too dangerous—and he knew it. Then again, Ryan was at a distinct disadvantage, and he imagined Miller must be laughing at his boastful threats.

Someone rushed through the living area at a gallop, and Ryan assumed either Tom or Doc Mitchell was coming to his rescue. When he saw Carol as a wolf, Ryan's heart did a flip.

Miller turned to face the snarling, growling female wolf

that was Ryan's mate, and as he did, Ryan tried to shove him off. Unsuccessfully.

Miller stayed where he was, his hefty size pinning Ryan down, but his attention remained focused on Carol.

She snapped at his flank with her wicked teeth, and he moved out of her way, still trying to keep Ryan—the greater threat once he shifted—pinned to the floor.

She moved behind Miller and bit his stiff tail. He yelped and Ryan's heart raced, but he still couldn't get out from underneath the big wolf.

She lunged at Miller's backside, like a small fish poking at a shark, and nipped his rump.

Again, he yelped, but this time, he turned to retaliate.

Unencumbered, Ryan shifted. His natural instinct was to growl and draw Miller's attention, to let him know he had real trouble in the form of an alpha male gray and give him a fighting chance, but he couldn't risk Miller tearing into Carol. The red who had changed her had torn into her once. Ryan couldn't have her traumatized all over again.

He leapt at Miller's back as Miller railroaded Carol into a corner of the office between a file cabinet and a chair. Her teeth bared, she growled, her eyes narrowed into slits, the blue color when she was human transformed into rich dark amber. She was beautiful and threatening.

Ryan grabbed Miller on the back of the neck, crushing his spine with one bite and regretting it as soon as the wolf collapsed. What if he'd hidden the vaccine? What if they couldn't discover a cure? How would they survive?

CHAPTER 27

A WEEK AND A HALF AFTER RYAN HAD KILLED MILLER, Carol sat at the kitchen table in Doc Weber's rental home, tapping her bare foot on the floor and reading through books written over the ages that discussed various herbal and other home remedies for getting rid of viruses or colds or wolfism. She wasn't any closer to finding a cure for the pack.

Darkness had descended on the house hours earlier, so fluorescent bulbs flooded the kitchen with light. Ryan was still annoyed with her for having come to his rescue in Miller's basement. But as soon as she'd realized that her vision of the room involving gunfire was the same place Ryan was investigating, she'd had to rescue him. She just hadn't realized *he* was the one doing the shooting and not Miller.

Tom and Sam still weren't talking to her, both mad that she'd taken off and nearly gotten herself killed. But she had been the only one not standing guard against the other red males! Besides, wasn't that what mates did for each other?

She took a deep breath and continued to study one of the books, while Ryan examined papers spread all over the other end of the golden-oak table. He was looking for a clue to where Miller might have hidden a vaccine.

On a whim, Lelandi had mentioned that Doc Weber had a personal library that he'd accumulated before he'd had much medical training. A lot of his remedies had been passed down from their ancestors. Carol figured that trying those remedies on the sickened wolves was worth a shot, since nothing else seemed to work. For days, she'd been studying the books and testing the remedies on any willing participant.

If a person didn't die from complications of the flu, which thankfully no one had, he or she would eventually get better. For the *lupus garous*, the real problem was being able to shift into wolf form and then not being able to shift back. She was trying herbal remedies for lessening the effects of the flu and supposed cures for shifting, if any of them seemed in the least bit sound. Piercing a wolf's hands with nails and striking a wolf in the head with a knife were supposed remedies for getting rid of the wolf problem, but she would leave them to myths and legends.

She rose from the table, crossed the linoleum floor, and opened the black fridge door. Inside, a bowl of diced onions sat in a thick, golden syrup of honey. She shuddered at the thought of anyone having to eat it.

A warm hand swept down her back, and she turned slightly to see Ryan looking down at her. His dark amber gaze was tender, and she knew that look in his eyes. It said she had been working at this for too long and she needed to sleep.

"In a little while," she said.

He took a deep breath and nodded. "I'm going to take a shower. Join me?"

"Sure."

He smiled, but she could tell he didn't believe her. She wanted to shower with him and enjoy what would happen between them if she did, but he probably assumed she'd never make it to the shower before he was finished.

"In a little while," she said again, trying to reassure him.

He kissed her forehead, let out his breath, and headed for the guest bathroom.

Carol closed the fridge door and turned on the teakettle. More of Darien's pack had shifted to their wolf forms, including Jake, and none could revert to their human forms. Tom and Sam were still fine. And Lelandi had said she had no urges to shift so was all right for now. Silva had been fighting the shift for a couple of days.

Those who hadn't shifted were taking care of those who had. Everyone who was left was short-tempered, feeling the tension, and worried about shifting and about family members who were stuck in their wolf forms.

A small tickle in Carol's throat had bothered her for the last hour or so, but it was probably just allergies. She prayed. She also felt a little warmer than usual, which she hoped only meant that the heater was on too high.

She thought of Nurse Matthew and Charlotte handling the patient load at the hospital while she wasn't doing her fair share. Sure, she was trying to find an antidote, but it seemed too much like being on holiday. Except that she was worried sick she wouldn't discover a way to stop the virus.

Doc Weber and Doc Mitchell remained at the hospital in their wolf forms. They urged Carol to use her experimental cures on them. Those ranged from herbal remedies like garlic and onion, echinacea, licorice—which didn't go over with any of the wolves—and vitamin C for improved antibodies to fight the virus in an infected person. She had even tested the medieval concept that exercising the wolf into exhaustion in his wolf form would force him to shift back to his human form. Nothing worked. Darien also had tried all the remedies in good spirit, although he wouldn't go along with the brutal exercise plan, probably figuring that was a bunch of medieval bunk.

Carol lifted two packages of licorice, one red and one black, and took a deep breath as she pondered the results of yet another attempt at creating a cure. She'd tested Darien, Jake, and both the vet and Doc Weber, but no one seemed to respond to the home remedies. The vet and Jake had both gone along with the exercise program, willing to try anything to snap out of the inability to shift back to their human form. But Darien was right. It didn't work.

Her mind frazzled, she poured herself another cup of ginger tea and took it back to the table. On page fifty-five of a set of handwritten notes on wolf myths and legends, she had found a possible cure, or death. She closed her eyes as she sat at the table and rested her head on her arm, willing herself to think. *Think*, what hadn't she tried that might work? Something that wouldn't possibly result in death.

Her thoughts shut down, and as if in a dream or out of the mist of her mind, a lush green meadow appeared.

The sun was shining down on Ryan as he lay on the grass. Hands behind his head, he had his eyes closed and his leg cocked, resting peacefully, until two small boys attacked him with child-like exuberance. The boys were identical in size, maybe three years of age, chubby, with dark hair like Ryan's, and smiles and dimples like his too. Startled out of his peaceful pose, he laughed and tackled them, tickling them amid giggles and squeals. Twin boys.

Before she could come to any conclusions about the vision, the fragrance of blended almond, lime, and mandarin soap drifted to her, and she returned to the world at present and turned in her chair. Freshly showered and totally naked, Ryan advanced on her in a strictly lustful predatory manner. Her gaze shifted to the package between his legs. He sure was hung. She might have missed showering with him, but he wasn't leaving her to stew over the dilemma of finding a cure all night. And she loved him for it.

She smiled at him, so handsome and caring and hunky, his mouth curving up a little, his eyes taking her in as if she was the most beautiful creature in the world—which as tired as she was, she knew wasn't possible—and his expression determined, bordering on sinful seduction.

No matter how frustrated and anxious she'd become with trying to discover a solution, Ryan was always her champion. He told everyone she was getting close to a breakthrough, when no one really knew how long it would take.

He encouraged her, adamantly insisting that she could do it, and by doing so, she knew he trusted in her abilities with all his heart. That bolstered her confidence in the face of failure. Pride reflected in his expression every time he talked about her efforts to find a solution. She wasn't sure if he did so to remind her she could fight this, too, or if he wanted her to know she was fully a wolf now—just like any of their kind.

Despite how tired she was, she saw he was ready for some loving. She rose from the chair to recharge her batteries too.

"Time to rest," he said, massaging her shoulders with dreamy strength.

She knew he meant *after* they made love.

"So soft," he whispered against her ear, his large capable

hands moving down her pale-blue cashmere sweater and settling on her breasts, measuring, feeling, circling. Then his lips curved up in a wicked way.

"Hmm, no bra."

The way he said the words in a hushed and seductive voice and the way he touched her made her feel naughty and decadent. She swept her hands up his naked biceps—strong, smooth, and tensing with her touch—and encircled his neck with her arms. She couldn't press against his length like she wanted, to feel his growing arousal and his desire for her building, not while his thumbs targeted her nipples, stroking and rolling the sensitive nubs between his fingers and stealing her thoughts, her breath, her willpower.

Already her loins tightened with need and her body quivered with desire—responsive, receptive, needy. She wanted him, wanted the feel of him mating with her, the closeness, the intimacy.

His mouth crushed hers, his hands moving from her breasts to the bottom edge of her soft sweater. He slid the luxurious fabric upward, his thumbs stroking her skin from her belly over her breasts, stopping to fondle her nipples for a moment in a deliciously sinful way, and then moving up her collarbone to pull the sweater off.

He dropped it on a chair and, head bent, leaned down to capture a nipple with his mouth, his tongue slick and hot as it glided over the raised hypersensitive nub. She moaned, felt her knees give, and would have been kneeling before him if he hadn't slipped his hands down to cup her buttocks and to hold her in place while he had his way with her.

She felt her bones melt, her blood and skin sizzle with his touch, and briefly worried that she was shifting…until his thigh pushed between her legs, pressed gently upward, and rubbed, giving her a jolt.

Oh God, she'd never last.

His heart was pounding as thunderously as hers, despite his slow and measured moves. He recaptured her mouth with his, their breathing heavy and labored. The scent of arousal, hers and his, entwined in a pleasing fragrance, added to the sweet and spicy aroma of the almond, lime, and mandarin soap he'd washed with.

His fingers tangled in her hair, his eyes dark as midnight, his thigh still pressed between her legs, holding her up and tormenting her. Then he unfastened her jeans button and, after that, the zipper. Once he'd unzipped her jeans and slipped his fingers into her soft curls, he pulled his mouth away from hers and smiled.

"No panties?" Again his words made her feel wickedly sinful.

As if he couldn't last a moment longer, he tugged her jeans down and left them in a puddle of blue denim on the floor.

"You're beautiful," he said and lifted her so that she was straddling him. "And all mine," he added, sounding wolf-ishly possessive.

No coherent words could come to mind as her legs were spread open to him against his belly, his chest hair mingling with her soft curls, his stomach rubbing against her feminine lips with every step he took. She clung to him as he moved fast, heading toward the guest room, his gait long and decisive.

"You're beautiful too," she said hoarsely, soliciting a deep-seated chuckle from him.

When they reached the bed, he didn't set her down and then join her, like she'd expected. Instead, in one deft move, she was on the mattress and he was still between her legs. He shifted away from her slightly and ran his hand up her inner thigh, teasing her into submission.

But she would not submit! Her hands swept over his arms and his back and lower to his buttocks. She squeezed, soliciting a shiver from him. She reached up and raked her hands through his damp hair while his eyes studied her, lust-filled, desirous, and hungry.

She pulled him down and licked his shoulder, loved the salty and sweet taste of him freshly showered, all man and wolf, and hers. He groaned, a sound that said she was pushing *him* over the edge.

As if he couldn't wait any longer, he began to stroke her between her legs, dipping a finger inside her and claiming her. He pressed his mouth against hers again, ravenous, passionate, greedy. His tongue danced with hers, their breathing fast paced as her fingers pressed against his lower back, her loins aching for resolution.

She arched her back, pushing against his fingers, demanding, begging. He stroked harder, relentlessly, watching her expression until she shuddered and fractured into a million wondrous bits of pleasure and gave out a cry.

Watching Carol come nearly brought him to climax. He dove into her tight sheath and pushed hard and deep—and deeper still. Her body was flushed and moist, and every inch was delectable, gripping him with ripples of orgasm. Her fingers dug into his buttocks, her desire pronounced in her actions and heady arousal.

He stretched her and claimed her, merging, melding,

and mating with her. Their tongues and lips tasted and teased, and he said her name softly against her mouth just before the final thrust—the eruption—when the heat sizzled between them.

She gave a tired smile, pulled him close, and held on tight.

"Mine," she said.

He rolled over and cushioned her against his chest.

"Mine" was his response.

After sleeping a few hours and still feeling the sensual glow that always lingered after making love with Ryan, Carol returned to the kitchen to begin working on the *Aconitum* cure. The plant was also called monkshood, leopard's bane, wolfsbane, and dozens of other aliases. Not only was it touted as an herbal cure for colds and fever, but it also slowed the heart rate and numbed nerve endings to pain.

However, the roots of the plant were poisonous, and while the mostly deep-blue or purple flowers were strikingly beautiful, they could also be deadly. So why did some wolf lore state that the flower was a cure for being a wolf? It killed wolves. But wouldn't it kill the human half also? Still, often legends arose from some truth. What if it would cure what ailed them?

The dawn was just beginning to appear, the darkness fading as the sun rose. Ryan was again reading through the files on Miller's computer, which Ryan had brought back to Doc Weber's house. Ryan's cell phone rang, and he yanked it off his belt.

"Yeah, Tom?" He glanced at Carol. She assumed it might be good news, but Ryan's expression was noncommittal as he stalked out of the kitchen to the living room to speak to Tom.

Carol started boiling the roots of the wolfsbane in a small stainless-steel pot. When Ryan walked back into the kitchen, she knew he was going on another fact-finding mission. Unfortunately, he'd done so at least once a day, sometimes more, and nothing had ever come of it.

She'd quit asking, and he hadn't offered explanations. The disappointment at not getting any closer to a solution was too much to deal with.

"I'll be back shortly." He leaned down and kissed Carol's cheek, but a new look of worry reflected in his eyes. She rose from her chair and took his hand.

"What's the matter, Ryan?"

"Nothing. Just another lead, as usual. I'll be back soon." He pulled her close and hugged her tight.

It didn't seem like "nothing." Knowing him, he was probably afraid to make her more anxious than she already was.

"You're not going into another wolf fight, are you? Without my help?"

He chuckled, kissed her generously on the mouth, and embraced her warmly.

"No more wolf fights for now. And I wouldn't think of not taking you with me to get me out of hot water if I needed it."

"Liar," she said affectionately.

He smiled. "Truly, no wolf fights. Just another lead."

She let out her breath, squeezed him back, and said, "All right. Bring me the vaccine, and I'll make it worth your while."

He laughed and cupped a breast. "You will anyway." He

rubbed her back, said his usual "Good luck," and headed out of the house.

If he said he wasn't going into a wolf fight, she believed him. Only sometimes, the unexpected happened. Something was bothering him, and she wasn't certain she wanted to know what it was. But she suspected he was fighting the shift, just like she'd been doing for days now.

———————

Ryan had been surprised as hell when he discovered that Miller had a bank account and safe deposit box at the Silver Town Bank. That seemed to confirm that Miller was plotting to take over the town. Ryan had wasted no time in getting a court order from the local judge that allowed him access to the safe deposit box. He hoped something in the box would reveal whether a cure of vaccine existed, although it was a long shot, and he didn't want to give Carol any more false hopes.

She was aware that something more than usual was bothering him. The real dilemma was his need to shift, which had been growing since the night before. He'd never worried about shifting, but as more of Darien's people were affected, his own concern had grown.

Not only that, but he'd noticed that Carol's body temperature had been warmer the previous night, and he thought she'd been running a low-grade fever. Although she hadn't mentioned anything to him about it. Even he had a sore throat this morning. He wondered if the virus was geared to push their wolf half into taking over once they were at some stage of being sick.

Thankfully, humans in the area were no longer shooting wolves. Darien's stiff policy of jail sentences, hefty fines, and rescinded hunting licenses had been enough of a deterrent. Also, those who had shifted into wolves were trying to stay close to their homes in the woods. Those who lived in town had been taken in by families living out of town to try to reduce the problem of human-wolf contact.

Ryan drove to the bank, parked, and stalked inside where Mason, the bank owner, quickly greeted him. Mason took him to the bank vault, where the safety deposit boxes were located behind a cage door.

Wearing one of his expensive gray suits, the gray-bearded banker led Ryan inside the vault. "I'd wring Miller's thick neck if you hadn't already killed him," the banker told Ryan.

"I wish we could have kept him alive, at least until we learned if he had a vaccine or not," Ryan replied.

"From what I've heard, it couldn't have been helped." Mason unlocked the metal box with its two keys and let Ryan open it. He scoured over the documents, receipts for medical supplies, rubber-banded bundles of one-thousand-dollar bills, and...

Ryan pulled a deed for a house in Silver Town out of the box. "Hell, apparently Miller had set up housekeeping here only a month after the big fight between Darien's people and the reds."

"Well, I'll be damned. No one ever thought to see if he'd purchased real estate here. Now what?" Mason asked, stroking his beard.

"Time to pay a call at his house at 150 Oak Drive. Thanks, Mason. I'll let you know if I find anything."

As Ryan headed out of the bank to his truck, he called

Tom with a heads-up and then drove over to Miller's home. It was a modest place with black shutters framing two large windows and massive oaks shading the grass. The lawn was a little shaggy, probably because Miller had been dead for ten days and a warming trend and spring rain had encouraged the growth.

Sheriff Peter Jorgenson drove into the drive, and Ryan gave him a silent nod of greeting. He'd planned to use his lockpicks, although he supposed that some of the neighbors might be human, and having a police officer on hand would be better. The sheriff was better yet.

"Peter," Ryan said as the sheriff climbed out of his vehicle.

"Ryan. Tom called and said to meet you here. Think this is where the gold is?"

"I sure as hell hope so."

Peter stifled a cough.

"You too, eh?"

"Hell, yeah. I don't think any of us are going to escape it."

Deputy Trevor Osgood drove up, lights flashing. He waved and joined them as Peter unlocked the door.

"Can you believe the bastard was living among us?" Trevor said, punching his fist into the palm of his hand.

"The guy had balls. I'll give him that," Ryan said.

When they entered the house, the smell of fresh paint assaulted them. New carpeting covered the floors, but the place was empty. No drapes over windows covered in mini-blinds. No furniture.

"Not moved in yet, looks like," Trevor said, sounding thankful, as though just the knowledge that Miller hadn't been living under their noses all along was a relief.

But the knowledge that Miller hadn't moved in ratcheted up Ryan's anxiety a notch. If Miller hadn't been here, he most likely wouldn't have left anything here. Still, they had to make sure.

While Trevor checked the bedrooms and bathroom down the hall, Ryan and Peter stalked toward the kitchen.

Everything looked brand new—appliances, cabinets, black granite countertop—despite the home being an older model.

"He was getting ready to move in, I suspect," Peter said, searching through the drawers and cabinets.

"Yeah, probably just waiting for us all to be infected and unable to shift back. Wonder what he would have done about the wolf half of us. Not many of us would have let him live if he'd ventured out of his house."

Ryan noticed that the fridge was running. He pulled open the fridge door. Through the glass top of one of the drawers, he spied several vials of liquid and packages of powder in a manila envelope.

"Might not be what we're looking for," Ryan said, pulling out a vial and looking at it like it was the most volatile thing in the world, "…but then again, it might be."

"Hot damn," Peter said.

Ryan opened a piece of paper from the envelope and read the first few lines of scribble. And smiled.

CHAPTER 28

THE FRONT DOOR TO DOC'S HOUSE OPENED, AND CAROL wondered if Ryan had found anything this time. She immediately straightened her back as she stood at the counter. She was boiling water in an electric teakettle in the process of making anise tea, one more possible herbal remedy for fighting a viral infection.

Again, she considered the wolfsbane solution she'd cooked and hidden in the crisper of the fridge. She wouldn't risk giving *that* remedy to anyone else. She did consider drinking a bit of it herself, now that she was sick with the flu, to see if it might be a cure.

She tilted her head in the direction of the footfalls. They were a woman's, much lighter and more delicate than Ryan's heavier step. She thrust the container of wolfsbane back in its hiding spot and closed the door.

Then someone else's footfalls sounded. Two women? At first, she thought it might be Bertha, bringing her and Ryan a snack as she'd been doing for the past several days, trying to help out in any way that she could, but they'd eaten breakfast an hour earlier.

Carol turned stiffly to see who was coming. Her skin felt warmer than normal, and she suspected—although she couldn't find a thermometer in Doc's house to confirm it—that she had another low-grade fever. She felt tired and out of sorts, her head throbbing, and she was deathly afraid that anytime now, she'd shift.

The only reason she hadn't yet, she figured, was because she'd shifted to help Ryan fight Miller. Before that, she'd shifted so she could play fishnet tag with North and his men. That might have knocked out the urge for the time being.

With any luck, maybe she'd find a cure before she felt the compulsion again.

The footsteps grew closer. Couldn't be Silva. She was sick and terrified of shifting. She didn't want to get near Carol and risk contaminating her. Or Nurse Charlotte. She was too busy dealing with patients to come to the house.

Which left Lelandi and some other women in the pack who Carol didn't know well. Lelandi had better not be coming here to see her!

"Who's there?" Carol called out, not wanting Lelandi to come any closer, if that was who it was.

The footfalls continued through the living room in the direction of the kitchen.

"'Tis I, Rosalind," Ryan's sister said, her voice bright and cheerful.

Carol's mouth dropped. *Oh, hell.* She didn't want anyone to lose faith in her ability to find a cure now that she was sick and could be on the verge of shifting at any time, but she didn't want Rosalind exposed to what she had either.

"You can't come in," Carol said, her voice firm.

"Lelandi said it was all right."

"Lelandi's wrong." Carol frowned. "Who's with you?"

"Lelandi," Darien's mate said, sounding amused.

"Lelandi, you shouldn't be here. Neither of you should. I…I'm sick."

They were nearly to the kitchen. Carol turned off

the teakettle, but she didn't know what else to do. It hurt to stand or sit or even lie down. Her joints all ached. Her throat was sore. She felt miserable.

"Don't come in," she warned.

Lelandi and Rosalind ignored her and entered the kitchen, each carrying a brass container of red roses. Rosalind was wearing a pale-pink sweater and matching jeans. Her curly, long brown hair bounced on her shoulders, and her amber eyes sparkled with excitement. Her smile was sweeter than Ryan's and not as devious as his often was.

Her red hair tied back in a bun, Lelandi wore a loosely fitted emerald sweatshirt and sweatpants. Carol wondered if Lelandi's jeans were getting a little too snug around her waist with triplets on the way. Lelandi gave her a knowing smile.

"Ryan has good news. But you've beat him at the game again."

Carol slumped on the chair, feeling light-headed. Tears blurred her eyes. Even if Ryan had found the vaccine, it would only protect wolves from getting the virus, not cure those who had it already.

"What are you doing here, Rosalind? You shouldn't be here," Carol said, defeated though hopeful that Ryan *did* find the vaccine and that it would help those who weren't sick.

"I couldn't stand being in Green Valley and not knowing how this was all going down. Lelandi told me you were looking into herbal remedies. I have a greenhouse and wanted to bring all kinds of fresh herbs for you to use in your search for the cure."

Carol sighed. "You shouldn't have come. What if you

get sick too?" Then she frowned and looked at Lelandi. "If Ryan found the vaccine, how would *I* have beaten him at the *game*?"

Lelandi beamed, then crossed the floor, pulled Carol from the chair into her embrace, and hugged her soundly. Carol wanted to break loose and dash away from her. But Carol didn't have the strength. Was Lelandi mad?

Rosalind waited, but the way she was standing so rigidly and grinning from ear to ear, Carol wondered if it was because she knew for sure Ryan and she were mated. But that would all be for nothing if she didn't find a cure!

"Darien shifted a few minutes ago," Lelandi said, tears misting her eyes. "God, Carol, you did it. That first remedy you tried—the one he balked at and I had to force him to drink? The spicy ginger tea? Combined with the raw onion chunks left soaking in honey overnight that he growled at me over, and the echinacea...all the different remedies together worked. It just took a while, but...he's back to his usual self. Well, a little gruffer than usual. He would have come down here personally and thanked you..."

Tears streamed down Carol's cheeks like a river run amok. She couldn't grasp the ramifications of what she'd done, and she wasn't sure she could accept it. What if they turned back? What if this didn't last?

Rosalind joined them. "Ryan found a jewel when he fell in love with you," she said and tugged Carol into a hug. "I've always wanted a sister who could beat him in something."

But it wasn't a game. She embraced Rosalind back, pleased to have another sister to add to her family in any event. She reached over and drew Lelandi into an all-girls' hug.

"Are you sure, Lelandi?"

Tears streaked down Lelandi's cheeks now, too, and she nodded vigorously.

"Oh, hell yeah. He's giving orders, yelling at Tom for allowing you to let North into the exam room and nearly taking off with you; giving Jake grief for shifting and getting stuck, even though he knew it couldn't be helped; and scolding me for allowing you to mate with Ryan without letting him know first."

She smiled. "We'll miss you, Carol. Will you be all right when Ryan takes you home to his pack?"

Rosalind took Carol's hand and squeezed. "Silver Town's not that far from Green Valley. She'll visit. We both will, if it's all right."

"For the all-girls-night parties," Carol said, trying to smile.

Rosalind gave Carol another hug. "Sounds like those could get out of hand, and I'm in. After you and Ryan are all right and no one from our pack will get sick with this"—she grinned even more broadly—"you can come home. Don't tell Ryan, but I'm moving to a condo in town, closer to my garden shop. The house will be yours and Ryan's. He'll say no, because he wants to keep an eye on me, but I need a little freedom, and…well, this is going to be perfect."

"I…I—"

"Darien is so proud of you," Lelandi said. "So very proud of you. He'll tell you himself after he finishes ordering everyone around. At least those who haven't shifted yet." She motioned to the doorway. "Ryan ran the vaccine to the hospital, and Charlotte and Matthew will be giving vaccinations to anyone who isn't sick. Rosalind and I were already vaccinated.

"Doc also shifted back—we suspect maybe even earlier

than Darien. We didn't know it until just a few minutes ago because he was so tired that he slept through the whole thing. He'll help with the vaccinations and wants to tell Ryan to join our pack and forget taking you away.

"Of course, Darien would say no to that. It's one thing for Ryan to come here to help us out with an important matter. It's another for Darien to have to butt heads with him all the time."

"Carol?" Ryan called as he entered the house. "Have I got good news! We found the vaccine."

Smiling, Lelandi and Carol wiped away residual tears as the women all waited for Ryan to enter the kitchen.

Ryan's smile faltered when he saw Rosalind and Lelandi with their arms around Carol's waist. "I got waylaid at the hospital and thought the two of you had gone home," he said to Lelandi.

"We were on our way there when Darien called Lelandi with the news. Carol found the cure," Rosalind said proudly. "So we had to tell her right away. Once you and she are cured and ready to come home…well, everything will be right with the world."

He looked from Rosalind to Lelandi. She shrugged. "Darien's raising Cain with everyone—North and his pack members; the two gray females, Becky and Marilee, for their shenanigans; and Tom for allowing North to nearly take off with Carol at the hospital."

"He shifted back." Ryan smiled with a bit of the devil in his expression. "He's mad at me for taking Carol as my mate without his permission, I can just bet."

"Um, yeah, but he'll speak with you after he makes sure Carol's cure has lasting power."

Ryan chuckled darkly. "And now?"

"Doc Mitchell hasn't changed back yet, and he's having fits over it. Doc Weber said the two of you can stay in his home as long as you like. He'll stay with Doc Mitchell in his big, old house in the country until the vet shifts back."

Carol felt relief and exhaustion, knowing that she no longer had to push herself to find a cure and that Ryan wouldn't have to keep looking for a vaccine. She slumped down on the kitchen chair and wanted to sleep for the next year without waking to do anything.

Ryan saw the telltale signs that Carol was truly sick. He assumed she'd been trying to hide it from him earlier. Now he saw how her eyelids drooped, her eyes glassy and her face pale. She looked worn out and sick. Like he felt.

"What's the cure?" he asked, ready to give it to Carol first.

She motioned to the fridge, teakettle, and herbs and spices sitting in containers on the counter. "A half-dozen remedies together. But I've detailed everything in my notes on the computer."

He glanced at the packages of licorice sitting on the countertop. "Not the licorice." He frowned at her. "Or the onion soaked all night in honey, surely."

She smiled a little and reached for his hand. "At least we don't have to try wolfsbane."

"Wolfsbane?" Rosalind and Lelandi said at the same time.

Carol shrugged. "It could have killed us. I need to throw that remedy out before anyone drinks it by accident."

Everyone looked at her as if she'd lost her mind.

"Or it could have been a cure, according to wolf lore. It was used for medicinal purposes eons ago. And as a poison."

Lelandi asked, "Where is it?"

"The bottom-right crisper in the fridge, blue container."

Rosalind went to dispose of it.

"Until we can move to Green Valley, Carol and I will stay here," Ryan said, damned thankful they hadn't had to try wolfsbane. He hated the taste of licorice, and the idea of onions soaked in honey was sure to turn him off eating either for months.

"What about Puss?" Carol asked and sneezed.

"Maybe Puss should stay with us a while longer while you get your rest," Lelandi suggested.

Carol nodded. The fight was out of her. She needed to rest.

Ryan gathered her up into his arms, feeling how warm her body was and knowing she was running a fever.

"No one is to disturb us…for anything."

Rosalind grinned. "I never thought I'd see the day that my brother would be mated."

Lelandi patted Ryan's back as he headed for the guest bedroom. "Take good care of her."

"She'll be good as new before you know it."

But Carol wasn't good as new in short order. She was run down, stressed to the max, and totally worn out. She lost her voice, coughed constantly, ran fevers, and ached all over. Ryan, who wasn't nearly as sick, was still feeling poorly. He

had to watch the way he coughed and grimaced every time
he swallowed. Yet he took care of Carol as if he were her personal nurse, bossy sometimes and coaxing at other times.

He brought her fresh boxes of tissues and glasses of
water and orange juice and sore-throat lozenges and expec-
torant medicines. He forced down pots of ginger tea, onions
minus honey, honey on toast—hopefully with the same
benefit—small doses of licorice, and garlic. He tried all the
remedies she'd used with Darien and the others who had
contracted the virus, except for the exercise routine.

Three times the previous night, she'd had the damnable
urge to shift, and the heat had again struck her. Three times,
Ryan had made love to her, and to her amazement and joy,
he'd coaxed the urge to shift right out of her. If she'd known
that hot sex would keep the shift from occurring, she would
have dragged him from the woods the first night she'd seen
him and sneaked him into the guest bedroom to ply his
erotic moves on her.

Now it was daylight, and the heat once again infiltrated
her muscles and joints—and even her bones. She hadn't
had a fever in two days, so she knew the heat wasn't due to
that. This went deeper. When she tugged at the covers in a
frantic way and then tried to pull off her long T-shirt, Ryan
noticed her distress. He left the chair he'd been sitting in
while he watched over her and sat on the edge of the bed,
his hand caressing her shoulder.

"Did I tell you about the time my partner drove after an
armed robber on foot, and the robber dove over a fence into
someone's backyard?"

She shook her head. She loved how he could lessen her
compulsion to shift by telling her tales of his exploits as a

police officer first and then as a PI. But she was afraid the effect wouldn't last forever, and she feared that the antidote wouldn't kick in soon enough.

"My partner didn't apply the brakes in time. The fence was hiding not only the robber but also an attractive nuisance."

"A swimming pool," she guessed, smiling.

"Yep. I was in foot pursuit. Instead of trying to catch the robber, I ended up having to rescue my partner from the swimming pool as his car plummeted into the heated water."

Carol smiled. Ryan gave her an elusive smile back and kissed her forehead.

"Did the robber get away?"

"He was so stunned that he was still gawking at the rescue as I pulled my partner free. By the time the robber thought to make a hasty retreat, I'd tackled him. He ended up in handcuffs—and soaking wet."

She chuckled, loving to hear about her mate's past and growing closer to him every day. She hoped and prayed and wished she'd be back to normal soon. Then he'd take her home—to his home, his pack, and his family. She hated leaving her job behind. Yet until she could get her shifting under control, she doubted she could handle work.

The urge to shift gone, she tugged down her T-shirt, and Ryan covered her back up with the blanket.

"Sleep, my Florence Nightingale." He ran the back of his hand across her cheek in a gentle caress. "Sleep, and we'll talk later."

When she woke again, she felt much better, not having coughed all night long. Her throat was no longer scratchy, and her energy was back, but Ryan wasn't in the bedroom.

Was he bringing her lunch or dinner or breakfast, depending on the hour?

For once, she felt famished. What *was* the hour? She glanced at the clock. One in the afternoon. She closed her eyes, uncertain what day it was. Had the phase of the new moon begun? Would the *lupus garous* be back to normal?

Carol crawled out of bed, stared at her translucent nightgown, and wondered when she'd put that on. She pulled it off, dumped it on the bed, and took a long, hot shower while speculating on how everyone else was faring. Had the vaccine worked and kept the last of their kind from falling prey to the bioengineered virus? Had the cure taken effect for everyone? Were Doc Mitchell and Jake back to their normal selves? Time to rejoin the world and find out what was going on.

She towel dried herself, wrapped the towel around her hair, walked out of the bathroom—and froze.

Ryan stood in the room with a bouquet of cheery pink roses in one hand and her cat cradled in his other arm. Almost smiling, Puss looked like he had a new pal.

Her heart did a little flip. Ryan had brought her flowers. She didn't realize how much that would mean to her. But it meant the world.

And Puss. She wanted to take him in her arms and squeeze him tightly.

Ryan smiled brightly at Carol. "I like what you've done with your hair, and"—he waved the flowers at her nude body—"the rest of you."

She'd forgotten all about that. Knowing just what he had in mind, she chuckled. "If you think I'm returning to bed after I've been in it for days now, you've got another think coming."

Part of her wanted him to change her mind, but the more sensible side of her said it was time to get to work doing something other than going back to bed. She stalked toward the dresser, hoping she had some clothes in it, but Ryan caught her with his free arm and pulled her tight against his body. The tea-scented, velvet rose petals tickled as they brushed her shoulder, and Puss licked her arm in greeting with his sandpaper tongue.

"While you were in the shower, I changed the sheets. Just in case."

He was a dream come true. And how could she deny she wanted to make love with him again? The day could wait. She snuggled against Ryan and reached up and stroked Puss's head. His motor instantly began to rumble.

"Is everyone all right?"

"Yep. Because of all the strain you've been under, you've taken the longest to recover."

"How long?" she asked, frowning.

"Nearly two weeks. North and his renegade pack members have joined Lelandi's uncle's red pack. If they cause any trouble there, they'll live to regret it. Becky and Marilee took off once they were well. No one knows where they went and no one cares. A few—well, let's say more than a few—of the bachelor males are pissed I mated you."

Carol smiled. "Guess it's good I'm leaving then."

"I have a proposition."

"Hmm?" Sex came to mind, as it often did. But what he said next surprised her.

"I've contracted with a *lupus garou* doctor to open a clinic in Green Valley. He said he'd try it out and make sure it was the kind of place he'd want to raise a family. He wanted to talk to you about being his nurse. Doc Weber had already told him what an asset you were.

"Until you've been a wolf for a year or two and can really get your shifting under control, a clinic run solely by wolf types would be the best solution. Patients would be strictly wolves, and our pack will welcome having their own clinic for *lupus garou*-related problems. One of the clerks at the hospital is in my pack, and she'd be thrilled to work for you as your receptionist and billing clerk."

"But…"

He frowned a little. "We really need a medical team that can take care of wolf patients. You could even further your training to become a physician's assistant if you wanted. Or a doctor even."

She thought it was a wonderful idea, but she still thought he wanted something more…intimate. "Here I thought you were going to proposition me for something else."

He grinned and leaned down and kissed her forehead.

"Hmm, what had you in mind?"

"Where's your kilt?"

"Next time, I promise." He slipped the bouquet of flowers into a vase of fresh water and then set Puss down on a soft cushion on top of a chair. Her cat immediately jumped down, wound his way around Carol's legs and then Ryan's, and then ran across the floor and curled up in a window seat.

Ryan snorted. "He has a mind of his own."

"I'm afraid you won't be able to show him who's boss." She began unbuttoning Ryan's shirt, slowly, provocatively.

"I've come to the conclusion that in the family—that means between you and Rosalind, and now the cat and me—I'll have a difficult time being in charge."

She laughed and pulled his shirt free from his pants. "That's as it should be, my Highland hero."

"Hmm, you saved me from a mad scientist, remember?"

"Well, we're even then," she said, unbuckling his belt as he caressed her naked breasts in a loving way. "You saved me from a fishnet."

He chuckled. "I'm going to have to teach you to swim. Have I told you I love you today?" He kissed her nose, pulled off her towel turban, and dropped it over the back of a chair.

"Before you made love to me, while you were making love to me, and after you made love to me sometime in the middle of the night. Yes, you did."

"Good. I can't say it enough." His thumbs chafed her nipples as she took hold of his arm and pulled him toward the bed.

She caressed his chest. "Ah, Ryan, I don't know anything about being a pack leader's mate."

"You couldn't be more perfect."

She snorted in a feminine way. "Right. I don't know how to howl, I can't swim, and—"

He kissed her thoroughly, his tongue stroking hers—hot, hard, and urgent, his hands making her breasts swollen and tingly, and she forgot what she was about to say. All she knew was they *were* perfect for each other. She would learn how to control her shifting somehow, how to raise a couple of were-kids, and how to lead a pack with Ryan at her side. One thing she didn't have to learn was how to love Ryan with all her heart.

Ryan could lose himself in Carol's sweet body, her willing mouth softening under his kisses, her nipples rosy and peaked and tantalizing, and the way she moved her body against his, arching and touching and pushing for action. He'd thought she might be sore from all their lovemaking the night before, but she'd been so eager, and he couldn't get enough of her once she'd felt better again.

He'd really thought to give her a break. Flowers, bringing Puss to her, giving her news about a job. He hadn't expected to find her fresh from the shower with her skin flushed and her hair done up in a turban. She was gorgeous. And she craved having him. Despite the pretense that she didn't want to return to bed. By the way she sounded so hopeful that he'd want her back in bed—and when would he not desire that?—he *knew* she was ready for more loving.

He loved her insecurities and strengths, the way she accepted him for all his foibles, and the way she loved him back. He now knew why he'd been obsessing about her for the past six months. He'd found the woman he couldn't live without, and he'd been fortunate that she'd wanted him with the same obsessive compulsion, no matter what reservations she might have had.

Carol caressed his back, her silky touch stealing his thoughts, her eyes blue pools of desire that called him like a siren's seductive song. Nothing else mattered but pleasuring his mate before he took her home to his pack, his people, his life.

His Little Miss Nightingale was the stuff of legends, the soothing balm that stirred his soul. Together, forever, they would solve life's little mysteries and make their dreams come true.

WOLF IN MIND

A SILVER TOWN WOLF NOVELLA

CHAPTER 1

Ingrid Bjorg had arrived early at Mayor Ryan McKinley's office and was doing her usual administrative-assistant thing before they opened for business. Sipping on a cup of lavender black tea, doing the daily Green Valley crossword puzzle, and catching up on emails for the boss. *Check! Check! And check!* Well, at least she was halfway through the puzzle, but she would finish it before the office opened. She was convinced there was a hidden message in it that would be fully revealed by the end of the month. She'd already worked out some words comprised of the intersecting letters between words written down and words written across.

She'd worked the paper's crossword puzzles before, but this month was the first time she'd seen a pattern of words emerging from the intersecting letters. She assumed the crossword creator was making up a hidden message for his devout followers to solve.

She'd hoped to get it done before Knox Granbury, the assistant mayor and a fellow wolf, arrived. Ingrid had no intention of mentioning the hidden message again to anyone in the office. But then Knox arrived and cast a glance at her pencil poised over the puzzle.

"Need any help with it?"

"No." She didn't mean to be so curt with him, but his tendency to tease about her morning crossword ritual annoyed her.

His dad had been stationed in the army at Fort Knox,
Kentucky, and his parents had named him after the Fort
Knox Bullion Depository, a fortified vault building located
next to the army post where a large portion of the federal
gold reserve was being held.

She swore he could charm any woman with his mischievous smile and golden-haired good looks—any woman but
her, of course.

He liked to tease her about the meaning of her name:
Ingrid meant fair-haired, and Bjorg meant help, save, rescue.
To Knox, that meant she was a fair-haired damsel in distress.
She always countered with the fact that his name meant he was
a round-topped hill. Then he had to remind her his name truly
meant he was worth his weight in gold. She'd barely curbed
the urge to call Knox obnoxious on more than one occasion.

He poured himself some coffee from the coffee maker
and started looking through her stack of crossword puzzles
for the month.

As far as she knew, he didn't do crossword puzzles, ever,
and he was always coming up with cockamamie words that
wouldn't have fit the puzzle no matter how many times he
offered them. She knew he did it to annoy her.

"Okay, so you seriously think there's a hidden message
in these?" he asked, sounding sincere for once.

She knew she shouldn't have said anything to him about it.

"You don't believe me, so why don't you just go about your
own business?" She sat back down at her desk. Only five minutes left to go, and she wouldn't finish the crossword puzzle in
time. She swore Knox only arrived early to bother her.

"You know, Carol would tell you if someone intended to
give you trouble."

Ingrid scoffed. She knew Ryan would have mentioned it to his mate. "I *didn't* say it was a hidden message for *me* in particular. Like it meant I was in some kind of danger or anything. Sheesh. And besides, just because Carol is psychic, that doesn't mean she can see all future happenings. Only those that seem to pertain to her in some way, and even then, not all the time. I just think the crossword puzzle constructor is trying to send a message to his loyal fans for fun, to see if anyone can catch it. It doesn't mean it's anything sinister.

"In fact, I kind of think it might be a love message. Each daily crossword puzzle has two or three secret words, and strung together, they make up sentences, if I'm right." She let out her breath in a huff and got up from her desk chair to get another cup of lavender tea so she could put up with Knox. "Don't you have anything to do that requires you to accomplish some real work today?"

"Ryan could have one of his private eyes check into the cruciverbalist," Knox said further, ignoring her comment.

Ryan had his own private investigation agency and still took cases on the side when he wasn't doing his mayoral duties: appointing department officials, preparing and presenting the municipality's budget, and providing overall responsibility for the safety of the city's citizens. He'd already closed two clubs deemed unsafe for violating numerous health codes, and he was in contact with the police and fire department often. Luckily, he hadn't had to call a state of emergency since he'd been elected, though he was always ready to order an evacuation and plan for transportation if necessary.

"The crossword creator is called a constructor." Ingrid set her used tea bag aside on the saucer to reuse one more time for her next cup of tea. "I was reading an interview with one of them, and he said there was a race among them to find the first new buzzword before the others came up with it. He said the biggest annoyance was having to use the common vowel-heavy words to make the crossword puzzle work."

"Hmm. Why do you do them?" Knox sifted through the puzzles.

"They help boost your memory and concentration."

He looked down at the crossword she'd half finished today. She scowled at him. "If you hadn't interrupted me, it would be done. It helps increase your vocabulary and general knowledge and problem-solving ability *and* can reduce your stress level—when you don't have to deal with someone who is annoying you while you're doing it."

He smiled one of his most charming smiles. "And makes you see hidden messages."

"Go. Away."

Ryan walked into the suite of offices, and both of them said "Good morning" to him.

"Good morning." Ryan raised his brows when he saw Ingrid's hand gripping a pencil as if she was ready to use it as a weapon on Knox and Knox resting his butt against her desk as if he was hanging around for a while longer.

"Puzzle trouble?" Ryan asked as he headed into his office.

"Only Knox not leaving me alone so I can concentrate on it. I'm sure you have something worthwhile for him to do. Anything at all would be extremely helpful."

"He has the job of looking into the crosswords' hidden message for me."

"Ha! Don't you go giving me a hard time about this too. I'll call Carol and have her speak to you about it." Ingrid thought the world of the nurse who had discovered the cure for the bioengineered virus that had caused terrible trouble for the pack in Silver Town.

"Carol and I talked it over, and we both decided Knox needs to look into it."

Ingrid's jaw dropped. She had never considered her pack leaders might truly believe there was something to this. But that didn't mean there was anything menacing about the messages. Now she wished she hadn't brought it up when she thought she'd found the beginning of a hidden message earlier this month.

She glanced at Knox. He gave her a crooked little smile. His blue eyes sparkled in the sunlight streaming through the windows of the office.

"I didn't say it had anything to do with anything bad," Ingrid said.

"No, but we want to make sure there is no hidden meaning that spells trouble. Now, Knox, I need you to make sure everything's on schedule for the two-hundredth anniversary parade for the last day of the month."

"Yes, sir," Knox said. "I'll head on out to check the new parade route. With all the construction they're doing on the previous route, the parade coordinator had to make some changes."

"Okay, good."

The phone rang and Ingrid answered it. "Yes, I'll let him know." She finished the call and said to Ryan, "That was for the dinner you and Carol are going to tomorrow night. Everything's a go."

"Okay, good," Ryan said.

Knox took hold of Ingrid's old crossword puzzles. "I'll return these once I learn if there's really a case here or not. Let me have that one"—he pointed to the one half-completed, sitting on her desk—"when you're done with it."

She lifted it off her desk and stretched it out to him. "You can finish it when you have time."

"My memory doesn't need to be improved."

"Says you. And your vocabulary isn't half as good as mine."

Knox smiled a little and headed into his office with her completed crossword puzzles, leaving the half-done one for her to finish.

"Don't lose them!" she called out. She didn't think Knox would have a clue about how to find the hidden meaning in the words, and she wanted to make sure she had it right when she finished the last puzzle this month.

———

Knox had a lot more in common with Ingrid than their wolf backgrounds, blond hair and blue eyes, and working for Ryan and being a member of his wolf pack. Knox loved to do crossword puzzles. But while growing up, his friends and father had made such a big deal about having his nose in a crossword puzzle all the time instead of going outside and romping with other wolves that he had become a closet puzzle solver, only doing them when no one else knew about it.

Ingrid was right about all the benefits of completing the puzzles, and he didn't know why he gave her grief over it. Maybe because others had given him trouble over it for so long, he just couldn't admit he loved doing them too.

He hadn't believed the puzzles were encoded with a secret message, but then Ingrid saw things differently than he did. Of course he'd already finished today's puzzle before he arrived at work. When she asked him and Ryan for help, Knox couldn't give her the answers. She wouldn't have the satisfaction of figuring it out for herself. And he knew she loved that, just as much as he did.

He checked with the parade coordinator and found everything was going fine. The parade route, which had been changed due to road construction, would suffice. When he returned to the office and while he had a free moment, he began really looking over each of the cross-word puzzles Ingrid had done. Sure, he could have looked at his own, and he had, but he hadn't seen anything that would clue him in as to what she saw.

He thought if he just asked her outright, like he'd done this morning, it would give him something to go on. But then she wouldn't give him the message. Not that he blamed her. She didn't believe he was really interested in helping her. When he looked closer at the letters, he noticed she had let her pencil rest on each of the intersecting letters for the words that went down and across, leaving a mark.

Then Knox got a call and had to check on the status of the different floats in the parade and the various marching bands that would be participating and where everyone was going to be in the lineup. He wanted to continue decipher-ing the messages in the crossword puzzles instead. He was as driven to solve puzzles as Ingrid was.

He told Ryan and Ingrid where he was going, though every time he did, she said, "You don't really have to give me your schedule. Ryan's your boss. Not me."

He smiled. It was almost a joke between them.

As he left the mostly glass building, he thought about the virus so many of the Silver pack members had come

down with recently and how Ingrid had ended up with the
flu. He'd been certain she'd had the same virus the other
wolves had suffered from. Ryan and Carol had been trying
to find a cure for it. Knox had been so worried about her,
he'd even stopped by to check on her at her home, but she
had refused to let him in, fearing she might have the virus
and not wanting to give it to him too.

He'd appreciated her concern and thought she liked
him, just a little. He'd even left a pot of freshly made chicken
soup on her doorstep. He'd never made chicken soup for
anyone other than himself or his family, but he hadn't mentioned *that* to her, not wanting her to think he was sweet on
her, which might have pushed her away.

As soon as Ingrid had mentioned the secret message in
the puzzle two weeks ago, Knox had been concerned and
had immediately asked Carol if she'd envisioned any trouble
for the community. But she hadn't. Not that she could see
every difficulty coming up.

He sighed as he got into his red Camaro. When he'd first
come to the pack, he'd immediately liked Ingrid. She wouldn't
give him the time of day because she'd been dating another
wolf. Then she and the wolf had broken up, and he'd moved
out of state after getting too much harassment from fellow
wolves in the pack, including Knox, for breaking Ingrid's
heart. Luckily, Ingrid hadn't known he was a part of it.

In truth, he was glad her former boyfriend was gone. Not
that it had given him much of a chance with her. She was still
getting over the breakup and was usually annoyed with Knox.

Women often found him funny and irresistible. So what
was he doing wrong when it came to Ingrid?

CHAPTER 2

"You know he likes you," Ryan said to Ingrid, sounding as serious as could be while Knox was out of the office.

Ingrid scoffed and finished typing up some paperwork. "Knox is one of the wolves who pressured my ex-boyfriend to leave the pack."

"Because he didn't like the way Jethro treated you, and he didn't want him in the pack reminding you of it." Ryan took the papers she'd printed out for him, read them through, and signed them. "He's not the only one who chased him off. Carol did too."

Ingrid had suspected as much.

"She told him she foresaw he would have a great job in Montana. The next thing we knew, he was on his way there."

"Did she really?" Ingrid asked, surprised.

"No. She said he could have a great job in Montana, or anywhere really. But Montana is a nice long way from Green Valley, Colorado."

Ingrid laughed. "I can't believe so many of our wolves would do that. I heard another five of our wolves were involved in it. I didn't realize Carol had given him the final push. Good riddance to the wolf, I say."

"They care about the welfare of all our wolves in the pack. He shouldn't have been dating human women when he was dating you, and we even learned he'd dated another she-wolf from the Silver pack at the same time, who didn't know he was seeing you. She was ready to terminate him when she discovered the truth, forget about having him sent on a wild-goose chase to Montana."

Ingrid smiled. "We could probably share stories, though I'm sure I really don't care to hear about him any further."

"So are you going to give Knox a chance?"

Ingrid sat back in her chair and folded her arms across her chest and gave Ryan a look that said to leave this alone.

He laughed and inclined his head to her. "I will leave it up to the two of you."

Ingrid frowned. "Carol doesn't see anything about us, does she?"

"No." Ryan chuckled and returned to his office.

Good. Ingrid hated to think her friend had psychic visions of her getting together with Knox. That should be personal.

Then a dark-haired man wearing a button-down shirt, khakis, and loafers walked into the office and smiled at her. "Hi, I'm Chas Ward, a freelance writer for the *Green Valley Times*. I'm here to interview the mayor today," he said quietly, as if he didn't want to alert Ryan he was there just yet. He glanced at the crossword puzzle—she hadn't stuck it in her drawer like she usually did.

"You're still doing the crossword puzzles?" Chas had been in here at the end of last month and had probably seen them on her desk, but this was the first time he'd spoken to her about it.

"Yeah, sure. I love them. Do you do them?" Ingrid hadn't met anyone who liked doing them.

"Uh, yeah, I sure do."

Ryan called out from his office, "Is that you, Chas?"

She knew Ryan had heard their conversation. Trying to

keep secrets from wolves wasn't easy, not when they were close by and with their enhanced wolf hearing.

"Uh, yes, sir, Mayor. Coming." Chas smiled at her. "I'm interviewing him," he said as if he hadn't already said that or that she wouldn't have been the one to schedule him to see the mayor.

Chas was cute in a sweet way, but not wolfish enough for her. He smiled again and hurried off to speak with Ryan while she answered a call.

When Chas finally came out of the interview, he stopped by Ingrid's desk on the way out. "What do you think of the crossword puzzles? Too easy? Too hard?"

She smiled at him. "They're fun. Just enough challenge. I always get started first thing and finish them normally before the office is open. They sort of jump-start my day."

"Oh, that's great. Um…"

"Ingrid? Can you get me the file on the promotion ceremony, please?" Ryan called out.

Her pack leader to the rescue! "Yes, sir."

Chas took that as his cue to leave. "Well, uh, see you around."

She didn't think so. Not unless he was part of their wolf circle, which he wasn't. "Nice to see you again." Since Chas had written several scathing articles about the old mayor and all the illegal activities he'd been involved in that had brought his downfall, she knew staying friendly with the freelance writer was important to help keep good press on Ryan.

Then she went to get the budget file for Ryan, since they didn't have a promotional file. She figured Ryan had said that to clue her in that he really didn't need anything from her.

Chas said goodbye to her again. Hadn't he already left? Smiling, she waved at him and took the folder into Ryan's office. They heard the door close behind Chas as he left the suite of offices.

"If this was an attempt to rescue me, thank you," she said.

"It was. If Knox had been here, he would have chased Chas off much less subtly than me."

She figured the same thing, Knox being a protective male wolf of her pack. "Good thing he wasn't here then. We need only favorable press. Was it a good interview?"

"Yeah, he asked a lot of excellent questions I had a lot of good answers for. After the former mayor went to prison, everyone's watching me."

"You're a wolf and wouldn't dare embezzle any of the city's money. Of course, they don't know that. Did you need anything else?" She waved the budget folder at him.

He smiled. "No, that's it."

She was returning to her desk with a bottle of water when Knox opened the door and walked in.

He lifted his nose, smelled the human's scent, and frowned. "Who was that?" Then he snapped his fingers. "Chas Ward, the writer. He wears way too much aftershave. And cologne."

"Yes, the one from the *Green Valley Times* who was interviewing our mayor." She wasn't about to let on she felt the same way about Chas's aftershave and cologne. A wolf's sense of smell was much better than a human's. She'd had sneezing fits when women came into the office wearing way too much perfume. "Did you figure out the message in the puzzle yet?"

"Still working on it. I had another job to do, you know."

"Right." She figured he hadn't even started on it, due to not enough time. Or interest.

Two hours later, Ryan's sister, Rosalind, who owned a flower shop, came into the office with a vase of a dozen red roses. "From a secret admirer," she said to Ingrid, her amber eyes reflecting the smile on her lips. Her long, dark-brown hair was pulled back in a chignon today.

"What? No way." Ingrid glanced at Knox, who was suddenly out of his office and in the reception area, frowning at the roses. She took his expression to mean he hadn't sent them.

"Secret, eh?" Knox said, sounding a little perturbed.

"How did he pay for them?" Ingrid asked, ignoring Knox.

Rosalind pulled out the card and handed it to Ingrid. "Someone left an envelope with cash and your name."

"The roses aren't from the ex, are they?" Ingrid asked. They'd better not be. She wasn't ever dating that rat again.

Rosalind shrugged. "Not that I know of. It says 'Secret Admirer.' And what that means, I haven't a clue."

"Are the roses from someone else in the pack?"

"Other than Knox, you mean?" Rosalind gave Knox a big smile.

Ingrid checked out his expression. He was still frowning.

"Don't you try and chase this guy off." Ingrid didn't want Knox to think he could bully anyone who was interested in dating her. As long as he was a wolf, of course.

Then he smiled. "Why would I do that?"

"Oh, I don't know. I've heard rumors several of you chased off my ex."

"Oh, that was necessary," Rosalind said. "He would

never have gotten a date from anyone else in the pack, and when we learned he had a girlfriend in the Silver Town pack? That was the living end. We don't want our wolves causing problems for their pack too."

"I agree with Rosalind. The guy was giving our pack a bad name, not to mention he had upset you." Knox folded his arms across his chest.

Ingrid was looking at the card on the roses. "It doesn't say anything. Except 'From Your Secret Admirer.' Didn't you see who delivered it?"

Rosalind shook her head. "The mailman. He thought someone had dropped it on the doorstep, and he picked it up for me and brought it inside."

"Great. Did you get anything on the security video outside your shop?" Ingrid said.

"No. There were lots of people coming and going out front. I couldn't tell from the videos if one of them had left the envelope at the door."

"Wow. Anyone could have gotten the envelope with the money in it," Ingrid said.

"You're right. I've got to run. I'll let you know if I hear from him again, and I'll listen to the scuttlebutt in the pack to see if anyone gives themselves away. You never know. It might be one of the bachelor males who is dying to ask you out, but he's afraid you're not ready to date yet after the situation with your ex, so he's softening you up beforehand," Rosalind said.

Ingrid smelled the sweet fragrance and touched the soft, velvet petals of one of the roses. "Hmm, well, if that's the case, I guess it's all right. They sure are nice and smell delightful."

"Oh, admit it. You're thrilled," Rosalind said.

Ingrid laughed. She was...to an extent.

Then Rosalind poked her head into Ryan's office and said, "You know you ought to buy your mate red roses every once in a while, since I'm your sister and I can always use the business, and it would be a nice thing to do for your mate."

"She will think something is up," Ryan said.

"You're impossible. She would love you for it." Rosalind said goodbye to everyone and left the mayor's suite of offices.

Knox was still eyeing her roses.

"What?" Ingrid asked.

Knox looked down at her unfinished crossword puzzle. "Finish your crossword puzzle. I'll take the calls for a while."

Ingrid was thrilled she could complete her crossword puzzle but so surprised at the offer, she just stared at Knox. Did he just say he'd take her calls? She thought he had to be joking, but when he returned to his office, the phone rang, and he answered the call before she could.

She sure hoped there wasn't anything disturbing about the hidden message and that was why Knox wanted her to finish the crossword in a hurry.

Completing the puzzle took her much longer than she thought it would. Knox had to answer the phone ten times, and half of those times, he had to hand over the call to her for something he didn't manage. She finally went into his office and gave him the finished, penciled-in crossword puzzle.

"Thanks." He sat it on the desk next to the others all spread out, and she saw he was writing down the letters to the intersecting words just like she had figured out to do.

"You *did* see the same message as I did." She was impressed.

"Uh, not quite. You have a real eye for puzzles. I saw where you rested your pencil on the intersecting letters each time."

She chuckled. "At least you're honest to a fault. So that means you are a good detective."

"I try to be. The number of times Ryan has had me work a case, they've turned out well."

"So is he going to have you learn who my secret admirer is?" In a way, she wanted to know who it was. It could be fun, or it could be creepy. But then it could spoil the surprise too. Just like knowing all the words in the message before she completed the puzzle.

"No, he is not going to ask Knox to look into the secret flower sender," Ryan called out from his office. "Unless you think it's someone with evil intent."

"I don't," she called out to him. "Just like I don't think the secret message in the puzzle is anything bad." Jeesh. How many times did she have to say that? She just thought it was something fun the crossword puzzle maker had made up. A little something to add to the puzzle for the month. She was dying to see what all the daily words were to learn what the whole message was.

"I will if either of you want me to look into it," Knox said as if Ingrid and Ryan hadn't already said he didn't need to. "No compensation necessary. Just a way to protect a fellow pack member if there's anything going on that could be worrisome."

"There isn't." And she didn't think that was Knox's only reason.

"Hey, Knox, I keep forgetting to mention it, but Carol asked me for that recipe for the homemade chicken soup you made for Ingrid when she was sick," Ryan said.

Ingrid raised her brows at Knox in question. "You told him you brought me soup when I was sick?" It was one thing to do something nice for someone, another to tell everyone else about the good deed.

Knox let out his breath in resignation. "I asked Carol if she thought it would be okay for you to eat it if you had the same virus the Silver pack members had. She's a nurse, you know, and she and Ryan were trying to find a cure, so I figured if anyone would know, she would."

"Oh."

"And he told her the ingredients to make sure they were all right, but he didn't tell Carol the exact amounts of the fresh ingredients he used. Carol wants to make some this weekend, so she wanted your recipe," Ryan said.

"Sure, I'll send it to her in an email." Knox smiled at Ingrid.

She frowned at him. "It was *homemade*?" She realized he'd put some real effort into it. She felt somewhat contrite that she hadn't made a big deal over it, though she'd been feeling like death warmed over, and nothing had appealed much, since she hadn't been suffering from the flu—just food poisoning. It had just been a relief she hadn't had to cook anything that took a lot of preparation when she could finally eat, and she hadn't had any cans of soup in her cupboard.

"Didn't it taste like it?" he asked, sounding like he thought he hadn't done a good enough job.

"I was sick. You can't fault me for not really noticing.

Though it *was* good, and thanks, belatedly. It was good of you to come by and check on me and bring me the soup."

"You're welcome. I just didn't want you to get dehydrated or starve because you were too sick to fix anything good for yourself."

She bit on her lower lip. Maybe she could kind of make it up to him, if he really was interested in her. "Do you want to go to the movies tonight?"

"What's playing?"

She pulled out her phone and looked for the shows out this week. "Oh, well, nothing looks that great. Kids' animated feature. A horror movie. A thriller I saw last week. Do you happen to have a movie subscription service? I wasn't watching enough TV, so I discontinued mine."

He fought a smile unsuccessfully, leaned back in his chair, folded his arms, and nodded. "What do you want for dinner?"

She smiled. Yeah, inviting herself over for a free dinner and a movie didn't sound much like thanking him for what he was doing for her. "Steaks, medium rare, mushrooms, spinach, and a baked potato. And we can go for a run tonight when it gets dark?" She figured she might as well ask for something she'd really like to eat if he was cooking.

"On Ryan and Carol's lands? Yeah, sure. It's a deal." At least Knox sounded enthusiastic and not like it was an imposition.

"It's the least I can do for you since you helped spearhead the effort to send my ex-boyfriend packing, brought me homemade chicken soup and checked on me when I was sick, and are trying to help me solve the message on the crossword puzzles."

"I'll figure out who sent you the roses, too, if you want me to."

Ingrid glanced back at them. "Sure, go ahead. See if you can become a bona fide private investigator. You can work for Ryan if you ever decide to quit this job."

"I'm already certified as a PI," Knox reminded her for the millionth time.

She patted his shoulder. "Good, then you'll be able to discover who it is in no time. What time did you want me to come over?"

"We close at five, and I need to run by the grocery store to get a couple of steaks. Want to make it six? That way, we can watch the movie and go running about nine." He texted his address to her.

"Okay, sounds like a good deal." Then her phone rang, and she returned to her desk to answer it, hoping the time she spent with Knox didn't turn out to be a bust.

After her ex's con game, she preferred her own company over seeing a male wolf for now. Besides, she didn't want to screw up a decent working relationship with Knox—if she decided she didn't really enjoy his company after hours and it hurt his feelings.

She sighed, hoping this wasn't the second worst mistake she was making in her life.

CHAPTER 3

KNOX WANTED TO LAUGH WHEN INGRID "THANKED" HIM by inviting herself over for a steak dinner and a movie. She was funny, and that was one of the things he liked about her. He figured she realized how it sounded, but that was part of what made it so amusing. He didn't mind. He was glad to have her over, only he needed to tidy up a bit.

At work, his desk was always neat. He glanced at her completed crossword puzzles stretched across his desk. Well, normally, he was always neat. At home? Sometimes the house looked like a tornado had whipped through there.

Today was one of those days. His dishwasher wasn't working, and a repairman wasn't coming for another four days. Knox had stacked the dishes up, intending to wash them in the dishwasher after it was repaired. Yeah, yeah, he knew it wasn't that hard to wash dishes by hand, but that was what a dishwasher was for—washing the dishes so he could take the night off after cooking the meal and working all day.

He'd done the laundry last night too. And…well, hell, it was all stacked on the couch ready to be put away. That was his goal tonight when he got home. He'd done it too late last night and had gone to bed before it was completely dry. This morning, he had pulled the clean clothes out of the dryer but didn't have time to put the laundry away. Not when he was in a hurry to do the crossword puzzle. He had to keep his priorities straight.

The bed wasn't made either, not that she'd see his bedroom. He figured why make it? The next time he'd be in his bedroom, he'd be ready to climb into bed, sheets and comforter pulled aside already for him. The bathroom that guests used was clean. He never used it. Thankfully.

As soon as it was time to leave work, he said good night to Ryan and said to Ingrid, "I look forward to seeing you in a little while."

"Thanks. Did you want me to bring anything?"

"Only if you want to. Otherwise, I think we'll be good." Then Knox walked her out of the building and waved goodbye, eager to have an enjoyable time with her. Maybe there wouldn't be anything between them as far as dating went, but he would enjoy the company tonight at least.

On the way to the grocery store, his car was listing on the road, one tire rumbling a bit, the ride suddenly bumpy. He pulled off onto the shoulder, got out of his car, and looked at the tire, flat as a Frisbee. He couldn't believe it. First the dishwasher, now this.

At least he had a spare tire. He opened the trunk and pulled it out. It was just as flat. He ground his teeth and called for a tow service. In a half hour, the man had arrived, pumped air into his spare tire, and gotten him on his way. Man, Knox was not going to be able to buy the groceries and get home in time to clean things up. He hated to make a lousy impression on Ingrid for their first social engagement, even if it was meant to be just a casual get-together.

He was rushing through the grocery store with a basket to grab what they were going to eat for dinner when he saw Carol headed his way. No, he couldn't chat. He was in a hurry. He wanted to at least dump his laundry on his bed so he could sort and put it away later, and he could quickly shove all his dirty dishes back into the dishwasher for expediency.

There was no line at the checkout counter, and he was eager to check out *now*.

"Hi, Knox." Carol looked worried, and that gave Knox pause. "Rosalind told me Ingrid got some roses from a secret admirer. Can you look into it for me?"

"Do you have any bad premonitions from it?"

"No, but...I don't know. I just feel like something's not quite right."

"Sure. Ingrid already asked me to check into it."

"Oh, good. I was afraid she'd feel we were prying into her business too much. First with chasing off Jethro Canton, the ex, and now this."

Knox smiled, but then he said, "Sorry, I've got to run. Ingrid's coming over for dinner, and I don't want to be late."

Carol glanced at the items he was purchasing for dinner and gave him a brilliant smile. "Enjoy yourselves."

He figured there wasn't any need to keep their impromptu date a secret from the pack. "We'll be running on your property about nine." They didn't have to ask permission, but it was a good idea to make sure not too many of them showed up to run at the same time.

"Okay, see you later if we see you. And thanks about checking on the roses. Ryan said you were looking into the situation with the hidden message in the crossword puzzle too."

"No problem, and yeah, I am. Okay, got to run."

They said their goodbyes, and when he hurried off to check out, there were five people standing in line, including one who wrote a check and had to find her ID but couldn't for several minutes. He didn't think anyone wrote checks anymore. Another was scrounging for some change in her purse when she went to pay for her candy bar. At least that was all she had to check out, if she could find enough money to purchase it. If he hadn't been so far back in line, he would have paid for the candy bar, done a good deed, and gotten the woman on her way.

Everyone else used credit cards or debit cards. Thankfully.

He finally paid for his purchases and rushed home, reminding himself that the first chance he had, he needed to get his regular tire's flat fixed before anything else went wrong.

When he arrived at the house, Ingrid was parked in his driveway, smiling at him.

So much for getting there ahead of time.

He was feeling frazzled, and he wanted to ask her to sit in the car for a moment while he straightened up the place.

But of course, he couldn't.

"I'm sorry I'm late. I had a flat tire on the way to the grocery store."

Ingrid smiled. "My week has been going that way too."

"Oh?" He carried the groceries to the front door and unlocked it.

"Yeah, my washing machine broke down, and I had suds all over the floor. Then my microwave went out. I'm trying not to think of what else could go wrong."

He smiled. "I know what you mean." When he walked into the house and she saw all his laundry sitting on the brown velour couch, he said, "Uh, I washed the clothes too late last night. I'll put those in the bedroom in a moment to sort through later."

"I do that all the time. You weren't expecting company. At least you don't have a litter of beer cans all over." She looked at all the dirty dishes sitting on the granite counter next to the double sink and raised a brow.

He guessed he could have let them soak in soapy water before he had the dishwasher repaired. He set the bags of groceries on the counter nearby. "The dishwasher broke."

She laughed.

He smiled. "I know. It's just the principle of the thing. The dishwasher has a purpose."

Smiling, she shook her head. "Go change into something more comfortable and then make dinner." She found a rubber stopper in the cabinet for one of the stainless-steel kitchen sinks and poured dishwasher soap and hot water into it.

"You don't have to do that." He pulled off his suit jacket in a hurry.

"When is your dishwasher being repaired?" she asked.

He set his jacket on the back of a kitchen chair, then removed his tie. "In four days."

She laughed again. He smiled, then grabbed his jacket and tie and headed back into the bedroom to throw on some shorts and a T-shirt.

When he returned to the kitchen, she glanced at his black T-shirt that said in white letters: Do Not Read the Next Sentence. In fine print, it said: You little rebel, you.

She smiled.

"You read the last sentence, didn't you?" he asked.

She laughed. "Of course. I imagine everyone would."

He began making dinner for them, and while the meal was cooking, he hurried to take his clean clothes into the bedroom and dumped them on the bed. He returned and saw her looking at the crossword puzzle on the oak dining table. *His* crossword puzzle, all neatly penned in.

Damn. He'd forgotten all about that.

"I didn't think *you* did crossword puzzles." She was smiling a little, one pretty blond brow raised.

He shrugged. "I have to do it every morning before work, you know. It's a mental process to get me going in the mornings."

She began cleaning his dishes. "When I asked you and Ryan for help, you already knew all the answers, but you wouldn't give them to me."

"Yeah, but I knew you wanted to figure it out for yourself. That's the satisfaction in doing them without any help."

"True. I can't believe you let on you thought the puzzles were silly."

"I don't think I said they were silly, exactly. Everyone I knew gave me a hard time about doing them when I was growing up."

She laughed. "They just weren't as astute as us. But it doesn't explain why you gave *me* a hard time about it." She figured it was because he liked her, but he hadn't wanted to give away his secret.

"Yeah, now you know my secret."

About the crossword puzzles? Or his liking her? "Do I have to keep it?"

He laughed. "No. And you don't have to do the dishes either." He finished cooking dinner and set it on the table. Then he brought over a pad of paper and a pen and set them next to his plate.

"Did you really not see the hidden meaning in the puzzle?" She rinsed off the dishes and silverware.

"No. You have a special knack for that."

She finished up the dishes and then came into the dining room, carrying glasses of ice water. "I didn't bring anything with me. I realized I didn't have the time to drop by the grocery store, since I wanted to stop at the house and change into something more comfortable."

She was wearing a pretty pink lacy blouse and blue jeans shorts—dressed for a date, not just to get comfortable. That could be a good sign. No matter what she wore, she always caught his attention.

"You didn't need to. We have enough food here, and I've got some chocolate cookies if we have an urge for something sweet after dinner."

"Do you have popcorn to munch on while watching the movie?"

Damn. He chuckled. "No. It wasn't on my list. Next time though."

CHAPTER 4

INGRID THOUGHT KNOX WAS SWEET TO HAVE WORRIED about the condition of his house, which was really super neat. Hers could be a mess when she wasn't expecting company. She couldn't even recall how she'd left hers this morning. He seemed to want everything to be special for them when she'd just invited herself over.

His house was well maintained and nicely appointed with a brown velour wraparound sectional sofa and a TV surrounded by bookcases. Prints of gray wolves in the woods hung on the other walls, courtesy of Jake Silver, who was a photographer and had taken pictures of some of the Green Valley wolves on a lark on Ryan and Carol's property. Ingrid loved the pictures and thought she should get some like that too.

She and Knox sat down at the oak dining table together. She suspected he usually ate dinner and watched TV at the same time if he didn't have company because of the TV tray set up next to the couch and a coffee cup still sitting there. She would do the same if she didn't prefer reading a book.

She was glad he didn't suggest sitting on the couch. Even though she wasn't going to call it a date, this was her first date with him, a way of seeing if they might be compatible. "That's okay that you don't have any popcorn. If we do this again sometime, I'll bring some with me."

This was fun, she had to admit. Already she wanted to have another date like this.

She hadn't thought she'd enjoy spending time with another male wolf anytime soon, but she felt comfortable with Knox. Maybe because she'd seen his house before he had picked up things and it wasn't a total wreck. It was the real him, and she liked getting to know the real man behind the suit. Maybe because he'd gone all out to make the dinner something special.

"Sure, you can bring the popcorn next time." He seemed pleased she was interested in doing this again. He cut into his steak. "Who do you think might have sent you the flowers?"

She cut into her steak, cooked perfectly, a warm pink, nice and tender. "I was thinking about that. How about the guys who helped chase off my ex? Excluding you, of course." She took a bite of her steak.

"I wouldn't do anything like that secretly." He began making notes on the notepad.

"You only do crossword puzzles in secret."

He chuckled, then took another bite of steak.

She pointed at her steak. "This is *really* good."

"The steaks are. I haven't had one in a while. Seems like I'm always eating fish or chicken." He raised his pen off the table, ready to write some more names on his list to check out. "What about the ex?"

"He's a possibility. Maybe he found the pack in Montana didn't want him. I wouldn't put it past Carol to send word that he might be trouble where the she-wolves were concerned. He wouldn't be welcome in the pack then. And maybe he didn't find a job there like he thought he would. Or maybe where he ended up, there are no *lupus garou* packs."

"Could be. Has there been anyone else you've met or worked with recently who might have taken a shine to you?" he asked.

"Well, you know a lot of men get real friendly sometimes because they want to see Ryan, but he's busy."

"Names?"

"Nobody recently, come to think of it. And all the positions are filled. Oh, I know, there's a pub that is concerned Ryan's going to close them down for health and safety issues. I don't know. I'm really reaching here."

"Name of the pub?"

"Spuds and Suds. They serve all kinds of different food and mainly beer and wine. Mickey Smithson is the owner, and he came in and was real nice to me, trying to get in to see Ryan about closing down his pub. He didn't have an appointment."

"Did Ryan see him?"

"Yeah, but he told Mickey exactly what *I* had told him. He had to pass the next health and safety inspection if he was going to stay in business. There's no getting around it. Mickey could send me a truckload of flowers and that wouldn't change. So it's probably not him."

"The guy who creates the crossword puzzles?"

Ingrid laughed. "Seriously?"

"I'm beginning to think it's a secret love message. What about the writer who interviewed the boss today?"

"Uh, yeah, Chas liked that I was doing a crossword puzzle, and he likes doing them too. He kept hanging around my desk."

"Okay, sounds like we might have our man."

"Well, if it is him, be nice. I've met him a few times when

he's come in to ask Ryan questions for the paper about articles he's doing on the city and ongoing policies, plans, and
entertainment. He's a little timid, I think. So don't go scar-
ing him to pieces if you ask him about it."

"Yeah, sure." Knox had better mean it. "I'll ask the men
in the pack if any of them sent you the flowers because
we're concerned it might be something sinister. Someone
will probably say they did it, and that will be the end of the
mystery."

"That could be bad. I can see some wolf being embarrassed because a sweet gesture was considered something
ominous."

"I don't have to do it. You just say the word." Knox picked
up their dirty dishes and carried them into the kitchen. He
set them in the sudsy water she'd left in the sink so he could
use it to clean the dishes after dinner.

"Nah, go ahead and look into it. But don't say we think
it's something sinister. We can all laugh about it later if we
learn one of the men in our pack sent them." She took their
water glasses into the living room and set them on coasters
on the coffee table. "Thank you for dinner. It was great. I
was planning on having a tuna-fish sandwich tonight."

"Then you changed your mind and wanted to watch
some TV?"

She smiled. "Well, you were assigned the job of investigating my secret admirer and the hidden message in the
crossword puzzles. I thought it would be nice to thank you
by keeping you company tonight."

"I'm enjoying your company. Thanks. Did you want
anything stronger to drink? Or a soda?"

"No soda. And we're running as wolves and driving, so

nothing harder to drink. The water is fine. Have you ever wondered what would happen if a *lupus garou* was drinking alcohol as a human, stripped and shifted, and got picked up by the pound as a wolf, and he tested positive for drinking over the limit?"

Knox laughed. "No. I've never thought of it that way. But now I will every time I have a beer and think about running as a wolf."

She smiled. "It's certainly something I consider before I drink and run as a wolf. Not that they'd ever test a wolf that way, but what if?"

Knox washed the dishes from dinner. Ingrid had thought of offering since he had bought the beautiful steaks for dinner and cooked for them, but since she'd washed about a week's worth of dishes for him, she decided to let him do them this time.

Afterward, they sat down on the soft brown sofa—if it had been hers, she could curl up on it and fall asleep—to decide on something to watch.

She sat closer to Knox than she'd intended on a first date, and their bare legs touched. He looked like he wanted to put his arm around her, and she was tired after a restless night, so snuggling against him appealed, as long as she didn't fall asleep. How would that look on a first date?

She moved to cuddle against him, and he put his arm around her shoulders. They found they both liked thrillers and mysteries, so they chose one based on a true story. Those were the best. "If I fall asleep, wake me. I didn't sleep soundly last night, but I don't want to fall asleep now and have difficulty sleeping tonight."

"If I hear you snoring, I'll wake you."

She laughed. "I don't snore." She sure hoped she didn't anyway.

Thankfully, the movie was filled with action and suspense as two murderers escaped from a penitentiary and headed for Canada. The story kept her riveted to the very end.

"That was a great movie," Ingrid said, stretching while she pulled away from Knox. "I love stories based on truth. It seems so unreal, yet there you have it."

Knox nodded and turned off the TV. "Yeah, it was a great movie. And the bad guys got it in the end." Knox rose from the couch and helped Ingrid up. He rubbed her arm. "Did you want to ride with me to Ryan and Carol's home so we can run as wolves?"

"I think I'll take my own vehicle. They live out in the country, and I can drive home after our run instead of returning to your place and picking up my car."

"Okay, that will work."

"Thanks for dinner and the movie. It was fun." She had thoroughly enjoyed it, and she could tell Knox had too. She took his hand and looked up at him, wanting a kiss. He was too tall for her to just kiss him without him inclining his head.

He smiled and obliged.

Knox kissed her gently, but the passion soon built between them. So much for leaving it at something sweet and nonbinding. She traced the seam of his lips with her tongue, and then they were melding mouths, tongues exploring, bodies colliding, and she was feeling hot and needy. Just as she felt his cock growing with interest. Her hands stroked his back, and his hands drifted to her lower back and rested there as they finally broke off the kiss.

His eyes were dark with desire, and she could hear his blood pumping as hard as hers was.

"We'd better go run before it gets too much later," she said.

"Thanks for the company and doing the dishes. This was fun. If you don't have any plans for tomorrow night, there's a good documentary about a man who lost his son, but the police weren't looking for the murderer, despite the town having the highest murder rate in the country for its size and the lowest rate of solved murders. So he intends to find his son's murderer."

"Okay, sure. I think I'm free tomorrow night." She knew she was, but she didn't want it to sound like she never had any plans. After she'd broken up with her ex, that was the way it had been. Though she'd done some things with the ladies in the pack a couple of times.

"Well, you let me know for sure, and we can decide on a meal."

"Sure, or I can bring something this time." She didn't want him to think he had to always buy her dinner. Even though he made more money than she did, she could fix a meal for two also.

"Either way works for me."

They were soon driving out to the countryside on the dark night, the stars lighting their way, but no moon because it was a new moon phase. Knox followed Ingrid to the spacious ranch and property. They reached their pack leaders' home, a two-story ranch home with big covered porches all the way around it and large rocking chairs for everyone to sit on. Rosalind's

Victorian-styled greenhouses were situated to the right of the house, perfect for her floral gardening and lovely to look at. Rosalind had planned to move out of the house, but Carol and Ryan had convinced her to stay with them.

The porch lights and several lights inside the house were on, welcoming them.

Ingrid got out of her car as Knox got out of his. "Should we ask if they want to run with us?" she asked.

"We can ask, but I suspect they won't want to impose," Knox said.

She went up to the door and knocked, Knox joining her.

"Then we'll have to let them know they wouldn't be." She didn't want anyone in the pack getting ideas about them.

Rosalind answered the door. "Hey, I hear you're running as wolves. Ryan and Carol and I are watching TV. It's the new moon. Carol can't shift, so Ryan isn't running as a wolf."

"Did you want to go with us?" Ingrid didn't want Rosalind to feel left out if she wanted to run too.

Rosalind gave her a big smile. "No. I'm enjoying the movie. Have fun. I just wanted to let you know we aren't ignoring you. Come in and you can use a couple of the spare rooms to strip and shift in."

"Thanks," Ingrid said and went into one of the rooms while Knox used another. She figured it was good to keep up appearances.

Knox and Ingrid soon came out of the rooms and left the house as wolves to run through the treed land and to the river nearby.

Knox was a beautiful wolf with a black saddle and white chest, black mask on his face, but partially tan legs and tan and white on his face too. He was regal looking, big and protective.

Whenever she'd gone running as a wolf here, Ingrid had always run with a few pack members at a time. Not with the whole pack of thirty all at once because they didn't want to catch anyone's attention if someone was on the land who shouldn't be. The five thousand acres was privately owned by Ryan and Carol, but that didn't mean hunters or others wouldn't trespass on the land.

Ingrid had come out here with Jethro because it really was the safest place for them to run as wolves. Unlike Silver Town, Green Valley was not run by wolves, so they had to be careful around the humans in town. Wouldn't they have been surprised to learn their mayor and the rest of his staff were wolves!

Ryan would have liked to have appointed wolves for all department heads, but they just didn't have enough quali-fied people to fill the spots.

Ingrid and Knox ran together at first and then slowed to a walk, exploring and then running again, chasing each other, just like any wolves would do out on a run.

Then they saw a cougar. It surprised them as much as it surprised the cougar. It was a male, so Ingrid wasn't worried they'd chase off a female who might have some cubs some-where nearby. They barked and ran after the cougar, chasing him out of the territory.

The cat outdistanced them in a hurry.

But then she heard the telltale sound of the cocking of a rifle. And then a second one. For a split second, she thought of the movie they'd watched, of the convicts on the run and the lawmen trying to hunt them down.

Knox heard the guns, too, and the two of them raced to get out of harm's way. As soon as they'd run far enough, though they could hear two men running through the brush trying to locate them again, Knox stopped, lifted his head, and howled to alert Ryan they were in trouble. But Ingrid continued to run toward the river so they could put it between them and the hunters.

Then Knox caught up to Ingrid. She'd reached the river and was contemplating crossing it. Would they have enough time to reach the other side and then the safety of the woods? The men probably wouldn't want to cross the stream, deep as it was. They'd have to swim across and surely get their rifles wet.

She was glad Rosalind hadn't come with them now.

Ingrid thought she and Knox should split up to try to avoid the hunters. Maybe one of them would get out of this alive. She motioned with her head for Knox to go in a different direction from her.

He shook his head.

All right, well, *she* was swimming across the river then. She ran into the water, and when she couldn't touch the bottom, she began to swim, wolf paddling as fast as she could against the current.

She glanced back, thinking Knox would be swimming with her but maybe just behind her a little. But he was waiting on shore, damn it! What if the hunters located him? They'd shoot him!

She suspected he planned to keep them from shooting her while she was so vulnerable as she tried to reach the opposite shore. When she reached the riverbank, she hurried out, shook off the water, and waited for him to join her. She couldn't do anything for him now, and she hated feeling useless. If the men appeared at the river's edge, she could dive into the forest for cover. But Knox would be defenseless.

Why didn't he just come with her when she began the swim? They'd both be safely on this side now!

CHAPTER 5

HIS HEART POUNDING HARD, KNOX HEARD THE HUNTERS coming. Since Ingrid was safely out of the water and within a wolf's leap from the protection of the woods, he finally started swimming across the river.

He'd stayed on the shore as long as he could to make sure the hunters didn't reach the river and shoot at Ingrid while she was swimming. He could have taken one of the men out at least, hoping to allow Ingrid time to escape unharmed. He sure wished he could get a visual on the men. Maybe he'd know them by sight, and if he lived through this, he could report them for illegal hunting and trespassing.

He thought he would make it across in time to get out of their range, but he was halfway across the river when he heard one of the men shout, "There, in the river and at the river's edge. Two of them!"

Crap!

Knox hoped the hell Ingrid wouldn't wait for him at the water's edge and would run to safety. To his profound relief, she finally dashed off, and he could see her stop safely in the woods, observing him. She looked as anxious as he felt.

Then one of the men fired his rifle, the rounds pinging into the water close to Knox. His heart practically skipping beats, Knox did what wolves normally *wouldn't* do. He dove under the water and swam as far as he could before he had to come up for air. The pads of his feet finally felt the rocky bottom, and he knew he was close enough to race out of the water. He came up for air, rushing out of the river at the same time, water flinging off his fur as he headed to the woods closest to him. Gunfire rang out, the rounds striking the ground around him. *Ping! Ping! Ping!*

Running as fast as he could, dodging back and forth, unlike a real wolf would do, he felt invincible, though he knew that feeling would be short-lived if one of the rounds hit him.

And then one did. Right in the damn hip. He staggered with the impact, and Ingrid was crouched, ready to lunge in his direction to come to his aid. He growled at her to stay where she was, safe from the rifles' range. They only had one target for now, and he wanted to keep it that way.

After howling for help, he was certain Ryan would be calling up the pack and everyone would be out here trying to catch the hunters before they killed Knox and Ingrid. As soon as Knox stumbled into the safety of the trees, Ingrid howled to let Ryan know where they were and that they were still in danger as long as the hunters were out here.

The two men paced across the riverbank, irritated they hadn't killed their prey.

Ingrid sat next to Knox and licked his cheek and then pressed her face against his bloody hip, trying to stem the blood. He wasn't in pain yet, thankfully, the adrenaline still racing through his blood keeping him from feeling anything. He wasn't feeling woozy, like he was losing too much blood. He wanted to go way around through the woods and cross the river to the pack leaders' house, but he figured the best thing to do was to stay put and wait for help to arrive.

His healing genetics would start to heal the wound right away, though he still would only heal in half the time a human would. So it wasn't instantaneous, certainly not for bad injuries. He was just lucky the bullet hadn't hit a major artery.

"Hell, I can't believe as many damn shots as we fired, we didn't take down the wolf. Let's go across. He's not going anywhere. He's just sitting in the woods with the other one."

"No way, Brother. We'd get our rifles wet, and what if the smaller one attacked us? Or the wounded wolf did?"

"They wouldn't dare. Not when we're toting rifles."

Knox was still panting, trying to catch his breath when he heard the shouts of men off across the river in the woods, men from their wolf pack, thankfully. The hunters were swearing up a storm while they tried to hightail it out of there and not get caught at illegal hunting and trespassing.

Knox perked up when he finally saw Ryan at the river's edge. Knox hoped someone else would catch the hunters.

He woofed, letting Ryan know where they were, just beyond the river, hiding in the trees. Ingrid was still pressing her cheek against his wound, really good thinking since they had nothing else to stem the bleeding. She was a pretty gray wolf, smaller than him, her face whiter than his. Her chest and a good part of her fur were tan, with just a few black guard hairs in the pattern of a saddle on her back. She had a little bit of black on her ears and head, giving her a look of noble distinction.

"Are either of you injured?" Ryan asked because both of them hadn't woofed in greeting.

Ingrid shifted and placed her hands on Knox's hip. "Knox was hit in the hind quarter. I'm trying to stop the bleeding." She shifted back and rested her head against his wound again.

"I'm coming across with medical supplies in a minute. Just hang on." Ryan called someone on his cell phone. "We're near the south fork of the river, about a quarter mile north of there. Knox is wounded and across the river in the woods. I'm not sure how bad. If you can bring a medical pack in the waterproof kit, I'll take it over to him. And we need to bring him back over here on a stretcher. Ingrid's okay, but she's staying with him. Okay, out here. We have a dozen men searching for the hunters, and they're on the run."

It seemed like it took forever for Carol to bring Ryan a medical kit, while Rosalind was carrying a stretcher. Ryan kissed Carol, then carrying the pack, he began to swim across the river to reach the other shore.

When he finally reached the riverbank, three men from the pack arrived. Two of them grabbed the stretcher and swam it across to the other side where Ryan was. No matter the emergency, the wolves always acted as a team, everyone doing their part to help others in need.

Ryan sprinted to the tree line and was soon taking over so he could bandage Knox the best he could. Because of the location of the wound and Knox's fur being wet, it wasn't easy.

"You're sure you weren't shot?" Ryan asked Ingrid. The fur on her right cheek was bloody from where she'd been leaning her face against Knox's wound.

Knox couldn't have appreciated her more for wanting to help him, to even try to come to his aid when it had been way too dangerous.

She shook her head.

Ryan looked down at Knox. "I'd tell you to shift to make

the bandaging easier, but you'll be warmer in your fur coat. We'll get you into the house, and Carol will take care of you. She's already called the pack leaders of Silver Town to see if they can send their doctor."

That was one great thing with the wolf packs. They didn't have a wolf doctor in Green Valley yet, the arrangements to build a clinic and set one up in practice here still in progress, but the one in Silver Town didn't mind making house calls for injured or sick wolves even as far away as Green Valley.

Knox hoped he wasn't bad enough off to need hospitalization though. He hoped he'd heal quickly and be back at work soon. Ryan could call in someone to fill in for him, but Knox didn't want to be off the job for too long. Not to mention he didn't want another male wolf hitting on Ingrid if he wasn't there to watch out for her. He had to smile at the notion. He was in full-blown pursuit of the she-wolf, even if she didn't know it.

Then the other men carrying the stretcher ran to reach them, both as wet as Ryan. They were Max Browning and Fen Kilgore, two of the men in the pack who worked for Ryan in his PI agency.

Despite how he was feeling, Knox wanted to question them as to whether one of them had sent Ingrid the roses. He would have shifted and asked if he wasn't already starting to feel so much pain. He wasn't sure he could manage a shift and not pass out. How would that look to the woman he was hoping to see much more of romantically?

He needn't have worried about passing out if he'd tried to shift. One minute, he was lying as a wounded wolf on the leaf-littered woodlands floor, and the next minute, he was soaking wet again, as if he'd swum across the river on his own power. Now he was being jostled back and forth on the stretcher as the men headed to the pack leaders' home. Not having remembered anything about the men carrying him across the river, Knox figured he must have passed out when they lifted him onto the wet stretcher.

Then he had another lapse in memory and woke in the room Carol had set aside for injured wolves, complete with medical supplies and a hospital bed. Sometimes they had emergencies and taking their wolves to Silver Town was out of the question, so this worked well for them. Carol wanted to be a doctor so she could do more for her wolf patients. Now that she could live a longer life because she was a wolf, she intended to do so for their pack.

For now, she would stabilize Knox before Dr. Weber from Silver Town arrived.

To Knox's surprise, Ingrid was at his bedside, doing whatever Carol told her to do. At some point, Ingrid had shifted and put on her clothes, her long blond hair still wet, hanging about her shoulders.

She looked worried for him, but then she frowned at him and pursed her lips before speaking. "Why in the world did you wait to cross the river? Why didn't you swim across with me at the same time? Then you could have fled to the woods like I did, and you would never have been in this mess." She motioned to his figure, lying with a sheet over him. He was now human, having shifted with some difficulty, and naked underneath the cover, except for the bandage on his wound. "Oh, wait, you wanted some vacation time off from work and didn't know how to ask for it."

Carol smiled.

Knox knew Ingrid was frustrated with him because he had been injured and not because he had so bravely waited to deter the men from shooting at her. Sure, in hindsight, he could have crossed the river with her, but neither of them knew if the hunters would have shown up before that happened.

He wasn't going to explain his reasoning to her when he knew darn well she knew why he'd done it. He smiled back at her instead.

Ingrid's annoyed expression didn't change.

He sighed. "Thank you for being there for me."

Ingrid came over and clasped his hand that didn't have an IV attached to it, giving him a gentle squeeze. That meant the world to him, and he knew she wasn't really mad at him. Well, maybe a little annoyed.

Ryan came into the room. "How's he doing?"

"Pulse rate and blood pressure are good," Carol said. "He'll be as good as new soon."

"Do I need to have one of our men come in as a replacement for him for a couple of weeks?" Ryan asked.

"No," Knox said. "I'll be in tomorrow. Next day at the latest."

Everyone looked at Carol to see her take on it. She shook her head.

Ryan patted Knox on the shoulder. "You get your rest. I'll have someone take over your duties until you can return to work."

Knox ground his teeth. He knew Ryan's word was final, both as his pack leader and his boss at work, but he didn't have to like it. And he knew Ryan would have one of their wolves do the job.

"Make sure it's someone who doesn't give me grief about doing my crossword puzzles," Ingrid said brightly. As if she was just fine working with someone else.

Hell, now Knox couldn't even see her socially until he could be up and about. He couldn't run with her as a wolf again for some time, though he thought she might not want to run with him again after what had happened to them.

Three bad things had happened. His dishwasher had crapped out on him. His tire had gone flat. And now he'd been shot. Enough was enough. It was time for something good to happen.

CHAPTER 6

INGRID FELT HORRIBLE ABOUT KNOX GETTING SHOT and not having been able to do anything about it. It had ruined a beautiful wolf run and a really great evening. Worst of all, they still didn't know who the hunters were.

She'd been so upset he'd been hurt because of trying to protect her that she had been annoyed with him when she shouldn't have been. Which was why she had squeezed his hand to let him know she cared about him and wanted him to get better quickly.

When Dr. Weber arrived, he removed the bullet with Carol's and Ingrid's assistance. When Knox finally came to and smiled at Ingrid, letting her know he would be on the mend and he was glad she was there, she raised her brows at him.

He gave her a bigger smile.

"You know what you have to do for the next three days or so," Dr. Weber said to Carol. Then he gently clasped Knox's shoulder. "You'll be like brand new before you know it."

"Thanks, Doc. I will be."

"As long as you do what I tell you to do," Carol warned.

Dr. Weber agreed with Carol with a stern nod.

When Dr. Weber left, Ryan and his sister came to check on Knox.

"He needs to sleep," Carol said. "But he did really well."

That meant Ingrid needed to leave, too, but Carol turned to her and said, "You can stay here at the house for however long you'd like."

Ingrid had already considered staying overnight, but she wasn't prepared for an overnight visit. "I'll be at work all day tomorrow. I don't have a change of office clothes with me or anything else. I'll drop by after work and check on Knox," she said. It was late and he needed to sleep. So did she. She guessed she could have left really early in the morning to go home first, but she wouldn't get as much sleep then.

"Okay, we'll see you tomorrow night," Carol said. "Knox, I'll be back in a little while to tuck you in for the night."

Ryan and Rosalind said good night to him, and then Ingrid was alone with Knox.

He looked so drowsy from the operation that she quickly leaned over and kissed his lips. "More of that when you're feeling better."

He smiled and instantly looked like he was ready to get out of the bed and kiss her back.

"Sleep so you can get better quicker."

He sleepily nodded, then closed his eyes.

"'Night, my protective wolf." She kissed him on the forehead. Then she headed out of the room, disquieted about what had happened. She just hoped they'd find the hunters soon.

When she left the room, Ryan approached her. "Did you see the men well enough to recognize them?"

"No, but one of the men's voices sounded vaguely familiar. And he called the other one his brother, unless it was to say he was his buddy. They wore camouflaged shirts and pants and caps. That's all I could see."

"All right. Did you need me to drive you home and have someone else drive your car there?"

"No, I'll be fine. Thanks." The adrenaline had seeped

out of her cells a couple of hours ago, and she felt even tireder now.

"If you need me to get someone else to watch the desk for a while in the morning, I can do that," Ryan offered.

"Thanks, Boss. I'll be in."

Ryan, Carol, and Rosalind gave her hugs, and she hugged them back, then drove off.

On the way home, she couldn't quit thinking of the cougar she and Knox had scared off. They'd probably saved his life. She couldn't quit visualizing Knox swimming in the river as a wolf, trying to reach the shore while the men were shooting at him.

She was just glad the men hadn't hit Knox more than the once. That was bad enough.

That night as she retired to bed, she wanted to think of only the fun she'd had with Knox and not about the shooting. She imagined she'd feel uneasy about running through there when she and Knox wanted to run as wolves again. And she did want to do that with him. But not until the men were caught and charged with the crime, because she was afraid they'd return to shoot the wolves they'd seen. Which meant any wolves in the Green Valley pack would be at risk.

For three days, Ingrid had seen Knox after work, and he had been on bed rest for the most part, though he'd been walking around the ranch house during the day before she arrived, trying to get his strength back. But by evening when she went to see him, he'd been in bed, looking like he'd overdone it. She always kissed him goodbye, and that seemed to cheer him immensely.

"He's cranky," Ryan told Ingrid at work today, "because I won't let him come back to work. Here are the keys to his place. He thanks you for dropping by his house when the dishwasher repairman comes to check it out this afternoon."

"Thanks for giving me the time off to do it. I know once Knox returns home, he'll be glad that it's fixed."

"He will. He asked me how you're feeling about being back to work after all this happened."

"I know. I've told him work keeps my mind off it, but I think he believes I'm just trying to hide what I feel."

"I told him you're still working the puzzles and doing everything you're supposed to do for me, so you're fine."

"Okay, good. After the repairman repairs Knox's dishwasher, I'll drive over and see him. Have we had any word about the hunters?" Ingrid asked.

"No. Knox is the only one who saw them close up, and he didn't recognize them. All we have to go by is their scent, and that won't be easy to do."

Max Browning returned to the office, smiled at Ingrid, and then related what he'd learned about the job Ryan had sent him on. She hoped Max wasn't getting used to the job, because as soon as Knox was home, she was planning on giving him some first-class care of her own at night so he could be back to work hassling her. And she'd hassle him right back.

Then a fellow pack member and friend of Ingrid's, Lettie Miller, dropped by the suite of offices. "I hope you're planning on seeing Knox soon. A bunch of us have dropped in from time to time to cheer him up during the day, but he *only* wants to see you. He's a grouch."

Ingrid chuckled. "I'm seeing him again tonight."

"Good. We all love him but"—Lettie smiled—"he's grumpy Ryan's making you work during the day so you can't see him. I've got to go. I just wanted to drop these flyers off with Ryan."

Ingrid looked over the top one. Lettie owned her own small print shop and was always doing orders for the mayor's office for one thing or another. And also for any wolf who needed something done—birth announcements, wedding announcements, party announcements, posters for Rosalind's floral shop and greenhouses, and more.

But these flyers featured an offer of a $10,000 reward for information leading to the arrest of the hunters who had trespassed on the mayor's private property and shot the assistant mayor who was walking in the woods with his girlfriend. The only way to really take these men to task, if they could find them, was to make them responsible for shooting a human, not a wolf.

The news about Knox's injury had already been in the local paper, and the police were still making inquiries. So were Ryan's staff who were working as private investigators.

And the rest of the pack was helping out in any way they could when they had a moment to do it. Several people were coming to post the flyers at businesses and all over town.

Carol had told Ingrid that Knox had received tons of get-well cards from people all over, a couple of stuffed teddy bears, flowers, and offers from several human women to take care of him when he came home. That had amused Ingrid.

He was getting so much attention, both from pack members and well-wishers from the community, that he didn't need hers too. He'd be spoiled rotten. Though she was glad he always seemed to be happier when she showed up and had dinner with him at the McKinleys' place. They would watch a movie together, including the one he'd mentioned wanting to see with her before this had happened, and Rosalind had even made them popcorn. She could be such a sweetheart.

Knox had been working the crossword puzzles from Carol's paper so he could keep up with them when he felt like it. After visiting with him for a couple of hours, having dinner with the family and Knox, and watching the movie with Knox, Ingrid would go home and look at her TV and think about how much she'd enjoyed their one date night four nights ago.

The wolf run had been the best, until the hunters had come into the picture. She was having nightmares about that. She figured Knox might be also, but she hadn't wanted to mention it.

It wasn't long before she took off early from work to reach Knox's house before the dishwasher repairman showed up. At least this one said he'd be there between noon and five, so she didn't have to take off for the whole day.

She unlocked Knox's door and entered the house, then locked the door. She knew the dishes would still be sitting on the counter where Knox had set them out to dry after he'd washed them. She put them away. Then she walked into the bedroom to put away the laundry so when Knox returned home, he could climb into bed and get comfortable.

The bed was unmade like hers would often be, which made her smile. She put away the laundry stacked on his bed: socks, boxer briefs, T-shirts, dress shirts, bath towel, and jeans. Then she pulled the linens off the bed and put them and his towels in the wash and started them so he could have fresh sheets and towels when he returned home. Then she made up his bed with fresh sheets from the linen closet.

Knox's home phone rang, and she quickly picked it up, thinking it was the dishwasher repairman, but it was Knox on his cell phone.

"Hey, the repairman hasn't come yet," she said, figuring Knox wanted her to hurry up and come see him since she got off earlier from work today.

"Thanks for dropping by to do that. He called my cell phone and said he'd be there between one and one thirty."

"Oh, good. That means I won't have too long to wait."

"And you can get here earlier, right? What's that noise in the background?" Knox asked.

"I'm doing a load of your laundry. Sheets, towels. When you're ready to come home, you'll have a working dishwasher and a fresh bed to sleep in."

"You didn't have to do that. But thanks. I guess another dinner is in order."

"When you're feeling well enough. How come you learned to cook? My dad didn't know the first thing about it." It was nice Knox could cook, and the meal was great too.

"My mother said the way into a woman's heart was to be able to cook great meals. She always appreciated when my dad gave her a break and cooked dinner. She and Dad both taught me how to cook. His mother said the same thing to him when he was growing up."

Ingrid smiled. "I like that."

"It hasn't gotten me anywhere yet, but I enjoy cooking. Lettie said you're coming by to see me after the repairman does his magic."

"I sure am. Did you want me to pick up a change of clothes for you for when you can leave Carol's care?"

"Yeah, sure, thanks. Carol said I could go home tonight if I had someone helping me out."

"I work." She didn't want Knox thinking she could ask Ryan for all that time off from work during the day.

"Right. Carol said she could have someone take care of me during the day. I'm getting more mobile. But she just worried if I should take a spill or start running a fever or something. I would need someone to stay with me at night for the same reason."

"You're asking me to stay with you at night until you're better?"

"Yeah, the perks are you can watch my TV and see all the programs you can't get at your house."

She laughed. "Have you been doing all the crossword puzzles since you've been there?"

"Yes. I've finished up all the ones I started on and now I've been doing them studiously."

"Okay, after the repairman leaves, I'll pack a bag at my house so I can stay at your house after work, and I'll bring you a change of clothes and bring you home this afternoon."

"Thank you. I will be forever grateful. Carol is a wonderful caregiver, but she wakes me all night long to check on my stats."

"What do you think I'll be doing?"

He chuckled. "I'm hoping you'll sleep and let me sleep too."

"I'll do whatever the nurse orders."

"Thanks for taking me home and doing this for me, really."

"No problem. You brought me soup when I was sick. If I'd let you into my home, I know you would have taken care of me. Though I was afraid you might have come down with what I had and then I would have been taking care of you."

"What are friends for?"

"Right. Hey, I hear a truck pulling up. I'll let you know what the problem was with your dishwasher when I learn of it."

"Okay, thanks."

Then they ended the call, and the repairman rang the doorbell. She opened the door, and the balding man wearing a service uniform for the repair company smiled at her. "Your dishwasher isn't working?"

"Uh, my friend's isn't. You wouldn't happen to know him, would you?"

"The assistant mayor? Nah, though I heard what had happened to him. That was awful." The man pushed some buttons on the computerized dishwasher. The lights came on, but nothing happened. She was sure Knox had already done that.

"I'm a hunter myself, but I stick to the rules. No trespassing on private property. Go only during the hunting season. Take only what I'm allotted. I know guys who think it's all right to hunt on someone's private property because no one should have the right to restrict them. But do they pay the taxes on the property? No. Do they take into consideration people could be out enjoying a hike on the land?" He took the inside panel off the door of the dishwasher. Then he turned to look at Ingrid. "You were with him walking through the woods?"

"Yep." She shrugged. "We work together. We thought it

would be a fun thing to do after having dinner and seeing a movie."

"Well, that's a lousy way to end an outing. The gossip I heard in hunter circles was that the men were shooting at a couple wolves that tried to attack them. And they said they hit one of the wolves."

"There weren't any wolves out there, and if there had been, they'd be running away, trying to get out of the hunters' sights, not attacking them."

"I agree with you there. So you didn't see the wolves?"

"No. I have no idea what they thought they saw. Those men shot at phantoms for a pure need to kill something, then made up a story about wolves attacking them. Did they have any wounds to prove they'd been attacked? After one of the bullets hit Knox and he was bleeding, why wouldn't the wolves have come after him, if that's what wolves do, which they don't?"

"Well, it sure makes it easier to tell the story and get some pats on the back if you can say the animal you're hunting attacked you," the repairman said.

"You wouldn't happen to know who the men are, would you?" Ingrid suspected he might.

The repairman shook his head. "I heard it from my younger brother."

"Then he would know who they are."

"Maybe." The repairman made some adjustments, then put the dishwasher door back together and tried starting it.

It started running.

Yes! "Is it working for real now?" She was hopeful it was.

"Yes. The wires that plug in to tell the dishwasher the door is closed were loose."

Too bad Knox couldn't have discovered that himself.

"No charge for parts. Just the cost of the trip fee. And tell Mr. Granbury the warranty is good for thirty days, should he have the same issue. He already paid for the trip charge ahead of time, so no more charges today."

"Thanks. So I know you probably all stick up for each other, the hunters, I mean, but what if these"—she stopped herself short of calling them *bastards*—"men shot at other people and wouldn't take responsibility? What if Knox had died? What if we'd both been wounded and were unable to seek help? It was just a good thing I was able to call the mayor on my cell phone and ask for help. The hunters have to take responsibility for their actions, or they can get away with anything. Even return to the mayor's land with the intent to kill the wolves they think they saw and shoot someone else."

The repairman pulled out a card and wrote a name and number on it. "That's my brother. He works at the paper as a freelance writer. Chas Ward. He's a hunter too. He said someone told him about it. He didn't mention names, and I didn't ask. But maybe he can tell you who told him, and you can talk to that hunter."

"Thanks. I really appreciate it."

"No problem. I like what the mayor and his staff are doing for Green Valley. Crime is down, and I'm glad he's getting rid of some of the eating establishments that aren't up to code. You know, none of us would know just by looking at the places. The old mayor was easily bribed and let people get away with everything short of murder. Maybe even that if he was paid to look the other way. The embezzlement, tax fraud, at least that landed him in prison."

Ingrid shook her head. Ryan wouldn't chance something like that. He couldn't afford to go to jail as a wolf.

Then the repairman gave her a receipt for the job on the dishwasher and left. She called up Knox. "Good news. No extra charge on the dishwasher. If you could have taken it apart, you could have fixed it. Loose cord to the door, signaling it wasn't shut."

"But the close-door light wasn't coming on."

"Yeah, well, it wasn't connected enough for that, I guess. Anyway, I'm leaving your house and headed to mine. I don't want you to have to sit in the car while I'm getting a bag packed. Oh, and other good news, the repairman is a hunter, and he'd heard stories about the shooting incident."

"Hell, Ingrid, you'd make a great PI yourself."

"Thanks. But I like what I do for now. I'll see you in a little bit."

She put the sheets and towels in the dryer before she took off to her place. She'd have to remember to put them away when she returned to his house and set out his clean towels too. There was nothing worse than when she went to take a shower and her freshly washed towels were still in the dryer halfway across the house in the laundry room.

After packing a bag at her place, she went to the pack leader's house, and Carol greeted her at the front door.

"Our patient is so ready to return home." Carol smiled, looking eager to discharge her patient.

"I sort of got that from the talk we had on the phone."

"Yes. You sure cheered him up when you said you'd watch over him at night."

Ingrid had been wondering if he shouldn't just stay at her house, since she was more familiar with her kitchen and all, but his place was a little closer to work, and he did have the good programs on TV. He probably would want to rest on the couch during the day and watch some TV. Not to mention he should be in his own master bedroom with his bathroom close by if he had any mobility issues.

Knox smiled brightly at her when she came into the room. He was dressed and sitting in a wheelchair. She hadn't expected that. She looked at Carol.

"He's been using crutches today. He should be off the crutches by tomorrow. I think it would be easier to get him out to the car in the wheelchair." Carol took charge of the wheelchair and started wheeling him out to the front door.

Ingrid swore Carol was ready to get rid of her charge in a hurry. She glanced down at Knox, and he gave her one of his more mischievous smiles. He better not have been a grouch with everyone just because he wanted to go home and spend more time with her.

"I'll bring all his stuff out after we load him up in the car," Carol said.

"I thought you needed me to bring you a change of clothes," Ingrid said, tossing his bag back in the car and realizing she hadn't needed it as she helped him out of the wheelchair. He groaned a little, and she wasn't sure she had what it took to be a nurse. She felt awful for him.

"I didn't want to wait to get changed."

She smiled at him. She understood the feeling. "What did you want for dinner? I should have asked before and picked something up at the grocery store."

"Anything I've got on hand that's handy. I'm feeling good, hungerwise. At first, I didn't have any appetite, but now I can eat anything."

"Boy, can he," Carol said, smiling, bringing out his get-well cards and notes in a big bag. "He has donated the plants to Rosalind since she has a green thumb and the teddy bears and other stuffed toys to the police department to hand out to kids they come into contact with who are injured or abused."

Ingrid smiled at Knox. "That's really nice of you."

"Those kids can use something to make them feel better, too, even if it's a small gesture."

"I can bring over some of my food from the fridge." Ingrid looked at the huge collection of cards Carol put in the back seat. "Looks like you didn't miss me at all."

Carol chuckled. "Have fun, you two, and, Ingrid, if he starts running a fever or anything doesn't seem right, give me a call. He needs to keep that dressing clean, but it's healing up nicely, and I imagine by tomorrow or the next day, he won't need to wear one. Take it easy, Knox. I don't want to see you back here to treat complications because you're trying to do too much."

He smiled. "Believe me, now that Ingrid's taking care of me, I don't want to get her into any trouble."

"Good," Ingrid said. "Because I don't want to have to call Carol and Ryan and report you for misbehaving."

That earned her another one of his endearing smiles.

She said goodbye to Carol, and he thanked her for everything, then Ingrid drove them back home. She realized his car wasn't at Ryan and Carol's home, and she asked, "Did someone park your car at home?"

"Yeah, and when I told them about the flat tire, they had it fixed too. This is the greatest wolf pack."

"Oh, good. I agree and I'm glad." Once she got him

home and settled on the couch with a pillow and blanket, she went in to see what she could fix for dinner. "Would spaghetti be all right? You have all the ingredients I need to use to make it."

"Yeah, sure, that would be good."

"Garlic toast and a salad?"

"Great. I'm sorry for how this all worked out."

"Hey, we had fun. It wasn't our fault we ran into hunters illegally hunting on private property. How do you feel?"

"Really, much better. I have some trouble sleeping, but during the day, I swear I can feel the wound healing. You won't have to stay here for more than a couple of days."

"Okay, well, I need to get Carol's say-so on it first. Do you want to sit on the couch while you eat or up at the table? Which would be more comfortable?"

"At the dining room table. So I don't spill the spaghetti all over me."

"All right. I can still spill spaghetti sauce on me while sitting up at the table. I had a boss once who said she couldn't eat spaghetti at lunchtime at work because she invariably splattered some of the red meat sauce on her blouse."

Knox smiled. "Sounds like me."

Ingrid brought out everything she needed and set the ingredients on the granite counter. She cooked the hamburger, then added sautéed onions and tomato sauce, some frozen chopped bell peppers, mushrooms he hadn't used for the steaks, and spices including an Italian seasoning. Once she was done boiling the noodles, she strained them and added the meat sauce on top. "Parmesan cheese sprinkled on top?"

"Yeah, thanks."

She served the spaghetti, then started the garlic toast, and while it was cooking, she quickly tossed some salad fixings he had in the fridge. Then she served up the salads and the garlic toast.

"Hmm, that smells good."

"Thanks. My mother taught me to cook. She said the way to a man's heart is through his stomach."

He chuckled and got off the couch. He was trying not to groan out loud, but Ingrid heard him groan a little.

"I could have helped you."

"Really, I'm fine." He moved over to the table with a slight limp. No crutches.

That was good. But she was eyeing him, ready to lunge forward and grab him if he started to go down. He reached the table and gingerly sat down.

"Does it hurt to sit?"

"Just a little." Then he started to eat some of the spaghetti. "Wow, this is good. Homemade sauce. I have the spices and all, but I usually just use a jar of the ready-made spaghetti sauce. I like this though. You'll have to give me your recipe."

"I just throw it together, but I can make up a recipe for it, I guess. Okay, so when does a wolf swim underwater and zigzag across a sandy beach?" she asked.

"When it's a *lupus garou* in a shooting gallery."

"I sure hope we catch the men who did that."

"We have to. They're bound to return again, except to hunt the wolves this time, and no telling who they'd shoot and maybe kill."

CHAPTER 7

THAT NIGHT, KNOX WAS SO GLAD TO BE HOME. NOT THAT it had been uncomfortable at the pack leaders' ranch, but it was nice not having Carol checking up on him all the time. Here at home, he really enjoyed Ingrid's company as she helped him settle on the couch after dinner and gently propped his legs on the footstool and fetched his slippers for him.

Then she brought him over a glass of water and handed him the remote controller. "We can watch whatever you'd like."

"I hope you're not going to try and spoil me," he said, searching for something to watch while she cleaned up the kitchen and put the leftover spaghetti away.

"If I were in your…um, slippers, I'd want to be spoiled too. After you tried to keep me safe from the hunters, it's the least I can do."

"I thought you were mad at me."

"I was upset because you were shot. I know it's irrational to think of it like that, but you would have been safely across the river at the same time as me if you hadn't waited so long."

"Any alpha male wolf would have done the same." He didn't want her to think he was the only one who would have protected her.

"But they weren't there. You were."

"I think you might like me."

She snorted.

He laughed.

Once she finished cleaning up the kitchen, she snuggled up next to him on the couch. This was the way it was supposed to be. "Oh, I left the business card with Chas's phone number on the kitchen counter for you. He's the freelance writer who talked to someone about the hunters shooting at the wolves. Maybe he knows their names."

"You told me that. Chas, the guy who was interviewing Ryan?"

"Yes."

"Has he been back to speak with you?"

"He's coming in tomorrow to clarify some questions the editor wanted him to answer on the interview."

"Then I'm coming in."

"No. You aren't." She looked sternly at him, and he looked just as sternly back at her. "I thought if you're feeling like it tomorrow, you might call Chas, but if you'd rather, I could give the card to Ryan, and he can send his PIs to investigate."

"I'll call about it. Thanks. So the story is we didn't see any wolves."

"I thought about saying we saw them when I talked to Chas's brother, the appliance repairman, but the wolves were running away from the hunters, like wolves would do. They weren't anywhere near the men and certainly didn't attack them. But I was afraid others would want to search for the wolves, either to study them or to shoot them, if I said we'd seen them. None of us would be safe then. So instead I thought of discrediting the hunters."

"I think that's the best way to deal with it. I doubt the

two hunters can be trusted to stay off the property, but it might keep others away. I think no matter what you said, the hunters might return to the land to see if they can find the wolves, kill them, and take pictures of the dead wolves or attempt to take their carcasses back to prove the wolves existed." He squirmed a little to get more comfortable.

She sighed. "Except if they kill our kind, they'll end up with dead humans."

"Exactly. Which is why we need to find them first and charge them with a crime. Carol said Ryan has put up a bunch of motion cameras for wildlife, just to watch for any sign of the hunters or anyone else on the property. But it's a lot of acreage to cover."

"That's good but that's true. I bet they won't get into much trouble. I can hear them convincing the judge it was just an accident. 'We didn't mean anything by it. And we didn't even know anyone was injured,'" she said.

"Except it's been all over the news, and they haven't come forward and confessed to the accidental shooting," Knox said. "And the word has leaked to the press, courtesy of the mayor, that killing a wolf in Colorado would earn the offender a year in prison and fines of up to $100,000 per offense—just a reminder to hunters that it's illegal to hunt the wolves if anyone had seen them running on the property."

"That's good. It would be hard to admit you shot a man when you know you shot a wolf. But telling the local citizens about the fines might keep others from thinking of trespassing to shoot the wolves. I bet the men who shot you get off with a slap on the hand no matter what."

He didn't want to say so, but he figured the same.

After the show was over, Knox needed to take a shower and retire to bed. He wished he was more in the mood to be on a date with Ingrid. Instead, he was so tired he felt like he was barely holding it together.

He thought he could do this on his own, but he wanted to let Ingrid know his plan. "I'm going to take a shower before I go to bed. I have two spare bedrooms, either of which you can use, unless you want to join me in the master bedroom."

She tilted her head and gave him the look that said he was pushing his luck, even though he was injured and couldn't do much about it. "You know, we've only had one date. And it was more like a get-together."

"That ended in disaster. I know."

She sighed. "It was *not* a disaster. It was the nicest date I've ever had. Until the very end. Do you need me to help you with showering?"

He smiled and knew his expression was on the wolfish side and not like he was an injured wolf who solely needed a caregiver's help.

She cleared her throat. "I don't know. I'd say you're looking really well."

"How about if you watch me or, I mean, just stand by in case I lose my balance and begin to fall or something."

She frowned. "Will you?"

"No. Well, hell, the way things have been going lately, maybe."

She smiled. "Sure. I'll be there for you if you need me. Carol would be upset with my caregiver services if you slipped and fell in the shower and broke something and she had to take care of you again. I'm sure I'd be fired from the job."

He chuckled, then slowly walked back to the bedroom, hoping to be as good as new in a few days. He enjoyed Ingrid's company, but he didn't want her to feel like he was a burden. And being injured and not being able to do all the things he was used to doing, without hurting, was a total pain.

She helped him strip off his clothes in the bathroom, and then she reached in and started his shower for him. When the water was the right temperature, he stepped into the glass enclosure and closed the door. She stood nearby, not watching him at first. Not until he began soaping himself up.

He wanted to ask her if she wanted to do the honors, but hell, then his cock started to rise. Not because he was washing himself, but just with the notion *she* would be washing him.

She chuckled. "Uh, it looks like you're getting better by the second."

"You don't want to know what I was thinking of that made that happen." He smiled back at her.

"The notion of me washing you? Yeah, you guys are all so transparent."

He chuckled.

"Oh-oh, I forgot the towel. It's in the dryer. Be right back." She made a mad dash for the laundry room, got his towel, and then brought it into the bathroom.

After he finished rinsing off, she handed him the towel. Once he had dried off, she took hold of his arm to make sure he wouldn't slip. She didn't need to, but he appreciated it. He finally reached the bedroom, and she rebandaged the wound, though he thought by tomorrow it would be fine without the bandage.

"So what do you think about the sleeping arrangements?" he asked as he climbed into a pair of pajama shorts with her help, hoping she might stay with him.

"I'll sleep in the bedroom closest to yours. Just holler if you need anything. I'm a light sleeper." Then she gave him a kiss. It was sweet, but he wanted more. To show her he truly was on the mend and could protect her again if she needed him to.

He wrapped his arms around her and kissed her like he'd wanted to ever since they'd first kissed. She opened to him, getting into the kiss as much as he was savoring kissing her. Her arms were gently wrapped around his neck, her warm lips pressing against his. Her tongue slid into his mouth, and he wanted to groan out loud, his cock reacting with enthusiasm.

He wanted her to come to bed with him. Not to make love to her—because he didn't think she was ready for it, and he wasn't sure he was after being shot—but to enjoy the intimacy further. To snuggle only. Despite the fact that his cock was telling him he was ready and willing for any action he could get.

Then she pulled her mouth away from his, her startling blue eyes looking up at him. He thought she appeared a little surprised they could feel this kind of connection again, that she could arouse him this much after he'd been wounded.

"Um, okay, you need to get your rest to heal." She patted his bare chest. "And I'm going to get your sheets out of the dryer, put them away, and go take my shower. I have to go to work tomorrow."

He wished she was the one ministering to his needs tomorrow. He knew he'd heal faster under her care. "True. If you have a nightmare, I'll chase your demons away."

"*You* are the one bound to have nightmares."

"Then you're more than welcome to come chase *mine* away."

She smiled, and Knox didn't think she was going for it.

After taking her shower and going to bed, Ingrid wondered who Carol had lined up to take care of Knox during the day. She wished she could, but she really needed to work. Ryan was lost without her. Dressed in a long T-shirt, she put Knox's sheets away in the closet and saw the light was already turned out in his bedroom. He had to be tired. She was glad he was home again, and she was looking forward to seeing him after work every evening as long as he needed or wanted her to come see him.

She kept thinking about Knox and how he had been so stubbornly heroic in trying to protect her from the hunters. She'd prayed he would make it beyond their range, but when he had been shot and stumbled, her heart had practically given out. Then she thought of Knox washing himself in the shower and of her taking on the job. She smiled, thinking she would have loved to, if he hadn't truly been so tired and she was afraid he'd want to do more...before she finally drifted off to sleep.

Two hunters wearing camouflaged clothes, both armed with rifles, were excited about seeing the wolves. "The other one got away, but this one won't."

She recognized the man's voice. Mickey Smithson, the guy who owned the Spuds and Suds Pub. She'd been so worried about Knox getting out of the path of the bullets that she'd kept her focus on that. And not on who the men might be. Hoping Ryan would get there with reinforcements in time, she howled for help.

"Ingrid," Knox said, his voice hushed.

She heard his voice from far away. He was so badly wounded, she knew Knox was saying her name on his last breath. She cried, big, fat teardrops rolling down her cheeks.

"Ingrid, everything's okay. I'm okay." Knox's hand caressed her wet cheek, partially waking her.

For a minute, she stared up in the darkness at his face, his expression concerned, brow furrowed, the thought of him being wounded and not making it...and then the dream... It was a dream. She was so glad it was only a nightmare.

She took his hand and pulled at him to join her in bed. She hadn't planned on this. Hadn't seriously thought she'd have nightmares about the shooting again. But she wanted him next to her so she could make sure he was safe if she had another one.

"Are you sure you want me to join you?" he asked.

Maybe he believed she wasn't awake enough to make a conscious decision about it. "Yeah, unless you're in too much pain and having me beside you might hurt your injury."

"No. I'll be fine if I sleep on this side of you."

"Good. Then if I have another nightmare about you being shot, I can reach over and pinch you and know you're okay."

He chuckled and climbed into bed with her. But he didn't seem to want to leave it at that and reached over to have her rest against his uninjured side. "Better like this so you know I'm all right than having you pinch me."

She smiled, then frowned. "I didn't really howl, did I? I was doing it in my nightmare, but not for real, I didn't think." Then again, how else would he have heard her and come to check on her?

"Yeah, you did."

She groaned. "I don't think I've ever howled in my sleep before."

He smiled, got comfortable with her, and kissed her forehead. "It's all good."

As long as she didn't injure him, she agreed.

CHAPTER 8

THAT MORNING, INGRID WOKE WITH A START AND realized Knox wasn't in bed with her, she hadn't set an alarm, and she was late to work. But what happened to the person Carol was supposed to send to watch over Knox?

Oh, Knox must have left the bedroom so no one would be the wiser that they'd slept together last night. She'd been so tired that she hadn't thought about that aspect of it when he'd joined her.

Then she heard Knox in the master bathroom, running the water in the sink. She had hoped he would sleep in. After getting dressed, she left the bedroom and found Rosalind sitting at the breakfast bar, quietly sipping some coffee.

Rosalind smiled at Ingrid. "Knox told me not to wake you. He called Ryan and told him you'd be coming in a little late."

Knox must have let Rosalind in, so she wouldn't know he and Ingrid had slept together. *Whew.* "I won't get my crossword puzzle done now." Actually, she didn't even have her morning paper. It was at her house. She noticed Knox had written up more of the message from the puzzle: that make| us want to| get to know| them better|| Pen in hand|

Rosalind smiled. "I'll bring my paper with me for you to do if I'm still needed tomorrow. I suspect I won't be. Knox looks good, but he should have someone stay here at least tonight."

Knox joined them and made cups of coffee for Ingrid and himself.

"Morning, Ingrid."

"Hey. Did you sleep well?" she asked.

"You bet." He gave her one of his naughty smiles.

Ingrid felt her cheeks warm considerably. "I'm running late. I'll see you tonight if you feel like you need me to come over."

"Yeah, that would be great. And I do."

Tonight, she wouldn't be watching him in the shower, soaping himself up. And she wouldn't be sleeping with him either.

She took a sip of her coffee and was about to hurry off. She didn't want to kiss him and give Rosalind ideas. But then she thought, what the heck? She wanted him to know she cared about him, even if they had an audience. "Do what Rosalind tells you to do." She kissed him and hurried to the front door and then thought about the dream. "I dreamed that the hunter shouting with enthusiasm that they were going to take you down was Mickey Smithson...owner of the Spuds and Suds. But I can't be sure. It might have just been a dream, you know, mixing up meeting with him the other day and knowing he's upset with Ryan over potentially losing his pub."

"I've never met the man. I could go over there and speak to him and see if I can recall his voice." Knox pulled the crossword puzzle out of his paper and crossed the floor to give it to her.

"Are you sure you don't want to do it yourself?"

"I can get another one."

"I can give him my paper," Rosalind said.

"Okay." Ingrid smiled. "Thanks. About seeing Mickey, wait for me tonight, and we'll go over there together."

"Not to eat dinner though." Rosalind wrinkled her nose. "They have serious health deficiencies, and Ryan will most likely close them down."

"We'll see if we can just talk to him," Ingrid said. "I agree about the food. Are you going to call Chas to see if he knows who was hunting out on the pack leaders' property?"

"Yeah, I'll do that too. I'll call you later to let you know what I learn."

"Okay, good. See you later." Ingrid hurried out the door.

She finally arrived at work, but all she could think about was the nightmare she'd had. Did she have it right? That one of the shooters was Mickey?

Maybe that was why he was trespassing on Ryan's property—because he was irritated with Ryan for promising to shut his pub down if he didn't take care of the violations.

Before Ingrid made a pot of coffee for Ryan and Max and a cup of tea for herself at the office, she called the appliance repairman to see if he knew if Mickey was even a hunter. Her dream had unsettled her, and she couldn't stop thinking about it. "Hello, this is Ingrid Bjorg, with the mayor's office."

"Yes? I fixed Mr. Granbury's dishwasher. Is he having problems with it again?"

"It's working great. Thanks. I hate to bother you, but is Mickey Smithson a hunter?"

"Uh, yeah."

"Okay, thanks. Oh, do you know if he has a good buddy he likes to hunt with?"

"His brother, Mitchell."

"Okay, thanks." Then it might have been Mitchell speaking, not Mickey, if their voices were similar. If they were hunting out on Ryan's property a few nights ago.

She ended the call and called up Knox. "I learned that Mickey is a hunter, and Mitchell, his brother, hunts with him. I still might be mistaken about the voice, but...if I'm not? We had talked about him earlier in the day. Maybe because of that, I dreamed he was in the nightmare. Did you call Chas to see what he has to say?"

"I was going to call him after lunch. Did you want to come here and have lunch with us? Rosalind's going to make pork ribs, rice, and broccoli."

"Is there enough for three of us?"

"Yeah, she'll be making more than enough."

"Okay, sure. I'll ask Ryan if I can have some extra time off at lunch."

"You can," Ryan called out from his office.

With everyone's wolf hearing in the office, she couldn't get away with much—like trying to talk privately to anyone.

"I forgot to mention Chas is returning this morning to ask more questions of Ryan," Ingrid told Knox.

"I'd forgotten about that. Okay."

Someone started knocking at one of the suite's glass office doors. Ingrid turned to see Rosalind with a crystal vase of what looked to be about two dozen beautiful red roses. "I've got to go. I'll see you at lunch." She hurried to the door to let Rosalind in, then locked the door behind her.

"Oh, my, not from my secret admirer again," Ingrid said.

"Not this time. By the way, Ryan called together the pack, all but the two of you, and asked if anyone had sent the earlier roses to you, so Knox wouldn't have to do it."

"Oh, no. I hope no one felt put on the spot."

"No. Several said if they'd sent you roses, Knox would have been sure to do something about it, and they didn't want to have to tangle with him."

"Really?" Ingrid smiled, realizing he really had liked her for some time.

"That's what they said. It looks like no one from the pack did it."

"Who are these roses from then?" Ingrid took hold of the envelope attached to the roses.

"Knox."

Ingrid smiled at Rosalind. "Really?"

"I do believe the bachelor males who were waiting for you to be ready to date again realize they've lost out. So what do you think?"

"They're beautiful." Ingrid pulled out the paper that was folded several times to fit into the small envelope. She read out loud, "'Thanks for taking care of me this week. I'm healing by leaps and bounds just knowing you'll be here spending more nights with me.'" She wanted to laugh. He probably only needed her to stay tonight. She smelled the roses. "Hmm, they smell divine. That was so sweet of him."

"I think when he saw some secret admirer had sent you flowers and how much you appreciated them, he decided to make his bid. I probably won't need to stay with him beyond today and tomorrow, if that, but I wouldn't let that keep you from staying with him at night."

"Speaking of which, who's watching him?" Ingrid smelled the fragrant roses and felt like she'd touched a bit of heaven.

"One of the guys dropped by to check on him and harass him a bit."

"You know it's not a done deal between Knox and me."

"Hey, you're further along with Knox than you were with the ex. You're staying the night already." Rosalind smiled.

"Out of necessity," Ingrid reminded her.

Just then, Max, temporary sub for Knox, arrived at the office and frowned at the crystal vase of flowers. "Are the roses from the secret admirer?" He looked like he was a wolf ready to track this mystery guy down.

"No, they're from Knox," Ingrid said. "Aren't they lovely?"

"Hell, why didn't I think of that?" Max cast her an evil smile.

"I've got to go and relieve the guy watching Knox. I just wanted to hand deliver the flowers before the office opened. I think things are really looking up for the two of you."

The door suddenly opened, and they all glanced in that direction to see Knox coming into the reception area.

"What are you doing here?" Ingrid asked before anyone else could ask the question. Knox was supposed to be resting!

"Lettie drove me here. You said Chas was doing some follow-up questions with Ryan this morning. I thought it wouldn't hurt for me to ask him in person about the hunters who shot at us. Since it's Ryan's property, he should be in on the conversation. Maybe between the three of us, we could get more of a handle on this." Knox looked at the roses and mouthed a thank-you to Rosalind.

Rosalind smiled and took a seat in the well-appointed reception area with its leather chairs and oak tables. "Well, since I'm supposed to be watching you, I'll just stay here until you're ready to leave."

Large photographs of Colorado wildflowers decorated the walls, courtesy of Jake Silver, gray wolf, of Silver Town, whose beautiful nature pictures hung in galleries all over the state of Colorado.

Ryan showed up at the suite of offices next and eyed the huge bunch of roses first.

"From Knox," Ingrid assured him.

Then Ryan's gaze shifted to Knox, who was getting himself a cup of coffee. "Chas is coming to interview you again, right, Boss? He talked to the hunters who were shooting at wolves. I'll question him about the hunters in your and Ingrid's presence."

Ryan glanced at Rosalind.

"I'm with him"—Rosalind motioned to Knox—"since I'm supposed to be watching over him, and I'm the flower deliverer."

Max raised his hands in a gesture of supplication. "I'm working for you, Boss."

"Okay, well...carry on." Ryan shook his head and went into his office.

Knox said to Ingrid, "Do you really think you can identify Mickey as the shooter from the sound of his voice?"

"It wouldn't be enough to use against him in court, but with our wolf hearing, probably," Ingrid said.

"Did I hear you say Mickey Smithson might be the one who was shooting on our property?" Ryan asked, coming out of the office.

Ingrid didn't want to accuse the wrong person. She needed to learn more first. But since Ryan was their pack leader, she explained about her nightmare and how she'd learned Mickey and his brother were both hunters.

"Okay, keep me informed. I won't press charges until we know for sure who was out there trespassing."

"Carol didn't have any psychic predictions about this?" Ingrid thought she might because the shooting was so close by and involved two of her pack members.

"Carol had a nightmare about a shooting taking place on the property the night before, but we'd been watching a thriller where hunters were chasing victims in the woods, and she thought that was all there was to it. Just a nightmare. After the shooting, it was too late to do anything about it."

"Did she see anything in the nightmare? Or premonition?"

"Two hunters, two wolves. One of the wolves had disappeared into the woods, and the other was hit but made it to the woods safely, and then I woke her."

"Wow, okay."

"Unfortunately, she doesn't see every detail often. She didn't know which wolves were running, and she couldn't say much about the hunters. We just figured it was a nightmare, or I would have restricted wolf runs on the property." Ryan returned to his office.

"Would you like tea or coffee?" Ingrid asked Rosalind. Ingrid bet Carol was feeling at fault for not warning them about the danger, but she didn't really know her vision would come true.

"Tea would be good, thanks," Rosalind said.

Max fixed himself and Ryan cups of coffee, then took them into Ryan's office to see what he needed to do this morning.

Ingrid handed Rosalind a cup of tea and said to Knox, "The roses are beautiful. I just love the fragrance."

"They remind me of you."

Max left Ryan's office and rolled his eyes at Knox, then headed into Knox's office to work.

Ingrid couldn't get used to Max using Knox's office. She'd be glad when Knox was back at work. She gave him a hug and kiss for the roses. She suspected where this was going, even if she wanted to slow down the relationship a bit to make sure they were right for each other.

Gingerly, Knox sat down next to Rosalind, and Ingrid was afraid he was hurting. She began working on Knox's crossword puzzle. "Thanks for being so sweet to give me your crossword puzzle, Knox."

"I figured you needed something to occupy your time before work started."

She glanced at the time. She had a minute before opening. Having unexpected guests had thrown her off schedule, besides getting up late.

"Well, speak of the devil..." Knox said, and Ingrid and Rosalind looked at the glass door.

CHAPTER 9

CHAS HAD ARRIVED AT THE MAYOR'S OFFICE. HE OPENED the door and gave Ingrid a big smile. He immediately saw the roses, and his smile faded. He looked crestfallen, which Ingrid hadn't expected.

"They're from me," Knox quickly said and waved his hand at the new roses, laying claim to them.

"You're Knox Granbury, the assistant mayor who was shot," Chas said, crossing the floor and reaching his hand out to shake Knox's. "I was so sorry to hear that. It was an awful thing to have happen." He sounded sincere.

Knox stood and shook his hand. "Yeah. After you see the mayor, I'd like to have a talk with you if you have a moment."

"Uh, yeah. Sure."

"Did you send the lovely roses to me a few days ago, Chas?" Ingrid suspected Chas might have done it from the expression on his face when he saw the new ones. "It was such a lovely gesture and made my whole day."

Chas glanced back at the new roses and then at Knox and said to Ingrid, "Uh, yeah. I didn't know you were dating anyone. I'm sorry."

"Don't be," Knox said. "This is kind of a new development for us. By you sending her flowers anonymously, it made me realize I needed to get on the ball and send her flowers of my own."

"Uh, yeah, sure. Maybe I should have said they were from me." Chas shoved his hands in his pockets. If he'd been a wolf, he would have been a beta for sure.

Ingrid smiled. "I think so. That's what women enjoy." It wouldn't have mattered to Ingrid, because he wasn't a wolf. But for some other lady, he ought to give his name.

"I can see you now, Chas," Ryan called out, as if they had all forgotten about his appointment with the freelance writer.

"Be right in, sir." Chas walked into Ryan's office and sat down to ask more questions for the interview.

Everyone was quiet while they talked until Ingrid had to answer the phone and Max had to handle other business.

After Ryan finished answering Chas's questions, Ryan called Knox and Ingrid into his office while Rosalind offered to man the phones.

"Okay," Ryan said, getting down to the real business at hand. Ingrid figured Ryan *would* take over the questioning. "Who shot Knox and shot at Ingrid?"

"Ingrid too?" Chas asked as if that was worse than Knox getting shot.

"I was out of range of the gunfire, thankfully," Ingrid said. "But yes, Knox and I had been walking along the river, and then two men started shooting at us."

"You were walking late at night in the woods? In the dark?" Chas asked. "There wasn't even a moon out that night."

As wolves, sure. They could see in the dark.

"With our flashlights, sure. It was romantic," Ingrid said, reaching for Knox's hand and giving it a squeeze. "We turned off our flashlights when they began shooting at us, thinking that they couldn't see us. But we were wrong. I made it to the woods before Knox did. He was a true hero and was trying to draw their fire."

"Oh." Chas ran his hand over the back of his hair. He might not have been brave enough to do that for a woman he was interested in dating.

"They must have had night-vision scopes when they shot at us," Knox said.

"Yeah, they do. Mickey and his brother, Mitchell, were bragging about shooting at a couple of wolves. One had escaped them to the woods on the other side of the river. The other was crossing the river, and they shot at him, finally hitting him. I don't see how they would have been involved in shooting at two people walking along the river."

"They said they found the wolves on my property?" Ryan asked.

"Uh, no. They said it was a place where they could legitimately hunt," Chas said.

"Naturally," Knox said.

"You think there's any chance they were trespassing on the mayor's property to hunt because he's given Mickey the ultimatum about his business?" Ingrid asked.

Chas didn't say anything for a moment, then he said, "Yeah. He and his brother have been doing a lot of spouting off about the mayor trying to put them out of business. They've lost a lot of business as the rumor has spread about the uncleanliness of the Spuds and Suds. You know, in the past, former Mayor Rickson would have just taken a bribe and looked the other way. He did on the other two businesses you shut down, Mayor."

"Would you be willing to testify against the brothers?" Ryan asked.

"That they said they were shooting at wolves, sure. I can only testify to what they said."

"We have the evidence of the shootings," Ryan said.

"Okay. I mean, as fellow hunters, we're on friendly terms, but my brother and I don't agree with their tactics. They often drink whiskey on hunts, smoke a joint or two. You know"—Chas paused and rubbed his forehead—"we did consider they had been drinking a lot and that's why they thought they saw wolves. We've heard them brag about trespassing on your land before, and they trespass on other private property to go hunting. I think they believe they're still living in the Wild West and can do whatever they want to and get away with it. They didn't say they were on your land this time, and I suspect that's because they don't want anyone else to go out and hunt the wolves down."

"Because they want to," Ryan guessed.

"Sure. If they really thought they'd seen wolves, I wouldn't put it past them to go looking for them on your land again and try to nail them. If they're claiming they shot a wolf, but it really was our assistant mayor instead and you've got proof? Then yeah, I'll testify against them about what they said and to their character when it comes to hunting. Besides, it's illegal to hunt wolves. When they tell us they're going hunting, the rest of us make sure we're not out on the same night as they are."

"Not wanting to be shot by the trigger-happy brothers?" Ryan asked.

"Yeah. They have a reputation. At least they could have said they saw movement and thought it was a deer. A couple of wolves? Give me a break. Still, I don't believe they thought they'd shot a man, or they wouldn't have been talking about it so freely."

"Unless alcohol and maybe drugs were involved like you said," Ryan said.

"Uh, yeah. That's what it had to have been. I'd check and see if they even have valid hunting licenses if I were you," Chas said. "Not that it really matters much since it's not even hunting season."

Max called out from the other office, "On it."

Everyone was quiet for a moment, then Chas said, "Man, has he got good hearing."

The wolves all smiled.

Then Ryan thanked Chas, and so did Knox and Ingrid. Chas seemed to want to say something more to Ingrid, so she moved them out of the office so Ryan could get on with mayor business.

"Hey, I loved that you were doing my crossword puzzles. I didn't mean to overstep my bounds with sending the roses," Chas said as if that was still bothering him.

"Ohmigod, you're the creator?" Ingrid was astounded and pleased to meet the man who was making them up.

"Constructor," Knox said. "They're great."

"You do them too?" Chas sounded surprised.

"Yeah, every morning. So about the secret message?" Knox asked.

Chas paled. "Uh, well, I was writing it for a…uh, woman I…uh, like."

"I hope she is figuring out the secret message, and you let her know it's you and that the person you're sending the message to is her," Ingrid said, assuming he was just making up the story about another woman he was interested in to save face.

"Uh, yeah. I will. I have to go. Deadlines won't wait." Chas hurried out of the reception area.

"I'd say that was a case of unrequited love if I ever saw it," Knox said.

Ingrid gave Knox a hug. "Go home and I'll see you later."

Rosalind quickly took Knox's arm and led him out of the office. "Talk about a case of unrequited love. Let Ingrid get back to work."

Knox smiled back through the closed glass doors at Ingrid, and she chuckled.

After working a couple of hours, she had a lull in business and called Knox. "Hey, how are you doing?"

"Good. Really feeling good. Rosalind made me take a nap, and I think that really helped."

"Then you might not need me tonight?"

"Have you got other plans?"

She smiled. "No, but I don't want you to feel obligated to have me over if you want some alone time."

"Hell, no. I might take a turn for the worse."

She laughed. "Okay, I'll be there after work." She glanced at the clock. "Oh, it's nearly lunchtime. I'll be there in half an hour." She saw Ryan leave his office. "Got to go. The boss needs me."

"Okay, see you in a little bit." Knox ended the call.

"I'm going to take a longer lunch to have it at Knox's house if that's okay with you. Rosalind is making us something to eat," Ingrid said to Ryan.

"Sure. Take all the time you need. Max and I will hold down the fort until then."

To Knox's surprise, when he entered the kitchen to check on the meal's progress, Rosalind had only made enough food for two. "Did you forget that Ingrid was coming over?" He was trying not to sound upset.

Rosalind patted him on the shoulder. "While she is here, you won't need me. Do you have a grocery list? I'll run out and pick up some things for you for when I'm no longer here and until you feel like driving."

"Oh, okay, sorry, Rosalind." Then he smiled, knowing just why she was leaving him and Ingrid alone. He hastily wrote a list, and when they heard knocking at the door, Rosalind went to get it.

"Hey, Ingrid. You're just in time." Rosalind grabbed her purse and took Knox's list in hand.

"You're leaving?" Ingrid sounded surprised.

Rosalind smiled. "I figured this was the best way to handle it. I'll pick up groceries for Knox while you're here keeping an eye on him. I must confess that while Knox was lying down, I ate my portion of the meal."

Ingrid gave her a hug. "Thanks. I owe you."

"Nah, it's what we do for each other." Then Rosalind left.

Ingrid hurried to the kitchen to serve the meal. "I have an extended lunch, but I don't want to abuse it."

"I agree." Knox was delighted he got to have lunch alone with Ingrid. "I'm doing really well." He wanted her to know he was ready to move the courtship along, but he still wanted her to come over at night, as long as she wanted to.

"I'm so glad." She reached over and squeezed his hand. "Thanks for the beautiful roses. I'm glad they arrived before Chas did. I was beginning to think the message in the crossword puzzle was romantic in nature, directed at a particular woman."

"Yeah, *you*."

"He did say he was sending it to some other woman."

"Ha! Did you see how he looked when I brought up the business about the message?"

"You shouldn't have." She gave him a look that said he should be nice to the man.

"I had to. I was put in charge of finding out who created it and if it was menacing or not." Knox gave her a kiss.

"Hmm." She kissed him back. "At least your injury isn't communicable." And then she kissed him thoroughly.

He wished she could just stay with him the rest of the afternoon and Rosalind could take over for her, but he knew Rosalind had to take care of her own business too. Though she had plenty of others helping her out in the interim. Rosalind returned with the groceries, and Ingrid had to return to work. But Ingrid gave him a final hug and thanked him for the roses again, and he thought they had a good start on their courtship phase, despite him being shot on their first date.

CHAPTER 10

"I PICKED US UP A PEPPERONI AND DOUBLE CHEESE PIZZA for dinner," Ingrid said, carrying the large box into the house as Knox let her in that night.

"That sure smells good. Great idea." He swore he'd never felt anything like this before with a woman, wanting to spend every minute of the day with her. He realized how much he'd missed not being able to see her at the office all day, even though he'd seen her briefly this morning.

Knox nuzzled her cheek with his, his arms wrapped around her as she faced the island and set the box on the counter. "I missed you."

She smiled and turned her head for a kiss, slipping around until she was face-to-face with him and wrapping her arms around his back. "I missed you too. I can't believe how much, now that you're not there at the office."

"I'll be glad to be back at work. Of course if you were here with me during the day, that would be a different story."

She laughed. "I figured we'd eat and then right afterward we'd head over to the Spuds and Suds to see if we recognize Mickey's voice. We'll have to come up with some story for why we're there. We can't eat or drink there, and we don't want to question him about the shooting. Unless we just order drinks and don't drink them."

"I agree." He kissed her mouth eagerly, wanting to take this further, but he hoped after the movie, she'd at least sleep with him tonight. He was ready to have her stay with him always. He couldn't believe he'd fallen so hard for her, despite having had a crush on her since he'd joined the pack.

"We'd better eat before the pizza gets cold," she said, breaking free of the kiss. "Business first." She patted his chest.

He wanted to skip any business having to do with Mickey, but he knew she was right. They needed to resolve this. "I'll get us some water. When you left, I helped Rosalind put away the groceries. She picked up popcorn for movie nights."

"She was so sweet to do that."

"Yeah, I forgot to add it to the list."

They sat down to eat and had finished the last of the pizza when the doorbell rang. She looked at Knox, but he shrugged.

"I have no idea who it is." He got up from the table, and when he reached the door, he looked out the peephole. "Hell," he said quietly. "Mickey Smithson himself."

"Doesn't sound good. I'm texting Ryan." Then she put her phone up on the bookcase where it could record the living room.

She nodded to Knox, who had his phone out too. He put his recorder on and placed the phone in his pocket, then opened the door.

"Yeah?"

"Hi, I'm Mickey Smithson, part owner of the Spuds and Suds."

"What can I do for you?" Knox asked, drawing him into the living room.

"Want a soda?" Ingrid asked.

Knox was glad she'd offered that and not a beer. The guy smelled liked he'd already had at least one. Knox wished he'd returned to the scene of the shooting after he was better to know the man's scent. But...hell, Ingrid would have smelled the men's scent when she returned to the opposite side of the river with him on the stretcher.

"Beer?" Mickey had dark-brown hair fluffed on top and shaved on the sides, with a trim beard and penetrating blue eyes. He was a stocky build, broad-shouldered, and maybe six two in height.

"Sorry, man, we're fresh out," Knox said.

"Water?" Ingrid asked.

"Coke, if you've got it."

She went to fetch one out of the fridge, then returned to give it to Mickey. Knox saw her take a deep breath, her gaze switching to Knox, and she smiled. They had their man, or at least one of them.

Knox took a seat with Ingrid on one of the love seats, while Mickey sat down on the couch and drank several long swallows of the soda, then put the can down on the coffee table. "I heard you've been asking about me and my brother hunting illegally on your boss's property. We've never been there. We shot at wolves, and that's the God's truth."

"Some others say you've been on the mayor's property before, illegally hunting," Knox said.

"Who the hell said that? They lied," Mickey said.

Knox wasn't about to divulge Chas's name. The guy was timid enough, and he could imagine Mickey bullying him.

"We heard your voice and recognized it," Ingrid said. "'He's getting away,' you said."

"Yeah, see? It was a wolf, and he was swimming across the river. You saw it too then. I hit him on the other side, or my brother did. I'm not sure. Damn wolf was zigzagging all over the place like he was crazy. Rabid maybe."

"We were on the mayor's property when you were shooting at us. We're not saying you were out to kill us, but you did shoot Knox. And you have to cease and desist trespassing on the mayor's property to hunt or otherwise."

Mickey stared at Ingrid as if he finally realized his mistake in admitting she'd heard their conversation in the vicinity of where Knox had been shot. "No way in hell are you going to pin this on us." Mickey rose to his feet. "I don't know what you think you're trying to pull. The mayor's already got it in for us about the pub. Now this? We shot at wolves! No one can say anything different."

"And that's illegal," Ingrid said.

Mickey's phone rang, and he yanked it out. "What? No way in hell. They can't do that. I'm headed over there now." He waved his phone at Knox. "You can't prove we shot you or were on the mayor's property."

As he stormed out of the house, Knox said, "Thanks for stopping by and speaking with us," then shut the door and locked it. Ingrid was retrieving her phone from the bookcase, and he turned his recording off too. "I didn't expect him to show up here."

"Me neither, but it worked great. I recognized his scent from the other side of the lake and had smelled him in the office before, but I wasn't thinking straight after you were shot. Once I smelled him here, I knew it was him. And his voice too. He has a distinctive Boston accent."

"Right." Knox threw out the rest of the can of soda and returned to the living room. "You were brilliant, getting him to admit to being on the mayor's property."

"I was, wasn't I? It took him a minute to figure out the mistake he'd made. I'm sending the recording to Ryan."

"I'll send mine too." Knox sent his with a note that Mickey had left in a hurry.

Ryan called him back, and Knox put the call on speaker.

"We've got him. The police are doing a search of Mickey's home. A person reported that they'd nearly run into a black pickup barreling onto the highway the night you were shot. He hadn't reported it initially because there hadn't been a collision, but he had written down the tag number in case the driver was driving recklessly up the road. When he learned Knox had been shot at that same location, he called in the tag number and said the truck had left the property in such a hurry, he might have been involved in the shooting. Good witness too. He's an out-of-town police investigator, off duty, and noted the time."

"Hot damn," Knox said. "And it was Mickey's truck?"

"Yeah. They have a search warrant for his truck too. They're looking for the rifles he and his brother used. We turned over all the spent shell casings and the bullet Doc Weber removed from your hip, Knox."

"Well, I can testify it was Mickey's voice, but I think if we had a police detective witness their truck leaving there in a hurry at the right time like they had done something wrong, and the ballistics match their weapons, we'll be good. I did recognize his scent as one of the men who had been shooting at Knox. So I know it was him. He implicated his brother also," Ingrid said.

"Hell, good job on interviewing him and getting it recorded. Yep, he implicated himself when he said you'd heard him then. That he actually had spoken those words. And that he was in the same place you and Knox were—which was on pack property—illegally. I'll send these to the detective in charge of the investigation."

"Thanks, Ryan," Ingrid said.

"Yeah, thanks, Boss. I think we finally have this guy," Knox said. They ended the call, and a few minutes later, Ryan called again.

"They picked up five rifles at Mickey's house. They'll have to run ballistic tests on them, and they'll let me know."

"Great," Knox said, hoping this was truly the end of it.

"We won't know for a while about the outcome," Ingrid said, "but hopefully with any luck, they'll at least be charged with an accidental shooting and they'll stay off the property. If not, maybe we'll catch them on the wildlife CCTV cameras Ryan is having installed all over the acreage. My bet is that they'll return to the same area where they saw the wolves, thinking they might be from that territory."

"Hopefully not. Are you ready to watch a movie and have some popcorn?"

Ingrid smiled. "Yeah. Get us some wine, and I'll make the popcorn. I still can't believe we're doing this when you'd harassed me so much at work."

"Why do you think I harassed you so much about things?" Knox poured them both glasses of red wine.

"Ryan says it's because you were stuck on me."

"More than stuck on you." Knox set their glasses of wine on the countertop while the popcorn was popping, and he took her into his arms. "We have chemistry."

"And we both love crossword puzzles."

He smiled. "You're funny."

"You are too. You have my sense of humor."

"It's perfect for relieving tension on the job. You're

dedicated to work, but you don't let that stop you from having fun. That's what makes work fun for me. You. I always look forward to going to work because of you. It helps to have a great pack leader for a boss too. But you are what makes it really fun. Not a day went by that I didn't think of you and want to court you. But first you were tied up with your boyfriend, and then you were getting over it."

"And still you couldn't wait to date me."

"You're damn right I couldn't."

"Well, I'd say we have been dating for nearly a week now. I'm all for keeping it up."

"That's the way I feel too." He carried their wineglasses into the living room and set them on the coffee table while she brought over a big bowl of buttered popcorn.

After wine, popcorn, the movie, and cuddling, it was time to call it a night.

"You know, I didn't realize it, but tomorrow is Saturday," Knox said. "I can't keep track of the days when I don't work for a time at the office."

Ingrid's jaw dropped, then she smiled. "You're right. Everything's been so crazy, I kept thinking I was working tomorrow. What do you want to do? How are you feeling?"

"I wouldn't mind getting out, but doing a lot of walking probably isn't reasonable after what I just went through."

"We could stick around here and play games. I see you have a stack of board games. We could have takeout or eat here. Binge-watch a series. Whatever you're in the mood for."

"That sounds like a good deal."

"Let's go take a shower and get ready for bed," she said.

He hoped she meant what he thought she meant. He was certainly counting on it.

CHAPTER 11

Two weeks later, Knox was back at work, leaning his backside against Ingrid's desk once again while Ingrid was working on the puzzle and the new message this month. He'd finished his at home before he brought her into work. He was so thrilled when she'd moved in with him and put her house up for sale. They still hadn't made the commitment to be a mated wolf pair, but he thought he could convince her any day now. At least he hoped so.

They'd deciphered the rest of the crossword puzzle's secret message from the previous month: is not enough|| We must take| action now|| Bring on the| summer sun| the joy of| life and| live a little||Diana love |from Chas

Ingrid had been right all along. The secret message was a love note, only Knox still suspected it had been written with Ingrid in mind. He hoped Diana was real and that Chas was enjoying some time with her, but he suspected it was just made up. What else could Chas do if he'd sent roses to Ingrid and written a love note to her over the better part of a month, then learned she was dating Knox?

Ryan came into work, looked at the two of them, and sighed. "Haven't the two of you mated yet?"

"She keeps asking me, but I want to make sure she's ready for it," Knox said.

Ingrid tilted her head to the side. "*Knox.*"

"Okay, so I keep asking her and she says…"

"Yes. I was going to wait until tonight to say so when you

asked me again because we have the weekend off." She gave him a brilliant smile.

Knox couldn't believe it. Was she *serious*? "Seriously?"

Ryan got on his phone. Wait, Ryan wasn't going to tell the whole pack, was he?

"Hey, Max, I need you to take over for Knox for the rest of the afternoon. Yeah, though it isn't a done deal. I know. I'm sending them home." Ryan called someone else. "Can you take over for Ingrid for the rest of the day? Thanks, Sis, and yeah, send a dozen roses to Carol, and if she suspects me of mischief, *you* are in trouble." He chuckled, then ended the call. "It's done. When Max and Rosalind get here, the two of you are taking care of business."

Ingrid smiled. "You're the best boss ever."

"You're serious?" Knox asked Ingrid again.

She got up from her chair, and Knox stood up from her desk, and she took hold of his hands, looking up into his eyes with her brilliant blue ones. "Yeah, you better believe it. I can't take any more of you asking me when I know there's only one way I want this to go."

"You want to mate me."

"Yeah, because I love you."

"That's music to my ears. I love you, too, you beautiful wolf." Though they'd told each other that for several days now. Then Knox kissed her, but the phone rang.

Before Knox could release Ingrid to answer it, Ryan got it.

Knox and Ingrid smiled at their pack leader. Knox was certain whoever the caller was would be shocked to hear from the mayor himself without having to speak to Ingrid first.

"Mayor McKinley speaking." Ryan nodded. "Yeah, it's

right here." He looked through the calendar on Ingrid's computer. "Yeah, you're good." He glanced at Ingrid and winked. "Yeah, Ingrid will be back to work on Monday. Okay, bye." He hung up the phone. "One of your admirers."

"Not Chas."

"Yeah. He'll be glad to know you two just got engaged. You can tell him the next time he calls or drops by. I'm beginning to think that's why he was always trying to get stories out of me. Not because he was glad I was a good mayor but because he wanted to see you," Ryan said.

"I'm glad you're a good mayor. Thanks for giving us the rest of the afternoon off," Ingrid said.

"It's good for the pack. And you know we'd do anything to help each other out when we can."

They'd planned to take a hike in the woods, have a picnic lunch, swim in the river as humans, maybe a movie and dinner out this weekend, but now Knox wanted to spend all his time with her in private, making love to her. Though he was sure they would get a lot of that in, too, no matter what other activities they did this weekend.

Then Rosalind hurried into the office. "I was in the vicinity. Max is on his way, I take it?" She smiled broadly at Knox and Ingrid.

"Yep. We'll handle things until Max gets here. Oh, did you ever learn what the message finally said?" Ryan asked Ingrid.

"It was a love message, and Chas ended it with 'Diana, love from Chas,'" Ingrid said.

"So he found a new woman to pursue," Rosalind said.

"If she reciprocates," Ryan said. "And it's for real. Go. I want this done. Now."

Ingrid laughed and gave Ryan a hug. And then Rosalind was there for a hug.

Ryan hugged Knox and slapped him on the back. "No mistakes."

"Not making any. Or I'm sure you'll hear about it." Knox hugged Rosalind. "Thanks for all your help with everything."

"Invite me to your wedding and we'll be good."

"Maid of honor," Ingrid said, pulling Knox toward the door. "Ryan can give me away."

They saw Max coming in the door. "Hell, I know what this is all about. I'd love to work a job where they'd give me time off to have a wolf mating."

"You'd have to find the right she-wolf, Max." Rosalind smiled at him.

He raised his brows at her and smiled.

"I said the 'right' she-wolf." Then Rosalind sat down to work, Max asked Ryan what he wanted him to do, and Ingrid and Knox hurried off to Knox's car.

Knox had a real spring to his step when he rushed Ingrid to the car.

"You know I won't change my mind between now and when we arrive home." Ingrid sounded totally amused.

Knox smiled down at her. "I know. But I just can't wait."

"You're like a little kid in a toy store."

They both pulled off their suit jackets before climbing into the hot car.

Seat-belted in, he drove them home. "You bet." He was trying to watch his speed.

She was watching it too. He smiled at her and reached over and squeezed her hand. "I love you."

"I love you, Knox. You so annoyed me when we first began working together. I'd tell my boyfriend, and he'd get mad. He must have known you liked me. And you were always doing little things for me. Except answering the phone. I knew when you took care of the phone that one day so I could work my crossword puzzle, that was it."

"I should have done it earlier. And you made me wait three weeks to learn you were hooked on me too?" Knox said in a teasing way as he pulled into the garage a few minutes later and shut the door.

"Yeah. I mean, we had to be sure. What if we had thought we would be totally compatible and learned it wasn't so?"

"Because of your relationship with the previous guy." Knox took her hand and led her into the house.

"Well, yeah, but I had to be sure about us too." After a nightly routine of unconsummated sex once he'd healed sufficiently, she was sure. They hadn't been able to consummate the sex until they'd agreed to the mating though.

He stopped her in the living room. "Are you certain?"

She smiled and pulled him toward the bedroom. "Yeah, unless *you* aren't."

"Hell, *I'm* sure." Knox swept her up in his arms, and she wanted to caution him about his wound, but he hadn't groaned.

She guessed it was sufficiently healed.

He carried her to the master bedroom where the sheets and comforter were all tucked neatly around the bed.

That was all they'd needed to help them make their bed mornings before work. Each other. As partners in cooking and cleaning, they'd had soap-suds fights and cooking mistakes, forgetting to add ingredients or adding too much—too many chefs in the kitchen. He'd chased her around the house with the vacuum cleaner, and she'd hosed him down while cleaning the cars, and more. But they'd always come out laughing, and she knew they were meant to be a mated couple.

He set her on the floor in the bedroom, and then they started to yank back the comforter and sheet. They both heeled off their shoes.

Before they stripped off any more of their clothes, he pulled her into his arms and looked down at her with longing and need. "The day you came into my life was the best day ever. The only caveat was that you were still dating a guy."

"You made sure *that* was no longer a problem." She tilted her head up for a kiss, her hands caressing his dress shirt.

"You bet."

They usually ditched their work clothes first thing when they got home, slipped into something more comfortable, enjoyed a dinner they both prepared, watched a movie, then did this. But today, they were home early from work, and they had more important business to take care of.

He leaned down to kiss her, his hands caressing her shoulders covered in the pale-blue silk blouse. She'd worn it on purpose—though her suit jacket covered her completely, and she usually wore a camisole under the blouse so her blue lace bra wouldn't be visible to the discerning viewer should she remove her jacket—because she'd planned the seduction of the wolf after work tonight. So no camisole and her prettiest blue lace bra was peeking out behind a film of blue silk. He didn't seem to notice. She wanted to laugh. He was too focused on seducing her mouth.

She leaned into the kiss, her hands moving to his lower back, then lower where she slipped her hands around his ass and pulled him tight against her needy body. He felt heavenly, and he groaned as his building erection pressed her eager body. She opened her eyes, worried the groan might have been due to him hurting. But he hadn't been hurting for the last week.

When she lessened the pressure of her mouth against his, he opened his eyes, a questioning look in them.

"You groaned."

He smiled. "Yeah." And got back to kissing.

She smiled against his lips and then got serious again. He was her dream wolf, the elusive wolf she'd sought for years and who had arrived when she was dating already. She'd known she shouldn't be interested in another wolf at the time, but Knox could melt her heart with one of his rakish smiles. Oh, sure, he used it on other she-wolves in the pack, but somehow when he did it with her, it seemed she was the only one he was really interested in getting to know better.

She hadn't known if Knox and she would be right together, but man, oh, man, it didn't take her long to figure it out.

She tongued his masculine lips and pressured his mouth to open. "Hmm." The sweet cherry soda he'd been drinking before they'd left work tasted delightful. "You taste divine," she whispered against his ear, then licked his neck.

His hands drifted to her fanny, and he gently squeezed her. "So do you." Then he was lifting her skirt, but she shook her head.

She should have just given into the lust and let him tear off her clothes. But she'd paid a lot for her suit, and she didn't want to get it all wrinkled. Go figure.

He quickly turned his attention to the button and zipper on the back of her skirt as if he had no qualms about taking care with her clothes. While he was busy trying to manage that, she began yanking out his shirttails from his trousers and then unbuttoning his shirt, eager to reach his bare chest. As soon as she had unbuttoned the rest of it, she slid her hands up his naked chest and sprinkled kisses all over it. He paused, absorbing the feel of her mouth kissing his skin. He finally managed to remove her skirt, and he paused again to enjoy her kisses.

"Ingrid," he said in a way that indicated he thought she'd been naughty, and she looked up at him to see what he meant by it. "You didn't wear your camisole under the blouse." He'd *finally* noticed. He pressed his hands over her blouse and squeezed her breasts covered in lace.

She smiled, albeit a bit wickedly.

"You *did* plan this all along. And I had *no* idea. All day when I was working with you... I must be getting old."

She laughed. She'd had a devil of a time keeping the secret. Then they were kissing again, and she was peeling his shirt off him so she could slide her hands over his shoulders and biceps. He had just enough muscle—hot and hard and delectable.

His concentration switched to the pearl buttons on her blouse, and he began to unbutton them, one by one, taking a moment to slide a hand over her breast and taking a gentle squeeze. It was killing her for them to take their time, yet she needed this slow seduction, loved feeling his hand caressing her breast through the lace, her heart pounding with intrigue.

Time to unfasten his belt while he was busy with her blouse. He had to remove her slip before he would see her sexy blue-mesh-and-lace garter belt. She'd certainly never worn her thigh-high stockings and garter belt for work before, and he'd never seen them on any other occasion. She couldn't wait to witness his expression when he discovered them.

She heard his heart beating hard while she unzipped his pants and pulled them down his narrow hips. He stepped out of them, and she tossed them on the back of the chair where he'd laid her skirt. Her blouse joined them. Then he was kissing her lace-covered breasts, suckling, licking the erect nipples. The sensation made her wild and hot and needy.

She ran her hands through his hair and arched her pelvis at his erection, straining for release from his black boxer briefs. She pressed herself against the swollen appendage, intending to feel his desire for her. He groaned and cupped her face and kissed her again.

She was kissing him back but working on his boxer briefs, pulling them down his hips, forcing him to lean over further to keep their mouths locked.

His freed cock was poking at her belly, and she pressed against him, rubbing, craving him inside her now. She reached up to unfasten her bra, but he stayed her hands and unfastened it for her, then slid the bra straps down her arms and kissed each naked breast.

When he switched his attention to her slip, she was eager to see his reaction when he removed it. She slid her hands down his naked backside, just anticipating the reveal.

He started to pull down the waistband of her slip and stopped when he saw the blue lace garter.

"Whoa." His blue eyes lit up with excitement, and he smiled at her. "Like Christmas in July."

She laughed and he pulled her slip off the rest of the way.

"Hot damn, honey."

She chuckled. "Just for you."

"Yeah, I'll say." He kissed her mouth and then leaned down to kiss her pale-blue garter. "Beautiful."

She ran her hands over his back. "You are too."

"Let's see. I've never done this before."

He slid his hand seductively between her legs, rubbing her as if he'd forgotten about the garter and stockings and removing them. He coaxed a moan out of her. She was wet and wanted to pull him into bed with her now.

She cupped his buttocks and squeezed. He began unsnapping each of the snaps on the garter. Then he slid a stocking down one leg. His hands were a wonderful, heated caress on her bare skin. He was kissing her thigh, her knee, her shin, and then did the same to the other.

Then he pulled off her garters. And her panties after that. He yanked off his socks next, and they hugged and kissed, naked body to naked body. She loved feeling his hardness, rubbing up against him before he scooped her up and set her on the bed. He was beside her in the next instant, kissing her shoulder and running his hand between her legs, then spreading her feminine folds and plying her with his love strokes.

She arched her back in response. He was lifting her into the heavens with his touch. And then he was kissing her mouth again, tonguing her, and she was soaking up the essence of him, kissing him as eagerly. Their pulses were rapid as he continued to stroke her.

She felt the power of his touch, pushing her to the edge, and she relished the feeling, grabbed hold, and released with a happy moan. Waves of orgasm slid through her, and she felt dazed and satiated for the moment. But then he was kissing her again, readying himself to mate her all the way. She was so ready for this. Delaying the inevitable had only heightened the pure magic of the mating moment.

He pushed her legs apart, centering and sliding inside her, filling her to the core.

He felt wondrous on top of her, protective, possessive, hers. Inside her, thrusting, he was a powerful and skilled lover. Her hands slid down his bare backside, caressing his buttocks. But she wanted him deeper. She wrapped her legs around him, and he fulfilled her need, pumping into her harder, faster, penetrating further.

Their pheromones spilled around them, inciting them, their heartbeats pounding. His body undulated against her in almost a sexy dance, his hand drifting to her buttocks, pushing her up toward him, making the connection even greater.

"Love you," he said, barely breathing the words against her ear.

She managed to get out "Love you right back" before his thrusts stole her thoughts and took her to that higher exquisite plane of existence where she would experience the wondrous orgasmic explosion all over again.

It was coming, she was anticipating the feeling and grabbed on as soon as it hit, crying out this time, and felt his explosion bathing her deep inside in wild, wet heat. He groaned as he completed the last of his thrusts, "Oh, baby, you are mine."

She smiled up at him. "Ditto, you sexy wolf, you."

And then he kissed her and pulled her against his body to cuddle. Ingrid couldn't have been happier.

Knox snuggled with his beautiful she-wolf. Ingrid was Knox's life, and he would cherish her always. He couldn't believe the sexy wolf had been prepared to do this tonight no matter what. When he'd finally noticed she wasn't wearing her camisole and was wearing the hot lace garter and stockings, he was about ready to come.

He caressed her arm and wondered if she wanted to get up and eat dinner, but she wasn't letting go of him, and he knew what was next on the agenda. Lots more wolf loving. Just the way they liked it.

EPILOGUE

INGRID WAS GLAD THE SMITHSON BROTHERS BOTH WERE brought up on charges for assault with a deadly weapon pertaining to shooting Knox, who was well liked in the community, but she knew it wouldn't stick.

The brothers were found guilty of a misdemeanor for not having a valid hunting license and fined for hunting out of season. They were charged with second-degree criminal trespass and given eighteen months in jail and a fine of $500 apiece because the criminal intent was to shoot wildlife without a license, out-of-season, on private property, and they ended up shooting an innocent man. They were warned again if they saw a wolf and killed it, it would be a costly mistake.

Ingrid and Knox had testified about the men shooting at them, and several others testified concerning the brothers' past hunting history. Nearly the whole wolf pack had attended the trial that was also packed with concerned citizens. When the brothers were sentenced with jail time and fines, Ingrid and Knox agreed with the sentencing.

Chas met up with Ingrid and Knox. "Hey, I'm writing an article for the paper on what went down, and I'd love it if I could get an interview with the two of you to get your feelings on the sentencing."

"Sure. Will tomorrow be all right?" Knox asked.

"Yeah, that'll be great. See you at the office at…?"

"I'll look at the schedule," Ingrid said, "and give you a call. Be sure and report in the newspaper about trespassing on private property and about the fines and jail time you can receive if you kill a wolf."

Chas nodded. "Absolutely. Oh, and I heard the Smithson brothers' sister stepped in and cleaned up the Spuds and Suds and the mayor gave the place a clean bill of health."

"He sure did, and she's running the place while the brothers serve their jail time," Knox said. "By the way, about the secret message to Diana—"

Chas smiled. "She's a bank teller, and I learned she loved doing the crossword puzzle and saw the hidden message."

"But you sent the roses to Ingrid," Knox said.

"Uh, yeah, but I realized I didn't stand a chance with Ingrid when I found out you were seeing her. But Diana was free and…well, a week before I finished the message, I asked her out. She…" Chas's ears turned a little red. "She thought I had been writing it to her since I bank there all the time. Anyway, we've been dating ever since."

Knox and Ingrid smiled at him.

"Did you send her flowers?" Ingrid asked.

"You bet. Only I took your advice and sent them to her with my name on it. She loved them." Chas smiled.

"I'm so glad for you," Ingrid said.

Knox agreed.

Then Knox and Ingrid thanked Chas and said goodbye and hurried off to join the pack at the pack leaders' ranch for a celebration.

"I think Chas still has a crush on you," Knox said.

"I think he's got something going with Diana. He doesn't even know the *real* me."

"Not like I do." Knox smiled.

"You sure do."

All the wolves gathered for a celebration at the pack leaders' home that night.

"Hell, that's great that Chas is going to mention the charges for killing a wolf and about trespassing on private property in the paper. Though we have signs posted all along the property's borders and notices about the fines and jail time for killing an endangered wolf, we also have cameras we can monitor to have trespassers arrested and prosecuted. But I'd say that was a good day for us. A win," Ryan said. "I know we all wanted them to have more time in jail for shooting Knox because to us, we are one and the same, wolf and human. But to them, we are no more than a wolf, and an attempted murder of a wolf will never be seen as the same thing. We figured this was the best we could get under the circumstances."

Ingrid agreed and hugged Knox. "I think it brought us together quicker. We might still be waiting on a mating if it hadn't been for the shooting." She smiled up at Knox.

"No. Way." Knox kissed her.

She laughed. So did several others.

Max said, "No, he was saying once Jethro was out of here, he was next in line to date Ingrid. We knew from his determined expression and from the way the two of you always acted toward each other during work hours, you were really meant to be together all along."

Everyone agreed.

"We just had to make sure the two of you saw it for what it was," Rosalind said.

Ryan saluted them with a glass of wine. "Several wolves wanted and were qualified for your positions. Why do you think I chose the two of you over everyone else who was interested?"

"Matchmaking? No way," Ingrid said.

Carol only smiled.

Knox laughed. "Well, I for one am glad, because I got the wolf of my dreams."

"Hmm, Knox, me too. I guess in the end, everything turned out the way it should have." Ingrid finished her glass of water. "Who wants to run with us as wolves?"

It would be the first time any of them had run as wolves since Knox had been shot, afraid other hunters might trespass to see or hunt the wolves. Afraid even the Smithson brothers would return to prove they'd been hunting wolves and not Knox and Ingrid.

A dozen planned to run with them, and Ingrid was glad because she knew she would still feel hunters were out there, ready to gun them down. She adored her fun-loving, heroic wolf and wouldn't give him up for anything. And being wolves was part of the whole magical package.

Knox had been waiting for this moment to run with Ingrid, to prove to her they didn't need to be afraid any longer. He was glad others wanted to be with them, spread out but nearby in case he and Ingrid needed anyone's help. Everybody had been on edge about running again.

Most of all, he was glad he could finally run with his mate, since they'd only had their first date when the shooting had happened. He was eager to show her how much fun they could have when they weren't being chased by rifletoting hunters.

He loved Ingrid with all his heart, and this was just the beginning.

ACKNOWLEDGMENTS

I want to thank Deb Werksman, my editor, and the rest of the Sourcebooks staff who put out the best books ever, from editing to book covers and every step in between. And to Donna Fournier and Darla Taylor, who help me to see my mistakes! And to my fans who share with me their love of worlds that aren't exactly normal!

ABOUT THE AUTHOR

USA Today bestselling author Terry Spear has written over sixty paranormal and medieval Highland romances. In 2008, *Heart of the Wolf* was named a *Publishers Weekly* Best Book of the Year. She has received a PNR Top Pick, a Best Book of the Month nomination by *Long and Short Reviews*, numerous *Night Owl Romance* Top Picks, and two Paranormal Excellence Awards for Romantic Literature (Finalist and Honorable Mention). In 2016, *Billionaire in Wolf's Clothing* was an *RT Book Reviews* top pick. A retired officer of the U.S. Army Reserves, Terry also creates award-winning teddy bears that have found homes all over the world, helps out with her grandbaby, and is raising two Havanese puppies. She lives in Spring, Texas.